The Washington Triangle

By
Shaun Duffy

PublishNation
www.publishnation.co.uk

Bradley Lowery, your bravery, smile and inspiration will live with me forever.

I would like to thank Sandra Riley and Joy Duffy for the contribution they made to towards the end of my eight year journey writing this.

To Suzannah, great art work thank you.

To Steve Becks Bilton, you really are a one off, I thank you for that!

To my mam, thank you for teaching me that a few great friends will always make you rich.

To my dad, I hope you have enough left in the tank to be able to read this. #F**K Alzheimer's

Thank you to all my family for the love and support over the years, it has been a rollercoaster, but it has been a canny ride eh?

To my mates, you know who you are! Washington, Sunderland, Hampshire, Scotland, Manchester, Blyth, Nottingham, Corfe Mullen and Melton Mowbray…We've laughed and laughed and then some. Have just loved my life!

To the Angels that look down on us…

To Norman Stocks, thank you!

Finally, to all Americans who read this. I hope you firstly enjoy it and then do something with it, come and live it!

Chapter 1

1789

The smell of scorched flesh cut through the air in the secret room. The President looked on as the Butler prepared the last iron. Offered one more slug of wine before the cloth gag was placed in his mouth, number four was ready. He was the last. The three before him writhed in agony, their soles burned for life.

The President nodded and the iron was ready, fizzing and spitting. The noise settled as it travelled to its target. The straw on the floor had been kicked to one side, leaving only the cold stone to worry about any forging spills. A drop of sweat from the Butler dripped from his brow and bounced onto the sizzling iron. Its effect was minimal, a hiss and puff. The Butler admired the lava like glow at the end of the iron. In truth though, he took no pleasure from this exercise. Number four sat in front of him, one foot firmly on the floor, one perched up in the air.

'Are you ready?'

Number four closed his eyes and bit hard on his gag. He screwed up his face and nodded. *God bless you.* The Butler removed number four's sock and then plunged the iron into the sole of his foot. He held it still, number four did his best not to move. The blistering heat caused the skin to pop like bubble-gum. The moisture was being sucked out, turning to steam. The hissing sound the branding made caused them all to gasp and squirm. Number four screamed into his gag, his concealed terror was horrendous to watch. He rocked from his hips, counting in his head. One, Two, Three …It was the longest seven seconds of his life.

The Butler quickly speared the iron back into its holder. Number four was desperately holding onto the chair. His black finger nails digging into the pine. The Butler leaned over him and lifted his chin. His eyes were closed. *Stay with me son.* He patted him on the shoulder and number four opened his eyes. He looked deep into them. They were now wide open, wider than they had ever been opened before. His pupils were spectacularly dilated. The whites of his eyes now displayed little bloodshot specks.

It was finally over; number four was now branded, his ordeal over. His manic breathing slowed. He spat out his gag and craved more wine. The Butler was on hand to allow the request, but swiftly removed the carafe.

'Two swigs are enough my son. You need a clear head, we all do. You did great' The Butler said, patting him warmly on the shoulder.

'I'll get you a bucket.'

Number four joined the other three by placing his foot in a tin bucket of dirty, cold water. It was only the smallest of relief; time would now be the healer.

All four of the branded brigade sat upright facing the President. They were ready to serve.

The Butler was ordered to dress their wounds. As he removed the buckets, candles flickered from all sides. The shadows they formed faded in and out.

The bandages were modest; their job was not to heal the wound. Their job was to hide it. The pain of the procedure was etched on their faces. All four had accepted their fate. This was an honour that had been bestowed upon them. They were the chosen ones.

The Butler's work was done for now. He pulled up a chair and sat alongside them. Four had become five. They sat in silence, the first time for a while and waited. He stood before them, arms folded, their master, their President, their saviour.

His appearance here was not documented. He was to be invisible to the outside world. Even in such bad light, he was still unmistakable to his followers. His dominant frame wrapped in a long black coat, topped with a black hat. His bushy, curly, white hair poked out at the sides. His voice was unmistakably gruff.

'I cannot express my gratitude enough to you all. Your sacrifice is just staggering. The fact that you are prepared to honour me and our great country in this way leaves me feeling humble and proud. You know what is at stake and you know what your role is.' The President paused a moment. He lifted his chin and pushed out his chest. He grew by another inch to his height. He felt enormous pride at what was happening. A rush of adrenalin thrust through his body.

'What you men are about to embark on, will in time, be historic.' The President was every bit a statesmen. He outlined where their new lives would begin. He called it the compass program. One would settle in the north, one in the east, one in the south and one in the west. The Butler had a different role to the others. He was to settle in the middle of the compass. He was the pointer to which gravity would pull.

Before the Butler could do that, he had one more job to do. It was the most important job of his life. The success of the President's master plan was now his to enforce.

The President walked over to the men and shook their hands. It was a very personal handshake and it was a very personal moment. His right hand locked into an embrace with their right hand. His left hand, clamped over both of them. There was no conversation, just a serious nod. Intense eye contact captured the final moments. That was enough; the bond had just been created.

The President looked down at the dusty wooden table next to him. A fat candle shone some light on a wooden box, the wax was burnt away in the centre; a hot liquid puddle offered him a faint reflection.

The box was no more than eight inches long, six inches wide and four inches deep. Unlike the table it was on, the box was new and clean. It was polished, its shine catching the candle's flames. He picked it up and cradled it in his hands. He held it gently, a life's work sat inside it.

The President prayed into the box quietly. *Please God, deliver this safely. Watch over my fellow believers and let us return humanity back to the righteous.*

The distant cry of ravens could be heard. They echoed around the hills that surround the isolated safe house. *A sign, thank you God.* The President whispered once more. A grand smile entered the proceedings, a smile of desire and purpose. He addressed his most trusty aide, the Butler and held out the box.

'You know where to go with this and you know what to do with it. Upon your return I will appoint one more person, a servant to watch over you.' The President looked down at the box and kissed it gently. He nodded to the Butler. The Butler stood up on command; it was an honour to receive the special package. He handed it over to him. *God be with you.*

The Butler accepted the box with the absolute commitment to carry out the President's wishes. He looked down at the box and quickly realised why the President had kissed it. The moisture from his lips had left an outline around a carving at the top of the box. It was an intricate and perfectly carved piece of craftsmanship. It proudly displayed the Washington family coat of arms.

The President stood back and made his final address.

'Once the Butler has buried this box, the four of you will shield it from the world. Then your blood lines will shield it from the world. As I look into the future your bravery will be beyond calculation. The *Document of Truth* inside this box will one day be opened and read, have no doubt. When that day comes, we will be able to pay back to the world, all that we owe.' The President was resolute, but extremely exhausted from the previous few months experience. He drew on every sliver of energy that he had inside him and used it in that room.

'You five people will save America in the coming years. Follow the plan and our country will be a world force. Fail and we could become a poverty stricken hell. God will guide us on this journey. He will decide what person is worthy of opening this box. He will decide what time in the future is right for them to do it.' The President looked up and pointed high into the heavens.

'He has spoken to me and he has told me. When the world is ready our teacher will appear.'

Chapter 2

Present day

The aroma of a Cohiba Cuban cigar was being inhaled by one person, the man smoking it. Its leaf had turned to ash at its tip. The smoke from the ash rose upwards, climbing an imaginary spiral staircase. The man that was holding it in his oversized, wrinkled right hand appreciated the woody taste. He twirled it slowly between his lips to moisten the tip, using his thumb and index finger to balance it in his mouth. The smoke slid down his tongue and then roamed freely out of his mouth. His dirty moustache, stained from years of nicotine abuse, acting as a filter.

Folis Heenan was smiling to himself. His left hand nestled tightly inside the lining of his jeans pocket. He gently rubbed the texture of a handkerchief tucked inside there. It was merely a subconscious act. He was staring straight ahead out of a first floor library window at his home. It overlooked his impressive twenty metre outdoor swimming pool. Manicured lawns and borders swept away from the house and then sloped down through the estate. No one could see inside his garden, but he could see out. He pondered to himself. *What will today's little trip to the cellar bring me?* His eyes became distracted for a brief moment from the trance like state he was in. The breeze had whipped up an army of ripples over the pool. They marched like rows of well drilled soldiers. His head followed them on their parade, turning from twelve o'clock to two o'clock, before they disappeared into their barracks.

He stubbed out the cigar with amazing accuracy. Six prods around the edges in equal measures and then he bounced it in the centre twice. He squeezed the cigar into the base of the ashtray, pushing down hard to completely extinguish it.

He picked up a glass that sat next to the ashtray. It was a quarter full of the good stuff, neat single malt Scottish whiskey. He looked outside and rolled the whiskey around in the glass. His attention was drawn to two birds, starlings. They looked like they were dancing and playing with each other. Their stealth like beaks seemed to kiss in the air, their spotty feathers flapping elegantly.

The birds disappeared into the distance. He threw back the glass and drank the lot. Not even blinking at the effects it had. He had drunk enough cheap plonk in his time, more than enough, now he warmed his insides with only the good stuff.

It is now time, he said to himself. He withdrew the handkerchief from his pocket. It was bright red in colour, his favourite, the colour of blood. He dabbed his forehead four times. Just like the cigar, it was done in equal measures. It was a precise routine that he had done many times before. Far left, centre left, centre right, far right. This cleaned up the beads of sweat building up from the unseasonal heat. The outside temperature had reached thirty nine degrees centigrade. He spoke to himself in an angry manner, as if it was he and only he that should have the power to control the weather. *These temperatures are too hot for this time of year. It is the middle of September and we have July temperatures. The tourist's moan it is too hot on normal days, God help us today!*

Folis Heenan is a man of great authority. A man who always believes he is right, even when he is wrong. It is never wise to challenge him; even as a child he had a very nasty temper. He only ever thinks about one person in this world now, himself. Although he has one Achilles heel; hamsters! As a child he saved one from dying, hand feeding it scraps that he had scrounged from dust bins. From that day forward, the little runts became his best friends.

He is now fifty four years old with many tell-tale signs. His face more red than brown, no matter how much sun exposure he gives it. He has many scars, some on his face. All of them are now bleached white and etched between several deep, saggy lines. His strawberry spotted nose boasting years of alcohol abuse. The greasy mop on his head was thinning badly.

He was born in the soulless ghetto of Voroshilovgrad, or Luhansk as it is known today. It is located on the Ukrainian-Russian border. It is a place of extreme temperatures and holds the record for the coldest temperature recorded in the Ukraine. Minus forty one point nine degrees Celsius. There was little doubt that was one of the reasons that he now lives in sunnier climes. It also helps that the local authorities and his neighbours, take no interest in his business dealings.

He had it tough back then, but his energy and focus, is now fixed firmly on the present and the future. He has grown outwards over the years, in equal proportions. His love of fast food and drink has seen to that. He always wears an open neck shirt, white or white; he does not care. Below the waist he wears jeans and cowboy boots, his trademark attire. He never wears a tie; he has a thing about men that wear ties. He also has a fetish for his cowboy boots and owns over two hundred pairs. This goes back to his childhood days. He would watch cowboy movies on the family's black and white portable television. He would sit with his dad, the man he called his hero and watch them for hours.

Back then, all he wanted to be when he grew up was to become one of them, a shooter. The truth is that part of that wish had become a reality.

Heenan walked down the grand stone staircase leading from the library to the ground floor, each step carefully placed in its centre, worn away from years of duty. His footsteps echoed off the walls and floor, as he passed five self-portrait paintings that hung on the staircase wall. He commissioned one every five years. The first was on his thirtieth birthday. The sixth would be staring shortly, his fifty fifth.

He was heading for the cellar and heading for a date. This date like many others before, had been kept waiting a worrying amount of time. At the entrance to the cellar was a large, majestic handmade oak door. It had four black hinges the size of car jack's holding it up. Behind the door waiting in the cellar was one terrified man, his date, or as Heenan called him, his playmate.

He was unaware of the value of this playmate. Lady luck had offered him something special, something very special. This playmate was valuable, more valuable than anyone or anything that had been thrown in his cellar before. He just didn't know it yet.

Heenan entered the cellar. He closed the great door behind him. The creaking noise from the hinges echoed around the room.

In the centre of the cellar floor was a blue plastic tarpaulin sheet, about twelve feet square. It was new; with classic tell-tale signs, two perfect creases running through the middle, making the sign of a cross. The shiny wax finish winked at the lights on the ceiling.

In the centre of the tarpaulin was a chair, a red plastic chair. Sat in it was McVey. He was hand cuffed. His hands were behind his back, his arms resting against the back of the chair. Each leg had been tied at the ankle, to the chair leg with white plastic ties.

McVey was already a broken man. He was increasingly unsettled in the chair. His nerves and fear were making him twitch awkwardly. His head twisted from side to side at the slightest noise that funnelled its way into the room. Beads of sweat dripped painfully slowly into his eyes, as he wrestled with his fate. His tatty brown summer suit was torn, dirty and creased.

The cellar was dome shaped with white washed walls. The white wash covered the red bricks that were used in its original construction. The room was very well lit. Heenan had installed new lighting when he arrived there six years ago.

McVey wrestled once more with his restraints, his teeth now clenched together. Heenan fixed his eyes in an evil stare and cast it at him. His arms were folded tightly, his plump and full midriff acting as a rest for them. His fat forefinger tapped away on his upper arm.

He advanced to McVey, his cowboy boots creating a nervous sound. Every step, met with a wince, as he approached the tarpaulin. The eight paces he took were the longest McVey had witnessed. He unfolded his arms and then slid his hands into his front pockets. He stood there, his eyes taunting his playmate. McVey stopped resisting; his wrists close to being cut by the plastic ties. He followed Heenan's every move, looking at his body language for any clues to his fate.

Heenan decided it was time to start the interrogation. He spoke quietly and calmly, almost a whisper.

'Tell me how you thought you could pay me back. You have a very bad gambling habit, do you not?' McVey caved in instantly. He feared that his past spending spree had caught up with him and he was right. He started to tremble; a serious beating would be the best outcome that he could hope for.

He had already been slapped about and deprived of sleep, water and food for twenty four hours. This was just the next stage. His nerves heightened as he tried to reply.

'Lllook I'm sorry ok, yes I have messed up ba-badly, I know I have, but you have got to believe me when I say I can fu-fix this. I can pay you back, all of it.' McVey looked up at Heenan in hope for mercy. Heenan was in no mood for beggars. He let out a little sigh and then moved on with the questioning. As before, his tone was calm, fluent but menacing.

'Tell me about your work?' This question threw McVey and he questioned himself. *Why is he asking that? I owe him money from a gambling debt. This does not make any sense to me.*

'My work, I don't understand, what about my work?' Confusion came over McVey's face. He started wrestling his restraints again, this time he sliced the edge of his wrist. He yanked his hand back in pain, making it worse for himself. Blood started to trickle down his hand. A few drops left his fingertip and fell onto the tarpaulin. Heenan lifted his left hand from his pocket and pointed to the blood.

'You are making a mess of my new sheet.' He bent down and pushed his finger into the small pool of blood. McVey looked disturbed. *Jesus, this guy is crazy, he is an animal.*

McVey watched as Heenan tasted the blood. He looked down to his side as more drops fell onto the tarpaulin. Heenan smiled, it looked false to McVey and he was not wrong.

'Unless you want me to taste more of your blood, tell me about your work!' Heenan removed his right hand from his pocket and rested his forefinger and thumb on the end of his chin. He waited for McVey's reaction as he rubbed his facial stubble, back and forth, another subconscious act. McVey took that as an opportunity to challenge him. It was more from desperation than anger.

'I don't have a job or a business anymore; I have not had either for some time, surely you know this?' Heenan circled slowly around McVey's chair, crunching the tarpaulin underneath his feet. McVey followed Heenan's every move with his eyes, petrified at what might come next. McVey appealed loudly once more.

'I swear to you, I do not have a job or a business to tell you about' McVey was struggling to hold back the tears of shame and terror. *How have I let my life come to this?*

Heenan had stopped in front of McVey, a matter of only a foot away from him. He leaned forward slightly and looked down on him.

He prodded him in the forehead, the blood from his finger now circled on McVey's brow.

'You told Bridie you were an oil stocks investor, so tell me about that.'

'I know I did, I was just trying to impress her, I don't know anything about the oil industry, it was just a cover story I made up and that is the truth.' Heenan launched forward grabbing McVey by the neck, squeezing him hard with both hands. His face screwed up in frustration, at the lack of information that he had obtained so far. He whispered in his ear, his face twisted with evil.

'Tell me about your work, this is your last chance!' McVey was choking, he sucked in any air he could, his face turned purple as he gasped for breath. He finally managed to squeeze out three words. His face turned a darker shade of purple by the second.

'I don't know!' Heenan released his hands; he exhaled as he stood back three steps. McVey hung on for dear life, drawing in big gulps of air. He was fighting the urge to pass out, but the big gulps of air were just enough to keep him conscious.

From his outstretched arm, Heenan pointed a fat finger at McVey and then blasted at him.

'You had your chance to make this easy for yourself.' He turned around and walked off the tarpaulin and unclipped a two way radio from his belt. He put it to his mouth. As it rested on the edge of his moustache, he pressed the intercom button and spoke into it.

'Yuri, are you there?'

There were two crackles that echoed around the room before a reply.

'Da'

'Yuri, I want answers.'

'Da, I'm on my way.' Yuri said, in a husky Baltic broken English tone. Heenan clipped his radio back on his belt and then turned back to McVey.

'I will be back once you have told Yuri what I need to know.' McVey bowed his head, knowing deep down that this was about to get worse for him. He muttered helplessly. *Please no, sir please no, c'mon, we can work this out. Don't do this to me.* McVey looked up; he took a deep breath and shouted at the back of Heenan's head.

'Please believe me.' Heenan ignored him; he pushed open the door, marched out, slamming it on his exit.

McVey had run up a large gambling debt with Heenan. He had blown more than $300.000 of credit. It had started nearly two years ago, when he visited a casino owned by Heenan in the South of France. Just like any other addict he started small, but soon got hooked on the chase, for the revenge of his losses. The problem for McVey was that he had met Bridie. She was two inches short of six feet. She had blonde flowing locks, with shimmering skin, a stunning body and legs that could grace the cover of Vogue. Her husky deep voice would melt the heart of most listeners.

Bridie was a sleeper who worked for Heenan in the casinos. Her job was to identify targets that could be of value to him. She would then groom them to become dependent on the casino and on her.

McVey had claimed to be an oil stocks investor and it was this that Bridie was interested in. McVey was an easy target and he fell right into Bridie's trap. In the last two years, under Bridie's spell he had lost everything. His home, his savings and now he was in danger of losing his life. Bridie ran a very slick operation. She was a cold professional on the inside, but appeared warm and seductive to her targets. It would be fair to say, that by the time her targets were introduced to Heenan most of them regretted ever meeting Bridie. Some of them would go onto pay the ultimate price.

Yuri had been working on McVey for nearly thirty minutes. He had removed his jacket and ripped open his shirt. First he beat him about the face, causing deep bruising and several cuts. He then used electric shock treatment. He clamped two probes on him, one to each nipple. He shocked him for five seconds at a time, at sixty second intervals, each time increasing the voltage capacity. This caused burn marks the size of an orange around his nipples and made him drool like a baby. Some of the drool was blood, caused from the beating and some were bodily fluids, brought up by the electric shock treatment.

He then placed a clear plastic bag over his head, suffocating him within seconds of his life. He was now on his final assault, slicing him open with a razor sharp knife. The knife he was using was a trophy to Yuri. He had taken it from a guy after a street fight many years ago. He had been wounded in the attack, but he had fought back and overpowered him. He had taken the knife from him and then used it to kill him. Street justice, he called it.

McVey had been sliced open in many of the body's sensitive areas, the last one being right under the base of his nose, just above his lip. This is particularly sickening; as it leaves you temporarily blind. McVey was fast becoming unrecognisable.

Heenan entered the room once more just as Yuri was wiping his trophy blade. McVey was screaming in pain, his child-like pleas wasted. There would be no mercy here. Heenan looked down at the blood stained tarpaulin and smiled. He waited for a pause in the screaming, lifted his head and glanced at Yuri.

'What have you found out?'

'He knows nothing about the oil industry, I am sure of it, he would have said by now. I don't think he has any useful information for you. Sorry boss'.

Heenan took a bottle of mineral water from the fridge. This large white metal box, looked out of place, sat lonely in the corner. He had shown no emotion at what he had seen; apart from a wry smile. He unscrewed the blue plastic cap and took two sips.

'Can you push him any further?'

'Not really boss, not without killing him.' McVey bowed his head on hearing this, blood dripping from his chin. Heenan took another two sips of water, nodding at McVey and spoke to Yuri.

'Don't waste any more time on him. Kill him, but take his eyes out first to settle his debt to me.' McVey managed a hollow plea, crying faintly.

'Please no, don't do this.' His plea was ignored by both Heenan and Yuri. Yuri walked up to McVey, grabbed the hair at the back of his head and then put the tip of his knife to his right eye. McVey screamed and blood shot out of his mouth, some of it landing on Yuri's face.

'Wait! Wait! I'll tell you, I'll tell you something, just put the knife down.' McVey was exhausted. He broke down at the realisation that he was about to give away the secret of his life's work. All to save the quality of life he had left. It was the coward's way out and he knew it. He was disgusted in himself for even thinking it, but he was willing to do it. The pain had to stop.

As Heenan finished another sip of water, he cleared the way for McVey.

'You'd better not be wasting my time.' He spat out blood from his mouth.

'I'm not, I swear to you. Please water.'

'If you are lying to me, I will take your eyes out myself, make no mistake of that.'

'Water please.' Heenan walked over and tipped the remainder of his bottle of water over McVey's head. McVey cried in pain, as the water found its way into his cuts. His face diluted of the red blood bath that it had become.

'Now talk.' Heenan demanded, as he threw the empty plastic bottle at him. McVey spat out once more.

'Take off my right shoe and sock and then look at the sole of my foot.' McVey was devastated he was giving in. His life had spiralled out of control. He was now a wreck of a man. He sat and imagined the gates of hell opening up and being dragged in. Over two hundred and thirty years of blood line was about to be compromised.

Heenan nodded to Yuri, his interest now aroused. *What have you got here, for me then, little man?* Yuri wasted no time in yanking the shoe and sock off. He cut the leg tie from around his ankle and then held his leg up for Heenan to see the sole. McVey looked up to the heavens and apologised to the world.

'What is this?' Heenan enquired. McVey coughed, his breathing difficult, he was now only talking out the side of his mouth. The side that was least damaged in the beating.

'Please, I need a drink of water.' McVey was beginning to blink fast, he was on the verge of passing out. Heenan showed no concern for his welfare. He took out his handkerchief and dabbed his forehead four times. Far left, centre left, centre right, far right. He stopped in anticipation of what he was about to hear and rested the handkerchief on the tip of his nose. Another subconscious act, one that Yuri was surprised to witness.

'Please water.' McVey whispered again.

'You can have some water if this is worth it.' Heenan growled as he stuffed his red rag back in his pocket.

McVey could hardly muster the energy to even speak. His face resembled Rocky Balboa, in the final scene from Rocky three. He whispered under his breath. *It's all or nothing now. Jesus Christ our Lord, I pray for forgiveness at what I am about to do.* McVey inhaled deeply, it was a hollow sound, like an old man taking his last breath.

'The markings you see on the sole of my foot are part of a series of secret cryptic messages. I am one of four people who have them. I can lead you to the other three.' McVey closed his eyes, his head dropped.

'Yuri, wake him up, get him some damn water.' Yuri grabbed a bottle and rushed over to McVey. He tipped it over his head; it ran down his chest and onto the tarpaulin. Heenan shouted at Yuri in frustration.

'No you fool some water to drink.'

'Yes boss, of course.' Yuri ran back and collected another bottle. He lifted McVey's head up enough to pour the water into his mouth. Instantly McVey came around and then he coughed up the water. As he coughed, he opened his eyes and nodded to Yuri.

'More, I need more.' Yuri looked at Heenan.

'Yes, for God's sake give him more. I want to know what this is all about.' McVey took two more gulps.

'Promise you will not kill me?'

'Yuri, pass me your knife, I am in no mood to negotiate with this low life.'

'Ok,ok. Once you have all the markings, I can help you work out what they mean.' Heenan took a step back and pondered for a moment. He turned around and walked over to the fridge. He tapped the top of the fridge three times. He spun around to his right, the ninety degrees needed to grab the big brass door handle. He stopped and paused once more, the last pause he needed. Three seconds on decision making. He twisted his head and looked at Yuri, who was motionless, awaiting his master's order.

'Clean him up. Get him some more water and some first aid treatment quickly. I want to know everything Yuri, everything!'

'I think he will need a doctor boss.'

'I don't pay you to think, just clean him up quickly.'

Chapter 3

Jack Hammonds had just finished his shopping and was leaving his local Wallmart, in downtown Sarasota, Florida. He glanced down at the time on his watch. It was sandwiched between several leather bands on his left wrist. It was 7.21 PM

Jack squinted as he scanned the area leading out to the parking lot. A sprinkling of motors littered the vast car park. His transportation was a motorcycle, his pride and joy, a red Norton Commando 961 Sport, with twin seats.

The distant sounds of shopping trolleys were the only distraction, as he shielded his eyes from the sun. There was a warm tinge to the horizon, as the big yellow beast retreated for the night.

The contents from his two shopping bags were cradled ape like, as he marched out of the exit. His size eleven, sky blue pumps pounded under his fourteen stone ripped frame. He was dressed in a light blue, loose fitting, cotton shirt. Its sleeves were folded back, to just above the elbow, enough to show off his impressive forearms. His unbuttoned, navy blue waistcoat hung over his navy blue jeans.

This was a specific trip to the shops for Jack; his bags were packed with fruit, vegetables, cereals, pulses, yogurts and fresh orange juice. It was the start of yet another health kick that he had promised himself.

He negotiated his way through a couple of cars and then past the trolley park. This was the quietest time to shop, something that Jack took advantage of. As he approached the crossing he stopped and glanced up at the sky, it had been yet another beautiful day. As he moved, his watch caught a chink of light from the sun. Another time check revealed it was now 7.22 PM

His sister had arranged a blind date for him. It was nothing too serious, just a trip to the cinema. He would be meeting his mystery lady in just under an hour.

A bit of a breeze swept across the car park as he marched to his baby. A flick of his thick dark hair lifted from his fringe. His precision side parting remained fully intact.

A black Sudan suddenly swung into a parking bay in front of him. A lady and a teenage girl enthusiastically bounded out of the car. Jack moved to the side to let the lady past. She looked up at Jack and then took a second look, this one being more obvious. She ran her fingers through her hair and smiled at Jack. She gazed into his eyes, long enough for him to notice her intent.

'Hi.' Jack said.

'Hi there, sorry about nearly running you over, I am in a bit of a hurry.' The lady was coy, even girly.

'Your husband's waiting for his dinner, is he?' Jack joked.

'Oh, I am not married anymore.' The lady showed Jack her finger, confirming that there was no ring on it.' The teenager turned stroppy, not happy with the nature of the conversation.

'God Mom, get a room, that's sick.' The lady rolled her eyes and smiled at Jack.

'Teenagers! It was nice to meet you anyway.' The lady grabbed her daughter's hand and scurried off. Jack watched the first few steps, he muttered to himself as he smiled inwardly. *Yep, still got it.*

There was the sound of an engine purring around the car park, louder than the average vehicle. Jack looked to his right to see where it was coming from. A black van with no markings was approaching quickly, far too quickly for his liking. He took a step back as it increased its speed; it was heading straight for him. *What a jackass.* He looked around for witnesses to this heinous car park crime. The lady and her daughter were now entering the store, no luck there. An elderly gentleman was the only other person close by, taking far too many attempts to park his car up.

He raised his hand to gesture to the driver of the van as he sped towards him. The driver jammed his breaks on and pulled up sharply at the crossing. Jack was incensed; he had stopped a mere three feet away from him. *You idiot, you could kill someone driving like that.*

'What the hell are you playing at?' He yelled at the driver. The windscreen glass was heavily tinted. This obscured any view that Jack had of the driver.

The back and side doors of the van swung open. Jack stood back; He looked around, still no other witnesses. Four men jumped out, two from the rear and two from the side door. *What the hell.* They were all wearing identical clothing. Black suits, white shirt, black tie and black sunglasses. They surrounded him, he took another step back, his brain was telling him that he was about to be robbed. His gut was telling him that they were too well dressed for a stick up. *I could outrun these guys as they are all wearing shoes, no match for me.* His shopping could be used as a distraction before he scarpered. The passenger door suddenly opened. Another suit got out; Jack was now unsure. *Stick or twist buddy, what is it?* The suit took off his sunglasses.

'I take it you must be Jack Hammonds if I am not mistaken? The suit without the glasses said. Jack was unresponsive, he needed time to think. He glanced down at the contents in his right hand; he started having second thoughts, about how much damage a bunch of apples could do. *These are hardly going to help me win a fight.*

'Well? I am waiting and frankly neither of us has the time to wait.'

'Yes, what do you want with me?'

'I'm Hunter from the Secret Service.' He held up his hand, showing his ID. Jack squinted at the photograph that was encased in a black leather wallet, which folded in two. He looked around at the other suits. *Jesus, what a bunch of waxwork dummies.*

'Good for you, what is this about?'

'You need to come with us; we need your help, please get in the van.' Agent Hunter pointed to the side door of the van with his outstretched arm. Jack looked around hoping for a rescue team to suddenly appear. He was out of luck.

'Look Mr Hunter I'm not going anywhere with you or your goons, until you tell me what this is about.' Jack displayed an arrogant confidence. The words just rolled out of his mouth in a dry husky southern accent. Agent Hunter calmly put away his ID and then unclipped his gun from its holster. He pointed the gun at Jack's face. His right hand had a firm grip on his SIG Sauer P229. He tilted his head a few degrees to his right, just enough to follow the terrain of his right arm. Jack dropped his shopping and lifted his hands.

'Whoa, whoa, whoa, hold on now soldier.' Jack said apprehensively.

'Get in the van now; we don't have a lot of time. We're on a very tight schedule as we have a plane to catch.'Jack looked around once more, still no passers-by. *Where the hell is everyone when you need them?* He decided to challenge Hunter; a display of nervous arrogance could be detected.

'A plane to catch, are you for real, I am not going on any plane, I have just got my shopping in and I have a date with a salad.' Hunter shook his head. He lowered his gun and then holstered it and then gave his agents an order.

'Get him in the van and confiscate his cell phone.'

Jack had been in a few scrapes in his time and often got out of them by acting the big man. Not this time, reality was dawning as he was shoved into a seat in the van.

Four suits settled into the back of the van with him, two sat opposite, and one either side. Jack quickly realised this was no hustle, this was serious.

The van sped away from the car park. It left two large rubber tyre marks on the ground. The driver took two left turns and then joined the freeway.

Jack sat looking at the four agents; they sat in silence, staring at him. His anger was brewing, he wanted an explanation.

'Look Hunter, what is this about, what is going on?' Jack dropped the arrogant tone and used a softer approach. Hunter calmly turned around from his front seat position and looked directly at Jack.

'We are headed to the airport where a plane is waiting for us.' Hunter showed no emotion. He looked tired and overworked. His bald head and milk white complexion well wrinkled after years of loyal service. The Florida sunshine had been of no benefit to him in recent times.

'Wait! Let's back up a minute here.' Jack tried to get off his seat, but was unceremoniously put back down. Hunter was unimpressed.

'Why do we need to get on a plane? Where are we going? And how can I be of help to the Secret Service?' Jack had quickly become exasperated; he put his hands on his head and shook it in disbelief, at the situation he now found himself in. Hunter was unnerved, just another day at the office for him.

'We need to go to Mexico and collect someone else, who like you, can help us with this matter.' This added to the confusion for Jack. *Why Mexico? Surely they are not getting a Mexican to help the Secret Service?*

'Hunter, why Mexico?' Jack demanded. Hunter pulled out a phone from the inside of his jacket pocket. He turned around to Jack and looked him in the eye. He said nothing; he just wondered what benefit this idiot could be to his country.

'I need to make a phone call Jack; we will be at the airport in thirty minutes. My boss will be on the plane waiting for you, he will give you more details as to what's going on. Just sit back and relax.' Hunter dialled a number and waited for an answer. Jack listened into the one sided conversation.

We have Jack. Yes sir he is fine. No, no problems. Which hanger are you at? Ok, we will be with you in about thirty minutes.

Jack had no choice, but to wait and see what played out and who it was on the plane. Hunter looked at the driver and gave him a short and definite instruction.

'Head for hanger one one seven.' The driver nodded acknowledgement.

Standing fuelled, cleaned and ready to go in hanger one one seven was a Learjet. Waiting impatiently on board for Jack's arrival was Agent Ridley, the man overseeing this part of the operation.

The van pulled up beside hanger one one seven. Jack was quickly ushered from the van. He stood and took in his surroundings. The sun was now down, dusk had arrived. The bright lights that flooded the hanger spread out through the hanger doors.

'Let's go.' Hunter issued his command and Jack was shoved forward by one of the suits.

'Move.' Jack pointed a finger at him in retaliation. *Watch it buddy.*

They marched the few yards across the expansive black tarmac and reached the hanger entrance. Jack stopped and looked at the jet; it looked small in such a huge space. The steps up to the jet awaited Jack's arrival. He had been on a Learjet before, a couple of times in fact, but not under these circumstances.

He was shoved inside the hanger, the same agent eager to move him forward. Jack fumbled forward and looked down at the floor. He stared at the polished shiny grey stone, as he built up an increasing anger for the pushy agent. *Do that once more and I swear.*

'Move it Jack, we don't have all day.' Hunter growled.

Jack took one step up, his right foot hovering on the second step. He paused and looked back at the agents. His emotions were spinning; he was pensive, angry, confused, but in truth, also a little intrigued.

Hunter shouted at Jack, the echo bounced off the metal roof.

'Jack, please, we are running short of time.' Jack looked up the steps as an agent popped his head out of the jet. The agent signalled him up. *What the hell do you need sunglasses on in an aeroplane for? What a dumb ass.* Jack looked back as Hunter stood right behind him.

'You want me to pull my gun out again?' Hunter was losing his patience with Jack. He obliged and started to walk up the steps. Hunter followed, leaving two steps between them. As Jack reached the top, the agent in the plane took a step back inside. Jack leaned in and looked inside; his heart was racing. *What the hell I am doing here?*

Jack had a clear view inside the jet. Sitting to his right, in a plush, cream leather seat was Ridley. He was deep in conversation on the telephone, but interrupted it when he caught sight of Jack.

'Excuse me sir, Jack Hammonds has just arrived on board' Ridley placed his phone on the small round cream table, in front of him and introduced himself.

'I am Ridley, very pleased to meet you Jack.' Jack politely nodded, at the same time weighing up his presence.

'Please have a seat next to me. I will be with you in one moment when I finish this call.' Jack sat down opposite Ridley; he looked around for any clues of what this could possibly be about. There were none, it was just a very posh jet, with more goons on board. Hunter boarded the jet and walked up to Ridley's seat. Ridley stood up and interrupted his call once more, this time to address Hunter.

'Thanks Hunter, good job. Go back to HQ. We will catch up tomorrow, once I have delivered this package.'

'Yes sir.' Ridley and Hunter shook hands warmly; two professional smiles accompanied two professional people. Hunter took one last look at Jack, who sat there on the plump cream leather seat and looked at them both. *Good luck with him sir.* Hunter's job was done and he was glad that the operation had been completely successfully. One more step towards another promotion. Ridley sat back down and continued with his phone call. *Thank you for holding sir. Yes, he is looking well. We will be at the White House around 7AM. We are heading for Mexico now. Yes sir, see you then.* As Ridley ended the call, Jack wondered if his hearing was playing up. *Did he just say we are heading for the White House?* Ridley offered Jack a large fake smile; he was just like the rest of them, just following orders from the top.

'Can I get you a drink or maybe some food Jack?' Jack frowned and shook his head.

'No thanks, I would just rather know what is going on and what the hell I'm doing on this plane.' Ridley adjusted his position slightly.

'What did Hunter tell you?' Jack leaned forward and put both hands out in front of him and rested his forearms on his knees, his palms facing together, as if in prayer.

'Not much really, just that you need my help and that we are going to pick up some Mexican. That's about it.' It was Ridley's turn to lean forward and as he did Jack responded by leaning back.

'Fair enough Jack, I'll fill you in on a little bit more detail, but even I do not have all the facts, I am just following orders.

'Who are you taking your orders from?' Ridley stared right into Jack's eyes and without a hint of emotion he replied.

'The President of the United States.' The plane door was slammed shut and the engines were fired up. It was time to taxi. Jack stood up, he was shocked at what he had just heard, even after the experience of the last hour, that was the last thing he expected. He mumbled to himself. *The President.* Ridley ordered Jack to sit back down.

'We are about to take off, sit down, buckle up and get some rest, you are sure going to need it.' Jack sat down and put his belt on, Ridley offered a little more insight.

'We are en route to Cancun in Mexico Jack, but not to pick up a Mexican as you just put it. We are going to pick up a woman called Holly Macdonald, who will also help us in this matter. We've been informed that you two are the best of the best at what you do. Between you and me, we hope the situation we find ourselves in will be resolved and quickly.' Jack interrupted Ridley.

'What situation do you find yourself in?'

'Please Jack, let me finish.' Jack nodded.

'Once Holly is on board we will fly to DC There you will be fully briefed on the detail of this operation.' Jack struggled with what he was hearing. Things were happening so quickly, but if Holly Macdonald was now involved then things were starting to make some sense.

'Holly Macdonald you say?' Jack rolled his eyes and looked to the sky.

'You know her?' Ridley asked.

'Never met her, but sure heard and read a whole lot about her.' Jack replied in a sarcastic tone, a tone that also carried a hint of jealousy. Jack looked out of the little window, the tarmac was rushing passed him as the plane left the ground.

The penny had finally dropped. *If he and Holly were wanted to help the President, then something priceless had gone missing.* Ridley watched Jack staring out of the plane window, he wondered. *Is this the man to help save the President and save the United States of America?*

The plane levelled off, Jack sat asking questions, not to Ridley, but himself. *What on earth had gone missing and what was Holly Macdonald doing in Cancun?*

Chapter 4

It was just another normal night at Coco Bongos. As usual it was packed to the rafters, as it is 365 days of the year. The Playa Del Carmen hot spot near Cancun was a must for Holly Macdonald and her three best friends to visit. Holly had seen a television documentary from an American journalist claiming 'Coco Bongos puts Vegas to shame.' The media hype stating that it was the best party venue in the world was too good to miss. Coco Bongos became their first choice destination for Holly's birthday celebrations.

Holly was blissfully unaware of the Learjet about to land at Cancun airport, as she and her friends had settled quickly into the party vibe. They had arranged their own private table on the second floor and paid extra for a private waiter. This came about as a result of a Trip Advisor recommendation.

Emma and Annie were the two heavy drinkers in the group, Holly and Angel preferred to dance rather than drink, the famous Sirocco shuffle, was their thing. Their preferred drinks ranged from Mojitos to Jack Daniels, to the local fire water, Tequila. Emma had asked the waiter for another line of shots, the third since they had arrived. As he brought them over, the Black Eyed Peas were blasting out from the speakers next to them. The vibration from the bass worked its way up from their toes. *'Tonight's the night, let's live it up.'* The waiter wormed his way through the crowds of merry club goers. Annie took the glasses from his tray and handed them out. She then took slices of lime and passed them around. They all stood up together and dipped their fingers in the bowl of salt that now sat lonely on the waiter's tray. Their glasses clinked, down the hatch, the collection of faces squirmed at the extreme taste of salt, then Tequila, then lime.

'Wooooo that hit the spot!' Emma screamed.

'That is my last for a while; I am going to have a Diet Coke next.' Holly replied, laughing and wiping her bottom lip.

'Don't be such a lightweight.' Emma said, as the rush of alcohol injected into her blood stream. She punched the air to the rhythm of the music, her hips rocking to the beat. Holly stuck her tongue out at

Emma and then joined in the hip sway. The Black Eyed Peas faded out and then Jackson 5 kicked in and took its place. The noise bounced off the walls and the place erupted. Multi-coloured balloons and streamers were sent from the heavens and loud sirens were set off. *Can you feel it, can you feel it, can you feel it.* It was time to dance, the Sirocco shuffle!

Chapter 5

Just twenty minutes' walk away from Coco Bongos stood a handsome local man in the lobby of the RIU Tequila hotel. He was taller than the average Mexican and well dressed in a light brown suit, with complementing brown shoes and white t-shirt to complete his outfit. In his right hand was a huge bouquet of flowers, a stunning mix of shades, shapes and sizes. A group of French Canadians were very enthusiastically checking in. They juggled with their paperwork, while gulping down the welcome drinks provided by the bell boy.

The Mexican stood patiently, even though he knew that he had pressing business to deal with. What seemed like an eternity was really no more than two minutes. Veronica, one of the three receptionists on duty, called him forward. The Mexican smiled as he arrived at the desk. He laid down the flowers in an obvious fashion, Veronica's eyes widened as she glanced at them.

'Excuse me Senorita, could you please tell me what room Holly Macdonald is staying in?' Veronica looked him up and down and then replied politely.

'I'm sorry sir; we are not permitted to give out room numbers.' The Mexican looked around and then turned back to Veronica. He smiled softly then leaned forward onto the reception desk. He turned his head slightly, his mouth now facing Veronica's ear. He spoke quietly to her, his hand cupped around his mouth to avoid being overheard by anyone.

'Of course I understand your position; it is just that I met the woman of my dreams last night and she is staying here in your beautiful hotel.' The Mexican gestured to Veronica to look at the flowers he had brought. She smiled and he sensed that she was succumbing to his Latin charm.

'We walked back together, after our night out to this wonderful hotel. We said goodnight just outside, at the taxi rank.' Veronica looked at the flowers once more. The Mexican knew he was winning her over.

'The problem is.' He paused, as he took note of her name badge.

'The problem is, Veronica; well I can't stop thinking about her. I would love to surprise her with these flowers.' Veronica smiled brightly; the Mexican pounced, he knew Veronica had finally succumbed.

'It's just a little bit of harmless romance, I'm sure you like a little romance now and again Senorita, do you not?'

The Mexican leaned back and paused, giving Veronica enough time to give in. She blushed, just a little, but enough for him to notice. Veronica looked around at the other receptionists. They were all busy and she knew her supervisor had taken a cigarette break. Her heart was beating faster, her pulse pumping quicker. *I could get fired for this.* She bit down gently on her plump lip, waiting for a sign. *C'mon, c'mon, I don't have all night.* Veronica inhaled and then quickly scanned for danger, it was all clear.

'Ok, let me see what I can do.' She said. The Mexican smiled. *She must have heard me.*

Her eyes were fixed on her computer screen, but her mind had wandered. *It's been a very long time since I've been romanced.* She smirked at her own thoughts. *Here we go, Holly Macdonald.* She leaned forward and spoke quietly.

'You understand that once you drop the flowers off, you will need to leave straight away? This is a five star, resident only, all-inclusive resort. I will get into a lot of trouble if you are caught without a wristband.' The Mexican took a step back and bowed gracefully at Veronica.

'You have my word, once I have delivered the flowers, I will be on my way.' Veronica tapped her computer one last time. She scribbled onto a piece of paper and handed it over to him. He glanced at it, before putting it away in his jacket pocket, Room 501. Veronica showed him to the end of the reception desk to gain more privacy and pointed in the direction that he should go.

'Go out of the far side of reception, keep to the right and follow the path. It's the second block on the right, it's on the ground floor and it's the first apartment on the right.' He picked up his flowers and then took Veronica's hand. He lifted it gently and kissed it, he raised his eyes, watching closely to see her blushing face.

The Mexican walked away from the reception desk at double speed. He negotiated his way around the fountain that dominated the centre of the lobby. He was about to leave the bright lights of the lobby behind, when he was stopped abruptly by a Canadian couple. Their eyes looked heavy and their smiles were far too exaggerated. The happy Canadian man stuffed his palm in to the Mexicans chest. The stench of rum on his breath was instantly evident to the Mexican.

'Wait up buddy, who is the lucky lady?' The Canadians stood there swaying, waiting for an answer. They were dressed in oversized, white t-shirts, both displaying messages in big black letters. "Ma bitch is 50 today" and "His bitch is 50 today."

It was time for Mrs Canada to pitch in. She put her hand on the Mexican's shoulder and leaned into him.

'Are those roses in the middle?' The Mexican was not amused.

'No, they are not roses, they are carnations.' *I can't even believe I am humouring these slobs.*

'Chip here never buys me flowers, in fact he never buys me jack!' The Mexican watched as her eyes rolled around her eye sockets. Mr Canada was not happy with her comments, but he needed his wife to steady himself.

'Heeyyy, cut it out man, I bought you this damn holiday didn't I?'

'Oh yeah he did, ooops, sorry. It's my birthday you know'

'I can see that.' *Bitch.*

The Mexican had seen his fair share of holiday drunks around this area, but being held up by two of them was really beginning to irritate him.

'Yes, this is very interesting, but could you please excuse me as I am in a hurry.' He moved Mrs Canada to one side and walked on past.

'Mighty fine bunch of flowers you got there, I hope she's worth it.' *I hope there is a sick bucket in their room tonight.*

The pathway was dimly lit at night. It was just enough for you to see your way and just enough for the wildlife to hide in the jungle trees and bushes that surrounded the resort. A bird noise caught his attention, as he approached his block. He looked up, but it was well hidden in the dark night. It reminded him of an old fashioned camera shutter clacking away taking hundreds of photographs.

As he double checked that he was at the correct block, a couple were coming up behind him. They all walked into the block together, all turning right. Only two apartments faced them, 501 and 502.

'Hey, you must be our new neighbour.' The lady said, offering a hand of friendship. The Mexican obliged.

'Nice flowers, are they for your wife?' *More tourists, I know you mean well lady, but just get in your room.* He nodded and smiled, hoping that this was the end of the polite evening conversation. The Mexican gestured to them to enter their room first. He was alarmed when he took his first look at the gentlemen. He had held back, while his good lady was speaking. He could feel himself staring at his face. *Dear mother of God.* He felt compelled to ask.

'Are you ok?' He did not get the chance to answer, his good lady was well in charge and he was well in the dog house.

'Is he ok? Oh my good God, do you know what this idiot has done today?' The Mexican stared at his face; he had not seen anything like it before. In front of him was a grown man, of at least sixty years of age. He had a perfect outline where his sunglasses had been all day. Around his eyes, his skin was lily white. The rest of his face looked deeply distressing, a mass of blisters and distorted skin sores, merged with swollen burnt skin and enlarged freckles. His good lady was not about to give him the lickings of a dog.

'Oh he is so stupid! He brought three tubes of sunscreen on holiday with him. Two tubes of factor two and one tube of factor four.' The Mexican could quickly see where this was going. The good lady needed to get this off her chest, her broad New York accent echoing throughout the corridor.

'He squirted all three out on the bench and then mixed them up, thinking that it would give him a factor eight, can you believe that?' The Mexican burst out laughing. Mr Sunburn could not even speak, it was too painful. It was no laughing matter to his good lady, their vacation was ruined.

'I am sorry for laughing, it does look so painful.' The Mexican held the door, as the couple entered their room.

'Goodnight.' He said which was met with a half-hearted goodbye. *Right, back to work.*

The Mexican put his ear to the door of room 501; he knocked firmly, three times. No answer, he knocked again, this time louder, still no sign of life. He turned around, walked back out of the block, to the nearest dust bin and stuffed the flowers into it. He looked around, all clear. He rushed back to room 501 and within thirty seconds he had picked the lock. He glanced around once more, before pushing the door open and entering the room.

The first thing that caught his attention, as he walked into the room was the mess. Clothes, make up, toiletries and hair straighteners, scattered across the bed and the floor. *How can people live like this?* He closed the door quietly behind him and walked into the dressing area. Four spirit bottles sat invitingly housed on the wall next to the wash basin. Left to right was vodka, tequila, whiskey then rum. They were local brands, but this was his country, they were his brands.

He picked up a glass from the table and then pushed it up onto the star shaped black plastic nozzle. Twenty-five cls of whisky was released into his glass. He pushed it again, then once more and then he threw the contents down the back of his throat. He wiped his lips with the back of his hand.

His face was the first to change, as his body reacted to the effects of such a large punishment. He clenched his fist and shook his head several times. He put the glass down and walked to the wardrobe. As he stood there for a second; he felt a rush from the whiskey. First, a lovely warm, lava glow lit up the back of his throat. From there, it slid down into his stomach and then finally it rested in his legs.

Inside the wardrobe was his mission, there it sat proudly bolted on the wall, the safe. He removed a small silver and black device from his jacket pocket and placed it on the front of the safe. The powerful magnet held it firmly in place. As he pressed the number zero on the safe keypad, a red light flashed on his little machine, followed by a high pitched noise. He continued to press all the numbers on the safe keypad, along with the hash and star keys.

As he waited for the safe to unlock, he could hear his superior's voice ringing in his head. *Get the passport; she cannot leave the country without it.*

Three simultaneously high pitched noises signalled success. The safe bolts retracted and the door released.

Inside the safe were various items of value, but the Mexican was only looking for one thing and he took it. *Right let's get out of here, without all the fuss of getting in here.*

The Mexican had successfully managed to escape unwanted attention, while heading back to reception. He put his head down as he scurried through the reception area, but his new best friends were still lurking around and still drinking there. Chip caught sight of him and yelled out loudly.

'Hey buddy, you get stood up or what?' The Mexican ignored him, but his loud voice was enough to make Veronica take notice. She too caught sight of him rushing through reception. Veronica waved, trying to catch his attention.

'Is everything ok sir?' She shouted. The Mexican ignored them all. His walk turned into a jog, as he ran outside to a waiting car. He jumped into the passenger seat and ordered the driver go, go, go. He looked over his shoulder to another two men in the back. He nodded, job done.

The Mexican looked at the neon lights extravaganza all around him, as the car approached Coco Bongos. The music was pumping out of the bar across the road, party goers from all over the globe were revelling in the midnight heat.

He ordered the driver to get a little closer to the entrance, a further twenty yards and that was the limit, as the streets were jam-packed.

The Mexican and his two back seat buddies got out and walked up to the entrance of Coco Bongos. Three separate lines of keen revellers waited in line, each line representing which floor they would be on to experience the show. Ignoring the waiting public they walked up to the front door. A selection of mountain like doormen stood in their way.

'Hey you three, there is a queue, wait your turn.' One of the doormen growled, holding his arm out pointing to the back of the queue. The Mexican was undeterred, he marched ahead. He walked up to the doorman with the big mouth and flashed identification at him.

'Get me your head of security please.'

Big mouth nodded and radioed the request in. The Mexican turned to his men.

'I know our orders were to remain covert on this, but I'm not wasting time arguing with these guys to let us in.'

'You're the boss.'

Within a matter of seconds another man mountain appeared, his security radio clipped inside his right ear. Big mouth pointed out the Mexican to him.

'I'm Carlos, head of security, how can I help you?' He dipped into his inside jacket pocket and pulled out the passport of Holly Macdonald. He handed it over to Carlos.

'I want her removed from here immediately.'

'Of course, I will see to it personally! I will bring her out of the side exit.' Carlos asked big mouth to escort the Mexican and his men to the side exit.

Carlos scoured through the eight CCTV screens in the security office. Within a minute he pinpointed Holly and her friends and radioed to his crew.

'All blue watch crew, go to block two in the upper seating area, repeat blue watch crew to block two in the upper seating area. Wait for my arrival, for further instructions. Eight security hunks converged on block two, a sight that did not go unnoticed to Holly and her friends.

Carlos quickly arrived and ordered them to surround Holly's table. He marched inside the cordon and issued his demands.

'Ladies, I'm Carlos, head of security, I need to escort one of you off the premises right away.'

'What the hell is going on, is this some kind of bloody joke?' Emma said, nearly laughing at the words she was hearing.

'This is no joke lady, believe me, the police are outside and they wish to speak with Holly Macdonald, as a matter of urgency.' The three girls looked at Holly.

'What do they want with me, is something wrong?'

'Lady, I don't have any details, we need to go now.' One hunk grabbed Holly by the arm, a bit too forcefully.

'Get off me, what are you doing, that hurts.' Emma jumped to her rescue but was quickly put back down on her backside. Carlos fired a warning to the others.

'There is no reason you three can't enjoy the rest of your evening, but interfere in matters of security once more and you will be thrown out.' Emma was not letting it go.

'Hey Carlos, stick your club up your backside and leave Holly alone, we are leaving with her.' Carlos lost his cool.

'Get them all out, Holly stays with me.' Holly pulled free, her arm bright red where the hunk had grabbed her.

'Wait!' Holly yelled as she looked at Carlos.

'Please Carlos, what is this all about?' Carlos looked directly at Holly.

'I have orders from the local police to hand you over to them, that's all I know.' Carlos was shouting above the Rolling Stones, who were belting out Satisfaction through the speaker right next to him.

'I don't understand, we only arrived two days ago in Mexico, it is my first visit here, what could the police possibly want with me?' *I have no time for this.* Carlos picked up Holly and threw her over his shoulder.

The fire exit was pushed open as Carlos marched through it. Holly was frantic; she was kicking and screaming, the girls had been ushered out of the opposite side of the building. Carlos bent down and dropped Holly at the Mexican's feet; she landed on her side, the grass softening her two foot fall.

'Hey, easy, who the hell are you people? Holly was a tough cookie, but this was really beginning to shake her up. Carlos handed Holly's passport to the Mexican.

'Thank you for your help.' Carlos nodded and retreated back to the club. The fire door was slammed; Holly jumped, she had recognised her pink passport holder.

'That is my passport, what the hell are you doing with it and how did you get it?' Holly looked at the Mexican for an explanation.

'Get up.' He offered Holly his hand; she snubbed it, she could manage without his thuggish help. She began to dust herself down, as he offered identification, she wanted answers not his badge. The Mexican ordered his sidekick to remove Holly's cell phone from her bag

'Whatever they are paying you, I will double it.' Holly pleaded, with a look of sheer terror on her face.

'Nobody is paying me anything Miss Macdonald. I am just following orders to get you to the airport security office. Some American high-ranking officials request your company immediately.' Holly had a flashback to the last time she was thrown out of a nightclub. She was only twenty years old at the time; she later found out that her dad was behind it. *Could this be him again, I would not put it past him, he probably thinks I will get kidnapped and sold off to South America.* Holly looked up at the policeman.

'Who are you and who is giving you orders to hand me over to the American officials?'

'My name is Chief Inspector Ramos Gonzales. I am taking my orders from the government Miss Macdonald.'

Holly was a stunning looking woman, but the fear written on her face aged her, right now. The events of the last few minutes had quickly sobered her up.

'This must be some kind of mistake; you must have me mixed up with someone else.'

'I do not make mistakes Miss Macdonald.' He replied abruptly.

Holly babbled nonstop for the twenty minute speedy journey to the airport, her probing questions fell on deaf ears. The one thing she did manage to do was to get Inspector Gonzales to wonder who Holly Macdonald really was. *She does not seem your average criminal.* He confessed to himself.

The car approached the impressive looking speed bumps to the airport building. Inspector Gonzales had toned down his opinion on this operation. He could not see how Holly could be any threat to his country, or be some fanatical criminal.

'I am sorry about the abrupt nature of your return to America Miss Macdonald. I hope that things will be alright for you and maybe someday you will return to our country.' Holly was trying to visualise what lay ahead for her, the Inspector's words offered little comfort.

'Do you really not know what is going on?'

'No I don't Miss Macdonald, I am purely following orders from my superiors.'

'I swear to you Inspector I do not know what all this is about, I have never been in any trouble in my life.' The Mexican gave Holly a concerned look; his attitude changing by the minute. The car pulled up at the entrance to the terminal, the Inspector and his two assistants got out and showed Holly the way. She looked up at the building that only two days ago had been such a happy source of memories.

They entered the terminal through the electric doors and something was starting to bother the Inspector. He was having doubts about the validity of the operation. *Could this be a big mistake?*

He stopped in his tracks and looked at Holly, holding her arm gently. He looked right into her eyes, showing her real concern.

'Miss Macdonald, now is the time to tell me the truth, have you done anything illegal that would cause you to be apprehended?' Holly was emotionally shattered; the intensity of her reply had faded somewhat, from her earlier exchanges.

'No, no, I have never broken the law in my life. I may have bent it a little, but nothing serious.' Holly appreciated his concern, the first bit of comfort she had felt for a while.

'I have to tell you Miss Macdonald, if you're telling me the truth, then this situation does not add up to me. Holly looked up at the Mexican, showing real concern.

'I am telling the truth.' Holly meant every word.

'Ok, let me go up to the security office on my own first and check this out. Just wait here with my men.'

The Inspector waltzed up to the security office and knocked firmly on the door. It opened, an airport official appeared, the Inspector showed his identification badge and then walked in. Holly stood watching her fate unfold with the other two policemen.

The Inspector appeared from the room, he looked glum and anxious.

'It all seems genuine Miss Macdonald; there is a member of the American Secret Service waiting to question you.' Holly stared at the office door.

'What does the Secret Service want with me? Did they say anything?'

'Just that they have orders to pick you up and take you to Washington DC.'

'But I live in New York, there must be some mistake.'

'Apparently not Miss Macdonald.' The Inspector opened the door and let Holly walk in first. He followed right behind, closing the door, his two officers outside.

The office was sparse; a table, two chairs and a large grey dust ridden filing cabinet.

The airport official in the room was quickly excused by the Secret Service Agent. Inspector Gonzales rested his tired body against the filling cabinet.

'That will be all Inspector, I will take it from here.' The Agent showed the Inspector the door. Gonzales nodded; he looked at Holly and nodded again. He stepped outside the room, as the agent closed the door right behind him.

'Take a seat Miss Macdonald.' He pointed to the seat opposite him. The Agent then flashed his ID badge.

'My name is Agent Underwood; I am to escort you on to a waiting plane. You are not in any trouble; in fact the opposite, we need your help as a matter of urgency. You will be given more details on the plane. You are not alone; another man is on board helping us too.' Before Holly could reply, the security door swung open and the Inspector stood there.

'What do you want now Inspector?' Underwood shouted in frustration. He looked at Holly.

'Are you alright Miss Macdonald?' Holly smiled.

'Yes I am, it's ok, I am going to be ok and please call me Holly.' The Inspector smiled and then took her passport from his inside pocket.

'You forgot this.' He leaned over and handed it to Underwood.

'Thank you.' Underwood replied through gritted teeth. The Inspector started pulling the door closed, Holly called him.

'Inspector!' He stopped and looked at Holly.

'Yes'

'Thank you.' Holly said, knowing the Inspector had just staged that for her sake.

'You're welcome Holly, goodbye.'

'Now that you are done with the flirting Holly, we have a plane to catch.' *I still think this could be my dad.*

Chapter 6

Folis Heenan lives in an eighteenth century mansion. It sit's perched on a hill, in the Turkish occupied area of Northern Cyprus. It has three hundred and sixty degree views. To the north, are the stunning turquoise waters of the Mediterranean. The other three sides offer a mix of rustic charm, rolling hills and fruit trees. The natural beauty on offer here is lost on Heenan, he lives here for many reasons, but nature isn't one of them. The only time he ventures further than his terrace is for his daily excuse for keeping fit, a ten minute paddle in his swimming pool and to feed his two pet hamsters, Bonnie and Clyde. They have their own purpose built run, at the head of the swimming pool. It cost a cool eight thousand euros to build, but it allows Heenan to be able watch them play from the comfort of his poolside seat.

He has a younger brother back home, but as far as he is concerned he does not exist, he is weak and worthless. He lost his father to lung cancer when he was fifteen and then lost his mother the following year to a brain disease. Treatment for both parents at the time was costly or impossible to get where they lived. They had no money and no hope. He still carries deep rooted scars, as he was unable to prevent his parents from suffering. It is that pain that drives him to the extremes in order to obtain money and power. It had been rumoured, that in 1986, he ordered the assassination of the doctor who refused his parents the treatment they needed for basic pain relief.

He now has an estimated net worth of over four billion dollars. Much of it gained from illegal dealings in arms, drugs and oil trades. Most of his business was done in Russia, the Ukraine and the Baltic States. Over the last decade he has focused more of his operation in Europe. He now owns several casinos and uses them for money laundering. He has all the comforts money can buy, but it's the commodities that money can't buy, that Heenan craves.

He is obsessed with protecting himself and has financed a small army to do it, with all of his men armed at all times. Over the years his list of enemies has grown, due to the brutal nature of how he runs his business.

Heenan takes risks all of the time, big risks. That means not all of them pay off and when that happens, someone will have to pay. He never settles until his debts are repaid to him, whatever the debt may be.

He hates the west with a passion, especially the United States. As far as he's concerned the United States should have been nuked in Cold War times. He has shouted many times in the past, that he wished he had access to that red button. If he did; he would have gladly pressed it a long time ago. One ambition Heenan did not achieve and now never will was to run for the Russian presidency. He picked up far too many political and KGB enemies, along his merry way to wealth gathering. The target on his back is now big, bigger than ever!

Chapter 7

Majorca is a beautiful island, full of contrasts, home to many famous celebrities. It has long been a favourite destination to several royal families and hundreds of thousands of holiday makers.

Nestled on the west coast is the idyllic Port d' Andratx. For the last three years, Mike Fox and his family have been living there in a traditional Majorcan villa. It is modest compared to some of the villas in the area, with three bedrooms and two reception rooms on a six hundred metre plot. It was chosen because of its hilltop setting, the view over the hills and out to sea were simply stunning.

Since arriving on the island Mike and his family have settled into the local way of life and made several friends, all of which he carefully selected. His kids go to the local school and both he and his wife do charity work for the local canine society. They are real dog lovers, but Mike could not justify having one at home.

They had moved around Europe a lot, mainly France and Spain. The past sixteen years had seen many changes for his family; every move was justified by his business commitments. Mike and his wife Ella have been together since their school days and she is the only person on the island he really trusts.

Yours sincerely, Mike. Another request for canine donations completed, his sixth today. His study was his sanctuary, his room, his man cave.

His phone beeped, a very rare occurrence, it only ever did once per day, this was the second time. He closed his laptop and picked up his phone. He swiped the screen and squinted down at the message. Suddenly, a look of utter disbelief swamped his face; he pushed back on his seat and then let out a deep sigh. He inhaled a deep breath and looked up at the ceiling. His hands gripped and then squeezed the top of his head. The rush of emotion that thrust through his bones was overwhelming. *Why now, I have just settled here, this cannot be happening again.*

A cobweb in the corner distracted him for a millisecond, from the whitewashed appearance of the walls. He dropped his head in despair and read the message; his golden suntan slowly disappeared, his weathered skin now shrouded in doubt. He shook his head in disbelief and read the message once again.

-B1689CXZ241- Confirm and then await instructions.

Mike sat and stared at the message for a moment. *I didn't think this day would ever come.* He fought with his conscience. *I promised her this was the last move.* He took a deep breath and replied by text.

–K5603YGD466

He threw the phone down on his study desk and then rushed outside into the garden, where his kids, Miles and Dylan were playing in the pool, with their mother.

'We have been compromised, get the kids out the pool and get some things together and be ready to leave in ten minutes.' Ella looked on in horror, her eyes filled with tears.

'You promised.' She yelled at Mike.

'Now is not the time Ella, c'mon, let's go.' Ella looked at the kids, her long blonde hair dripping from the pool games she had been playing with them. Her new aqua coloured two piece suit would only be worn once.

'Now Ella, c'mon move!' Mike shouted. Ella snapped out of her trance, using her arms as paddles to swish the water back, she rushed over to the kids, her feet giving way with every step she took on the navy blue floor tiles.

Mike rushed back inside, the study now stood before him. He paused a moment and had a flashback of a happier time. He stared at a painting that his son Miles, his youngest, had done for him. He fancied himself as quite the young artist and this was his finest piece, but there was no time for sentiment, the clock was ticking and ticking very fast.

He removed the painting from the wall to reveal a digital front entry safe and wasted no time in typing in the code. Two, eight, six, seven, one. Three high pitched beeps signalled a successful entry. A clunk followed, the sound of the bolt performing its duty. He grabbed the safe handle, in anticipation of the bolt releasing; he glanced down at his wedding ring. *Sorry baby.*

A ding, safe bolt released, he yanked it open, his wedding ring caught the edge of it. *Ouch, I just said sorry.*

He fumbled around and then grabbed some things and threw them on the study desk. He started to separate money from their documents. *Passports and cash, that is it Mike, passports and cash.* He convinced himself.

He stacked up euros, dollars and sterling and then stuffed them into a plain black holdall that had been stowed under the study desk. Mike shouted upstairs, while encouraging himself to go faster. *C'mon, c'mon*

'C'mon Ella, quickly, we don't have much time, we need to get out of here!'

'I'm going as fast as I can Mike.' Ella yelled back. She looked at her kids and cuddled them tight. They had been towelled down and had their quickest ever clothes change.

'Don't worry darlings; we are just going on a little adventure.'

Mike had no intention of changing his clothes, his black cap, t-shirt, cargo shorts, socks and trainers were staying on. He had to travel light, he had to travel quickly and nothing else mattered. Ella could never understand why he always wore black in the Majorcan heat.

He packed the plain black bag with as much money as it could hold and then slammed the safe door shut.

He pulled his chair back and sat for a moment, his life flying by, he waited, one more text was required before they fled. *Where am I going now?* Mike sat wondering where he was going to be sent, somewhere near, somewhere far, will Ella be happy, what about the kids schooling?

Ella carried two bags as she came rushing down the stairs, the kids followed, Miles ran up to his dad and grabbed him tight.

'Don't worry son, everything will be ok.' Miles looked up with huge wide eyes. Mike squeezed him and kissed his head.

'Go, go on, and get in the car.' Miles took his mother's hand, the phone beeped again. Mike looked at Ella, Ella looked at the kids.

'Go on, let me deal with this.' Ella nodded reluctantly; Mike picked up his phone and swiped the screen. He took a deep breath and then looked down at his message.

Go immediately to where the Ferry departed. Then, use a biro by the sea and stand between the centre columns, facing east. Shout out and listen to the echo.

Mike read the message five times, memorising it. He ran into the kitchen and pulled a hammer out the cupboard drawer. He placed his phone on the speckled grey floor tiles and then frantically smashed it into little bit's, cracking some marble tiles as the hammer destroyed the little piece of technology that had ripped his world apart.

He lifted off his dampened cap and wiped away the beads of nervous sweat that had built up on his forehead. He took one last look around at his home. *I did love it here.* Ella was reassuring the disgruntled kids as she buckled them in to the car. Mike grabbed the car key from the kitchen bench and rushed out. His cap was knocked off as he bounced into the driver's seat. *Sorry,* he half apologised for his crude entry, then fired up the engine. The kids were picking up on the nervous energy building up from their great getaway.

His foot was heavy on the pedal, as he spun off, the wheels thrusting, the tyres whipping up a gravel storm. A trail of dust blew up behind them and followed the car out of the entrance to the villa.

Mike quickly raced to full speed; he turned and looked at Ella briefly catching her eye.

'We need to go to Palma and charter a boat; we need to get off the island now.'

'What about a plane?'

'We have no time to catch a plane Ella.'

Ella knew this day might come, but like Mike and the kids, had firmly settled in Majorca.

'Where are we going Mike?' Mike was too focused on his driving to answer. The road ahead was about to wind sharply, one hundred and eighty degrees from the C-719 and join the Ma-1 motorway. He leaned in his seat as he cornered the last bend, he looked at Ella as he joined the motorway, he split his concentration between the road and Ella.

'Mainland Spain first, then we will be going to,' Mike became distracted, constantly looking out of his rear view mirror. A motorbike had appeared from nowhere and was approaching fast.

'Mike, where are we going after mainland Spain?' Ella asked. Mike was still distracted, something was wrong, Ella sensed it.

'Mike, you're scaring me, what's wrong?' He whispered to Ella, not wanting to alarm the kids.

'I think we are being followed by the motorbike behind us, in fact I'm sure of it.' Ella looked around.

'What are you going to do?'

'I am going to come off at the next exit, come back up the other side and join the motorway again just to be sure.' Mike pushed the car for all it's worth to the roundabout at the bottom of the hill, negotiated the roundabout and then joined the motorway. Mike looked in his rear view mirror, Ella looked over her shoulder. Ella did her best to reassure the kids everything was alright. *We are just having fun, aren't we daddy?*

'I think I've lost them.' Mike said and raised half a smile for his efforts.

'Yes, we are just having fun.' Mike smiled at the kids, checking his mirror to see if they bought it.

'Maybe the motorbike was not following us.' Ella whispered nervously.

'Maybe'

A steady fifty four kph was the reading on the speedometer as he approached Av. Joan Miro at the end of the Autopista De Poniente. The dual carriageway that led into Palma city had some traffic congestion, Mike knew it was inevitable. This was a small comfort to him as he could blend in with all the other cars. He kept his speed in check; he didn't want any more unwanted attention. He passed the first major traffic light crossroads and then swept left handed around the bend and onto the Av. Gabriel Roca.

Thousands of beautiful boats and yachts of all sizes covered the water's edge. It was a stunning sight to behold, but not one that the Fox family were in the mood to take in.

They were stopped at the next set of traffic lights; the red light just sat there and taunted Mike. The lights switched to amber, *at last*. Mike was off, his foot already covering the pedal; soon he released it, sixty kph, the mental limit he had just set himself. *I don't believe it* were the words Mike muttered out loud.

'What is it?' Ella asked as he stared into his rear view mirror.

'The motorbike is back.' Mike said quietly. Ella looked around. *The same colour as before, matt black and the rider has the same outfit and helmet on.* The motorbike weaved through the traffic and then sat behind them. The traffic was solid; Mike looked for gaps, the car swerved back and forth. *It must be him, how can I get out of this?* Each look in his rear view mirror confirmed his worst fears.

Mike noticed a gap emerging two cars ahead and squeezed between two cars, he caught the side of the car to his right, it clipped the kerb and rammed into the safety barrier. A domino effect followed as several cars crashed into the back of each other. The kids screamed, Ella did her best to calm them, Mike floored the car and it responded to his demands and quickly reached one hundred and five kph. The red Opel Astra had no more respect for the sixty kph speed limits.

The motorbike followed, finding it much easier to weave in and out of the traffic. The traffic was once again halting his plans; he glanced out of the side window. The sign at the Hotel Mirador caught his eye for a brief moment. They had renewed their wedding vows there last year; Ella knew what Mike was thinking. She squeezed his leg, Mike looked back at her, she mimed, *I love you.*

'I love you to Ella, I give you my word, I am going to get us out of this and we are going to settle down somewhere. I will go off grid and this life will be over, I am finished with it.' Ella smiled, the first for some time. Mike looked ahead and then back at Ella.

'I mean it Ella, it's a promise.'

'Mike, he is alongside you, he has a gun!' Ella screamed. Mike had no time to react; the rider fired a single shot, hitting him in the side of his head. The bullet shot out of the other side, just missing Ella. Mike slumped onto the steering wheel, the car swerved violently to its right, Ella grabbed the steering wheel, Mike's body made it impossible for her to pull the car back, the car was now heading straight for the safety barrier. *Noooooo!*

The car behind watched in horror as the red Astra smashed through the safety barrier at ninety two kph. It hurtled towards the marina, hitting the water hard, bumper first, narrowly missing a row of yachts. It slowly submerged, Ella was dazed, her head taking a bang on impact, she heard the screams from the back seat. She fought hard with her consciousness to stay awake. She looked down at her airbag. *Where are you*? She pushed anything she could feel looking for the seat belt button. Bells were ringing in her head, her eyes were playing tricks. Suddenly she fell forward, she had found the button.

The motorcyclist was long gone, as other drivers jumped out of their cars and converged at the safety barriers. Everyone was looking at each other for answers as to what had just happened.

A buoy and some rope were thrown from the edge by a frantic passer-by. Ella wrestled with her head rest and pulled it out from the seat. She had recently seen a news item on a similar situation she had now found herself in. It had shown that the head rest can be used to smash out the car windows. The bullet hole in the passenger window was not good enough for the kids escape, so she climbed into the back and rammed the two spikes at the side window. *It's ok kid's mama has got this, just look at me and do not look at dad ok*? The car continued to submerge; she rammed the window again, this time it smashed. Ella leant back and kicked off the last bit of glass.

The car started to take in water, the front quickly filling up. Ella grabbed the rope and tied it around Dylan and eased him out of the back window. He was hoisted up quickly. Another rope was thrown in. Miles sobbed for his dad; Ella comforted him, blood from her cut filled the side of her face. She kissed Miles and tied the rope around him and carefully pushed him out of the window. Miles was clear; Ella could see a buoy right next to her. She leaned out to get it, the car slipped back, she missed it, the car slipped some more.

Ella could hear the screams fading as the car submerged under water. Her visibility deteriorated as she took a deep breath. Help quickly arrived, three men jumped into the water, the kids were safe and they needed their mother. Ella squeezed herself through the broken window; she had taken in some water, dirty bacteria ridden water. She surfaced, coughing, but alive.

Chapter 8

One of the presidential helicopters waited at the airport, to take Jack and Holly the ten minute journey to the White House. The plane touched down in Washington DC 6.10AM local time. The plane journey had been a strange experience for all concerned. Jack and Holly had been given a briefing on the plane by Ridley, although it was all too brief for their liking. They had exchanged a few pleasantries. The only thing they found out that they had in common with each other, apart from their abductions, was that they were both an only child.

Ridley climbed aboard the helicopter, Holly followed, Jack stopped at the bottom of the steps. He looked up at the green and white hunk of metal. *I hate these things.* The co-pilot handed Ridley three pairs of ear protectors, Holly sat down and buckled up. She looked out at Jack daydreaming and waved.

'Jack, c'mon.' *So, it's true what I've heard, you are bossy.* Ridley gave the order to fire up the engines; Jack took his seat, buckled up and put on his ear protectors.

Ridley was the first one to compete with the noise level of the engine.

'You need to understand, that this is a top secret operation we are dealing with. You will be given more details by the President, but please, for the good of your country, help us and do it quickly.' Holly looked at Jack and then looked back at Ridley. She leaned forward to Ridley and yelled out over the noise.

'We will do our best!' Jack nodded, holding onto his ear protectors for dear life.

'When we land, you will be given an escort to the man in charge of the operation. Whatever happens in the future, or whoever you come in contact with in the future, he is the only person you take your orders from. Is that clear? Trust no one else.'

The helicopter landed inside the White House grounds. Two men appeared from nowhere and ordered Jack and Holly to follow them to a stairwell inside the White House.

At the bottom of the stairwell was a short corridor.

The lead agent stopped at a door, he looked around then looked back and then placed his hand on the digital palm reading machine that sat on the wall to the right of the door. It scanned across his hand and then back again, the neon green light that beamed across the scanner could be seen between his fingers. Five clicks were heard, one after the other in a rhythmic motion. The door popped open slightly and the agent pushed it back, creating their first view inside the White House.

They all marched in; Jack's first impression was a puzzling one. He questioned himself. *Why are three of the doors labelled and one of them not? And why is that door bright red?* They walked down the corridor, passing doors labelled, WH1, WH2, WH3. The lead agent stopped at the final door, the red door. He typed in a seven digit code on a keypad to unlock it, only three clicks this time, a point noted by Holly.

Behind the red door was a sparse room, both Jack and Holly were told to sit down. A survey of the room revealed a sea of grey, this time seats, either side of a large desk. The only thing to break the room's bleak appearance was a silver service tray. It was quite inviting; the smell of coffee wafting out of the spout of the silver flask was a welcome one for Holly. Jack noted four cups and saucers, all white china, a small silver jug of milk, four silver teaspoons, a silver bowl of sugar cubes, four bottles of water and a selection of plain biscuits.

'Please help yourselves'. The lead agent said, before he turned around and marched out of the room, closing the bright red door behind him. *Three more clicks.*

Both Jack and Holly had been wondering about each other. This was the first time they had been left alone and they both found it all a bit weird. They had heard lots about each other over the years and both had built an opinion of the other from a distance. Even after the in-flight pleasantries and the brief conversation they had managed, neither had changed their opinions of each other.

'You want a coffee?' Holly broke the ice.

'It smells good, why not.' Jack did not look at Holly when he replied; he was still surveying the room, looking for anything that could help build a picture, of why they were there. *It is true what they say about you then, you are pretty arrogant.*

'You're welcome.' She quickly replied, her tone descending into pure sarcasm.

Holly stood up over the tray to pour the coffee, as three more clicks were heard. They both looked at the door as it opened slightly. Two voices could be heard, but neither could make out what was being said. Holly looked at Jack, who was staring at the red door and then decided against the coffee and quickly sat back down. *It is true what they say, he is quite handsome, in a rugged sort of way.*

What had seemed like an eternity was in fact only a matter of seconds, before Jack and Holly caught sight of him. The President, their President, the President of the United States of America. They both stood as the President entered the room, Holly could feel her heart rate increase by a few beats. *Who is the other guy, I don't recognise him.* Jack asked himself.

The President greeted them both like long lost friends, smiling and then shaking their hands warmly. His member of staff was less forthcoming; he stood four feet behind the President. He looked glum and concerned, his cheeks were pinkish. His tiny facial veins were highlighted, his stress levels all too clear from first sight. The bags under his eyes told Jack a story, this was an overworked stressed out dude.

Once the introductions were over the red door was closed. *No clicks this time.* Holly noted.

'Jack, Holly, have you been treated well?' The President enquired. Both Jack and Holly gave answers that the President wanted to hear, but not how they truly felt about the last few hours.

'Yes sir Mr President.' Said Holly

'Yes sir Mr President.' Jack quickly followed. They were in the White House about to be addressed by the President on an urgent matter. Not what either of them would have expected yesterday.

'I am sorry you have been brought here under such difficult circumstances, but as you've had it explained to you, we have a situation that requires your unique skills and knowledge.' The President oozed confidence, if he had a major problem on his hands, he didn't show it, in either his manner, or enthusiasm.

'I cannot express to you how important it is to succeed, I do not have much time, but I wanted to meet you in person. I wanted to express to you, the importance of getting me the result I need.' The President turned and pointed to his aide.

'Johnson here will fill you in on all the facts. Goodbye, good luck and God speed to you both.' The President shook hands once more and left the room, as he closed the door, silence. *No clicks again. There must be one code to open then lock, when it's closed and another code to open and then stay unlocked.* Holly pondered to herself.

'Take a seat please.' Johnson's first words were direct, official and eager.

'You have both been chosen for this mission because we believe you are the crème de la crème, at what you do.' His tone was steady and convincing, but the look on his face and his body language were different.

'What I am about to tell you may seem a little farfetched at first, but believe me, every detail I tell you is 100% true.

'Ok.' Jack replied, hungry to hear what was going on.

'We have just been made aware that the President's Shield has been compromised.' Johnson said. Jack and Holly looked at each other, hoping that the other had an idea what Johnson was talking about.

'What's that?' Holly asked.

'It is not what, it is who. The President's Shield is a group of four men, each sworn to carry until their death, coded information on the whereabouts of a *Document of Truth*.

'What?' Holly gasped. Johnson ignored her and carried on.

'Each of them have markings on the sole of their right foot, these markings are meaningless and completely worthless on their own. However, if someone were to get their hands on all four men and decipher their markings, then they would be in a position to be able to destroy the President and destroy the United States of America.'

Jack and Holly were dumbstruck at what they had just heard come out of Johnson's mouth. Johnson paused, waiting for a response; he was disappointed, there was just silence. Jack and Holly knew of many conspiracy theories, urban myths, rumours, all sorts of tales, but this one had come right out of the blue to both of them.

Johnson rocked back on his heels an inch and then put his hands in his pockets. He continued, this time his tone was a little higher, his pitch a little faster.

'This could also destabilise our relations with the rest of the world. It would cause a domino effect of problems with other nations, including our closest allies.'

Johnson's navy blue tie was loosened and the top button of his white shirt was undone. This did nothing to halt the impression that Johnson was struggling with the weight of this problem.

Holly looked confused, Jack looked confused and Johnson was confused as to why they stood looking at him in silence. Holly could not figure out where this was leading to. *This is the White House for God's sake.*

'I don't understand, what could be so important that you need to keep it secret by using four men in this way? It all sounds a bit hocus pocus, is this some sort of joke?'

Holly was two days away from her thirty fourth birthday. She had planned to spend it in Mexico, with her friends, but that was well and truly in the past now. She had a velvety shine to her long wavy chocolate brown hair. She had the most beautiful clear skin, with sparkling brown eyes, that radiated around a room.

She had a privileged upbringing, her dad being a prominent Senator, before he retired two years ago. Her grandpa, who was Italian, moved to New York in 1946. He was her hero and they spent lots of time together when she was growing up, as her dad worked very long hours for his ambition to become Senator Natalie. Grandpa Marco was a great teacher and philosopher. He taught her many things, some she liked, some she loved. Her home study with grandpa far outweighed her personal development in life.

He was a great problem solver and spent many an hour teaching her ways to see things differently to other people. He taught her magic and the art of illusion. He also taught her chess, amongst many other board games. It was chess that she excelled in, becoming a junior world chess champion at just seventeen years old. This triumph was squashed, by the news of Grandpa Marco's sudden death, from a heart attack, the following day. She took comfort from the fact that he was there to see her win.

Holly's mother died giving birth to her. She never took to her step mother, who came on the scene when she was eleven years old. She rebelled against her father after the death of Grandpa Marco. She changed her family name of Natalie to Macdonald, which was the name of her grandpa's loyal servant, a German Shepherd Dog.

Her father was desperate for Holly to become a lawyer; he knew she had all the ability to succeed, but Holly would do anything other than what her father wanted her to do.

After working at an insurance company, at middle management level, as a claims executive for four years, she made a smart move. She started her own business; she would track down fraudulent insurance claims, something that had become big business in the 1990's. Her company grew and expanded quickly and many major blue chip companies used her services. She sold her business in 2004 for fifty-one million dollars, banking seven million dollars of that herself.

After taking some time out, she started a new business, this time as a specialist and on her own. She freelanced herself to track down missing persons. Sometimes for the police, sometimes for individuals and sometimes for lawyers looking to settle inheritance claims. Like Jack, she made a name for herself in this line of work; they had both become bounty hunters. Now, their paths have crossed and the bounty that brings them together could put the United States of America on the brink of collapse.

'This is no joke; believe me, if only it were I could sleep at night. The truth is though Holly, I don't know what information they have or why they are protecting it; I can only make an educated guess.' Johnson went on to explain further.

'Each President has discreetly passed on to the next all that they know and have heard about the Shield.' Jack jumped into the conversation, his manner becoming irritated.

'This is madness, what are we supposed to do with this poppycock you are telling us? It sounds like a load of Chinese whispers to me' Holly jumped in too, but she aimed her irritation at Jack.

'For God's sake Jack, give it a rest.' Jack looked in amazement at Holly. *What the hell, only seconds before she said a similar thing. Jeezz, I can tell she really likes me.*

Jack had studied forensic science at Harvard and after excelling there, he landed a job working in his local police force, as the Chief of Forensics. He became the youngest person to hold that post in Florida.

The trouble with Jack was that he is a dreamer. After three years he got bored with his work and decided to travel the world. Jack visited Europe and Asia and then settled in Africa, where he was offered a job looking for rare species of insects.

Jack's background in forensic science helped him greatly in the job. He loved it and he read books like his life depended on it. He read books about anything that could give him an edge, no matter how bizarre the subject seemed. Jack quickly made a name for himself in this field and two years later a wealthy business man made him an offer he could not refuse. He was asked to track down a family heirloom, a priceless antique and he paid him very handsomely for it.

After Jack successfully reunited the antique with its owner, word quickly spread of his talents in this field. The local police took a different view, his results made a mockery of some of their investigations, but this only heightened the demand for his services, from some very wealthy people.

Jack moved back to his home in Florida eighteen months ago, after his marriage broke down. His wife had claimed that he was married to his work. The truth was, Jack loved her very much, but the passion for his work at that time, was intoxicating to him.

'What is your role in all this Johnson?' Jack was puzzled, he needed answers.

'I am known as *Servant to the President's Butler*. It has been an unofficial position, for someone who has been close to the President since 1789.' Jack interrupted him, his interest awoken again.

'1789? That is when Washington was sworn in.'

'That is correct, my job is to always know the whereabouts of the 'Presidents Butler', who in turn, is the only person with the knowledge of the whereabouts of the President's Shield.' It was Holly's turn to interrupt.

'Does that mean the information that the President's Shield men have, dates back to 1789?'

'That is also correct; the President's Shield has been in place since 1789. Every serving President has been made aware of the need to protect the Shield. It has been their highest priority.'

'I still don't understand what you want us to do to help you.' Jack said.

'Isn't it obvious Jack?' Holly laughed nervously.

'Seriously, you're not saying you have lost the whereabouts of the Presidents Shield are you?' Jack puffed at Johnson. Johnson puffed straight back.

'No I am not Jack, it is much worse than that. I have lost contact with the Butler.' Jack looked down at the floor and shook his head; this situation had turned his life upside down. *If my baby has gone missing from the car park, over this heap of tosh, I will never vote Republican again.* Jack was back in the car park, about to climb onto his motorbike, when Johnson brought him back into the room.

'The Butler had informed me that one of the Shield had not replied to his message. The Butler communicates everyday with the entire Shield. He sends them a coded message by text. It is highly unusual, almost unheard of for a member of the Shield to ever miss a day of contact with him. It is unprecedented to miss two days.' Jack interrupted Johnson.

'Wait up a second, let us be clear here. We have been kidnapped and brought here to do your job for you. That is the bottom line isn't it Johnson?' Jack looked at Holly for agreement, still no endorsement.

'Does it seem like that to you Holly?'

'Can you please just shut up and let him finish.' Holly's response was blunt and to the point. Jack rolled his eyes in frustration.

'I was told you could be an ass, but I take people as I find them and I am inclined to agree with them at present.'

'What is this, pick on Jack day?'

'Like Holly has so eloquently put it Jack, please shut up and let me finish.' Jack rolled his eyes even further, before a very brief response.

'Fine.'

'I was informed by the Butler that one of the Shield had done just that, gone two days without a response, so I started to investigate. I have since found out, that two days ago the Shield member in question, one James McVey had run up serious gambling debts and crossed a man called Folis Heenan. It turns out this man is a major up and coming bad ass.'

'So you're saying your man may have been killed by this Heenan guy for a gambling debt?' Holly enquired. Her mind had gone into overdrive, while trying to piece things together to second guess what Johnson was going to say.

'I wish it was that simple Holly! My God I really do.' Johnson was rubbing his forehead; this was way more painful to get out than he thought it would be.

'I believe from my enquiries into Folis Heenan's methods, that he tortured our man, who then gave up details of the origin of the President's Shield and details of the Butler. I am still looking into how Heenan did it. I now believe that he could have all the information that the Butler had about the location of the Presidents Shield.'

'How do you know that?' Jack asked, a little more interested in the developments of the conversation.

'The Butler contacted me yesterday, to say the Shield was now totally compromised. He was pulling his men from their locations and issuing a code red message, leave at all costs.' Johnson began shaking his head and muttered under his breath. *Over two hundred and twenty four years have passed by and I am now part of the collapse of the Shield, Jesus Christ, why did this happen on my watch?*

'What was that'? Jack asked, screwing his face up at Johnson's schoolboy like mutterings. Johnson ignored his smug request and carried on.

'That was the last contact I had with him. He had confirmed another one of the Shield; Mike Fox had now been killed in Majorca, shot in the head while trying to escape. He lost control of his car and it sank into the marina in Palma. His wife Ella and their two children survived, but when his body was brought up to the surface later, his right foot was missing. '

'Do you know where they were headed?' Holly asked, sensing the pain Ella must now be feeling.

'No, only the Butler decides that and we could not obtain any information to help us work that out.'

'Is there anything else you can tell us?' Jack asked.

'The Butler told me he was going off the grid, until he could find out whom it was that he could trust. He had no further contact from the remaining two shield members. That was the last communication I had with him.'

'If that is the case we really need to speak to the President and find out what it is he knows. He must know more than he has told us.' Jack was trying his best to build up a picture of what had happened and how they could help, but it all seemed dangerously uncomfortable to him.

'Two dead, two missing and you want us to go out and find this thing, Jesus who do you think we are, Sherlock Holmes and Dr Watson?'

'Jack, you need to understand, it is not that the President does not want to tell you, he can't tell you, it is forbidden.' Holly came around to Jack's way of thinking; it was beginning to sound like a stitch-up.

'I'm with Jack on this Johnson; if we don't speak to the President I'm afraid this is doomed, before we start.'

'Hurrah, finally a bit of credit.' Holly ignored Jack's remark and fired another warning shot at Johnson.

'We need to speak to him, to have any chance of finding whatever it is we are looking for. This information is cryptic at best.' Holly sat back down and looked up at Johnson, waiting for his reply.

'I will see what I can do.'

'One last question Johnson.' Jack asked.

'Why is this door red, when the other doors are grey?' Jack's random question threw Johnson. He shook his head, walked over to the door and opened it. He paused and looked around at Jack.

'You work it out!'

Chapter 9

Brad Cummings had being living a very peaceful life on the island of Rhodes, Greece. He lived in a small lodging in the village of Lardos, in the south east of the island. It is located only a few kilometres from Lindos, a stunning whitewashed village and home to a maze of the most idyllic, narrow streets. Spectacular sunsets stand behind the Acropolis then tease their way underwater.

Brad was addicted to snorkelling and it was that addiction that brought him to Lardos. The crystal-clear waters of the Aegean Sea, provided ample activities for his pleasure. He shared a small, modest motorised boat with a British expatriate called Mark, who worked in the next village of Pefkos, a popular tourist destination.

Brad and Mark became very good friends over the years and they were often mistaken for brothers. They were very similar in height and build, but their hair styles differed. Mark's hair was black, short and sharp, dyed of course. Brad on the other hand, had the Aussie surfer look; although he always thought his green "go to bed eyes" were his best feature. Brad liked nothing more than getting his torso out in the Pefkos sun, his six-pack being a close second to his eyes.

They had a good little number going in the resort of Pefkos. Mark worked in a little hotel called the Matina. He ran the bar in the evenings, with a local guy called Stergos, or as Mark called him, the man with a thousand cousins. Mark was charming with everyone, warm, friendly and genuine. He would encourage holiday makers to join him and Brad on their boat, for some snorkelling or fishing. They could take up to ten people at a time. They charged ten euros per person for a two hour trip, which was great value compared to other boat trips. It was also a great way of meeting people and one of the perks was meeting single women. Both Brad and Mark made the most of their captive audience. They romanced and charmed their way through many holiday makers, who were very willing participants.

Mark woke up suffering from a major hangover, from the previous night's action at the Matina hotel. Another one of the perks of working there was the amount of holiday guests who bought him drinks. There had been two such guests staying there that week. Mark had nicknamed them the Cocktail Twins, as these girls could drink. They spent serious cash on cocktails and not just any cocktails. Mark would invite them around his side of the bar, to select whatever alcohol they wanted, mixed up in the silver shaker.

There was one other family that gave the Cocktail Twins a run for their money as far as the drinking stakes were concerned. They came in the shape of a young couple, who were celebrating their wedding with their families and celebrate they did. Mark had a flashback to last night's celebrations. The night shift security guard had given him a telling off, for allowing the whole wedding party to pile into the swimming pool at 2am. The Mansfield's, some clothed, some in their underwear, had taken over Mark's bar last night.

Mark had arranged with Brad, for the Cocktail Twins to join them for lunch, on the boat that day. They didn't charge them this time, it was purely a charm offensive. They arranged to meet on the jetty on Pefkos beach, just fifty metres down the dusty hill, from the Matina hotel. Although, in the forty two degree midday sun, that fifty metres seemed a lot further to the Cocktail Twins, with their King Kong hangovers.

Brad was in a deep sleep, his phone on silent. It had been on silent since yesterday evening. A trip to the local dentist for root canal work had proved a minor disaster. A slip of the drill and several internal stitches later he was released, bloody, bruised and tired. A severe migraine had set in; Brad's answer was a double dose of sleeping pills. Four tablets had him out for the count. He was still asleep when Mark started shaking him to wake him up.

The Cocktail Twins had arrived early; they had been waiting for five minutes already. Mark had rushed over to Brad's place; a couple of hundred yards across the square from where he lived. He had also slept in, but now wide awake; his hangover was competing with his testosterone.

'Brad wake up you idiot, we have a date mate, c'mon shake a leg. It's half twelve now, we are supposed to meet the 'cocktail twins' at half twelve mate.' Brad raised an eyebrow, his mind taking time to adjust to the sights and sounds he was confronted with. He rubbed his eyes and then squinted; he could just about make Mark out, against the backdrop of bright light shining into the room.

'Alright mate, chill out will you.'

'C'mon mate, they will not wait forever man, these girls are hot and you don't want to waste this opportunity.'

'Alright, alright I'll get dressed toot sweet.'

The boat was berthed in Lardos, but it only took a few minutes for the lads to chug around to Pefkos in it.

Brad plodded gingerly into the bathroom next door; he shook a small aerosol and sprayed three white clouds of deodorant into each armpit. After gargling a mouth full of purple mouthwash, he squirted a pinch of toothpaste onto his electric tooth brush and then buzzed away.

Brad stood looking in his full length bedroom mirror. The white vest and shorts that he had just put on were covered in last night's red pasta sauce. *That will have to do for today, anyway, I will take my vest off when we get on the boat.* He added a splash of his favourite aftershave, Paul Smith Extreme, *the one that girls could not resist.* He could hear Mark yelling at him to get a move on. He spoke to his reflection in the mirror. *Dear me Mark, these girls must be hot.*

In the rush of getting ready, Brad had forgotten his phone and it was not until they had ran down to board the boat that he remembered. *Bloody hell, why did I take those sleeping pills?* He always messaged the Butler first thing in the morning, but he was now oblivious to the fact that he had several unread messages.

As Brad and Mark were approaching Pefkos harbour, another boat came in from the distance, heading towards them. It was a very impressive piece of floating fibreglass, a Sunseeker Mangusta 130.

'You don't see many boats of that quality in these waters Brad.' Both Brad and Mark were admiring the boat, as it forged in their direction, at a rate of knots. The speedboat closed right in on them as they rolled up to the jetty at Pefkos beach.

'Brad, there is someone standing up on the boat waving at us'.

'I don't recognise them, do you?'

'No, I don't mate. I think they are shouting something at us'

'Wait up; I need to talk to you.' The man on the Sunseeker shouted, franticly waving at them, his cries drowned out by the noise created by the Honda engine that growled away at the back of the boat.

'Who is this guy Mark?'

'I have told you mate, I have no idea, maybe some new guy from the boat club.'

The Cocktail Twins' caught sight of Mark and Brad and made their way from the beach, down the jetty. Each step of their loose flip flops carefully placed between the wooden slats. They held onto each other, their wraps blowing open in the slight breeze. This offered Mark his first sight of the floral bikinis they were wearing. He was wearing his usual Ralph Lauren polo shirt, red of course, his team's colours. *Lovely jubbly girls. That will do for me. If you come on my boat and you're not wearing a Nottingham Forest top, then a bikini like that certainly gets my vote.*

'Wait.' Yelled the man on the speedboat.

'Why is he waving us back out to sea, that's a bit weird mate.' Mark told Brad, who agreed, Brad was strict on routine and this was very unusual.

'Damn it.' Said the man on the Sunseeker, his fellow shipmate offered him words of advice.

'This is too public, take her back for now.'

A quick turn and they were off, the front end of the boat rising like a horse on two legs. Brad and Mark looked on as the speedboat powered around the cliff edge and out of sight.

'Let's just get the girls mate.' Mark squeezed down on the throttle an inch, as they cruised the last few metres to hook up at the jetty.

Brad was spooked and it showed.

'Chill out man Brad, don't look so worried, we need to focus on the girls now mate.' Brad's mind was now on other things. *I need my phone.*

'Mark, I need to go back for my phone, I need to check a couple of things before we go out with the girls.'

'No way Brad, the girls are about to jump on board, just relax mate, what is up with you? Just use my phone to check whatever you want.'

'I can't Mark, it's complicated. We are going back right now and that's the end of it.' Brad's tone was assertive. He looked right at Mark, his facial features serious and still. Mark thought for a second and then realised that this little hissy fit was way out of character.

'Ok mate, no problem, whatever Brad, but we take the girls with us ok?'

'I really don't think that is a good idea.'

'That's the deal, take it or leave it.' Brad nodded in agreement; he just wanted his phone and quickly and to compromise was the quickest way to get it.

Mark held out an arm to welcome the girls on board their floating love nest. He put on his best, corny pirates accent to welcome them.

'Aye aye, me hearties.' He gruffed.

'Aye aye, captain.' Was one response, while the other one giggled in excitement. They each took a wobbly step onto the front of the boat, both grinning in anticipation for their little adventure. Mark offered them both two air kisses, followed by an introduction for Brad, in his best thespian voice.

'As you have guessed girls, this is Brad and as you have guessed Brad, these are the Cocktail Twins, aka Zoe and Boo.' Mark had done this routine many times before, but he could sense that on this occasion it would be hard work with Brad.

Zoe handed Mark a bottle of bubbly, freshly chilled, from the supermarket at the Matina hotel. Mark helped them to take a seat on the rocky boat and then prompted Brad to do the honours.

'Brad!' Mark shouted, finally getting his attention.

'Open the bubbly for the girls mate.'

'What? Ok, yeah, sorry I was miles away.' As Brad opened the bubbly, the girls got back to their giggly ways, Mark informed them of a slight change of plan.

'We are going to take a little detour my lovelies, Brad needs to go back to get his phone and check on his teddy bear's temperature or something. Just relax, get your suntan lotion on and get ready to have some fun in the sun.' Mark was trying to rally Brad. His effort was wasted; his mind was fixated at the point of the bay, where the Sunseeker disappeared.

Brad steered the boat out the harbour and back to the point where the Sunseeker disappeared. Mark and the Cocktail Twins quickly became oblivious to Brad's increasing concerns they had a bottle that needed attention. No glasses required, this bubbly could be swigged from the bottle.

Like most of the summer days in Pefkos, there were clear blue skies and calm waters. Brad took the boat out of the bay and past the point where the Sunseeker disappeared from sight; he could see it was clear. *No Sunseeker, I am getting paranoid.*

'I will be quick mate, I promise' Brad yelled as he scrambled off the boat at Lardos harbour.

'You better be mate.' He shouted at the back of Brad's head, as he ran off.

Brad's home was only a two minute jog up the road from the harbour. His mind was focused on only one thing, his phone, he couldn't think of anything else, as ran into the house. He rushed up the stairs and into his bedroom as quick as he could.

'Oh my God, no!' Brad shouted at himself. His phone was missing, his bedside table was empty, the place where the phone slept every night. Panic set in, his mind was catapulted back to the last time he had to run. He was only a child, but he can remember it like it was yesterday, but that was his dad being chased; now it was his turn to make the decisions.

Brad ran for the bedroom door, but stopped suddenly. He held his breath as he recalled a pre- sleeping pill flashback. *I took the phone to bed last night, Jesus; I am so messed up today, what is wrong with me?* He inhaled, ran back to the bed and yanked back the white cotton sheet and finally exhaled. A wave of relief descended over him, his phone was there, where he had left it. He picked it up and hugged it tight and allowed himself to collapse backwards onto his bed. *Panic over.*

Mark was finishing off his third joke with the girls, when he noticed the Sunseeker had berthed behind them and no one was on board. *Strange.*

'Two minutes girls, while I run up and get Brad to sort himself out.'

Brad swiped his phone to send a message to the Butler, his momentary sense of relief and calmness, was quickly crushed. It was quickly replaced by a surge of sheer terror as he read the display.

Six unread messages from the Butler, Jesus. He pressed message one, as a voice yelled at him from downstairs.

'Brad.' He sat up quickly; shocked to hear his name. *I don't know that voice .*He could hear footsteps rushing up the stairs. He jumped off the bed and lunged for his bedside draw. *My gun.*

'Stop!' The man yelled and then fired off a warning shot from his pistol. Brad froze; and then put his hands up, still clutching onto his phone. Church bells chimed, they echoed around the square outside the house. *I'm going to die at 1PM.*

'Turn around.' He ordered. Brad slowly obliged. The gunman checked a photograph that he had in his hand. *Good.* He looked at Brad between the eyes. *This is a present from my boss.*

Brad collapsed face down on the floor; he had taken a bullet to the head and one to the stomach. He clung on to the side of the bed, gasping on his last breath. He mustered one last act; he wanted to see his maker. He managed to pull and drag himself around onto his back, the blood from his wounds seeping into his bed sheet. *He looks Aryan.* The gunmen stood over Brad and smiled, his blue eyes looked captivating, as he unloaded a third and fatal shot.

Mark had bounced through the front door, which was left wide open.

'Bloody hell Brad, what is taking you so long?' He shouted, but no reply.

'Brad, hurry up, the girls will not wait forever mate!' *Where the hell is he?*

Mark ran upstairs to the bedroom and burst in to the room shouting Brad's name.

'*Ah my God, Jesus Christ, no, what the hell is going on*? Mark stood with his head in his hands and then fell to his knees as he looked at Brad's body, covered in a red blood stained sheet. He pulled the sheet back off Brad's head. *Is he dead? He's dead; I know he's dead, what the hell is going on? Who could do this this, Jesus I need to call the police. I'm going to be sick.* Mark cried, his best mate gone, as he sat in total shock looking at Brad. Mark looked away as he sobbed. *Oh my God his foot has been chopped off.*

Chapter 10

The President had agreed to give Jack and Holly five more minutes of his time. He had been reluctant, but he knew the ever spiralling chain of events needed to be brought to a halt and fast.

Johnson headed back to the room with the red door. Click, click, click, the door popped open and Johnson walked back into the room.

Jack and Holly looked calm; they had done their fretting for the moment. Johnson gathered himself, leaned forward and then handed a cell phone to Jack. Jack looked at the cell phone, he raised his eyebrows. *An Alcatel One Touch.* Johnson pointed at the cell phone in Jack's hands.

'I am the only person that you are to speak to regarding this operation, my number is stored in there and you can call me anytime, day or night. Is that clear?'

'Yes.' Holly replied.

'Hey, what about my cell phone, your goons took that off me.' Jack said.

'Both of your cell phones will be kept safe, don't worry and do not use email. We don't want anyway of anyone tracking your movements. Is that understood?'

The President appeared at the doorway, as Johnson was giving his lecture, he took stock for a moment, important decisions required moments of reflection.

'Please leave us Johnson.'

'But Mr President, I am in charge of this operation, I must insist.' The President cut him off, before he could protest any further.

Johnson followed the order, not happy at being left out of the conversation, but his professionalism and loyalty to his President was unquestionable.

'I will be outside should you need anything. The President nodded and then closed the red door. The President asked Jack and Holly to take a seat and then propped himself up on the corner of the grey desk. Holly admired his immaculate attire. *He looks every inch a President in that suit.*

'I'm sure once you know all the facts, you will have some questions and I will do my best to answer them, but you need to realise one thing before I go on. If we ever find out that either of you use the information, that I am about to give you, against the United States of America, you will be given the death penalty for treason.' The President paused a moment, Jack and Holly looked at each other; they had no idea what was going on and no idea how to react to it.

'I will get Johnson to give you a copy of the Espionage Act. You must sign it, do we have a deal?' *Do we have a choice?* Jack thought.

'We have a deal.' Holly replied, as she looked at Jack.

'Before I start, I would like to thank you both. We have put you in a very difficult situation and like the brave men and women before you; you have come forward to protect our great country. It is people like you two that make me proud to be the President.' *Come forward? That's a good one, abducted and pushed here more like.* Jack quipped to himself.

'If I was to start by saying (*we the people*). What would that conjure up in your minds?' This question surprised them both. Holly paused for thought, an attempt to retrieve an answer from the depths of her memory bank.

'The constitution, everything we stand for.' Jack replied, his voice stronger and wiser than in his last stupid remark.

'That is it in a nutshell Jack. That is what this is all about.' Holly's squint expanded into to a full blown look of confusion.

'I don't understand sir.' Holly quizzed. The President put his hands up to gesture his understanding, of Holly's confusion and continued.

'While the Constitution was being agreed, debated and drawn up in 1787, there was a disturbing set of events. All of these events were hidden from the American people. Still to this day, they are hidden from the American people. There was a stand-off between several delegates surrounding the Constitution, on some serious issues about trade and finances.' The President stood up, putting his hands in his pockets; he looked around at the red door. He lowered his voice slightly and shook his head.

'It resulted in a series of underhand measures; all of them were very unsavoury.' The President went on to explain things that happened at that time. He listed a host of disturbing events.

'Our country was poor, so poor that we stole gold bullion, from hundreds of ships. We confiscated thousands of crops from our neighbours, north, south and around the Caribbean. We blackmailed many countries over the pricing of goods. Prominent state figures, who did not comply with certain requests, were murdered. We lied to our own people about our wealth. We lied to our people about where we got our wealth from.'

'How on earth have you managed to keep this out of the public domain?' Holly asked.

'We have lied to the American people and the world about the Constitution, since the day it was introduced Holly. The one thing that our country has founded itself on is nothing short of a sham. It is the supreme law of this land. If it can be proved that the Constitution was not agreed by all the delegates at that time, then lawyers all over the world will tear our country apart. We have gone into wars for God's sake, using the Constitution as our justification.' The president went on to explain.

'After a failed attempt was made to kill George Washington by some of the delegates, he decided to document all the evidence he could find, against all the barbaric actions taking place. '

'Is this what the Shield is protecting?' Holly asked. The President nodded.

'George Washington was a very wise and clever man. He secretly had a *Document of Truth* made of all his findings, naming and shaming those involved and exactly what they had done. He also planned and ordered a secret mission, to steal the gold bullion from the state vaults. I guess he wanted to give it back to the countries we stole it from. Incidentally, that gold would be worth hundreds of billions of dollars in today's money.'

'What happened to the gold?' Holly asked.

'We don't know, but I believe it is written in the script, along with all of the other secrets of that time.'

'So the gold never reached its rightful owners, is that what you are saying sir?' Holly asked.

'Again this is what we presume Holly.'

'So, is this Heenan guy after the gold do you think?' Jack asked.

'Of course he is, but that causes another problem for us. If Folis Heenan, or anyone else for that matter were to somehow find the *Document of Truth,* well, it frightens me what could happen. We would have a catastrophic disaster on our hands.'

'Because of the gold?' Jack questioned.

'The gold is only a small part Jack and I don't want you to lose focus on that.' The president sat back down on the corner of the desk again.

'If the *Document of Truth* was found and then deciphered, our country would implode.' The President looked down at the floor for a moment, Jack and Holly looked at each other. *I wonder if you are as sceptical as me about all this Holly?* Jack asked himself.

The president removed his hands from his pockets, lifted his head and rallied once more.

'Our people would lose all trust in our legal system. The prisons would be in chaos, as everyone could challenge the Constitution. Other countries could fight us in the courts, over trade deals. We would have to compensate many countries, for the thefts and blackmail, that took place at that time and that could bankrupt the country. The stock market would collapse from beneath our feet in all the turmoil. In short, we would become a third world country overnight.' *Wait a minute, that book I read, The Great Shipping Quest, yes that was it.* Jack looked at Holly and then addressed the President.

'When I was in Africa working, I studied a lot of old works. Most were written over one hundred years ago. They were about how the world had changed through shipping. Suggestions were made about some countries wealth. Massive increases and decreases to wealth, in a very short space of time. At that time, there was a question over America's sudden ability to buy and trade in massive quantities, around the time George Washington was sworn in.' The President stood back up and jumped in, his fist clenched and his arm shaking.

'That is why we must find the *'Document of Truth'* before it falls into the hands of someone else.' He enthused.

'But, where do we start?' Holly asked. The President's answer opened up a whole new thread for Jack and Holly to take in.

'George Washington may have had a secret son. We think he chose him, along with three loyal disciples, to take on the role of the Presidents Shield. They were all entrusted, with an equal part of the information of the original location of the *Document of Truth*.'

'Original location, so has it been moved?' Jack questioned.

'I don't know, maybe, but we must keep an open mind. Some Presidents have tried to locate it, but I believe they have all failed. The Butler and the Shield have never given up on the wishes of George Washington.'

'I think we need some of this coffee sir.' Jack said, his sarcasm filtering back to irritate Holly once more. The President pointed to the tray.

'Please help yourself.'

'I will have one please Jack.' Said Holly. Jack did the honours of pouring the coffee, while the President offered more insight.

'Kennedy was the last President to have any idea of the location of the *Document of Truth*. I think he wanted to find it and use the gold to his advantage.'

'Did he locate the Shield by any chance?' Holly asked.

'I believe he had a team of men working on it, when he was assassinated.' Holly raised an eyebrow.

'And before you ask Holly, I don't know what happened to these men.' *You read my mind Mr President.*

'I also believe George Washington's Butler, was the one who was entrusted with hiding the *Document of Truth*. George Washington gave instructions to pass down his secret to the Butler's first born on their twenty first birthdays, that way he protected his blood line.

'What about the Shield?' Holly asked.

'Exactly the same Holly, they passed it down to their first born at twenty one years of age. They were branded on the sole of their right foot. All four markings give a set of cryptic information on the location of the *Document of Truth*. This was then branded on their first born at twenty one and theirs was removed.' Holly's face creased up at the thought of that process. She burnt her foot on an open fire as a child. It was a minor burn and very little can now be seen by the naked eye, but she can still transport herself back, to that exact moment of sheer terror.

'This Shield has served its purpose in my opinion and now only serves to damage our country. George Washington did what he thought was right, for our country and the world, but this has no happy ending now. Find me that *Document of Truth* please and then we can all sleep better at night.' Jack handed Holly her coffee and took a sip from his.

'I still find it hard to believe that this has lasted all these years, without being discovered, or that the Shield simply did not maintain the blood line.' Jack was blunt and honest in his appraisal, something that was not lost on the President.

'Ok Jack, there is one other thing.' The President sighed; a visible awkwardness had appeared in his body language, as he sensed some doubts.

'The woman, George Washington may have had a secret son with, was said by folklore, at the time, to be sent from God. That God would always protect her. It is said she had a halo, that watched over her, in the shape of a triangle.' Jack put his cup of coffee down on the desk, stood up and looked the President straight in the eyes.

'A triangle, what could that represent?' He asked, his tone sincere.

'Folklore tells us the triangle represents a message of faith, true faith, the kind you would do anything to protect. You see Jack; this situation has complex consequences. This could be far bigger than George Washington, the Constitution, or even my Presidency. It could have massive religious consequences too.' The President had pricked Jack's interest again, Holly was less impressed about the last comments; she had no time for religious nonsense. *A triangle halo of faith, c'mon.*

'That is it, you know everything I do.' The President made one final plea.

'Jack, Holly, your country needs you, I need you, please find me this *Document of Truth* before anyone else does.' The President smiled, it seemed genuine to Holly as she nodded. Jack hated most politicians, take, take, take was his mantra for them. The President walked to the red door and turned around.

'Remember, Johnson does not know all of the details I have just told you. When you find the *Document of Truth*, do whatever it takes to find a way to speak to me directly. Is that clear?' They both nodded, offering a firm Yes Sir.

'Mr President, you have my word we will do everything possible to get this back for you.'

Holly stated.

'Mr President, before you go, I have one last question for you.'

'Go ahead Jack.'

'Why is this door red and the others grey?' The President shrugged his shoulders.

'I dunno Jack, ask Johnson.'

Chapter 11

Achoo... achoo... achoo... Eden Mcguire was suffering from a surge in the pollen activity. The pollinators had caused his nasal hairs to fight each other, for the first rub from the side of his finger. He held off, but another bout brewed up and stopped him in his tracks. He leaned over and cupped his hands over his nose and mouth. He closed his eyes and launched another batch of several sneezes, each one reaching over ninety miles an hour.

There was a faint noise of a diesel engine coming from the distance, it sounded to him like it was from behind. He opened his eyes and peered down at his red socks and dusty red trainers. As he straightened up the noise grew louder and nearer. Now he could hear the clumping of the tyres over the dirt track. He glanced around to see a battered green 4x4 Land Rover, slowly rolling up behind him.

The driver of the Land Rover had his arm hanging out of the window; he was tapping away on the door, to a beat only he could hear. He slowed down and brought the rust bucket to a stop beside Eden. The dust coming off the big chunky black tyres puffed skywards. Eden had finished one sneezing session and was now fighting the urge of another, this time watching as the dust made a painfully slow exit skywards.

'You ok laddie?'

'Yes Mason I'm fine thanks, just a bit of a sneezing fit.' Eden laughed at his own minor misfortune. At the wheel was Mason Laurie. He was the overweight, puffy red cheeked, tweed-wearing local farmer.

'Aye laddie, the pollen count is off the scale today, even my sheep are complaining.' It was Mason's turn to laugh at his own humour. This time it was a full belly laugh, as he banged the side of the motor for his own applause. His puffy red cheeks burned even brighter from his laughter. Eden just smiled at Mason, shaking his head sympathetically.

'Are you having a drink tonight Eden?'

'Yes, I'll be heading along a bit later.'

'Ok pal, see you there.'

Mason drove off lifting another trail of dust from the rear. That dust challenged the pollen in the air, to see who could annoy Eden the most.

Glenelg is a tiny little village in the Scottish Highlands, far away from any fuss or scandal. The population pops its head above the two thousand mark in the summer, with wealthy second home owners making the five hour drive from the Scottish capital, Edinburgh.

Everyone in the village knows just about everyone else and not many people who were born there ever spread their wings and leave.

It has two major focal points. The first being the Glenachulish ferry boat, that goes over to the Isle of Skye. It has a certain romance to it. It is the last, manually operated, turntable ferry in Scotland. The second is the Glenelg Inn. It has a unique atmosphere, where every visitor is encouraged to pick up an instrument that is displayed, hung on a wall or just laying around the pub.There are guitars, mouth organs, flutes, trumpets, tambourines, triangles and not forgetting the famous and arousing bagpipes. The Glenelg Inn is a place where you can literally *play or even sing for your supper*.

Eden had returned from his run and showered off. He had made himself a light tea of scrambled eggs and smoked salmon. He was home alone this weekend; his wife away on a hen party weekend in Glasgow, with some of the other women from the village.

Eden and Alice had lived in Glenelg for over eight years and loved it. The locals had welcomed and accepted them as one of their own. This was helped, on a huge scale, by the fact that Eden had saved the life of seven year old Stuart McKay. Stuart was Mason Laurie's nephew. Stuart had been playing with a friend at the lochside, near his home, when he fell into the loch. Eden just happened to be passing at the time. He dived into the loch and rescued him. He was the talk of the village and never had to buy a drink in the Glenelg Inn for a very long time.

All of the local broadband, mobile and domestic landlines were out of order. No one knew why, but they had been out of use since early morning. It was the first time, that any of the locals could remember, this type of thing happening, for a generation. Eden had run down to the local payphone to call Alice. He had expected it would be out of order, but to his surprise he managed to get a dialling tone. After three beeps Alice answered.

'Hello darling, how is your trip going with the girls and more importantly, is everyone behaving themselves?'

'Hola, Hola, Hola' Buenos dias my darling'

'Hey, what's with the Spanish lingo?'

'Well, we are sitting in a tapas bar and drinking Sangria.'

'Wow, go girl. I bet I can top that baby. I will be partaking in a few beverages, in our local public house tonight.'

'Ah you decided to go out honey, good for you. And who was it that persuaded you to go, was it Mason or seven fingered Syd?'

'You're funny Alice, I decided all by myself, thank you very much.'

'One of the girls said all the phone lines were down in the village. I was wondering why you did not reply to my texts.'

'Yeah, bit of a pain, but hopefully fixed soon. Anyway honey, have a fabulous time and I will see you tomorrow evening when you get back. I love you.'

'Love you more'

'Love you louder'

'Faster'

'Longer'

'Deeper'

'Ok you win, bye darling.'

'Byeeeeeeee.'

Chapter 12

Jack and Holly had been moved to another room, less formal than the room with the red door. They sat opposite each other, at a white wooden table. The room had no natural light, but a one way window and a security camera that had Jack thinking. *Why move us to a room with a one way window and a camera, who is watching us?*

Johnson walked in to the room, with the paperwork for them to sign. Holly noticed his tie had been corrected. *I wonder if the President had a word with him?* Johnson slapped the paperwork down on the desk and thrust a pen in Jack's hands.

'Sign them please.' He asked abruptly.

For all her good looks and athletic figure, Holly was often very much understated in her dress sense. Smart, but casual, she would tell herself. She wore very little make up, a little blusher and lipstick and even that was only on special occasions. Her friends would tease her; she was more like a tom boy, than a lady. She never travelled anywhere without her trusty black satchel, it was small, a present from her first love, who tragically died in a skiing accident. The satchel housed many handy items, some personal, some for business, but all very necessary in her mind. The only thing she could not fit in there was a spare pair of Converse trainers. She had collected many pairs over the years, another thing that her friends teased here about, she would end up walking down the aisle in a pair.

After the formalities of signing the paperwork, Johnson gave them five minutes to come up with a plan of action. There was a Learjet on standby, to take them to any destination they wanted to go. The clock was ticking and Johnson seemed ruffled.

Jack and Holly agreed the first port of call would be the library, as some vital research was needed before finalising a starting point.

Johnson had a car whisk them off to the National Library, the Library of Congress. He called ahead and had a room set aside, that they could use, without being distracted.

When Jack and Holly arrived at the library they were offered a runner and they gratefully accepted. Someone who knew their way around would be a great asset.

The runner they were given did not look like a runner, far from it. He was over forty years old, overweight from a diet of fast food that hung around his midriff. His hair had receded at the centre of his head, but he had long jet black strands that dangled down at the side. The skin on his face was ash grey; sunshine had abandoned him years ago.

He had introduced himself as Walt. His colleagues called him the 'Oracle'. His knowledge and wisdom glowed like a beacon; he was forever making predictions (mostly correct) on politics, current affairs, celebrity deaths, even the weather. Almost all subjects were fair game to him.

The Oracle was given a list of the subjects and threads that they were looking at. He was told to bring them anything that he thought would be relevant or useful to them. They stressed the importance of the time constraints that they were under. The Oracle was off like a whippet. *Maybe his running talents were hidden under his body mass index.* Jack thought cruelly.

His New Balance trainers were worn on the outside of the heels and he rocked when he ran. This was a mission to the Oracle; it was not often he was offered an audience to show off his talents to. He was determined that they saw them in the best light.

Within two minutes he was back with his first book, slammed down on the table causing Holly to jump. He turned and put his arm up, not as an apology, but as a salute and testament to how quickly he produced the goods. He headed back out of the room, puffing out his cheeks, enjoying the challenge.

Over the next five minutes the Oracle produced seven books, each time it was done as if competing in a relay race. On his final return beads of sweat were trickling down his face. He pulled up a seat and wiped his brow with the sleeve of his brown woollen top. It looked like something out of the seventies, something that even a charity shop would decline, if offered. The material was the type that would cause a rash on the skin, just by looking at it.

'Ok then, what are we looking for, just hit me with it and I will find it' The Oracle asked in a firm and definite manner. He looked worn out, but he was serious, he wanted in.

'Look Walt, we really appreciate your help with the books and all that, but this is classified.' Jack quickly put a damper on the Oracle's enthusiasm. Tears welled in the Oracle's eyes; his moment of glory had been crushed. He got up and walked back to the door.

'Walt.' Holly piped up. The Oracle stopped on the spot and swivelled his body ninety degrees, grinning with anticipation, the gap in his front two teeth evident to them both.

'Walt, thank you very much for your help, we may need your help again and I would be very grateful if you could just wait outside the door. Would that be ok?' Holly used a calm and gentle approach to her question. Walt's face lit up again. The Oracle was given a much softer blow to the stomach this time, one he could cope with.

'Sure, I'll just be outside if you need me.' He smiled back at Holly as he re-organised a patch of his side hair into place. Jack rolled his eyes at Holly, but did not protest with her on this occasion. He knew he was a bit harsh on Walt, but he was too stubborn to say anything.

Jack and Holly whisked through pages and pages. They were hopeful that they could find something that would stand out as a starting point. They had been in the room alone for just over ten minutes, when Walt popped his head in the door. Holly looked up and saw his creased brow asking for entry.

'Come in Walt, take a seat, you might be able to pin point some facts for us.' Walt shuffled in; half his tongue cheekily sticking out of the corner of his mouth, then took a seat. Jack did not even lift his head from the book he was sifting through.

'What do you want to know? The Oracle is here to help.' Jack cackled quietly, he whispered to himself *Oh the Oracle is here, we are saved from world destruction.* The words he whispered carried their way to the ears of Holly and Walt. They turned and stared at Jack as he hesitantly looked up at them. Jack raised his eyes to his forehead, as he gently squeezed out a half-hearted apology.

'Did I say that out loud?' Both Holly and Walt merely nodded in confirmation. *Sorry,* Jack mimed.

'What can you tell us about George Washington, other than the obvious?' Holly asked, as she rested her hand on his forearm.

'Little known facts or rumours, that kind of thing.' He smiled and then bowed his head almost in embarrassment; his knowledge of George Washington was extensive.

The Oracle grabbed one of the books and flicked through it. He knew the exact page to find, to display his vast knowledge of the subject. Jack sat and watched with a hint of contempt, as he opened the book at the Washington family tree.

'This is what you need to look at first to have any appreciation of George Washington. This is where everyone goes wrong, they overlook the obvious.' The Oracle tapped the family tree. Jack looked very unimpressed. Holly raised her eyebrows and showed a little spec of confusion.

'What do you mean Walt?'

'We are wasting time with this Holly.' Jack blurted out. He sat back in frustration, flung his arms out and then dragged his hands back through his hair.

'Oh you think so do you?' The Oracle replied, a small dose of arrogance was detected in his raised tone. Jack rolled his eyes and looked up.'

'Shut up Jack, go on Walt' Holly regained control of the room.

'George Washington was the chosen one, I know it and a few other people know it. It's just that I can't prove it. Although…' He paused, looking down at the family tree.

'What, what do you mean although?'

The Oracle once again tapped down on the family tree.

'Chosen one for what Walt?' Jack asked dismissively. The Oracle looked around the room. Nothing had changed, but the conspiracy cogs in his mind were beginning to turn. He sat back in his chair and stared at the wall, suddenly transported back to the heady days of the Washington's. He snapped out of his little trance and looked back at them.

'The Washington Triangle.' He murmured.

This was the first time he had released these words from his conscience in public. Jack and Holly looked at each other; the three words the Oracle had just spoken, already held great substance and meaning to them.

'I have a friend in England; we communicate on a web forum. The forum is part of a website dedicated to like-minded people who follow the theory that the Constitution was rigged.'

'What website, what conspiracy?' Jack scoffed, not buying into another American conspiracy. Walt's thoughts wandered off, he was certain there was an answer and he was certain someone was getting close to finding it.

'Walt.' Holly said, as her and Jack looked back at him. He was temporarily transferred to another place in his mind.

'Walt!' Jack shouted. The Oracle bounced back on his seat on hearing his name this time. He looked dazed, something had got in to his head and whisked him away from the conversation they were having. He looked at Jack.

'Yes?'

'Walt, are you ok my dear?' Holly put her hand on his shoulder.

'Yes, yes, sorry, something just came over me.'

'Yeah we noticed.' Jack said.

'Jaaaack.' Holly snapped. *This partnership is gonna be swell.* He muttered to himself.

Jack could not help himself; he was sarcastically funny by nature. He did not mean anything by it; he just could not keep his mouth shut at times.

'The Washington Triangle is real; I don't care what anyone else has to say about it, I believe it.'

'Ok Walt, we believe you.' Holly took a swift glance at Jack, as she spoke to Walt; he knew that he was being told to butt out.

'Can you explain to us, just what you know about the Washington Triangle please?' The Oracle nodded purposely. *I can my dear, all day long.*

'Look at the family tree; you need to understand the growth and the honour of it. Let's go back to 1183 in particular.' The Oracle went on to outline the significance of the Washington name and its true meaning.

'In those times, if you took on responsibility of the Lord of the Manor, you adopted the village name.' Suddenly, the Oracle had Jack and Holly hanging on his every word.

'William de Hertburn undertook an exchange of land in 1183, from his home in Hertburn, Stockton, in the north of England. The exchange was for the village of Washington, which was also in the north of England. This allowed him to take the village name and thus became William de Wessyngton.'

'So, Wessyngton becomes Washington I take it?' Jack asked, with Holly nodding her agreement.

'Correct.'

'So, are you saying you believe this to be the birth of the Washington Triangle?' Holly asked.

'I believe so. William de Hertburn became William de Washington and he my friends is the last traceable ancestor of George Washington.' *Am I missing something here?* Jack asked himself and then Walt.

'That does not explain why you would call something the Washington Triangle.'

'No Jack, your right, but there is more. The Washingtons were Lords of the Manor from 1183 to 1376. In 1183 they created a coat of arms and carried that coat of arms through the centuries. It is still in use locally to this day. It is known as the *Washington Coat of Arms*. It was known back in the day, as the *Mullet and Bars*. The present day translation for *Mullet and Bars* is '*Stars and Stripes.*'

'Whoa, whoa, back up a minute here partner. Are you really saying that the '*Stars and Stripes*' come from this coat of arms?' Jack asked with an air of disbelief. The Oracle puffed out his chest in defiance and firmly interjected.

'The *Washington Coat of Arms* was carried through the generations by the blood line. The Washington family moved further south in England, to Northampton. It was there that Lawrence Washington built a new house for his family, the Manor of Sulgrave. It was completed around 1560, hundreds of years after Washington. If you look at the Manor of Sulgrave, it is very similar to the Manor of Washington. The Washington coat of arms was placed prominently above the entrance to the Manor of Sulgrave. Lawrence was a very wealthy man; some say he was a wool merchant, but I have other ideas.'

'Wow, Walt, you really know your stuff.'

Holly chirped enthusiastically.

'Yes I do.' He said confidently.

'Ok Walt, you have got my attention, anything else you can enlighten us with?' Jack asked, coming around to the font of knowledge that the Oracle clearly had on the subject.

'If you look back in time, the Washingtons were rich and well connected, this includes the British monarchy.' Walt took a breath, he felt himself speaking faster, the excitement of his VIP audience arousing his emotions.

'John Washington, the great, great grandson of Lawrence emigrated to the new world in 1658, Virginia being his destination. The first thing he packed, to travel on the ship, was his coat of arms. This was the first time it had been seen outside of England. John Washington's great grandson was General George Washington. His coat of arms was carried into battle and legend has it, that on the verge of defeat, he knelt before his men and prayed to the coat of arms. The rest as they say is history; he won and gained us independence!' Jack and Holly were mesmerised, lost for words. Walt took that as a sign to carry on.

'I believe like many leading academics do, that the *Washington Coat of Arms* from 1183 became the basis of the American flag that we have today.' Jack and Holly were still wrapped in silence, processing the detail that the Oracle had given them. Walt continued.

'The Manor of Washington still exists to this day and is now a National Trust protected building. It is open to the public to celebrate its history, to view its amazing place in history. It even celebrates American Independence Day every year. It is just a shame the world is so ignorant to its place in history.'

'Have you ever been?' Holly asked.

'Actually, I am saving up hard to make the pilgrimage there one day and see it for myself. Every American should visit it once in their lifetime; it is our heritage, our primary existence. 'The romance of the tale had crawled under the skins of Jack and Holly.

'C'mon Walt give me your best conspiracy theory.' Holly enthused. He smiled. *Ok, if you want both barrels, you can have it.*

'1183 created the blood line of the Washington's. That same year the Washington family created the Washington coat of arms. That blood line gave us the man, who gave us independence. That man went on to be our first President. Washington DC was given its name in honour of George Washington. His coat of arms, the *Washington Coat of Arms*, became the basis of our national flag, the *stars and stripes*.' Jack put his arm up to question Walt.

'As much as I have enjoyed listening to this story, I still don't get where you see a triangle.'

'Don't you, it is really obvious if you just look.' Walt took a pencil and paper off the table and drew a triangle on it. He wrote George Washington in the centre of it; the 1183 Washington coat of arms at the top point: Washington village, England to the lower left point and Washington DC to the lower right point.

'What we have here Jack is amazing, it is such a strong connection.' Holly had bought in to the Oracle's theory.

'Oh yes, Holly we are looking at another Washington Triangle, but this time there is no halo.' Jack remarked smugly.

'Another Washington Triangle, what on earth do you mean?' The Oracle asked, showing the first signs of confusion on his face.

'You're not the first person to spot a Washington Triangle my good man, we had already found one.'

'Where?'

'Ok you two, knock it off. He is just joking with you Walt.'

'Is there anything else you can tell us Walt?'

'President Carter visited Washington village in 1977 to celebrate two hundred years of independence. He planted a tree along with the British Prime Minister, in the village right next to Washington Old Hall. Our manor house and George Washington's ancestral home.'

'But what significance could that have?' Jack questioned, this time his interest was genuine.

'I don't know Jack, but c'mon, it is a long way for Carter to go just to plant a tree.' Holly replied.

'Not when you're celebrating two hundred years of independence and the founder of that independence had his family roots there.' The Oracle said.

'He made a very brief speech on his arrival and I am positive that there was a hidden message there. It was dressed up as a welcome gesture, but I don't buy that.'

'What type of message?' Holly asked.

'The type no one is ever supposed to find out about I suspect. I have no evidence, but I have watched that speech over and over again and there is a message in there somewhere, mark my words.'

'Can we see the speech please Walt?'

'Sure I can get it on my iPhone, it just so happens to be in my favourites file.'

'Of course it is.' Jack quipped.

'It is the first three words of the opening, which I believe has some significance, or could be a coded message, to someone out there, just listen.' Jack and Holly leaned forward to watch the screen and listen to it.

'HA'WAY THE LADS.' The Oracle pressed pause on the recording.

'Is that it?' Jack quizzed.

'That is it, three words; I am telling you that those three words carry so much weight in history.'

'Thank you so much for all your help Walt, you have been great.' Holly smiled and shook his hand.

'Yeah cheers Walt' Jack reluctantly agreed.

'Do you mind leaving us now?' Holly asked sensitively. The Oracle picked up the pen and paper from the table and scribbled on a note pad, then ripped the page out.

'Sure thing, glad I could help. Look, here is my direct number, should you guys need any more information from the Oracle.'

'Thanks Walt. Holly said.

'Don't forget if you ever go to Washington, England, I have a contact there from the forum, someone who knows things, has seen things.' Jack leaned over and shook his hand, thanking him for his help and this time it was genuine. The Oracle walked out of the room and closed the door behind him.

'What do you think Jack?'

'I think old nut job there does know his stuff after all, but it is still a bit airy-fairy for me to want to jump on a plane and go there. I'm not a big fan of conspiracy theory forums.'

'I agree.'

'You do?'

'Yes Jack I do, don't sound so surprised.'

'Ok, you write down where you think we should start, I'll do the same, see where that leads us.' Holly laughed.

'That is so childish.'

'We need to start somewhere, time is ticking away.' Jack grabbed a pencil from the grand table and scribbled on some paper.

'I say we go to Majorca and speak to Ella Fox. She is the only person alive that could give us any details on her husband. Maybe get an idea what was on his tattoo, what he was like as a person and did she have any idea who was behind this?' Jack looked at Holly; it was a look of disappointment.

'I said write it down.' Jack showed Holly his piece of paper, with the words Majorca written on it.

'Majorca here we come then!' Jack smiled.

Jack placed the cell phone, that Johnson had given them, on the table and dialled the pre-set number and put it on speakerphone. Johnson answered after two rings. Jack looked at Holly and put his hands out, to give her the honour of speaking. She explained to Johnson that they had gathered a basic foundation of knowledge to help them and Majorca would be their first stop. Johnson acknowledged their request, agreed to make arrangements to speak with Ella Fox and had the jet placed on standby for Spain.

'We will be in touch from Majorca.'

'Good, goodbye and good luck.'

'Goodbye Johnson.'

Chapter 13

Eden took the four hundred yard walk from his cottage to the Glenelg Inn. Mason and the other locals were standing at the bar on his arrival and gave him a hearty welcome.

It had just turned 7 PM and standing huddled in their usual spots were Tam, Wattie the sparky, Davey the painter Andy B, Andy D, Syd, or to give him his full title, seven fingered Syd and finally Rab nine toes. Rab got his name after an accident with a tractor and no one ever lets him forget about it.

'Guinness for me Sheila, thank you my darling.' Eden shouted over the chatter of the lads.

'It's my round Sheila; I'll get this one, same again for the others please.'

'Right you are Mason, coming up.' Sheila bellowed out. She was the busty and strong willed landlady of the Glenelg Inn. She could put anyone in their place if things got out of control.

'Who are your friends Eden?' Syd asked while nodding over in the direction of two strangers that had followed him in.

'Not sure Syd, never seen them before.' The two men had settled into a couple of seats in the back corner and then appeared to be browsing through the food and drinks menus. Eden looked around for a brief moment and shrugged his shoulders.

'No mate, no idea.'

'Came in right behind you Eden, you must have seen them.'

'No, I never seen them Syd.' Eden smiled, more so at the fact that Syd could go on like an old woman at times.

'Strangers in our pub it is then, I will go over and introduce myself, see if they are up to playing us a few notes or maybe sing us a song.'

'Jesus Syd, they have just walked in, let them get settled at least.' Eden said.

'Don't look the type to me.' Mason said, smiling at Syd's instant insistence, to make friends with every person that walked through the doors of the pub. Syd ignored the comments and walked over to them.

'Hi gents, I'm Syd. What brings you to these parts then?' They both peered over the menu, their faces said enough, no emotion, no movement, just a cold reply.

'Fishing.' Said one.

'Walking.' Said the other.

'Ok then, which one is it, fishing or walking?' Syd said sarcastically, because of the welcome he had just received

'Fishing and walking.' Said the first stranger.

'There's plenty of fishing and walking in these parts.' Syd said smiling, feeling awkward.

'Would either of you like to play one of our instruments? Or maybe sing us a song?' Syd knew he was failing in every way. His words and meaning completely lost on the strangers.

'Are you trying to make a fool of me?' The first stranger said, looking chillingly into Syd's eyes.

'No, no, no, of course not, no problem, I was just trying to be friendly.' With that Syd turned spun on the spot and walked back to the lads.

'Well?' Mason said as Syd re-joined the group.

'There's something about them I don't like and they have funny accents.' Mason laughed at Syd's summary of the strangers.

'What type of funny accents did they have Syd? American, like Eden's?' Mason said, causing a huge round of laughter. Eden put his arm around Syd's shoulder and moved him to the side to have a quiet word.

'What type of accent did they have?' Eden asked.

'Funny, you know, like out of a James Bond film, like a baddie. Maybe Russian or something like that'

'What did they want in these parts, did they say?'

Eden probed.

'To be left alone, by their attitude, miserable buggers. They said they were here for fishing and walking, but I don't believe them.'

'Why is that?'

'Just call it a hunch Eden, call it a hunch.' Syd said tapping his only forefinger on the side of his nose.

The first stranger stood up and spoke to the other stranger.

'Let's go, that is our man, I am sure of it.' As the two strangers walked to the front door Mason remarked with a smile.

'Well Syd, you have sent your two new best friends off fishing I see. Sheila will not be happy you're messing with her profits.' Mason received another round of laughter.

'They are no friends of mine Mason, that's for sure.' Syd said glumly.

The strangers walked outside to the car park. The first stranger nodded to the driver of a red Alpha Romeo, parked only twenty feet from the entrance. The driver popped the boot of the car; they walked over and the first stranger lifted up the boot. Inside the boot was a selection of guns, a meat clever and a light blue plastic cool box with a white lid. The first stranger took out two pistols and handed one of them to the second stranger. He then took out two silencers again handing one over. As he screwed the silencer on to his gun, he issued a clear instruction to the second stranger.

'I want this over quick and I want his right foot in that cool box. If anyone else gets in the way, take them out. Is that clear?'

'Da.'

The first stranger closed the boot and then climbed into the front seat, while the second stranger sat in the back. The first stranger took out a digital satellite phone from the glove compartment and made a call.

'Unblock the signal to Glenelg, we have Eden McGuire in our sights.'

'Give me thirty seconds and it will be done.' The unknown voice replied. He looked up to the big sign above the entrance, then tapped the telephone number from the sign into his phone and placed a call. Loud cheers greeted the telephone ringing inside the pub; the lines were back up and running. Phones started beeping with texts and voicemails. It had been many hours since anyone had heard them. Eden was about to look at his phone when Sheila shouted over to him to take the call.

'Eden my love, call for you.'

'Is it my darling wife by any chance Sheila?' Eden asked with a big smile on his face.

'No my love, it is some man asking for you by name, said it was urgent.' The pub fell silent as Sheila's words settled on the ears of all the locals around her. Eden took the phone from Sheila looking puzzled and anxious.

'Hello, who is this?'

'You have two choices Eden. Either you come out of the pub right now, without any fuss or we come in and get you and we end up killing many innocent people. To help you make up your mind, we have taken your wife hostage. Your mobile will ring any second. Answer it, as it will be your wife. You will have five seconds to speak to her and then my man will hang up. At that point you have ten seconds to come out quietly.' Eden's phone rang that instant. He looked down and it was Alice's number, he was numb with fear. He answered it, his head tilted down at the floor, his face crumbled with fear. That fear became instantly evident to his friends around him.

'Alice, Alice, are you ok?'

'Eden, I'm really scared.'

'Alice, listen to me...' The signal was gone. Eden squeezed his phone hard in his hand, tears filled his eyes.

'What's wrong laddie?' Mason asked, putting his hand on his shoulder in concern.

'It is too complicated to explain Mason. He looked at all his friends and raised his voice in defiance.

'I want to thank you all for the past eight years, but I have to leave right now. I ask one more thing of you all. Please, please no one follow me out that door.' Eden was pointing at the door; tears were rolling down his face. His friends were shocked, confused and distressed at the sight of their friend breaking down like this. They all looked at each other for answers. This was unexplainable to them all.

Eden took a deep breath, wiped back some of his distressed tears and made one last rallying call, once again pointing at the door.

'Promise me everyone that none of you will walk out that door after me.' No one was moving, no one was talking and all their silent eyes were on Eden.

'Ok laddie we promise.' Mason squeezed his shoulder in comfort and then gave him a great big bear hug. Eden moved forward and walked to the door as his friends stepped to one side. A text message came through on Syd's phone, a noise that had been heard a thousand times before made everyone jump and look at him. Syd put his hands up as a helpless apology. Everyone watched every step

Eden took. They were transfixed by what was happening in their local bar.

Eden turned around as he took the door handle, making sure that they had all followed his demand and stayed where they were. He took a last glance at what his life had been like, his face covered in a mass of fear and anguish. He turned back around and then took his final walk out of the door of the Glenelg Inn.

Chapter 14

Jack and Holly had arrived in Majorca. Johnson had arranged with the hospital management and their security staff, for them to have access to speak with Ella privately.

Ella was being treated, along with their two children, for minor wounds and shock. It was the shock more than any of the wounds that shook Ella to the core. She had barely spoken since her husband's murder.

A private hospital car picked them up at the airport and took them straight there. The driver parked outside the staff entrance and escorted them to the room where Ella was being treated. The guard at the door was armed with an automatic weapon, dressed in military uniform and built like a heavyweight cage fighter. He opened it and let them in. Holly looked him up and down. It was a reminder to her of the reality of the situation, that they found themselves in.

Ella was in a room with four beds, two beds about four feet apart and the same on the opposite wall. She sat on a high back foam chair that was in the middle of two of the beds. Miles and Dylan lay fast asleep, either side of her. She had been sitting, staring at the white wall opposite her, for some time. They had been given strong sedatives on their arrival, but they had now been reduced to a milder dose, to be taken every two hours. She was vacant, grey and lost in her own world of pain.

There were two distinct noises in the room. The air conditioning unit, constantly purring away, was one. That was quite comforting, compared to the relentless beeps, from the machines that were monitoring them. The ordeal had drained Ella and the children of every ounce of energy that they had. At six and eight years old, the children's understanding of the situation had been limited.

Holly was first to enter the room. She walked over to Ella, with Jack behind her and gently pulled up a chair, resting it in front of her, doing her best to limit the noise from the chair legs. She took hold of her hands and held them in hers. She spoke softly and warmly to her, offering her condolences. Jack just stood back and let Holly take the lead, his head down a little. He looked at the children, without wanting to stare. *Poor kids.*

The guard had been standing at the door watching them, Jack asked him discreetly if they could have a moment in private, the guard nodded and closed the door quietly. Ella showed no emotion to their arrival. Holly spoke softly to Ella, she too felt heartbroken for her.

'My name is Holly MacDonald; I am here with Jack Hammonds.' Holly looked around at Jack who had moved to the side of the bed, so Ella could see him. There was no response, no eye contact, no hand movement; her hands were cold and lifeless. Holly continued.

'I can't ever begin to imagine what you must be feeling right now. I know the last thing you want is for anyone to be bothering you, but we really do need your help.' Ella was still motionless. Holly looked at Jack for some inspiration, but instead he just nodded his confirmation for her to carry on.

'We have been sent by the President to help you.' Ella raised her head slightly, the first bit of movement. She rolled her eyes at Jack, then back at Holly.

'I don't believe you.' She muttered, with the minimal movement from her lips. Jack moved a few inches forward and then nodded.

'It's true.' He said. Without moving anything other than her mouth, Ella made a brief statement.

'Prove it.' Holly looked around again at Jack; again he nodded, to go on.

'Ella, I am asking you to trust us, we want to help you.' Holly squeezed her hands very gently, as a signal of her intent.

'Prove it to me; get the President on the phone now.' Ella continued to stare into space, lifeless almost. The reaction from Ella threw Holly.

'Ok, let me see what we can do.' Was the only thing Holly could think of saying. She looked over to Jack and whispered to him.

'Call Johnson and tell him.' Jack took the cell phone out his pocket. He turned around and walked a couple of steps away from them. He called Johnson, speaking quietly, covering his mouth with his hand, almost whispering to him.

'We are at the hospital with Ella and have a bit of a problem. She is very scared and will not speak to us without speaking to the

President first. She wants to know that she can trust us and frankly I don't blame her.'

'Give me thirty seconds and I will call you back.' Jack walked over to Ella and Holly. He looked sincere and advised them of the outcome.

'We should hear back real soon.'

'We really do want to help you Ella.' Jack said attentively. He looked at the array of machines, beeping away. His experience of hospitals was very limited. He had only been once before, following a motorbike accident, where he sustained minor injuries.

'I swear to you Ella, it was the President that ordered us to look into all of this. He even kidnapped us in the process to do it.'

'Jack!' Holly snapped quietly.

'What?' He replied, shrugging his shoulders.

'Ella does not need to know those details at the moment. Can't you see how distressed she is already?'

'Okay, okay, point taken.' Jack turned his attention back to Ella.

'We really do want to find the person responsible, who did this to your family.' This time Jack's words were compassionate.

'Who are you then? FBI?, Secret Service?, NSA?' Ella asked. Jack and Holly looked at each other and then Holly turned back to Ella.

'The truth is Ella, we are none of those. We work completely independently; our day job is to recover things. They could be lost, stolen, or just missing. We were picked up by Secret Service yesterday and taken to the White House to meet the President. We were asked.'

'Forced.' Jack said, hijacking Holly's conversation.

Holly gave him a filthy look.

'Thank you Jack.' Holly said. She turned her attention back to Ella.

'We were asked to help out in a matter of national interest.' Ella made the slightest of head movements, to look Jack in the eye.

'Tell me Jack, who is forcing you, to help in this matter of national interest?' Jack looked suddenly awkward. *Me and my big mouth.*

'We cannot say too much.' He replied.

'We are already overstepping the mark, saying what we have Ella.' Jack asserted a small amount of authority in his response.

The cell phone rang, a welcome distraction to the seriousness of the current situation. Jack answered it. He walked away, to the other side of the room.

'Hello .'

'Sorry Jack, the President will not speak to Ella. You will need to find another way to convince her.' Jack looked dismayed.

'You have to be kidding me Johnson.' Jack was gobsmacked. *After what he's done to us in the last twenty four hours, why will he not take one phone call?*

'I just don't get it Johnson, why not? It makes no sense to me.' Jack looked over to Holly and Ella. They sat eagerly waiting for his response.

'Me neither Jack, but just deal with it please and quickly.' Johnson was forceful, but Jack could hear genuine disappointment in his voice. Jack became angry, his blood sugar levels falling.

'Jesus Christ Johnson, I don't believe you're doing this to us.' Jack hung up, without waiting to hear any response to his outburst.

Jack walked over to Ella and Holly, he glanced at the kids asleep, before he stopped and looked down at the floor.

'What is it Jack?' Holly asked. Jack looked at the cell phone in his hand.

'The President will not speak to you Ella, I am sorry.' He said, in a downbeat and apologetic manner. He turned away in disappointment, but Ella's response surprised Jack and Holly. She sat upright, removed her hands from Holly's and folded her arms.

'I never liked the man, never trusted him or his policies and certainly never voted for him. I suppose you must be telling me the truth, or you would have had some stooge set up on the phone pretending to be the President.' Holly and Jack felt a wave of relief, at the sudden change of heart from Ella.

'I can assure you Ella, we are not that bright.' Jack said. This time the smart comment was welcomed by Ella and Holly. Half a smile appeared in the corner of Ella's mouth. *Quick thinking Jack.*

'Before I help you I want you both to promise me something.'

'Anything, just name it.' Holly gestured.

'Whoever is behind all this, whoever is behind the murder of my husband, bring them to justice in whatever way you can. Do you understand what I am saying?' Ella's eyes filled up, her emotions had been stirred. The hate for her husband's killer was now rising with every passing second. Holly looked at Jack and then looked back at Ella.

'We will do everything in our power to help in any way we can Ella, you have my word.' Holly stared right into Ella's eyes and squeezed her hands tight.

'Thank you; what would you like to know my dear?'

'I know it will be difficult to talk about Mike's murder, but any little detail you have, particularly about his past could help us.'

'Mike confided in me a few years ago, after I threatened to leave him, because we moved about so much. He told me all about this Shield thing. I take it you know about it, that's the real reason the President sent you?' Two awkward nods followed. *She is nobody's fool this lady.* Holly thought.

'We were childhood sweethearts and he knew I loved him unconditionally. I would never have left him; I was just looking for answers. I have never told anyone else and never will. It was a promise I made to him and I would have kept it, until I took my last breath, but his death changes everything.'

'When did you know something was wrong Ella?'

Jack asked.

'Mike got a message on his cell phone. He came running out of our villa; I was playing with the children in the swimming pool one minute and then all hell broke loose. He was panicking and ordered me to get our emergency things together, so we could leave straight away.'

'Where were you going?' Holly asked

'Mainland Spain, by boat first, then we would travel further afield after that, but we never finished that conversation before he was shot.'

'Did Mike have his cell phone on him when the accident happened? Jack asked.

'It was no accident Jack, he was murdered.' Jack put his hands out as a sign of apology.

'I am sorry Ella, wrong choice of words, I don't want to cause you anymore upset, than you've already suffered.'

'He kept reading the message over and over again to himself to memorise it. Once he had done that he destroyed the phone, he smashed it up with a hammer on the floor before we left the villa.'

'Is there anything you can tell us about the gunman?' Ella took a deep breath, this was indeed critically painful, reliving the moments before her husband's death.

'They were dressed in black leather and on a motorbike; I think that was black too. That is about it, it all happened so fast.'

'It is ok Ella, you are doing well. Can you think of anything else, even the smallest detail could possibly help us?'

'Like I have already said, one moment I was playing in the swimming pool, unaware anything was wrong and then we sped off in the car. Mike knew within two or three minutes that we were being followed. Twenty minutes later he was dead.' Ella broke down and cried. Holly leaned forward and embraced her; she could feel her pain, the pain of a broken woman. Holly sat back and then held Ella's arms. She looked in to her eyes and spoke sympathetically to her.

'I am so sorry.' Ella smiled, the first since her husband was taken from her. She wiped back her tears.

'Thank you, I need to stay strong for the children.' She leaned across and stroked Mile's hair. Holly caught a glimpse of her hospital wristband. *Fenella?*

'Is that your full name?' Holly asked, pointing to her wristband.

'Yes, Fenella is my Sunday name, but everyone calls me Ella now. It's a Manx name.' Holly had a look of surprise on her face. Ella was quick to pick up on it.

'Manx is a way of describing something or someone from the Isle of Man. I was born there.' Holly smiled.

Jack wanted Ella's permission for something; even he felt she deserved that much.

'Ella, would you mind if we go to the villa to have a look around, just to see if there is anything that can help us?' Holly looked at Jack. *He does have a softer side.*

'Do what you need to do, to catch the son of a bitch.'

'Can you explain to us where it is and how to get there please?' Ella looked at Jack and nodded. She stood up carefully and walked to the window.

Jack took notes, as Ella gave the address and directions to the villa. Ella watched the distant traffic from her window on the third floor.

'The main door is unlocked, just walk in. I am not sure I could ever go back there, you know.' Holly walked over and stood next to her.'

'Time is a great healer Ella; I hope in time, you and the children find peace in your hearts.' Ella turned quickly to Holly.

'It is not peace I want, it's revenge, remember your promise.'

Chapter 15

Heenan was at home sitting in his office. It housed two well-crafted pieces of workmanship. He had a great appreciation of handmade items, particularly fine furniture.

His desk was a one-off, as was his chair. Both had been commissioned individual works of art. They both carried a logo, something he came up with when he was young. It resembled a no entry sign, a circle, with a diagonal line across it. In the middle of the circle was a pistol that overlaid the outline of two hamsters.

This room, like every other in his grand palace was cold. A few pieces of stunning eye candy from the art world and then nothing, just empty space that was crying out for something else to fill it.

The only other equipment in Heenan's office belonged to technology. The type of technology that made him feel safe. Every gadget from the world of espionage was at his disposal, he spared no expense on staying alive and ahead of his enemies.

Heenan suffered from circulation problems, which affected his legs mostly. Apart from the fact that Northern Cyprus offered a safe haven to some of the world's biggest criminals, it also offered a beautiful climate that was sympathetic to his medical needs. This morning like most mornings he had received a leg massage from Zia, one of only a handful of outsiders that were ever let through the doors of his mansion. She had been intensively vetted. Prior to their little arrangement, Heenan had Zia followed, but she was clean and discreet, a quality that kept her alive.

Sitting temptingly on his desk was an olive pizza, made by his own private chef, ex-military and also on the protection payroll. He looked down at his thin and crispy pizza. It was twelve inches in diameter, with extra rosemary sprinkled across it, something he loved on almost everything he ate. He picked up one of the six slices and started to chomp away, when there was a knock on his office door. Heenan knew the knock, like most things in his life, he had insisted on identical knocks on his door.

'Come in Yuri.' Yuri opened the door and walked in. He stood facing Heenan, as he wiped his mouth clean of two strands of rosemary and a smudge of olive oil.

'What is it?' Heenan asked as he stuffed in another slice. Yuri paused and looked at the six computer monitors on his desk.

Heenan played the markets, his computer monitors showed real-time updates of oil stocks, currency values, gold prices and stock market news. His desk was twice the size of a normal desk; it needed to be, to fit all his monitors on.

'Good news and not so good news boss.' Yuri's voice dropped a notch with his last five words. Heenan dragged the slice of pizza out of his mouth, a cheese strand about four inches long dangled tantalizingly, while he slopped the contents around his mouth. Yuri put his finger to his mouth and gestured at the unruly strand of cheese. Heenan picked up his white linen cloth and snapped off the cheese string.

'Give me the good news Yuri.'

'We have in our possession the right feet of the other three members of the Shield. They are all being flown here right away.'

'That is good news Yuri.' Heenan paused and looked down at the pizza and then sighed. He decided against another slice.

'Now Yuri, I take it you are about to disappoint me with the not so good news, as you just put it?' Yuri winced as he cleared his throat.

'Well boss, we were unable to track down the whereabouts of Holly Macdonald and Jack Hammonds, they seem to have vanished into thin air.'

'Have they been reported as missing?' Heenan asked. Yuri did not show any emotion when he killed for Heenan, but when it came to disappointing his boss, he became fidgety and it showed.

'Our contacts in the United States say Holly Macdonald was on holiday in Mexico with her friends. The information we have is that she was abducted. Possibly mafia, possibly police, but it was definitely a local pick up.' Yuri said rubbing his clammy hands.

'This is not what I want to hear Yuri.' Heenan slammed his hand on his desk, the plate holding the remaining pieces of pizza jumped with fright.

'What about Jack Hammonds?' Yuri rubbed his brow and then offered out his arms for mercy.

'He has just disappeared too boss. Last anyone knew he was out shopping.' Yuri's speech quickened.

'We have checked the local CCTV and it shows him leaving the store, but his motorbike is still in the car park.' Heenan stood up and then banged his desk with rage again three times, one slice of pizza flipped over showing off its floury charred base.

'Jesus Christ! I do not pay you and all of your men to be told such negative things. Find me them today Yuri, or get me someone else that can.' Heenan blasted.

'Boss, I have made some enquires and there might be someone else that can crack this code.' Yuri then stood in silence, hoping his proactive actions may soften the outburst from his boss.

'Well, don't just stand there Yuri, get out there and find them and do it quickly.'

'Yes sir, right away sir.' Yuri made a slight turn on his feet, but then turned back around and raised one nervous finger towards Heenan.

'Boss there is just one more thing.' Yuri held his breath in anticipation of Heenan's reaction.

'What is it Yuri?'

'The Butler has also disappeared.'

'Aaaarrrrgggghhh' Heenan jumped up, he grabbed the plate and threw it at the wall, just missing Yuri, as he ducked out of the way.

'Yuri, don't come knocking on my door, while I am eating my pizza, giving me these problems. All I want are solutions, problems will give me indigestion. Now get out of my office before I shove that pizza somewhere the sun doesn't shine.'

'Da, da, da.' Yuri exhaled loudly and then turned around and walked to the door. Heenan shouted at him once more.

'If you had not pushed McVey over the edge and killed him, he could have helped us further with this situation.' Yuri nodded. *You ordered me to torture him boss.*

'Solutions Yuri, find me the solutions.'

Chapter 16

The taxi rolled slowly through the entrance to the villa which the Fox family had fled. As it pulled in to the front of the villa, Holly felt a shiver run down her spine. She had visited many families before, in her job locating missing people and tracking down distant relatives, but this was different, this felt personal. Jack asked the driver to wait for them, he nodded, his English was limited.

Jack was first to the door; it was unlocked, just as Ella had advised. As Jack tentatively pushed the door, he turned back and looked at Holly. She gave him a firm nod to go forward. The taxi driver looked on as they crept into the house.

The Majorcan Villa was full of colour, Mediterranean in design and full of family photographs, something that was not lost on Holly. As she stood in the vibrant deep blue and yellow hall, she browsed the collections; one photograph in particular caught her eye on a half-moon glass table. It was a photograph of Mike and Ella handing over a cheque for eight hundred and seventy five euros. As Holly looked closely, she could see the cheque was made out to the Canine Society. She picked up the gold plated frame and then spoke to it, touching the glass. *Is this a sign Grandpa?* She was stroking a dog, a German Shepherd; one very similar to her Grandpa's loyal servant. The dog sat proudly in the photograph, as if he was accepting the cheque. Holly looked closely at the name tag that dangled from the collar around its neck. It was silver, in the shape of a bone. *Tino. Hello Tino, are you going to help us find something here? Has Grandpa Natalie sent you to help me?*

'Holly, in here, I think I have found something.' Jack shouted from the kitchen area. *Thank you Grandpa.* Holly kissed the inside of her two fore fingers and touched the glass where Tino sat.

The broken phone lay shattered in a million pieces on the kitchen floor. Jack had sifted through the mess of black plastic casing and internal components. Some parts were still hidden under the shards of broken floor tiles. *You really went to town on this cell phone, Mike old boy.* Jack swept a couple of shards to the side and there it was.

What do we have here then? He asked himself. He picked it up and analysed it closely.

'What have you found Jack?'

'I'm betting it's Mike's sim card.

'Try it in the phone that Johnson gave you. It may be the same size sim.' Holly suggested.

'Good idea.'

'While you do that, I will have a look around.' Holly made her way back to the hall and then into Mike's study. She looked at the paperwork scattered on his desk and then browsed through the remaining contents of the safe. *Wow, you guys really left in a hurry huh?*

Jack removed the sim card from Johnson's cell phone; he dusted off the debris from his new found treasure and then inserted it. It fit, a relief, what luck. As Jack waited for the cell phone to boot up, Holly shouted through.

'Any luck Jack?' The cell phone beeped and a message appeared. *Sim card failed, great.* Jack shouted back through to Holly.

'No luck, it won't read it.' Holly walked back through to the kitchen to speak to Jack, she had an idea.

'No, but it might work in a Spanish phone, that has the same network provider.'

'Good idea.'

'Again.' Holly replied.

'Again what?' Jack asked.

'Good idea again.' Holly teased.

'This is not a good idea contest Holly.' Jack stated sarcastically.

'No? Mmmm, I sure got the impression you thought it was.' Holly mocked.

'Here is another good idea Jack, let's go to a local phone shop to see if we can get anything off this sim card.' Jack removed the sim card and replaced it with the original, he looked at Holly. *I will be the one to crack any jokes around here.*

'Ok Holly, enough of the obvious.' Jack

'Is there anything in the safe that could help us?' He asked.

'They left in some hurry Jack; there is still jewellery and paperwork in the safe.'

'Yeah, well Ella did say that.'

'Ok, let's check the other rooms and then we can find a phone shop.' Jack suggested.

'This village looks too small to have that kind of shop Jack. I say, head back into Palma and get one there.'

'Ok, I'm sure the taxi driver will know of one.'

The taxi pulled up outside the *Telephonica dos Grande* shop on the corner of Carrer Dameto and Carrer Cottoner. The driver was again asked to wait for them. Jack and Holly made their way into the shop, it was small and quiet, no other customers around. A little bell sounded as the door was opened.

'Hola buenos dias.' The shop assistant happily chirped up, from behind his glass counter.

'Do you speak English?' Holly asked

'Yes, a little.' He replied. Holly put her hands together, as if to pray and smiled warmly.

'Great. We have a sim card here and we need a new phone to put it in.'

'This is your sim card, yes?' The assistant asked. Holly had not expected such a question.

'Well it is my brothers and he needs it quickly, he has broken his phone.' Holly reprimanded herself for making such a rash statement. *Why did I say that?*

'Name and telephone number please, so I can check our records.' *Damn we never thought to ask Ella the telephone number for Mike's phone.*

'My name?' Holly asked sweetly, as she put her palm to her chest, trying to buy a few seconds of time to think.

'Your brother's name madam, you said it was his sim card.' The assistant asserted. Holly just smiled. The assistant pressed on.

'To check our records madam, I need your brother's name and telephone number.' Holly put her palms onto the assistants counter, she spoke quietly.

'Can't you just search his name, I am not sure of my brothers number off the top of my head.' The assistant looked down at Holly from behind the counter. He inhaled, twisted his head a little and stroked the end of his greasy ponytail.

'Ok.'

'Great, my brother's name is Mike Fox.'

Jack quickly observed that Holly had great people skills; she was smooth, firm, persuasive but also genuinely pleasant and kind. He had smirked to himself, his opinion of Holly growing. Her infectious personality confirmed to him that she could in fact be the right person for this job.

The assistant typed the name Mike Fox into his computer and then looked up at Holly.

'Address please.' Holly's eyes widened. *The address, what have I done with it? I know I gave it to the taxi driver, where is it?* Holly unclipped her satchel and looked for the paper with the address on it.

'One moment please, I have it here somewhere.' Jack leaned over the counter and handed the paper with the address on it to the assistant. Holly gave Jack a filthy look. *He did that on purpose, to get me back for teasing him.* Jack winked at Holly, a boyish smirk lit up his face. *He is so smug.* Holly thought to herself.

A few taps on the computer keyboard and the assistant had some news for them

'Yes this is one of our sim cards. You have a choice of seven compatible phones.'

'The cheapest smart phone you have will be fine thank you.' Jack quickly pointed out.

'That will be one hundred and forty euros please.' Holly looked at Jack and raised her eyebrows.

Johnson had given them a box, which had four brown envelopes in it. The first envelope contained two false passports, the rest were money, five thousand euros, five thousand sterling and five thousand dollars. This was their new temporary identity and a slush fund to help them complete the operation. Holly's old faithful bag stored them all. Holly handed the assistant three fifty-euro notes.

'Can you insert the sim card into the phone for me please?' Holly asked.

'Of course I will.' Holly smiled at the assistant and watched, as he unclipped the back of the phone. After removing the battery he slid in the new sim card, replaced the battery and then clipped on the back cover. The assistant handed the phone to Holly and then offered Jack the receipt, along with his ten euros change. Jack thanked the assistant; Holly put her hand out to shake his hand and then thanked him. Jack pointed to the corner of the shop, near the front window.

'Let's give it a try over there.' Holly agreed. As they walked a few paces to the corner they heard the sound of the bell dinging as the postman came bounding in. He dropped the pile of letters on the desk and left as quickly as he arrived. The assistant shouted over to Jack and Holly as they switched on the phone.

'I would estimate the battery life will only be an hour or two, so it will need a good charge.'

'Thanks.' Holly shouted back.

They both stood staring at the screen, Holly had her hand on Jack's arm and she held her breath as they watched the screen run through the start-up phase and then bingo! The welcome chime of a sim card being accepted to the network was music to their ears. They looked back and thanked the assistant once again, he had done them proud. Holly squeezed Jack's arm in excitement.

Jack searched the call log file, it was empty. He turned his attention to the message file. *How did we manage with these old phones?* Holly asked herself. Jack pressed messages received, there were two stored in the folder. Holly squeezed Jack's arm again, she moved her head closer to the screen, as he pressed the first message.

-B1689CXZ241- Confirm and then await instructions

'I am betting that this is the code red message that the Butler sent Mike when he found out they were compromised.' Holly nodded.

'Go to the sent message folder and see if Mike sent a reply.' Jack pressed sent messages.

–K5603YGD466

'That does not tell us either way, I'll bring up the other message that was received.' Jack said.

Go immediately to where the Ferry departed. Then, use a biro by the sea and stand between the centre columns facing east. Shout out and listen to the echo.

'Is everything ok with your phone?' The assistant enquired politely.

'Yes, thank you, we are just checking that it is working ok before we leave.' Jack looked over and gave him a thumbs up.

'Come on Jack I need a coffee, I noticed a coffee shop close by as we drove in. We can look at this in more detail there. We can give the taxi driver some money and tell him to hang on while we look into this.'

'Good idea, I would kill for a chocolate doughnut and a latte.' Jack replied, as he nudged Holly playfully.

The bay window seat in the coffee shop was to be their new home for the next few minutes. Two café con leche's and two chocolate doughnuts were the delights that were placed on their small dark wooden table by the young petite waitress. The bay window offered them a glimpse of part of Palma harbour. It was very close to where Mike Fox had been assassinated. Holly picked up a sachet of sugar from her saucer, ripped off the tip and then sprinkled the brown granules in to the white creamy topping. Jack looked over the table at Holly and smirked.

'What is it?' Holly asked.

'Sugar? Really Holly? I would not have taken you for the sugar type.' Holly poked her tongue out, more with humour, than anger.

'I don't normally take it; I just need a fix, hell, why am I explaining myself to you anyway. 'Jack's smirk grew bigger. Holly looked out at the yachts and their great masts, some bobbing up and down on the water.

'I wonder what went through his mind just before he entered the water?' She asked, stirring her coffee, daydreaming about the past events.

'The bullet I would imagine.' Jack was quick to pull back on his comment; he winced at his own lack of decorum.

'There is no need to speak ill of the dead like that Jack.'

'Sorry.' Jack rolled his eyes in embarrassment and then changed the subject immediately.

'Have a look in the archive and draft messages folder; see if there are any messages in there that can help us.' Holly took a sip of her coffee and then handed the phone over to Jack. She gave him back the same cheeky wink he gave to her in the phone shop

'It's all yours Jack, fill your boots.'

Jack sank his teeth into a good chunk of his doughnut and chomped on it, while he checked for other messages. There was nothing. The only thing he was able to confirm was the timing of the three messages that they had retrieved. They suggested what they had first thought; it had to be the Butler.

As Jack wiped away a chocolate smudge from the corner of his mouth, he thought it was time for some direct action.

'Let's call the number.'

'Let's do it.' Holly replied. Jack dusted the scraps of food from his hands and then re-coated them, as he forced the last of the doughnut into his mouth. Holly grabbed the phone from the table.

'I'll do it then.' Holly snapped. Jack looked at Holly, his lips closed, but his mouth rolling round in circles. He emptied his mouth and then cleared his throat.

'Sorreeee.' Holly shook her head in mild disappointment at his cave man attitude.

'It's ringing.' Holly whispered in excitement. The excitement was short lived, there was no answer. *I thought that was too good to be true*. Holly told herself.

'What shall we do now?' Holly asked Jack.

'Well we have established that this number is still in use, so if it is indeed the Butler's phone, then we should keep ringing it.' Holly looked out once again over the marina, sipping her coffee. Suddenly, she jolted backwards; an unexpected noise came from the phone, two sharp beeps, then two more straight after. The volume was at maximum and had taken her by surprise. Jack grabbed the phone. *An incoming message*. He pressed it as quick as he could. It read:

BCWYWF EAFHOIO RUAUSR ELTH

Jack showed Holly the message.

'A puzzle, I love these, let me see.' Holly unclipped her satchel and took out a notepad and a pencil. Always use a pencil; her grandpa taught her, mistakes can quickly be erased. She began to mumble to herself, as she scribbled furiously, it looked to Jack like she was using shorthand, not that he had extensive knowledge on the subject. Holly threw her pencil down on the table.

'He will need to do much better than that Jack, I've cracked it. The message is

Be careful what you wish for.

'How on earth did you do that so quick Holly?'
'It is all down to the way you see the puzzle Jack, my grandpa taught me that, many years ago.'
'He must have had a special gift.' Jack said.
Holly smiled warmly; she took herself back to the photo of Tino the dog in the hall. *Thank you, grandpa.*
'He did Jack, he left me a message at the villa, he speaks to me in different ways, even though he passed away many years ago.'
'And what is your grandpa telling you to do now?'
'Oh, I don't need his help for that Jack, I can work that one out for myself, we reply with a puzzle.'
'Fine by me, this is your expertise Holly, knock yourself out.'
Holly sensed that Jack genuinely acknowledged the skills she had just applied.
'I am going to keep it short, but just give him enough to let him know what our intentions are.'
'Him? Your assuming it's the Butler.'
'It's him Jack.' Holly said with conviction. She compiled the message and then showed Jack. It read:

GHMAJH OOAANAAD OLCLDCMS GLDDKMLYOO ENNS.

'I have no idea what that could possibly mean.' Jack said. Holly pointed at the screen.
'Look at the first part of the message that he sent us Jack, *BCWYWF*. Then read the message that I translated from the puzzle, *be careful what you wish for* '
'Oh I see, it is the first letter of each word, how simple, but brilliant. So your message back to him is the same?'
'Yes, the first part is always the first letter of each word; the rest of it, is the letters you need to complete the other words. They run in sequence. Holly went on to explain further to Jack, the workings of the puzzle.

GHMAJH OOAANAAD OLCLDCMS GLDDKMLYOO ENNS.

So, you now know that *GHMAJH* is the first letter of each word of the puzzle and that the puzzle is six words long. Once you have your first word, of which mine is *GOOGLE*, you then start to assemble the rest of the words. You always start a word from the first section and then take one letter from each section, sometimes taking a second letter from a section, depending on the length of the word, until that particular word is complete. For example, my second word is *HOLLY*, so if we remove Google from the puzzle we end with this.

HMAJH OAANAAD LCLDCMS LDDKMYOO NNS

Now, this is where some people make mistakes. They fail to follow the puzzle. Watch what happens when I remove Holly from the puzzle. The next word is Macdonald and is longer than six letters, so you need to continue, without using the first section.

*MAJH AANAAD **CL**DCMS **DD**KMOO NNS*

You continue on until you have your message in full which is: *Google Holly Macdonald and Jack Hammonds'*
'Genius Holly, just genius.'
Time seemed to stand still as they waited for a reply. When it did come, the arrangement of the puzzle had been changed, it seemed rushed to Holly, too simple. It read:

UOY ERA EREHW.

Jack looked down at the message.
'That's an easy one, a mirror message, just read the letters backwards.' He said.
'It is, I was just thinking that this message seemed rushed.' Holly messaged using the same format.

ACROJAM AMLAP.

An instant reply was received.

YHW.

Holly replied

XOF ALLE.

Holly had anticipated an instant reply to her last message, but it did not materialise. Their coffees had gone cold; they waited and waited, but no reply. Holly sat tapping the table with her finger; the sounds of china clinking and café chatter were not enough to break her trance. Jack was pondering to himself. *What if someone had gotten to the Butler?*

Holly made a vain attempt to call the number, no answer. She sent two further requests by text, still no answer, the mood quickly dampened.

Chapter 17

The time had come for Jack and Holly to make a decision on their next move, but their options were somewhat limited. The recovered sim card, that they had hoped would provide a breakthrough with the Butler, had fallen silent. The sim card held no further clues; it was time to call Johnson.

'What should we tell him Holly?'

'How do you mean Jack?'

'Well, should we tell him about the sim card and the Butler or just keep it to ourselves for now?'

'Why would we keep it to ourselves? We have nothing to hide.' Holly showed signs of being a little confused at Jack's line of questioning. Jack looked around the coffee shop; he had seen enough movies, where the good guys are being listened in to. He leaned towards Holly and spoke quietly.

'We don't know anything for certain yet. Rather than speculate, let's wait until we get some real information before we call him'

'I'm not so sure Jack.'

'C'mon Holly it's pointless calling him with pure speculation. We don't even know who it is on the other end of the phone yet. Maybe it is the Butler, maybe it's not.' Holly looked away, out to the marina; she did not want Jack's 'go to bed eyes' influencing her decision. *I hate to agree, but he has a point.*

'Ok Jack, but you can call him later.' Holly replied, as she wagged her forefinger at him. Jack smiled, he liked getting his own way on any subject, but getting his own way with Holly was difficult, she was a good match, but he revelled a little in his mini victory.

Beep beep, beep beep.

Once again, Jack and Holly jumped, at the unexpected loud beeps. They sat and looked at each other, an unexpected surprise. Holly quickly opened the message.

'It's another puzzle Jack, from the same number.'

'What is it Holly, do you recognise it, do you think it is him again?' Holly started making some notes, Jack was anxious to see what this message would bring them. Holly started talking aloud to herself.

'Another puzzle, but this one is a little bit more taxing than the last two, but I should have it cracked in no time.'

Several minutes had past; Jack was encouraging Holly with words of support, but all Holly wanted was silence. She scribbled furiously once again, talking to herself nonstop. She consumed letters and numbers like they were her favourite food.

Holly stopped what she was doing and sat up. She looked at Jack; her face was thoughtful, full of questions, not answers.

'He is asking us a series of questions.' Holly said.

'Like what?' Jack replied.

'Who recruited us, why us, what we know?'

'What have you said back?' Jack asked.

'I have told him the truth Jack, best way, don't you think?'

'I guess.'

The phone fell silent again. Jack kept checking his watch; people came and went in the café, but still no messages. They decided to walk down to the marina to see the place where the car had crashed. There was nothing else left that they could think of doing. Jack walked to the counter to pay the bill. The assistant looked Jack up and down when he handed over a fifty euro note. She wiped it with a yellow pen; a faint smile appeared when it passed the test. A ringtone suddenly echoed around the café. Jack swung his head around to his left and looked at Holly.

'It's him Jack. Holly shouted. 'Well, I think it's him.'

'Answer it Holly, it's the only way we will find out.'

Holly stared at the phone for a second, as it vibrated on the table, lighting up as it rang. Two young couples at other tables glanced around and then gave her filthy looks. The volume was up full and not a welcome sound in the cafe. Jack gritted his teeth, he was uncomfortable about the time it was taking Holly to answer and the unwanted attention the ring tone was now attracting.

'Answer it Holly.' Jack lunged forward, grabbed the phone and handed it to Holly.

'Hello.' Holly said calmly.

'Speakerphone please.' Was the clear instruction from the caller, a male voice, serious, forthright and mature. Holly switched to speaker and confirmed to the caller that it had been done. There was to be no small talk. Holly quickly turned down the volume so only Jack and her could hear the voice asking the questions.

'I have a list of questions that I am going to ask both of you. You will have three seconds to answer each one. Any longer and I will know you are imposters.' Jack leaned forward to speak into the phone.

'Ok buddy fire away.' He turned and looked at Holly. His shoulders hunched and his hands held out to express they had nothing to lose. The Butler proceeded to ask a list of questions about their personal lives, travels, successes and favourite things. All the questions were compiled from the information he had just found on the internet. It was a Wikipedia mastermind test.

They had both answered nine out of the ten questions, one question still remained unanswered and that puzzled them both.

'Good, I threw in a curve ball question to you both. I wanted to see if you would lie or just guess the answer.'

'Have we passed the test?' Jack asked, holding his breath while waiting for an answer. There was silence, several seconds, Jack became impatient.

'Are you the Butler?' He questioned.

'Holly, Jack, I am indeed the Presidents Butler. It saddens me greatly to admit it, but this situation has grown arms and legs and I have no idea where it will lead now. What I know for sure is that I trust no one at this moment in time and you shouldn't either. I mean no one.'

'See Holly I told you.' Jack whispered.

'Sssshhhh.' Holly thrust her forefinger to her mouth.

'Somebody deep inside the White House or Secret Service has infiltrated the Presidents Shield.'

'How do you know?' Jack was sceptical about what the Butler was saying, it was his nature, but he had a feeling right from the start that things were not quite what they seemed to be.

'There is no other explanation of how this could have happened so quickly. I did not give up the Shield; I did not give up any person or any information that could have resulted in this. McVey did not know my whereabouts or the whereabouts of the other members of the Shield, so it is the only explanation of how Folis Heenan could have obtained this information.'

The Butler went on to reveal that he knew his computer had been hacked, the same day that McVey went off the radar. He told Jack and Holly that a virus had been dropped into his computer. A skull had appeared on the screen taunting him, displaying the message, happy birthday Mr President.

'My computer held a cryptic registration of some GPS co-ordinates. These were the co-ordinates of The President's Shield, this is what they hacked.' The Butler paused for breath.

'Can we meet you please?' Holly asked quietly.

'It is not safe for you to meet me; it is only a matter of time before I am tracked down too. I have taken precautions though.' The Butler replied.

'When you say trust no one, what about Johnson and the President? Jack enquired.

'I mean trust no one; I am not saying they have knowledge of this. I just can't rule them out at the moment. As unlikely as it seems, those are the facts as they stand.'

'What do you suggest we do now?' Holly asked.

'Well, I have a backup plan. The reason that the Shield has survived all this time is that everyone has had a backup. We are just the first layer; we are part of a bigger organisation.' The Butler, although exasperated, seemed relieved to be able to share this information with someone.

'Who is this organisation and why have they not been able to help you?' Holly asked.

'The organisation is called 1183.' There was a pause from both sides. Holly had a flashback to the Oracle. *Walt kept going on about 1183 in the library.*

'I knew it.' Jack said triumphantly. 'I said from the very start that the Shield could not have survived on its own.'

'No you did not Jack, you just questioned it.' Holly snapped back.

'What can you tell us about 1183?' Jack asked.

'Very little to be honest, well-funded, well-connected, they seem to have eyes everywhere, that's about it.'

'But why have they not sorted all this out?' Holly asked.

'Good question Holly, but I am afraid, just like Johnson and the President, I don't know who to trust so I am staying dark for the time being.' Something was bothering Holly, enough to want an answer.

'What or who are 1183 protecting?' She asked.

'It is a well-known fact that George Washington was a prominent Freemason and was arguably the most influential person in America's history. Apart from being a great leader and the first President, he gave us our identity, our capital and most importantly our faith. It is that faith which is now under threat.' Holly interjected.

'But we are a nation of many religions now.'

'I did not say religion Holly, I said faith. If the *Document of Truth* is found and used against us, then we lose our faith and that applies to all Americans, irrelevant of whatever beliefs or religion they belong too.'

'Do you have any idea where it is?' Jack asked, not believing for one moment that the Butler would give it up, even if he did.

'No I do not, but I do have something that you could start looking into.'

'What is that?' Holly asked, as she sat bolt upright in anticipation of what she was about to hear.

'Once every five years The President's Shield and the President's Butler meet up to continue the bond and to make sure everything is rock solid. I had arranged our last get together in Durham, a small city in the North East of England and very close to where 1183 was founded. Legend has it that many of the early meetings took place at Durham Cathedral, one of Europe's leading Norman buildings and one of England's best loved buildings. I choose that place because of the significance of it. I needed to bridge the gap between the ever growing, relentless quest for technology and the root of our faith.

'Does the President know about 1183?' Jack asked.

'Of course he does, but he has no control over it. It is an independent organisation.' Holly felt the conversation going off track and wanted to bring it back.

'What happened when you met up?'

'We met six weeks ago and it was obvious to me that McVey was not right. I needed to do something about it, but I also needed to keep it to myself, until I could prove that something was wrong.'

'What did you do?' Jack asked,

'I arranged for us to stay for a night at a place called Seaham Hall Spa. It was only a few miles away from Durham, on the coast. I arranged for all of us to have a full body massage, a kind of bonding/relaxing time. The Shield had no idea what I was up to.'

'What were you up to?' Holly jumped in to ask.

'I went for my massage first. I left a holdall bag on the table next to the massage bed. There was a recording device in it. It was fixed to the outer bag and there was no way anyone could tell what it was. I was able to video the markings on all of their feet. I asked the masseuse not to touch the bag and that I would collect it later.' Holly touched Jack's arm.

'So you have copies of all the markings, we need to see those right away.' The Butler did not seem to listen to Holly's request.

'I am not proud of what I did and I would have never shared that information with anyone. I studied it that night and then deleted it, that information is only in one place, my mind's eye.'

'Sir, we really, really need to see this information if we are to stand any chance of helping you.' Holly pleaded. The Butler sighed, he knew his time was limited, maybe even his life.

'I have a suggestion, but we need to act quickly.' He said.

'Anything, we will do it.' Holly replied.

'Go to the nearest hotel and text me the fax number. I will write down all the markings and send them to you. The fate of America will then lie on your shoulders.'

'No pressure then.' Jack said sarcastically. Holly scowled at Jack, although she was now starting to get his excuse for a sense of humour. Jack held his palms out and mimed '*what?*' as if he was entitled to use sarcasm in that situation.

'We will go right now and I will text you the number.' Holly beamed.

'Ok, but be quick, we may not have much time.'

'One last question, if I may please. Where were you sending Mike Fox and the rest of the Shield to? Jack asked.

'We really have no more time for this; I could get caught at any minute. Get to a fax machine and I will explain everything when you have the fax.'

Chapter 18

Heenan had never ever thought about his chest freezer before. Now that it contained the feet of the President's Shield, it was the only thing he could think about. He had become very irritated by the lack of recent progress. One question in particular was irritating him, it kept swirling around in his head and he wanted an answer to it. *Who the hell is going to decipher this?* There was a knock on his office door.

'Come in Yuri.' *And you better have some good news for me.* He mumbled to himself. Yuri walked in, closing the door behind him, he smiled, his wide jaw expanding as he stood to attention.

'Well, what is it?' Heenan asked.

'Good news boss and more good news, we have traced a professor from London who studies this kind of thing.' Heenan became even more irritated at Yuri's lack of respect, for this piece of history that he had obtained. He jumped up from his seat and yelled at Yuri.

'This kind of thing?'

'Sorry boss wrong choice of words.'

Heenan went back to his seat, his flushing face settling a little.

'Go on Yuri, who is this professor?'

'I am told he is the best in Europe on ancient readings and mathematical equations.'

'You had better hope he has the ability to help us decipher this puzzle.' Heenan snapped.

Heenan was pleased, almost relieved, at this turn of events, but he would not share this with Yuri. There was still too much work to be done yet.

'How quickly can you get him here? Heenan questioned.

'The professor is currently in Edinburgh, due to do a speech at the castle at any minute. I have an itinerary of his movements for the day. I have a team en route to extract him.' Heenan slammed his hand on the desk yet again in frustration of Yuri's lack of clarity.

'That is not the question I asked Yuri, do you not listen to the words that come out of my mouth?'

'Sorry boss, we should have him here by midnight.' Heenan nodded his reluctant approval and rubbed his little fat hands in anticipation.

'And what was the other good news?'

'I have located the Butler; we should have him within two hours.'

'At last Yuri, at last, no mistakes, you hear me? The Shield has now been destroyed; next I want to take down the President and then America.' Before Yuri could answer, a little squeak could be heard from under the desk. Heenan leaned over; his pet hamster Bonnie had paid him a visit. He picked it up and cradled it. Heenan looked at Bonnie lovingly, stroking her and then offered Yuri some unexpected good news.

'Get me Bridie.' Yuri's eyes lit up, relief, someone to calm his boss down.

'Yes boss.'

Yuri had a very good working relationship with Bridie. Over the years, she was a calming influence on Heenan, the only person that ever did and he was always glad when she was involved. This was the most erratic and demanding he had seen Heenan for a long time, maybe ever.

Heenan did try to become romantically involved with Bridie, but even his vast resources were not enough to lure her. Ironically, it was that episode which cemented his respect for her. Now that Heenan knew Bridie could not be bought, she became untouchable and irresistible in his eyes.

Chapter 19

The head receptionist at the Catalonia Majorca hotel, on Carrer Garita, had welcomed Jack and Holly to the hotel.

'How may I help you today?' The receptionist asked in English, but with a heavy Spanish accent, slow and sexy, her voice deeper than the average lady.

'Hi there, we have a very important fax that we need to retrieve. Could we have it sent here and if so, could we have the number please?' Holly enquired.

'Of course madam, here you go.' Holly was handed a compliments slip, Jack stepped in and took it from her. He smiled and then nodded, as he looked into her eyes.

'Gracias Senorita.' He said seductively as he took the slip.

'Is there anything else I can help you with today?' She replied. Holly had heard enough.

'C'mon Casanova, we need to send this number to the Butler.' The receptionist smiled at Holly, Jack was less amused.

'Did you have to make me look stupid Holly?'

'No Jack, you did that all by yourself. Now let's go.' Jack looked around and pointed to a bar area.

'Why don't we go over there and a get a cold drink?' Holly agreed, so that they could send the fax number to the Butler.

The bar area had two sections to it. The indoor area, which was a standard, plush area with one metre square, cream, shiny marble floor tiles, cream walls, cream, brown and orange furnishings and brown wooden table and chairs. The second section was al-fresco. The same brown wooden, table and chairs, covered the terrace area, but beneath them, were burnt orange, non-slip floor tiles. The terrace offered one thing that the indoor section did not, the view!

This was the first time, either Jack or Holly had taken a moment to reflect on how their lives had changed forever and in a very short space of time.

'The views are stunning.' Holly said, shielding her eyes, her hand held above at her forehead, saluting the sunny blue sky.

'There must be a billion pounds worth of yachts down there.' Jack replied, daydreaming that one day, one of them would be his.

'I had a yacht once.' Holly said, as if it was a typical every day conversation topic.

'You did?' Jack replied, smiling in amazement.

'Tell me more Holly.'

'I bought it about five years ago, when I sold my business. It cost me over one million dollars. I only used it three or four times, it ended up being one big headache to me. It was just a waste of money. Anyway, I sold it the following year for just over nine hundred thousand dollars. It is a very quick way to lose money Jack that is for sure.'

The waiter arrived at their table, as Jack was building up to investigate Holly's past further.

'Would you like something to drink?' He asked, armed with a pen and fresh white notepad, his slim build casting a slender shadow that cut across the table. The waiter was immaculate; he was dressed in a crisp white short sleeved shirt, which had one button undone at the neck. His lower half had black drain pipe trousers and freshly polished shoes.

'Fresh orange juice please.' Holly said, squinting from the sunlight.

'Mineral water please.' Jack said and then got straight back to the conversation.

'You know how to sail then I take it. That is a pretty cool thing to have up your sleeve.'

'Yes, cool and expensive.' Holly laughed. Jack crossed his legs, sat back a little and then wagged his forefinger at Holly.

'You know Holly, I had a pretty low opinion of you before we met, but you're ok.' Holly smiled at the comment, her first genuine warm smile. Jack leaned forward and lowered his voice, bordering on being flirtatious.

'You are nothing like the person I had imagined in my head.' Holly's smile grew bigger.

'What had you imagined Jack? That I was an over opinionated, self-righteous, stubborn, selfish liberal?'

'Yeah, pretty much.' Jack laughed. He ran his hand through his hair, puffing his chest out, the male mating call in full cry.

'To be fair Jack, if you had met me when I had my yacht, then I think your opinion would have been about right.' Holly looked out at the yachts. She pushed her fingers through her hair, Jack noticed. *She is mirroring me, she really likes me.*

'I have changed; a lot, I have slowed down, both mentally and physically.' Holly was lost in the moment, lost in her past and speaking from the heart. As she stared out at the yachts, they spoke again, their words turned to memories, ones Holly would rather forget.

'I have started to see life a little differently recently. I spend more time with my friends and I am much more relaxed as a person.' Holly snapped out of her little trance and burst out laughing to herself.

'Well I was until I got kidnapped in Coco Bongos.' Jack sensed he was listening to the real Holly; he had let her speak freely and felt a real connection. He was guilty of pre judging her, like she was of him.

The waiter arrived with the drinks. He had an oversized black round tray for the two drinks. He placed a round white paper coaster down at each setting and gently placed the drinks down for them.

'Cheers.' Jack said, smiling as he lifted his glass to chink Holly's.

'Cheers Jack.' Jack wanted to know more, he was seeing a different side to Holly, a more open one and one he liked.

'You said you spend more time with your friends, but what about your family?' He asked, showing a caring side, one which Holly had not seen from him until now.

'My Mom died a long, long time ago and my Dad; well let's just say I don't really have any contact with him now.'

'I'm sorry to hear about your Mom Holly, but why do you not have contact with your Dad?' Holly's face changed, something bothered her about that question, Jack could tell instantly by her reaction.

'Please Jack, can we drop it, that topic is not up for discussion.' Jack apologised, it was not his intention to wind Holly up, not on this occasion and not when they were having their first real conversation. Holly looked at Jack and changed the subject.

'Tell me about you Jack, I must admit you are pretty much like the person I thought you would be.' Holly laughed at herself again.

She was a strong lady and had acknowledged to herself and to her friends, that she had taken life far too seriously in the past. She had changed and she was still changing.

'You mean tall, dark and handsome right?' It was Jack's turn to laugh.

'You got one out of three Jack.' Holly smiled; she felt a warm sense of flirtation, something that had just crept up on her without realising it. She took a sip of orange and gazed warmly out to sea, her legs were crossed, her right leg bouncing gently over her left. She was in the mood for teasing.

'C'mon Jack, open up!' Jack smiled; he too could feel that the situation had developed into more than just an average conversation.

'Not much to tell Holly, apart from I am now single. Although, I was supposed to be on a date, about an hour after I was picked up by this mob.'

'Was it a recent thing, that you became single Jack?' Holly smiled, knowing fine well it was.

'Everything in my life is recent at the moment Holly.' Holly curled the ends of her hair around her finger.

'I am sure there will be someone out there who will be bowled over by your boyish, selfish, charms.' Jack tilted his head back.

'Ouch.'

'Can you hear that music coming from the bar? Holly asked Jack. Jack then started to sing quietly to Holly. *Take me home country road, to the place I belong, West Floridaaa.*

This sensitive moment was brought to an abrupt end by the sound of the cell phone ringing. Jack looked at the caller, the Butler.

'Hello.'

'Did you get the fax?'

'Not yet, I will check with the receptionist, one second.' Holly picked up the phone and ran over to the reception.

'Has the fax arrived for us?'

'Nothing madam, I will double check.' The receptionist went into the back room and swiftly came back out.

'No madam, nothing.'

'Thanks.' Holly spoke into the cell phone.

'No fax has arrived here, are you sure you have the right number?' The Butler double-checked, the number was indeed correct.

'Damn it, it is probably my machine playing up, I will resend it.' The Butler hung up before Holly could speak. *This is not good; he may have to email the hotel instead.*

'Please have a seat, I will hear the noise when it comes through and bring it straight over to you.' Holly nodded.

'Thanks again.'

Chapter 20

It had been a trusty old fella to him, but it was playing up just at the wrong time. The Butler was standing over his fax machine, frantically pressing buttons and opening the trays, trying to work out why the fax had not sent.

Outside the front door of his Boston apartment was a small camera. It was installed just above his door. It had been spray painted to blend into the background and was virtually invisible from a few yards away. It had a wide angled lens that captured the full view of the outside, up to around twenty five yards away.

The Butler was getting very frustrated with himself, as he slammed away at the fax machine buttons. *C'mon, C'mon, don't do this to me now.* He glanced over to his laptop, perched on his desk, alongside his fax machine. He could see a man, dressed head to toe in black, slowly creeping along the side of his wall, towards his front door. He knew his time was running out one way or another, but he was desperate to send this fax. *Please let me do this one last act in life; give them a chance to save us, please.*

He continued franticly to push every button, one by one. He double checked the power sockets; everything was powered up as it should be. *What is wrong with you, you stupid damn machine?* He lifted the lid and checked inside again, the fourth time now. He looked back at the laptop and he could see the man inching closer. He watched as the man removed a small black backpack from his shoulder. He turned back and yelled at the fax machine. *Jesus Christ beep or something you little piece of grey plastic crap.*

Outside, the man very carefully unzipped his backpack; he was now no more than two feet away from the door. He took out a lock picking tool. The Butler looked on, agonising at his every movement. He stopped pressing buttons and just stared at his laptop. The man was now kneeling in front of the door. He started to pick the lock, inserting two metal probes into the mechanism. He rubbed one of his probes, up and down inside the mechanism, as he held the other still. Two clicks echoed from the lock. The Butler was rooted to the spot as he looked on. He pushed his hair back with both hands, fear swamping him. It was too late to send the fax. *My time has come and I have failed, sorry Shield, sorry America.* The man gently leaned his bodyweight against the door, turned the handle and pushed forward. Nothing happened. He pushed a little harder, but still no movement. The Butler had four dead bolts that ran the full width of the door. The intruder was not getting in that easily.

The Butler looked back at the fax machine. He went through the same frantic routine. *Please let me do one more good deed, please, please.* Nothing happened, not a beep, not a flicker, nothing. He looked back at the laptop again and could now see the man removing what clearly looked like an explosive device from his backpack. *The bolts on the door will not stop that. Please God grant me one last request, please send this fax now.* The Butler looked on anxiously, his fear consuming him. The device was delicately attached to the door. It was in two parts, the largest part looked like a square marzipan cake wrapped in clear film, with two wires fixed to it. The wires then looped around to a little terminal. Both were firmly stuck to the door with black masking tape. The Butler resigned himself to the inevitable and sat down. He wrapped his arms around his knees and then continued to await his fate, as he rocked back and forwards gently.

The intruder carefully walked backwards along the corridor, six carefully placed steps. He dipped back into his backpack one last time and removed the one thing that he needed to complete the job. The Butler had finally run out of time, he removed a very small, silver trinket box from his trouser pocket and opened it. He peered down at it and then took out its only contents, a small white pill. He put it in his mouth, took one gulp back and swallowed it. *This is it my friend.* He said to himself, as he sighed deeply. He crawled up off his knees and in one last moment of utter defiance, he slammed his hand on top of the fax machine and roared. *Nooooooooooooooo.* He sat back down teary eyed, to suffer the last moments of his life.

A high pitched noise burst out of the fax machine and then another and then a green light appeared at the top. The Butler spun around and looked back at the laptop. The intruder had just pulled out the aerial from his device; he put his backpack on the floor and then put his finger over the round red plastic button. He was ready to go, ready to blow the door. Just then, his phone rang, which was only heard through his earpiece. It caused him to flinch, the timing could not have been worse. He looked at his phone, which was strapped to his bicep and could see the name 'Base' flashing from it. He slowly laid the device on the ground and answered the call.

'Da.'

'Do you have him?'

'I will in a matter of seconds, I am about to blow up his door.' He whispered.

'Call me when you have him.'

'Da.'

The Butler sensed that he had one last attempt to send the fax; he knew he had only seconds before the tablet killed him or the intruder captured him. He mustered up one last burst of energy and repeatedly pushed the redial button.

Boom, the front door was blown right off. The Butler slumped to the floor on his knees; the blast and the tablet had disorientated him. He started to dribble from the side of his mouth; the tablet was now rushing through his bloodstream. He leaned up, grabbed the fax machine and pulled it down from the table. He hugged it tight and then began to cry.

The dust and debris had swamped the entrance hall and filtered its way through to the rest of the apartment. The man ran in, he was faced with three doors to choose from. He switched on his torch and looked inside the first one. It was of no interest, a cupboard, with one coat hanging in it.

The Butler was now dipping in and out of consciousness; his head was bowed, as the intruder found his way in. He walked over and stood over him. He lifted up the Butler's head by his hair and could see the white foam spilling from his mouth. He tightened his grip on his hair, pulled it hard and lifted the Butler off his feet. He looked him in the eyes.

'What have you taken?' He demanded. The Butler managed half a defiant smile, as the tablet completed its mission. His eyes were locked open, but he would see no more in this world.

Chapter 21

Jack caught sight of the head receptionist as she walked over to their table. She had a slow seductive walk, her hips rocked side to side like two well-oiled pistons. Dressed in a white shirt, that had three buttons undone at the neck, something that could not be found in the staff dress code. She wore a light brown skirt, short enough to see just above her knees, showing off her Spanish bronzed and toned legs.

She had a fax clasped tightly in her right hand. The same fax that the Butler had died for. The same fax that he prayed for, as he took his last breath.

'This is it by the looks of it Holly.' Holly's head turned to her right to see the receptionist, as she approached their table.

'Your fax Senorita.' The receptionist said, smiling as she handed over the paper.

'Thank you so much.' Holly replied. Jack gestured and then thanked the receptionist. She smiled back at Jack, a warm, sunny, beaming smile, then twisted one hundred and eighty degrees on her black court shoes and swaggered off, back to her duties.

'Well, here goes Jack, let's hope this is our answer.' The fax was on one roll of paper, so Holly unrolled the fax from itself. Her eyes were immediately drawn to the top of the fax. *Save us, find it, hide it.*

'Is that a message from the Butler, or part of the puzzle?' Holly said out loud to herself.

Jack pulled his chair around and leaned in towards Holly to look at the fax. Silence descended, distant bird noises were all that filled the warm air, as they took their first glimpse at the drawings and writing on the fax. This puzzle was different to anything either of them had seen before. Was it a puzzle? A code? A location? A message? A warning? A riddle? Or a mixture of all six?

As expected, there were four tattoos' on the fax to look at. All four had a zodiac symbol, each one was different. This was followed by what appeared to be jumbled up markings, again each one different to the next. Three out of the four tattoos' had names of a city on them, again different cities on each one. All four had a faint line around the edge of the tattoo. Finally, there was a list of numbers, what appeared at first sight to be sequenced, again each one was different.

Jack and Holly had been studying the fax for a couple of minutes, but their concentration was broken, as their phone rang. Holly looked at the number flashing.

'The Butler.' Holly said. Jack pressed speakerphone and then launched straight into an excitable conversation.

'We have received the fax thank you, but we have a number of questions for you.' There was no response, only silence. Holly decided to have a go, to get his attention.

'Hello, Mr Butler, I said we have.' Holly's sentence was cut short by Jack. He covered her mouth with his hand, shaking his head in the process. The silence had spooked him, Holly knew, she nodded as he moved his hand away. The uncomfortable silence continued for a few more seconds, before the caller spoke.

'Who is this? Who I am speaking too?' The voice had an eastern European ring to it. *That was not the voice of the Butler, so who the hell was it?* Jack whispered to Holly. They both held their silence.

'If you co-operate with me, then you might stand a chance of living, if not, then you will certainly die. I will only ask once more. Who are you?' Holly looked at Jack to take the lead on this one; he nodded and then slammed his finger down to end the call. They both let out a sigh.

'They must have the Butler.' Holly whispered, as if the caller could somehow still hear her. Jack was still deep in thought.

'They will be able to trace this sim card now, or at least know where the fax was sent. We are finished here; we need to get out of here and fast. I say we dump the sim card in the marina.' Holly stated. Jack had concluded something.

'Agreed, we must assume the Butler is dead. Whoever the caller was, they would have used him as leverage. If he had still been alive, he would have been used on that call.' Jack picked up the fax and looked at it and then looked at Holly.

'It's one step forward and two back Holly.'

'How do you mean?' Holly replied. Jack tapped his finger on the fax.

'We have this fax, but the Butler is now dead and we don't know where the Shield was heading. The Butler never got to answer that question'

'Well Jack, we must make this fax count, we must find a way of cracking this thing, we promised Ella.'

'Before we go Holly, can you write down the messages from the sim card before we dump it.'

'Yes, good idea.'

Jack was pulling Holly along into a fast walk as they breezed through the hotel. Their taxi was waiting for them, his meter still running and his best fare in years. They both raced into the back seats.

'Drive please, quickly, gracias.' Jack said, firmly tapping the driver's headrest.

'Where are we going sir?' The driver replied.

'Take us to the airport, but stop at the marina for one moment please.'

The Taxi sped away and onto Av. Gabriel Roca. They sped along to the end of the road and then turned off, just before the start of the Autovia Autopista De Levante. Jack and Holly slid a little on the black leather seats, as they rattled along, taking the corners swiftly. The taxi turned down Camino De La Escollera and then pulled up at one of the parking bays, next to the Yacht repair centre. Jack jumped out of the taxi; he glanced around at the spectacular amount of yachts before him and then threw the sim card into the water, as if his life depended on it. He climbed back into the taxi and ordered the driver to push on. Holly had taken a moment to reflect, as she watched Jack hurling the sim card into the marina. She took his hand, she was scared and she wanted some reassurance.

'Jack, this situation is pretty scary and I really don't know what our next move is, other than to get the hell out of here. Maybe it is time to call Johnson.' Jack exhaled as he squeezed Holly's hand gently. He turned to her, offering her genuine concern.

'Listen, we are in this together Holly, I will look after you and you can count on it.' Holly leaned her head into Jack's shoulder. Jack looked down and spoke to the top of her head.

'We can call Johnson from the airport and tell him what is going on to some extent Holly, but we need to be careful. That accent on the phone was eastern European; we both agree with that, my hunch is that our mystery caller was working for that Heenan guy that we were told about.' Jack pushed his head back on the seat and then looked up at the taxi roof for inspiration. He was out of luck. Holly had her own idea.

'I suggest we should tell Johnson the Butler is dead and maybe it was this Heenan guy who was behind it? But I think maybe we should hold back telling him about the fax until we have had time to look at it properly and make some sense of it.'

'Ok, I just hope we can come up with something soon. I do have one serious concern though.' Jack replied.

'What's that?' Holly replied. Jack dropped his head and looked at Holly.

'The Butler told us that this was an inside job and that his computer had been hacked, correct?

'Go on Jack, I'm listening.'

'We really need to think about what we say and to whom we say it. I have said it before and I am saying it again, something is just not right here Holly. What if the President or Johnson is behind this?'

'Look Jack, I do agree, that things are beginning to look a little different, but c'mon, I don't buy that the President or Johnson are playing us, that seems a little farfetched in my book.'

'We will see Holly. In the meantime I say we fly to England to shed some light on this 1183 organisation. We can study the fax en route' Jack replied. Holly looked out of the taxi window and caught sight of the big blue sign above their heads, as the taxi flashed by. *Aeropuerto.*

'I once had family in England Jack; they last visited us back in the States, on my 13th birthday. Uncle Albert and Aunty Linda.' Holly looked at Jack, her eyes looked heavy and then she continued.

'They were killed in a boating accident. I remember when my dad told me, I cried for days. Although Linda was my Aunty and I only ever saw her every couple of years, she became like a mother figure to me. She made the most amazing cupcakes and made me a beautiful chocolate birthday cake that day.

'That's tragic Holly; you certainly have had a rough deal with your family. Do you know where in England they lived?'

'No, we never got to visit them, they always came to us.'

Chapter 22

The professor was packing up his papers and saying his goodbyes at Edinburgh Castle. He was renowned for his lengthy student lectures, although this speech had only run over by a mere fifteen minutes. Not that long, considering one speech in Manchester last year, ran over by nearly two hours.

His last goodbye was to Kim Carson, the lady who had organised the speech that day. Kim worked for a publicity company in Edinburgh. They devoted part of their time and money, in bringing specialist speakers to Edinburgh, for their students to learn from. Kim had been working on bringing the professor to Edinburgh for nearly two years and she was ecstatic that she had finally secured his services.

'Do you have any plans this evening professor? My partners and I would love you to join us for dinner. We are going to the secret garden at the Witchery.'

'Please Kim, call me Gordon. I have always wanted to go to the Witchery, it sounds like an incredible place. I have heard really good things about it over the years. Unfortunately though, I have made other arrangements with my friends, who I'm staying with tonight.'

'Bring them along Gordon, the more the merrier and the evening is on us. What do you say Gordon?' Kim was a quarter of an inch over five feet six, but still looked up at the professor, even with her three inch heels on. He was a towering six feet four, but this did not stop him from smiling down on her.

'Go on then, you have talked me in to it. I am sure Denise and Steven would love to come too.'

'Great, I will send a car to pick you up, shall we say seven?'

'Yes, seven is fine with me, do you have the address?

'No, but if you give it to me I will call the driver straight away.' Kim typed the address into her iPad, as the professor read it out.

'It's Martin's Guesthouse, Granville Terrace, EH10 4PQ. My friends, Denise and Steven own it, so it means I can catch up with them while I'm staying there.' Kim offered the professor a warm hearty handshake.

'I am looking forward to meeting them and I will catch up with you later Gordon.'

'Yes, thank you.' *What a nice lady.* He thought to himself.

The professor removed his grey suit jacket from his chair and put it on. He loosened his grey tie and unbuttoned the very top of his creased white shirt. Dressed almost head to toe in grey, the professor was not the most flamboyant of dressers. His thoughts on his dress code were simple. Wearing a bright suit or funky tie could distract attention away from his lectures.

The professor marched out from the castle, baggage in hand and flagged down a black cab. It spun around the cobbles and pulled up at the entrance. Edinburgh Castle sit's at the very top of the Royal Mile. The professor had fond memories of the Royal Mile. He spent four consecutive years visiting the Edinburgh Festival in the 1990's. He would often walk up and down the Royal Mile, watching the endless array of acts on show to the public. All free of charge, which the professor was a great advocate of. The professor spoke very passionately about the Royal Mile festival activities and the festival in general, to anyone that would listen to him. He would enthuse to all about its character, with its cobbled streets lined with pubs, cafes, apartments, hotels and tourists shops.

The Royal Mile also has a spectacular collection of architecture, running the entire length of it. The professor would list them in order of his own personal preference, the way his mind's eye brought them to life. His hit list included The Scotch Whisky Experience, the new Scottish Parliament building, John Knox house, the Museum of Childhood, but the most unique part about The Royal Mile in his mind, was the top and tail, as he called it. Edinburgh Castle stood proudly at the top and Holyrood Palace at the tail.

The professor leaned forward and gave the driver the address of his destination. The taxi turned left off the Royal Mile, down Bank Street and headed down the Mound, before turning left onto Princes Street. The heavens opened and the cab driver flicked on the windscreen wipers. The conditions outside now looked as appealing as the professors grey suit. The taxi driver had decided it was time for a chat.

'Are ye up visiting these parts mate?'

'No, not quite, I have been giving a lecture at the castle.' The professor replied.

'A lecture, get oot of here mate. What ye lecturing on like mate?'

'Well it was about ancient worlds and how they came to communicate with one another.' The professor smiled, the broad and direct approach of the taxi driver, was amusing to him. Having visited Edinburgh many times before, the professor had become familiar with the local accent and the local humour.

The rain falling from the sky above became heavier, a common sight for any Edinburgh taxi driver. The driver flicked the wipers to maximum and then decided to turn the conversation from work to play and to his favourite topic.

'De ye like football mate?' The professor was quickly warming to the taxi driver. He thought to himself. *Who would have followed on from a castle lecture, to ask a question about football, other than an Edinburgh black cab driver?*

'I do, very much. I am an Arsenal fan.' The professor declared.

'Arsenal eh, they have had a strange few years now mate. Since you built that new stadium, I don't think you have been the same side.' The driver engaged eye contact, looking into his rear view mirror. Football was his passion; it was his life, inside the taxi and out.

'It has been a strange few years, you are right there. Which team do you support?' The professor asked, happily joining in the banter with the driver. He looked out of the rain soaked window. As his eyes caught sight of the John Lewis department store, sitting to his right, the driver turned off Princes Street and took a left onto Lothian Road.

'I'm a Jambo mate, a Jam Tart, a Maroon.' The driver said chuckling.

'Ah, you are a Hearts fan then. Arsenal's troubles pale into insignificance, with the dire straits Hearts have found themselves in over recent years.'

'You are right mate. It pains me to say it, but the Hibees along the road, really know how to run a football club properly.'

'Yes I have friends who are season ticket holders at Hibernian.'

'Do ya mate? Well that's it I'm nae talking to yee, if you associate yourself with folk who support that mob.' The driver laughed at himself.

'Only joking, I have loads of mates that are Hibs fans and anyway, I want me tip.' The driver put his thumbs up, looking back into his rear view mirror. The professor smiled at him, nodding his affection to his cheeky approach. The driver had made the short four minute journey to Martin's guesthouse seem a little more interesting to the professor.

The taxi pulled up at the roadside, on the double yellow lines right outside the entrance to the front garden. The professor could see the price on the taxi meter. He pushed a note through the little gap and told him to keep the change.

'Cheers buddy, have a gud night mate, nice chatting to yee.'

'You are welcome my friend and likewise.' The professor closed the taxi door and strode up the path to the front door of the guesthouse. Raindrops soaked the shoulders of his suit, as the relentless downpour had turned the sky black. The diesel engine spluttered as the taxi pulled away. The professor rang the bell and waited for a reply. He glanced around at his surroundings, frowning as the raindrops trickled down his face. He caught sight of Denise walking down the hall and wiped his face dry. He glanced around at the garden and noticed the new wooden garden bench that had been added since his last visit. The professor turned back and waved through the window of the front door at Denise, who was wearing a great big smile on her face. She opened the door and gave the professor a big hug.

'So good to see you Gordon, come out of the rain, you're soaking. It always seems to rain when you visit us dear.'

'Great to see you too Denise and I do believe the sun shone once in 2006 when I was here.' They laughed at the Edinburgh weather's hold over their lives.

'How was your day Gordon?'

'I had a great day thanks, plane was on time this morning, a warm reception at the castle, followed by a good lecture, well I thought so anyway and I only ran over by a few minutes this time.' They both laughed again.

'I have a dinner offer for the three of us, from my employers and you will never guess where it is?' Denise clasped her hands in excitement.

'Splendid, where are we off too?'

'We are going to the secret garden at the Witchery.'

'Wow, cool, I love that place.' Denise opened her hands a little and applauded the offer.

'Yes I know, I thought you would be pleased. Is Steven back yet?' The professor asked.

'No, you have just missed him, he is off to the wholesalers, but he will be back in an hour or so.'

'Ok, I will go and grab a shower and get changed.'

'That is no problem, I will get your key, I have put you in your favourite room, room four.'

'Ah thank you, you do look after me Denise.'

'Here we go, there is your key.'

'I will see you shortly Denise.' The professor made his way up the one flight of stairs, to reach room four.

Denise had made her way back indoors, but the sound of the front door bell stopped her in her tracks. *I bet Steven has forgotten his keys again, that bloody man would forget what day it was if it wasn't written on the calendar.* She thought to herself. As Denise got close to the door, she could see it was not Steven and she did not recognise the man waiting there. *We are full my dear, no room at the inn tonight I'm afraid.* She muttered under her breath. As Denise opened the door, she offered her warm greeting.

'Hello there, what can I do for you?'

'I am so sorry to disturb you madam, I am looking for the professor.' The man at the door asked, his accent thick and deep. Denise looked him up and down, something looked odd, very odd. *Why is he wearing sunglasses in the rain*? Although the rain had just eased a little, she watched droplets roll down his glasses. He stood there, a colossus of a man, black roll neck jumper, black body warmer, jeans and boots. His hair was sleek, waxed back, turning grey at the edges.

'Who?' Denise made a poor attempt to buy some thinking time. The man took his sunglasses off and placed them carefully onto his head. Denise looked up at his eye, there was a mark under the corner of it, she could not quite see what it was.

'The professor madam, he is a guest here with you tonight, I am led to believe.' Denise had become slightly defensive now, her arm blocking the entrance via the door handle.

'And who may I ask are you?' She asked abruptly.

'I am from Edinburgh Castle madam, the professor was speaking there today. We had a parcel delivered for him, but he did not pick it up before he left. Would you be so kind to get the professor, so I can get him to sign for it?' The man smiled, a forced smile she thought. *I don't like the look of you my dear and what is that mark below your eye, it looks like a tattoo.* The man interrupted Denise's observation time.

'Please madam, the professor, I'm in a hurry.'

'Oh yes, the professor, I know who you mean now. He is staying in room four. I will go and knock on his door and get him for you. Would you like to come into the hall while I go upstairs?'

'Yes that would be nice thank you.' The man walked into the hall as Denise held the door open. She took a second look at the man and noticed something was missing.

'Where is the parcel?' Denise once again looked the man up and down.

'Excuse me madam?'

'You said you had a parcel for the professor and he needed to sign for it.' Denise was frowning with confusion; there was no parcel in sight. The man put his arms out arrogantly and explained.

'I have madam, it is a fragile parcel, very expensive and I am only insured to transport the parcel. The professor will need to come out to the van to collect and sign for it.' Denise reluctantly accepted the explanation and ran upstairs.

The man then dialled a number on his phone; it was answered on the first ring.

'Get the parcel ready for despatch please.'

Denise knocked on the door of room four and the professor answered it quickly.

'Gordon, you have a delivery waiting for you downstairs my darling.' The professor looked puzzled.

'A delivery for me Denise, are you sure?

'Yes, there is a representative from Edinburgh Castle downstairs. Apparently it arrived for you today, but you never picked it up. He said it was fragile.' The professor was still puzzled.

'Nobody informed me of any delivery today and I have not ordered anything, I wonder what on earth it could be.'

'Oooh, well maybe you have a secret admirer Gordon, you never know. Denise said jokingly.

'I wish Denise! I don't think the wife would be too happy though.' The professor chuckled as Denise teased him. Denise walked back down the stairs and the Professor followed. The man was patiently waiting at the entrance and smiled as the professor approached him.

'Professor, I have a parcel for you in the van, but as I explained to the lady, I am only insured for the transport, as it is very fragile and expensive.'

'I have not ordered anything and I have certainly not been informed of any parcel.' The man took a step forward and offered his identification badge. It showed his name as Richard Christie.

'You don't sound like a Richard.' The professor remarked, as he checked his identification.

'My mother moved here from Russia when I was a child and re-married. She loved Richard Burton movies, so changed my name, no big deal.' The man said, barely moving his lips.

'Please professor, I am parked on double yellow lines and I would appreciate it if you come and sign for the parcel, before I get a parking ticket.'

'Very well, let us see what all this fuss is about.' The professor looked at Denise.

'Do you have an umbrella I could use please?'

'Of course, I have one here behind the door. Here you go.' Denise handed the navy blue umbrella to the professor. As the professor stepped out of the door, he popped up the umbrella; giant white letters appeared on it, The Royal Bank of Scotland.

The professor followed the man down the path, Denise shouted to him.

'I will put the kettle on Gordon and we can have a cup of tea while you open your parcel.'

'Thank you.' The professor shouted, waving back, with his one free hand. *That looked like a tattoo of a tear under his eye; I wonder what that could mean?* Denise concluded.

The man stopped at the end of the path, put his arm out and offered the professor the right of way, from the pedestrian pathway to the van.

'It is the white Mercedes van just ahead of you professor.' As the professor reached the end of the pathway he noticed the van had no company marking on it. He turned around; about to question it, when out of the corner of his eye he caught sight of the man's hand coming over his shoulder. Instantly he felt an object thrust into his neck. A second man pulled the van's side door open from the inside, just in time to see the needle doing its job. It had rendered the professor unconscious within four seconds. His tall frame was bundled unceremoniously into the back of the van. The van door was slammed shut. The man took one last look looked around to make sure the abduction was clean. He put his rain soaked sunglasses back on and climbed into the passenger seat.

'Go.'

Chapter 23

The taxi had arrived at the Son Bonet airfield in Palma, where their plane was waiting. The thirteen minutes it had taken to drive there, had allowed them to have a brief look at the fax. The information on the fax was complicated, random even; it would take time to make sense of it. Their decision to fly to England still stood.

Their private jet was one of only two that sat in the hanger. The pilots were resting in the VIP lounge, awaiting further instructions.

'We should call Johnson now and tell him our plans.' Holly suggested to Jack.

'What are our plans Holly? We need to agree on what to tell him, I just don't feel easy about telling him anything.'

'C'mon Jack, I thought we had this phone call boxed off?' Holly was annoyed, they had agreed to call and Jack was now changing the goalposts.

'So what do you suggest Jack, we say nothing and hope the pilot will kindly drop us off on a deserted beach, out of the reach of the United States Secret Service, Folis Heenan and his merry men?' Holly's outburst took Jack by surprise, but he put it down to her tiredness.

'You're just being ridiculous Holly; I don't know any deserted beaches we could go to.' He said smugly.

'If I did, I sure would not want to be there with you.' Jack winked at Holly and he could see she was rising to his bait. The calm, considerate person she had spoken to, when they got into the taxi had vanished, replaced by stubborn mule Jack.

The taxi pulled up at the hanger. Holly snarled at Jack, as she unclipped her seatbelt.

'Urgghhh, you think you are so funny don't you Jack?' Jack smiled and then raised his eyebrows, tilted his head a few degrees and nodded.

'No Holly, I know I'm funny.' Holly's temperature kept rising, her temper bubbling inside, time for an ultimatum.

'You either call Johnson or you're on your own Jack and I'm being serious.' Holly jumped out of the taxi and slammed the car door. Jack exhaled. *Jesus, where did that come from?* He paid the driver and climbed out of the car. He looked at Holly as he closed the car door. She had turned her back on him, not wanting him to see her eyes, filling up with tears. Jack gestured an apology, even though Holly had her back to him.

'Hey Holly, I'm sorry ok? I know I come across as an ass sometimes, but it's because I care, ok? He had finally dropped the act. Holly sniffled, turned around and wiped away a tear, her frustration evident.

'We need to make the call Jack; we need Johnson to sign off the plane, so we can fly to England.' Jack walked over to Holly; he put his hands on her shoulders and looked in her eyes.

'Hey, I'm sorry ok.' He said softly. Holly wiped another tear.

'It's just that I'm really concerned something is seriously a miss here Holly. I know we agreed the call, but on reflection, I would rather tell Johnson, the absolute minimum. At least until we understand a bit more, about what we are dealing with here.' Jack had become firm and assured, his defence was accepted, Holly's tiredness had taken over.

'Okay, okay. You can call him though Jack.'

'I will, but we don't know who has hacked into the Butler's laptop, that could be Johnson, we just don't know.'

'I said okay and I meant it, make the call. Holly flung her arms up to finish the conversation, time was creeping by.

'Make the call Jack'

'Hello.' Johnson answered.

'Hello Johnson, It's Jack, we are back at the plane in Palma. I'm calling you with an update on what we have come across. I'm going to put the phone on speaker, so that Holly can hear you. Ok, that's it done.'

'Hello Holly, hello Jack, what have you come up with?' Holly hijacked the conversation immediately.

'Johnson, Have there been any developments at your end that we need to know about?' Jack looked at Holly and mimed, *what are you doing?* He was amazed at her intervention after the grief he had just received from her.

'Maybe, I am not sure yet.' Johnson replied. A plane had just landed and the engine noise had blocked out Johnson's reply.

'What did you just say?' Holly shouted.

'There is some intelligence coming through as we speak. We are trying to establish its authenticity.'

'What intelligence?' Holly asked.

'We believe a Professor Gordon Nelson, from London has been kidnapped in Edinburgh by Heenan's men.' Holly's face instantly changed, a look of fear swamped it.

'Oh my god, I know him. I have met him several times; he is a friend of mine. We had dinner after one of his lectures in New York last year.'

'Yes, I know him too.' Jack said. 'He is the best person I know on historical data links. It looks like this Heenan guy will stop at nothing, to get what he wants.'

'I will keep you informed, now what have you found out for me?' Johnson enquired.

'We believe the Butler is dead.' Jack was blunt, a deliberate act to gage Johnson's reaction. Johnson reacted, but not quite how Jack had imagined he would.

'WHAT.' He foamed down the speaker phone.

'It's true Johnson.' Holly added.

'Oh good God, how on earth have you come to this conclusion? Jesus Christ I hope you have made a mistake.' Johnson raged, the Butler was his responsibility, how could this happen to him.

'It has all happened so very fast, hence only being able to give you this information now.' Jack blurted his reply, raising his voice slightly, still surprised at Johnson's volatile reaction.

'Look Johnson, after speaking with Ella Fox we went to their Villa. We were able to find Mike's sim card.' Johnson cut Holly's explanation, his voice and tone less aggressive.

'You got access to Mike Fox's sim card, good, what was on it?'

'If you let me speak, I will tell you.' She declared, her tone forthright, her tiredness now spilling over from Jack to Johnson.

'The sim card contained two text messages. The first was to tell him to get the hell out of there. The second was a coded message. We believe that message was the location of where to go next.'

'What was on the message?' Johnson asked. Holly reacted angrily.

'Jesus Johnson! I have just said it was coded.' Johnson was now furious with Holly. *How dare she take that tone with me?*

'I thought you two were supposed to be the best in the business at cracking coded messages?' Johnson fumed, the phone call had quickly escalated, time for a calm head and Jack was on hand.

'Look Johnson we are sorry, it has been a very stressful few hours. We are doing our best and we are both well aware of the stakes at hand, in finding the *Document of Truth* before Heenan does.' There was a moment of silence before Johnson replied.

'There is a lot of pressure and stress on everyone, but we must stay calm and communicate with each other civilly. Please Holly, carry on.' A verbal truce was called and it allowed for both parties to move on. Holly walked Johnson through the second coded message, word by word, line by line. It made no sense to him, or to any of them.

'We will head for England; there may be a thread that we can work on from our research at the library.' Jack stated.

'Very well, keep me informed.' Johnson replied.

'We will, but if you have any updates about the professor or anything else, then please get in touch ASAP.' Holly pleaded.

'Of course I will.' Johnson replied. 'You did well finding the sim card and contacting the Butler, good job, it is just a shame it never amounted to anything more. Speak soon. Goodbye.' Jack looked at Holly and shook his head. *Hold your nerve Holly*. He whispered to her.

'Bye.' Holly said, as she ended the call. Jack looked up; relieved they still held the trump card. Johnson seemed genuine to him, but he wasn't taking any chances.

England was now agreed, the pilots informed and the plane put on standby. Newcastle International Airport was to be the next stop. As Holly climbed the steps to the plane, she turned to Jack, her mind caught now focused on the future.

'I wonder what adventure awaits us in England Jack?'

'If the last twenty four hours is anything to go by, I would buckle up for a bumpy ride.' Jack replied. As Holly climbed on board the jet, piped music played quietly, but loud enough to grab Holly's attention. *Don't worry about a thing, cause every little thing, gonna be alright, rise up this mornin' smiled with the risin' sun, three little birds...* Holly looked to the sky. *Thank you grandpa.*

Chapter 24

Johnson was in the middle of updating the President about his conversation with Jack and Holly. The President's cell phone, began buzzing away, in the inside pocket of his Hugo Boss navy blue suit. As the President took the cell phone out of his pocket, Johnson stopped talking, he seemed bemused. *I didn't know he had a private cell phone.* The President looked down at the caller's details flashing on the screen.

'Please excuse me Johnson, I need to take this call, it is the British Prime Minister, about our upcoming meeting, no doubt.' The President watched on as Johnson left the room. The President looked at the screen, the display still flashing, unknown caller.

'Hello.' The President said quietly, as he paced slowly around the room.'

'Is this line secure?' The unknown caller asked.

'Yes this line is secure.' The President replied, as he looked down at the carpet, his cell phone, pressed firmly against his ear.

'Do you take me for a fool Mr President?'

'No, of course I don't. Why do you say that for God's sake?'

'I say that as you have just put it, because you have indeed taken me for a fool Mr President. Did you think that I wouldn't find out about your plan to double cross me?' The unknown caller's voice was stripped of any emotion; he was cold, but exact.

'What plan? What are you talking about? We had a deal and I am sticking to that deal, nothing has changed.' The President was concerned and moved quickly to reassure the unknown caller.

'Look, nothing has changed, you have my word.'

'Mr President, your word means nothing to me. I am afraid our deal is off. I should never have trusted you in the first place. You are just like the rest, all talk and no balls.' The unknown caller had caught the President off guard. He was not expecting such a quick backlash.

'Please, this deal is good for the both of us, you must see that?' The President pleas fell on deaf ears.

'Mr President, I have the photograph.' The President stopped in his tracks.

'W, what photo?' He asked tentatively.

'My, my, you really don't have any balls do you Mr President. You know fine well the photograph I am talking about. Goodbye Mr President.'

'Wait.' It was too late for the President's plea. *No, no, no, the dirty son of a bitch.* The President screwed up his face in disbelief, at the news he had just heard. He put his cell phone back in his jacket pocket, went to the door and invited Johnson back in. Johnson noticed he was distracted, while updating him on the events taking place. His observation was compounded when he suddenly and abruptly announced that he was closing down the operation to find the *Document of Truth*.

'Have the operation closed Johnson, it not open for discussion, it is a waste of time and money.' Johnson looked dismayed.

'Mr President I must disagree strongly, we have a coded message in our possession. I have just come off the phone with Jack and Holly. They made communication with the Butler. I was just about to tell you, before your phone rang.' The President looked surprised, his face relaxed a little as hope once again sparkled in his eyes.

'Where is he and what did he say? The President ·enthused. Johnson looked down at the floor; he needed to take a breath.

'What is it Johnson, what is wrong?' Johnson lifted his head and looked the President straight in the eyes.

'We believe the Butler was murdered Mr President.'

'Jesus Christ Johnson, the Butler is dead?' The President was exasperated; he looked around the room for answers, he rubbed his head with both hands, the pressure clearly mounting. Johnson needed to push harder.

'We have retrieved a coded message that was sent to Mike Fox, one of the Shield. Jack and Holly are working on it right now.' The President was unmoved; he stood starring at the carpet, thinking of what to do.

'Give Jack and Holly some time sir, they have made some progress.' Johnson pleaded, his face twisted, his arms outstretched, his palms clasped together. The President put his arms by his side and sighed as he prepared to deliver the dreaded news to Johnson.

'My mind is made up Johnson; wind up the operation and that is an order.' Johnson pleaded once more, in vain.

'But sir, we have so much to lose, if we concede defeat without a battle.' The President wanted to move on.

'We need to focus on the aftermath of all this, plan what we say to the rest of the world.' Johnson could not believe what he was hearing. None of it made sense to him. He started to question himself. *Why would the President want to close this down now? We have nothing to gain and everything to lose.* The President turned his back on Johnson and told him to leave the office.

As Johnson left the room, the President wasted no time in dragging his phone back out of his pocket. He dialled a number and then held a finger over the call button. He took a deep breath and then pressed it. It was answered swiftly.

'Yes?'

'We have a major problem and you are going to have to fix it.' He whispered, scanning the room as if the whole world was listening in on him.

'What type of problem?' The accent was hard to call.

'Our asset has gone sour on us. We need to take him out now.' The President rubbed his mouth, his nervous tension rising. He was losing control of the situation and it was really starting to affect his judgement.

'Understood, but it could be very messy.'

'Just get it done; you know what's at stake.' The President loosened his tie and unbuttoned his shirt at the neck.

'Consider it done, but don't say I didn't warn you that this could cause a fuss.' The President paced the floor, with his head bowed, holding the phone to his ear, as if his life depended on it.

'Do it, do it now.' He demanded. He ended the call and stood transfixed on the spot. He shook his head then looked over to his cream sofa, it was calling him. He walked over and gently put his right hand down to take his weight, as he slumped onto it. *Dear God, what have I done?*

Chapter 25

Heenan's men had arrived back at his home in Northern Cyprus. With them was a tired, confused and very frightened professor. He was led to the basement and put into the red chair. The same red chair that McVey had confessed in, the confession that started off this whole chain of events. The smell from his torture still lingered around the room. It heightened his senses to a limit he had never experienced before. He was pale grey with worry; which matched his crumpled grey suit. He had been about to change into his navy suit for dinner that evening, before Denise had knocked on the door of room four.

Heenan was informed of his arrival and swooped down the stairs to the basement. He clomped into the room, slamming the great door closed behind him, grinning like a kid in a candy shop.

'Professor!' He shouted, holding his arms out to him, as if he was a long-lost friend. The professor looked at him in disgust, terrified at what was to become of him.

'What do you want with me?' He asked pleadingly. He was desperate for an answer to this ordeal. There had been only silence on the journey from Scotland, although he had not long been conscious from the drug that was pumped into his neck in Edinburgh. His mind was swimming with fear and utter confusion. *Who were these people and what did they want? It must be a big mistake.*

'Please tell me, what is it you want with me?' His desperation was palpable. A grey map of sweat outlined the wet area of his white shirt. His trousers although creased somewhat, held their shape, his tie still pressed up against his top button.

The professor was a quiet unassuming man, who never used his position for petty gain, unlike some people he knew. He was a true family man. His second wife of twenty one years, Margaret, had three children, two of them to the professor, although he treated all three equally. His passion outside of his work was the same passion he had for his work. In fact his wife had a nickname for him. 'The busman.' This came about because every family holiday seemed to turn out like a busman's holiday.

He was obsessed with collecting unusual objects from all over the world and spent many a weekend in museums, collector's workshops and auctions. He was a member of a number of clubs. The most active of the clubs was also his favourite, the British Battle Re-Enactment Society, although even that passion had suffered recently, due to his work commitments on the lecture circuit.

'That is a good question professor, in fact that is the only question you should occupy your mind with. You are my new best friend now and you and I are going to change history together.' Heenan had continued with his fake smile, gesturing flamboyantly at the professor. The professor was already scared enough, but Heenan's performance added another level to the desperation he felt.

Heenan went through his OCD ritual once more. His handkerchief, changed twice daily by Yuri, was about to come under attack from his sweating salty brow. He dabbed four times, far left, centre left, centre right and far right.

'I don't understand how I could possibly help you change history; you must have me mistaken with someone else.' The professor looked up at Heenan from his seated position, his slim lanky frame, not covering the red plastic seat in the way McVey's did. He was trying his best to unscramble all the thoughts whizzing around his brain. Heenan offered the professor a piece of wisdom.

'You are going to solve a problem for me and for that I will let you and your family live.' Heenan sounded pleased with himself that he was offering such a deal. The professor ground his teeth together hard. The flippancy of how Heenan had brought his family into the equation stunned him.

'Please, don't hurt my family, they have done nothing to you, I have done nothing to you. I don't understand what all this is about; surely you must have the wrong person, please.' Heenan stamped the floor in anger; his cowboy boot whipping up a noise that echoed around the room. It startled the professor even more.

'Enough of your dribbling professor, you are beginning to bore me now.'

'What possible problem could I help you with? Are you sure you have the right person?' The professor had become teary, but he kept his head up while speaking to Heenan. The good old British stiff upper lip treatment was on show, but it was about to be shattered and rendered worthless. Heenan marched two steps forward and pointed directly at the professor. A look of devilment shrouded his face.

'I have the right person. You are going to get me what I want and you are going to do it quickly. ' He paused a second, enough time for a tear to roll down the professor's cheek. He lowered his tone, now cold, quiet and menacing.

'I would not have gone to all the trouble to locate you and bring you here otherwise, would I? Now, I want to make sure I have your full attention professor and that you are ready to help me.' The professor looked down at the blue tarpaulin; he could see dried red stains and could only assume what it was. *I can't believe this is happening to me.*

Heenan raised his voice once more and then nodded to Yuri, who lifted a laptop from the top of the fridge. He handed it to his boss. Heenan opened it and tapped the enter button. A distant sound of voices could be heard coming through the laptop speakers. Heenan turned the laptop around and handed it to the professor. It took no more than three seconds before the professor realised what he was looking at.

'No, no, no, no, please no.' He shouted. Yuri called a number and issued a command.

'Now.'

'Da'

The professor watched on through teary eyes, as the live video stream displayed his worst nightmare. He could see the front of his home as Heenan's henchmen entered it. His tears were unleashed at what he witnessed next. His wife and one of his children were gagged and tied up, terrified on the sofa. The professor reached out and touched the screen, his hands shaking uncontrollably. He tried to stroke the image of his wife and child; he yearned to hold them that very moment. Heenan stepped forward and snatched the laptop back off the professor.

'So professor, do I have your full attention now?' The professor just stared into space, his tears dripping down onto his suit jacket and shirt. *How could this monster know where I live, or where I was working? I don't understand what is going on?* The professor pleaded with himself. He was dejected and distraught; his thoughts still in the living room with his family.

Yuri walked over and slapped the professor across the face, the noise echoed; the cellar acoustics were fierce and real.

'You are being spoken to, look up.' Yuri demanded. The professor wiped away the mess that had dribbled from his nose and looked up at Heenan. He sniffed back through both nostrils, trying to compose himself.

'Yes, you have my full attention, what is it you need from me?' Heenan pressed two buttons on the laptop and then handed it back to the professor.

'Look at these photographs. The professor looked down at the laptop. He squinted in disbelief at the screen, tears still blurred his view, but the image was graphic, gut wrenching and one of a kind.

'Have you seen anything like this before professor?' Heenan asked. The professor leaned forward to take a closer look, studying the photos closely. He fought off wandering thoughts of his family and decided the only way he could help them was to get Heenan what he wanted, it was time to focus.

In front of him were the brutally, dismembered, right feet of the four members of the President's Shield.

'These markings are extraordinary, where on earth did you get them from?' Heenan stomped once more, his cowboy boot once again taking the brunt of his frustration. He shouted at the professor, grabbing him by the scuff of the neck and lifted him forward.

'I ask the questions, do you understand?' Heenan growled in his face, close enough for some angry saliva to fly out of his mouth, into the professor's face. The professor nodded, his eyes dropped back down to the laptop. He muttered quietly.

'Yes, I understand.' Heenen let go and took a step back.

'That is the right answer professor, because your family are relying on you.' The professor looked over at Yuri, who was stood rooted to the spot, his arms folded. He offered no help, no emotion, only a piercing menacing look.

'Yuri, pass me your knife.' Heenan said. Yuri pulled up his left trouser leg and took out the knife from the black leather case strapped to his leg. Heenan grabbed the professor's hand, separated his little finger from the rest and then scowled at Yuri.

'He is wasting my time; bring me that table to rest his hand on.

'Hold him still, while I chop off this finger.'

'Noooo, what are you doing?' The professor was frantic; his fifty eight year old facial skin was beginning to ripple deeply, the pressure of the interrogation had become overwhelming.

'No, no, wait; please, you don't need to do that, I have seen something similar to these photos. I will do whatever you want, just let go.' The professor, like many people before him had succumbed to Heenan's evil ways.

'You waste any more of my time professor and it will be more than your little finger that I will be chopping off.' Heenan passed the knife back to Yuri, knowing that his little stunt was enough to push the buttons of his new best friend.

The professor asked to see the photos again and then asked for water. Heenan nodded to Yuri, who walked the three steps to the fridge. He took out a bottle of water and handed it to him. The professor unscrewed the cap with his shaky left hand. He drank the water quickly, too quickly as it made him gasp for breath. He coughed some water back up, but quickly returned to gulp some more, his thirst was a close second to his fear. He composed himself and then offered Heenan the first piece of news, about his new found treasure.

'I have not actually seen this group of markings before, but I have heard rumours about them.' Heenan's eyes lit up.

'What rumours have you heard professor?' The professor wiped away the last residue of his tears.

'Just what legend has led us to believe?' The professor's voice was croaky; his nerves were hanging by a thread.

'Tell me.' Heenan demanded.

'Legend has it, that a group of men, sort of cult I suppose, were formed to protect some mysterious body. This cult was thought to have special powers that were sent from God and that God had given them immortal status.' Heenan laughed, a very sarcastic laugh.

'Do they look immortal to you professor? Their feet are in my fridge.' Yuri chuckled, his folded arms bounced up and down.

'That all sounds farfetched professor, are you sure you are not feeding me bull here?'

'I may be sitting here terrified, but I am no liar, I assure you of that.' The professor showed the first signs of his authority, but he was on dodgy ground and he knew it. Heenen smirked at him; it was the only pleasant look that he would be offered today. Heenan pointed at the laptop.

'Scroll down; there is one more photo I want you to look at. The professor sat looking at the markings on the sole of the Butler's foot. He looked up, an awkward confidence rushed through him.

'Yes, I am quite familiar with this marking.'

'Go on then, what is it?'

'This is the Washington Coat of Arms. It dates back to 1183 if I am not mistaken.' Heenan interrupted the professor to question his history lesson. How could it possibly date that far back, America is not that old. The professor looked stunned; he looked at Heenan and then looked at Yuri in disbelief. *Was this a serious question?*

'The Washington Coat of Arms that dates back to 1183 is not from America, it's actually in England.' Heenan looked confused. *England, what have they got to do with this?*

'It is the original Washington, a village in the north. It is the ancestral home of George Washington.' Heenan shrugged his shoulders, still confused.

'And?' Heenan said. The professor decided against ridicule, even though every ounce of his professional status wanted him to. *How could this man be so uneducated?*

'George Washington, the first President of the United States of America.' Heenan smiled and nodded to Yuri enthusiastically. Finally America was back on the table.

'Washington DC was then named after George Washington.'

'I see, good professor, we are starting to get somewhere. What else can you tell me?'

'There is someone in England that I have met. He takes you on personal tours of all of these sites.'

'What sites are you referring too?' Heenan enquired.

'All of the sites, where the Washington Coat of Arms are located.'

'And, how many sites are we talking about?'

'There are several, most based in the North of England, but some further south too. I have the company business card somewhere in my wallet.' The professor routed around in his wallet and pulled out a business card. Heenan squinted down at the card, his eyes requiring reading glasses now, although he had resisted them so far. He looked down and read the card.

'Danni Grundy, proprietor of the The Washington Triangle. Norman Stocks, head of operations and tours.' Heenan looked up and pointed at the business card to Yuri.

'It says here. Over eight hundred years of history await you. Join my team as we start at America's true birthplace, Washington village and travel all over England, discovering the path that the coat of arms took through time. We look at the legends it made and the Saint it created along the way.'

Heenan looked at the red, white and blue business card and flicked it with his fingers, he pondered as the professor offered more insight.

'I have been on it, twice in fact. Once as part of my work studies and the second time was a present from my wife.'

'Ok professor, I want to know all about this.' Heenan folded his arms; he was in for the long haul.

'Actually the coat of arms has travelled out of England.' Although he was stating the obvious, the professor did not want to suffer the wrath of Heenan any longer, it was time for the gentle approach history lesson.

'I was part of a group who led an investigation into medieval lost symbols. We scoured the world to investigate one-off symbols. Our job was to try and data link them to another symbol.' The professor grew in confidence. He knew his subjects extensively, he was a great story teller and it was this that led him to a very successful and lucrative career on the lecture circuit.

'The investigation was funded by an unknown source, from South America we believe. We were just paid through a middle man'

'Who was this middle man?' Heenan quizzed. His attention levels heightened.

'His name was Oscar Ṣanchez. He was unfortunately killed in a car accident, the day after we submitted our findings from our investigation.'

'And you did not find this suspicious professor?' The professor was taken aback by Heenan's comment.

'Suspicious? Of course not, why would I?'

'After a few hours with me, you will be suspicious of everything and everyone professor, that is if you live that long.' Heenan smirked again; his love of control over his fellow humans clear to see.

'And what did you find out?'

'Very little really, there was no evidence linking any of the markings and symbols, apart from one, that's why I bring it up. It was the Washington Coat of Arms. Our investigation led us to Havana, in Cuba'. Heenan jumped in.

'I know where Havana is professor.' The professor acknowledged Heenan's new found expertise with a passing nod.

'Good. We found the coat of arms in the 'Palace of the Captain's General Museum'.

'What is the significance of that museum to the coat of arms?' The professor was beginning to draw Heenan back into his world, a world he much preferred to the current one.

'That was the very strange thing about it. We made two visits to the museum. The first visit was very exciting, as we located a scroll dating back to 1898. It was part of a selection of items that belonged to 'USS Battleship Maine'. The Washington Coat of Arms was on the scroll. The ship was sunk by a series of explosions in Havana harbour in 1898. It is believed that this incident led to the start of the Spanish-American war. After the war had ended several years later, a special commission was set up to raise the ship and confirm how it sank.' Heenan was mesmerised, he bowed his head down at the professor.

'What did they find?'

'That it was indeed sunk deliberately and there were rumours about a secret cargo on board.'

'What type of rumours? And what type of cargo?' Heenan wanted answers to everything and wanted them now! His determination to destroy the President and America was utterly arousing to him.

'The rumour was that the ship was carrying a presidential package, a package that dated back to George Washington, but no one can be more specific than that.' Heenan took out his handkerchief and once more went through his ritual. Once he was finished he took a moment to collect himself, he could feel himself being lost in the professor's wisdom. He wanted more answers.

'You said you went twice to the museum. What happened on your second visit? The professor was uncomfortable about passing on the next piece of information.

'The second time was somewhat disappointing. We had taken some special equipment with us, to date the scroll and make sure it was genuine, but it was gone. We asked to speak to the curator, but we were abruptly evicted out of the building.' Heenan rolled his eyes. *Mother of God.* He muttered. He sensed that the professor's words were becoming more useful to him.

'Tell me more about this ship.' Heenan's mind wandered off in to a dream-like state. Could the special package have been *The Document of Truth?*

'All I know is that they were just rumours, nothing factual.'

'Believe me professor there is no smoke without fire, when it comes to rumours.'

'There were lots of rumours, but there was one that intrigued me.' Heenan's eyes lit up once more.

'This rumour circulated a lot at the time. It is said that the ship was sunk to steal the presidential package that was on board. The package was believed to hold secrets about lots of things and that included Cuba. They had been a massive trading partner in the past.' Heenan was now enjoying the current topic very much. The professor could have provided him with the edge he had always wanted over the President.

'After the second Havana visit our funding was stopped. We all went back to our day jobs and no one looked any further.'

'Well it's time to start looking again professor. What do you need to help you?' Heenan knew the professor would need a long leash to do his research, but it would be a very tight one.

'I need a laptop and connection to the internet. It will take some time, as I will need to look at many archive sites.'

'Yuri will watch your every move. If you try and contact anyone professor, I will order the death of your youngest child.' The professor looked up at Heenan. It was a sincere look.

'I understand. I would never put my family in danger' Yuri laughed at the professor.

'You already have!'

'Just one more thing professor, before I leave you.' Heenan took a cigar from his back pocket and stuffed it in his mouth; Yuri stepped forward and lit it. Heenan sucked hard on it, to get it going and then blew a huge puff of smoke into the professor's face, causing him to cough.

'If you love your family as much as you say you do, get me some answers and then you can all live happily ever after.'

Chapter 26

Johnson wanted an update from Jack and Holly before he made his decision, on whether to follow the President's orders or ignore them. Johnson was justified in wanting to make such allowances. *The President is not himself; he would want me to make allowances for his behaviour, while under so much pressure.* Johnson had waited the maximum amount of time he could, before making the call, but that time had ran out.

Jack and Holly had spent that hour; studying the fax, while en route for England. Their studies had so far been frustrating and fruitless, with no real starting point to work from. They debated several possible links, but they agreed that one by one they were not worth pursuing. They were clutching at straws and they knew it. The cell phone rang; the caller display showed it was Johnson on the line for them. *Who else?* Jack thought. Holly took the call and then switched it to speakerphone.

'Hi Johnson, what's up, you heard anything about the professor?'

'Nothing more on the professor I'm afraid.' Johnson sounded even more deflated than them, something was up, they could tell.

'Have you any more news to update me on?' Jack looked at Holly; he sensed there was something coming.

'No, we said we would call you as soon as we did.'

'Then I'm afraid the operation is closed, you are to return home. I will organise a safe house for you until this matter is concluded.' Holly stood and pointed at Jack. *Tell him.* She whispered. Jack refused, he needed to think. *What could possibly be behind this seismic shift?* He decided on an unusual softly-softly approach, Holly was interested to see where he was going with it.

'Hey Johnson, are you ok, what has brought this on man?'

'Unless you can give me something to go back to the President with, then it's over.'

'And is this your decision Johnson?' Jack was probing, his instinct urging him to peel back the truth, behind the dramatic change of events. Johnson paused before answering.

'I cannot lie, it's not my decision, it's the President's.' Jack wagged his finger at Holly. He whispered again. *I told you.* Holly was prepared to let him probe further.

'Do you agree with his decision?' Johnson paused again before answering.

'That is not the point...' Jack cut short into Johnson's statement and declared.

'That is the point, that is the only point, c'mon Johnson, be honest, do you agree with this?' Johnson could be heard clearing his throat.

'No, I don't agree with the President's decision Jack. But he is the boss.' Holly was ready to declare her hand.

'Stall him.'

'What?' Johnson replied.

'Stall him, do whatever it takes to buy us more time.' Holly demanded. Jack decided to back up his partner.

'C'mon Johnson we need more time, you know that. We are just getting started here.' Johnson was not hearing their rallying cry.

'I have held off calling you for an hour to buy some time, in the hope you come up with something.' Holly looked at Jack, she scribbled on some paper. *The President made this decision an hour ago, why???* Jack put his thumb up to Holly, they were in sync on this, something didn't add up.

'Johnson, help us out here man, we need more time.' Jack pleaded one last time.

'My hands are tied; this is the President's orders.'

'Johnson, why on earth would the President want to close this search down?' Holly asked.

'The truth is, I really don't know, he wants us to start planning for the consequences. ' Holly threw her pen and paper on the floor in disgust. She yelled in anger down the speakerphone.

'It's as if he knows something we don't Johnson. We are not stupid. You have dragged us into this mess, put our lives at risk and now, you want to dump us like yesterday's trash and hole us up in some safe house, for God knows how long. Well that's just not good enough.' Holly's face was flushed; pink tinged emotion had quickly swamped it. Jack stood up and embraced her. He whispered in her ear. Don't give up the fax, we have to buy more time, we need an angle, we can do this. Holly looked at Jack, her outburst of anger settling. *Okay.* Johnson conceded.

'You have thirty minutes, if I do not hear from you in that time the operation is shut down, is that clear?

'Yes, crystal clear.'

'Good, good luck. Jack pressed 'End call'. They both breathed a big sigh of relief.

'What was all that about Holly?'

'I don't know, but I am quickly coming round to your way of thinking on this Jack, something is seriously wrong with this operation and from where I'm standing it looks like the President is feeding us to the sharks.' Jack suggested that Holly should sit down.

'We have the fax up our sleeve, but what if Johnson is in on this too?' He asked Holly

'No way, Johnson is clean, he has proven his colours in my book, I trust him. Jack shook his head.

'I'm not so sure.'

'Well what is this master plan you have up your sleeve now then Jack? Jack stood up and took Holly's hand. He leaned forward a few inches and tilted his head to the side, as he moved his mouth, right up to Holly's ear. He cupped his hand to mask any unnecessary sound and whispered gently.

'I don't need to tell you my master plan Holly, I will show you it.' He raised both hands and placed them on the side of each cheek in a soft clasp. He brought his eyes back to look deep into Holly's eyes and slowly moved his hands down her face and rested them on the side of her mouth.

'Close your eyes Holly.' Jack said softly. Holly stared back at him; she was lost in the moment. Her eyes flickered slightly.

'What?'

'Close your eyes.' Jack edged forward; Holly could feel his breath drift across her face. She slowly closed her eyes as Jack's lips pressed softly against hers. Holly, with her eyes tightly closed totally succumbed to his kiss. Her legs turned to jelly, something her subconscious had been hoping for. Their lips separated, Jack moved in closer again; close enough to whisper softly once more. Holly opened her eyes and wondered what to do next. She was rooted to the spot.

'My master plan is simple Holly. Let us work on the fax again; between us there must be something we can decipher and hopefully we can do it within the next thirty minutes.' Jack moved back, giving Holly some space to breath. She could not stop looking at his eyes. She found herself caught up in a fantasy. *A Learjet, a handsome prince, a President who could not be trusted.*

'Well I suppose we could do that Jack.' Holly said softly, slowly coming around, from the induced spell that Jack had put her under.

'Great, let's get to work then.' Jack smiled and then sat back down smugly. Holly sensed a rush of sexual embarrassment. She felt naked standing there, she had lost control.

Chapter 27

'More coffee Senor Max?'

'Nada mas, gracias.'

Max was sitting reading a book in the lounge area of the Playa Pesquero Hotel, Holguin, Cuba. He paused from reading for a moment and looked up. He glanced around, while taking a sip from his latte. As he moved his head left to right he smiled to himself at the array of hotel guests and the attire they displayed.

There were two groups of tourists in the hotel, the British and the Canadians, mostly French Canadians. Americans were banned from travelling to Cuba after the revolution in 1963. Things had improved a little recently, thanks to a new treaty, but the death of a national hero like Castro still runs deep today and will for a very long time. Reminders of the revolution are everywhere and still a huge part of Cuban life.

The French Canadians take great delight in the fact that the Americans have restricted travel to Cuba and descend on mass because of it.

Max switched his vision from the lounge to the bar area. He never understood his fellow hotel guests, his mantra was simple. *Too many people showing too much flesh*. His eyes moved around to the Coffee Coach Bar, his favourite place on the resort. There were several reasons for that. It was part of an old train carriage, a theme that ran through the resort. There was a beautiful painting on the wall, which created the effect that you were on a train, looking out onto fields, as the train moved along. Then there was the superb array of Cuban coffees on offer. Finally there was Mailen. She worked tirelessly behind the Coffee Coach bar. In Max's world, she did this with humour and humility. She was pretty, confident and Max liked her, a lot!

This had been home to Max for over three years now. It is a place where people normally holiday for a week or two, so it did not go unnoticed to the staff that Max was there on a more permanent basis. Cuba was a safe place for Max. No Americans was good for him too. No Americans also meant no one would recognise him.

He dipped his last bit of shortbread biscuit into the dregs of his latte. He had never tired of the place; in fact he had been happier there recently, than he had been anywhere else in the past. He always kept a low profile with other holiday makers; not wanting unwelcome attention. He had grown very fond of the staff; he had his favourites of course, like anyone would. He tipped well and in return he was well liked and well looked after. Yanelis and Nelson looked after him in the Latino Restaurant, where he ate twice a week. The reception, bar and lounge staff all treated him with great respect. Behind the scenes though, staff did wonder who Max really was, but this was Cuba, you didn't ask.

Max had a routine which he stuck to every day. Maybe it was his military background, but his routine was slick and precise.

06.30 Alarm.
06.45 Shower.
07.00 News headlines.
07.20 Morning walk along the beach.
08.15 Breakfast.
09.00 Reading time.
10.30 Swim, fifty lengths of the small pool. This was timed to perfection to be finished before the
11.00 Water polo game started.
11.30 Latte, shortbread, read and people watching.
13.00 Lunch.
14.00 Siesta.
16.30 Latte, shortbread, read and people watching.
18.00 Shower
19.00 Evening meal.
20.00 Brandy or Havana Seven time.
21.30 Retire to room.

Max took his last sip of latte, as Mailen came over to collect his cup. As it was Thursday, Mailen like the rest of the staff wore their burgundy uniforms. Max looked up as Mailen approached. It was his favourite day, as the uniform matched Mailen's hair colour. Her hair was tied to the side in a ponytail, pinned up with a sparkly silver star hair clip. Max would often think to himself. *Maybe in another life we could be together.*

Max was living there under the name of Max Muller. His passport was Canadian. Max Muller was not his real name and he most certainly was not Canadian. Max Muller was Max Hoggarth, Max Christie, Max Hand, Max Wallace and Max Bowles, Max Quigley and Max Mills. He was also American, British, Swiss, German, Swedish, Dutch and Austrian.

Max had all the time in the world to ponder on the predicament Cuba faced. A communist country in the Caribbean since Castro and Co took control in 1959. It had changed so much since then. Most people would agree that education and health was its biggest successes in that time. He was torn between the structure that the country offered its people and the restrictions it imposed on them. There was one thing was for sure, Max had grown to love the Cuban people and they had grown to love him.

Max was a very wealthy man now, but this had come at a great cost to him. He was a specialist. The type of person the American government turned to, when no one else could help them on delicate international matters, matters that often required the ultimate sacrifice from some of the participants.

Max's last assignment went wrong, very wrong. He blames himself for the death of three of his closest friends, who were part of his six man team. The operation was to destroy a components factory in Panama. It was believed that this factory was a smoke screen for making chemical weapons, to be used against the United States and its allies.

Two spotters stayed outside, one front, one rear. Max and his other three comrades entered the factory together and then split off to search one small area each. Within seconds, a huge explosion ripped through the factory. Max was blown straight out of an office window on the second floor. He was lucky; he landed on a flat roof, one floor below, at the back of the factory.

What Max did not know was that this was a set up. He had hobbled away from the blast and got away. He was certain his comrades inside the factory would have been killed, as they were all further inside than he was, when the bomb went off. The two spotters did not show up at the rendezvous point as agreed. He waited all night, fighting through the pain of a dislocated shoulder, broken arm, sprained ankle and hundreds of cuts to his body.

Max then fled to Cuba, assuming the spotters were killed or captured and has been there ever since. That day was a big payday for Max. As usual, his salary was paid in advance, by a secret American government fund, to an untraceable offshore account in the Cayman Islands. As the leader of the operation he was on 250,000. The other five 100.000 a man. Max was unaware of three facts from that operation.

Fact one. The two spotters that did not show up at the rendezvous point were still alive.

Fact two. They were the ones that double crossed him.

Fact three. There was a second operation in play. His two double crossing comrades had been recruited by the Panama underworld. They were paid 500.000 each, a drop in the ocean to the local drug barons. The Panama underworld had hoped that this move would get the American government off their tail for the time being. Max was presumed dead, there was no way anyone could have identified any remains from that explosion. Max always emptied his account in advance of an operation and transferred it to a secret slush fund. That way, if the job went sour, he was off the radar with a pocket load of cash.

Since the day of the explosion no one knew that Max was still alive, his past life had disappeared. Things however, were about to change!

Chapter 28

The pressure of a thirty minute deadline from Johnson, had forced Jack and Holly to switch their focus. The sim card messages were now the priority, in the time frame they had. Every word from the second message was laid out in front of them.

Go immediately to where the Ferry departed. Then use a biro by the sea and stand between the centre columns, facing east. Shout out and listen to the echo.

'I have a question Holly. Why is the word Ferry carrying a capital F? Is it suggesting that this is the start of the code?' Holly looked up at Jack and smiled.

'Jack, you're right, I had assumed it was a typing error. Of course, it is obvious now; it could be a place or even a name. It has to be.' They began a new search on the Internet. *Ferry* was typed in to Google. There were 209,000,000 possibilities, so they scrolled to the bottom of the page.

Searches related to Ferry
ferry doverdirect ferries routes
ferry routesdirect ferries greece
ferry meaningcheap ferries
ferry definitiondfds ferries

'No, there is nothing there that I want to look at.' Holly said.

'Type in to Google *people called Ferry*, see what that brings.' The search had narrowed, this time 3,980,000, but the third link down on the page stood out. Jack read it out loud to himself.

Famous people names Ferry, Celebrities named Ferry – Nameslist.org
www.nameslist.org/people/Ferry

They clicked on the link. It brought up a list of famous people from various backgrounds, acting, directing, arts and costume design, but it was the second name on the list, that Jack was about to jump on.

'That's it Holly.' Jack beamed.

'What is it?'

'Roxy Music!'

'You have lost me Jack.'

'Bryan Ferry is the lead singer of Roxy Music, one of my all-time favourite bands, he is English and if I'm not mistaken, I am sure I read at some point, that he was born in the North East. Wikipedia Bryan Ferry right now.' Holly tapped on the mini iPad that Johnson had arranged for them to use on the plane. As the page loaded they looked at each other, a moment of hope had arrived at last. The page loaded and their hope turned to reality.

'I don't believe it. He was born and raised in Washington, Tyne and Wear, England. The Butler was sending the Shield to Washington. Now we need to find out why.' Holly enthused.

'Let's not jump to conclusions; there is still a big part of the message to decipher.'

'Yes, you're right Jack. Ok the next part reads, *use a biro by the sea.* Bring up a map of the area, is Washington by the sea? '

'Yes it is. Washington is part of the city of Sunderland which is right on the coast.'

'Great.' Holly said. 'The next part is, *stand between the centre columns, facing east. Shout out and listen to the echo.* Search for famous local landmarks, museums, derelict buildings, anything like that. I think the reference to the centre columns is a key component here.' Jack typed in to Google, *local north east landmarks with columns.*

'There is a Penshaw Monument that has columns, that comes up several times, I will it put it into Wikipedia, see what that tells us.' As Jack typed away, Holly could hear her Grandpa Natalie's voice talking to her conscience. *C'mon Holly, two syllables, you're missing the obvious. Pen shaw. Of course,* she muttered to herself.

'Jack, it is Penshaw Monument 100%.'

'How come?'

'In the coded message it says, *use a biro by the sea*, well what is another word for biro?'

'Pen?' Came the reply.

'Exactly and what is at the edge of the sea?'

'The shore line?' As the words rolled out of Jack's mouth the penny dropped.

'Pen-shore (Penshaw). Good job Holly, good job.'

'You need to thank my Grandpa, he told me.' Jack smiled at what he perceived to be Holly's modesty, but the truth was her Grandpa's voice was always in her head.

'What does Wikipedia say about Penshaw Monument Jack?' Jack read the first few lines, but Holly wanted it read out to her.

'Read it out Jack.' Jack smiled and then turned the iPad around and pointed to it.

'You read it Holly; I am starting to like the sound of your voice.' Holly rolled her eyes playfully.

'Penshaw Monument, a prominent landmark built in 1844 on top of Penshaw Hill. It is a half-scale replica of the Temple of Hephaestus in Athens. Owing to its proximity to Durham City, the area was allocated a Durham postcode, DH4, which forms part of the Houghton-le-Spring post town. It lies about three miles north of Houghton-le-Spring, just over the River Wear from Washington.' Holly looked up at Jack and smiled.

'We are getting somewhere now Jack, the President will surely call off the dogs and let us get on with this.'

'Yes, now we know the location, he is duty bound to allow us to investigate this further. Before we call Johnson, what else does it say?'

'Penshaw Monument, officially the Earl of Durham's monument, is between the districts of Washington and Houghton-le-Spring, within the City of Sunderland. The 1st Earl of Durham was also the first Governor of the Province of Canada.'

'Geez Holly, I didn't know that last fact.' Jack said sarcastically. Holly ignored him; her attention had turned towards calling Johnson with the news.

Chapter 29

Once a week, Max would check his emails on an old computer. It was a task that he did every Thursday afternoon after his latte. It was a laborious task, as the hotel did not have a fast Internet connection. This was Cuba after all. Max like everyone else had to sit and wait for the screen to appear. *Even when you have nothing else to do, it is one of life's biggest frustrations, waiting for a screen to load, even then it's just to read and delete a load of junk.*

Every week for the last three years Max would just delete, delete, delete. Today though was different. Max was working his way through his sixteen emails, deleting them one by one. He was about to press delete for the seventh time, when he noticed a name he recognised, a name from his past life. He sat in silence and just looked at the screen. He wondered if he should just keep on deleting and forget this email ever appeared in his inbox. *What if it is a tracer email? I could be giving up my location. Damn it!* Max wrestled with his conscience. *What if this is a trap, but what if it was real? He was my best friend and he saved my life, so I owe him. I should open it.*

Max convinced himself that he was duty bound to open the email. The man that sent it, saved his life on New Year's Day 1990, when they fought together in Desert Storm, Kuwait. Max always looked up to him. He was twenty years his senior and if the truth be told, Max regarded him as a father figure.

Max sat for a moment and wondered what could possibly be on the email and why would his great friend wait till now to get in touch? Max considered different reasons, but he would only know by opening it. *Should I wait until tomorrow? That way I can get roaring drunk tonight.* Max looked up to the ceiling, took a big intake of breath and then looked back at the computer screen. He was about to click on the open icon, when the sun shone through the window. He could see his reflection in the screen. *This is the healthiest I have looked for ten years, but Max my dear boy this email could change everything.*

Max had hazel green eyes, short dark hair, which was slightly greying at the sides and had good looking features which had benefited from his Cuban lifestyle. He kept himself in shape and held on to his athletic six foot physique. He had a photographic memory, lightning reflexes and was one of the best marksmen to grace the United States Forces. He spoke English, Spanish and German fluently. He also knew enough French, Dutch and Mandarin to get by. He was an expert in self-control; self-defence and could read a room very quickly. Max was also very lonely. His existence in hiding had its benefit's and although he was very content, he did question the long term future of the arrangement he had with himself.

The email was only three hours old. *This is it.* Max clicked and opened the email, the headline bar read:

-My dear friend-

The email was short and to the point.

-I hope this email finds you well. I know it has been a very long time Max, but I have found myself in a situation that I can no longer control. I really, really need your help and need it urgently, if you are available to provide it. Holly has got herself mixed up in a political situation that could lead to her being killed. I am in my Florida home until the weekend.

-Thank you Max
-Nat.

Max exhaled as he leaned forward to touch the screen, it was a gentle touch and one that he imagined would bridge the gap between now and the future. He was certain the email was his dear friend and that it was authentic. It was time to reply to the email.

-Senator Natalie

-I will be with you tomorrow, you can count on it.

-Max

Max rushed back to his room and headed straight for his safe. He took out a watch and put it on his left wrist. He took out five passports, a stash of cash, a knife and two hand guns. He quickly got changed. He dressed in jeans, white trainers and a floral shirt unbuttoned over a white T-shirt. He stuffed one hand gun down the sock of his right leg and the other behind his back, tucked into his jeans. He grabbed an overnight bag, jammed in some clothes, toiletries and equipment required for his little trip.

He pulled out several blank brown envelopes from a drawer and put different amounts of cash in three of them. As he left his room en route to reception, he pondered on his three years in Cuba and in particular the staff that he was now leaving behind. The staff he now called his friends.

For three years block sixty one had been his home. It was just three blocks away from reception, in no time he had made his way through the lounge area and then through the bar and finally past the Coffee Coach Bar, before reaching reception. Mailen was serving a customer when she noticed Max sweeping past her.

'Max! Max! Where are you going all dressed up? Max ignored the call for his attention. Max headed straight for Jose, his trusty porter who was standing daydreaming out of the front entrance. Jose looked over to see Max walking briskly towards him. Max put his right hand out to shake hands with Jose, who responded with a great big welcoming grin.

'Hola Senor Max.' Max held onto Jose's hand, putting his left hand over the top of Jose's arm. He looked him right between the eyes and brought him close.

'Jose, you tell me you can organise anything this side of Havana. Is that true?' Max held onto his arm and stayed fixed onto his eyes. Jose nodded.

'Yes Max, I can get anything you want for the right price, just name it.' Jose's face became serious, it was obvious to him Max meant business.

'I need to be taken to Florida by boat, under the radar, can you organise it for me?'

'Yes Senor Max, I can do that for you. When do you want to go?' Max leaned closer to Jose; he did not even blink in his reply.

'Now'

'Now Senor Max, wow, I will need a few minutes to make all the necessary arrangements.

'Of course Jose, I will be back soon. There are a few things I need to take care of first.'

'Before you go Senor Max, I need to ask you.' Max could sense where the question was headed and nodded his agreement.

'You want to ask about money?'

'Yes Senor Max, I know you are a very important person, I have always known and I do not want to disrespect you, but do you have the money to cover this request.' Max smiled then put his left hand on Jose's shoulder.

'Will ten thousand US dollars cover it Jose.' Jose gave a grin that lit up the reception area.

'That will more than cover everything Senor Max. I will have a taxi ready to take you to my cousin's home, he will organise a boat for you.'

'Good, I will be back soon.' Max broke off the shake and patted Jose on the upper arm warmly.

Max had one more important thing to do, before he said his farewell to Cuba. He walked back into the hotel reception and headed for the Coffee Coach Bar to see Mailen. She had watched his every move since he walked past her, wanting to know why Max had veered from his predictable routine. As he approached the Coffee Coach bar, Mailen put down the cloth that she was using to clean the counter top. Max put his hand up and waved and then he signalled to her to join him. He dropped his bag from his shoulder and put it between his feet. Mailen approached him and Max smiled warmly, he held out his hands for Mailen to take them. She grasped them, but this was out of character for Max and she wondered why?

'What is going on Max?' Max noticed just how beautiful her chocolate coloured eyes were and how neatly her lipstick outlined the curves of her lips.

'I need to leave Playa Pesquero, Mailen.' Her eyes widened with confusion and a great frown appeared on her brow.

'How long will you be gone?' Max took his time to savour how close he was to Mailen and how beautiful she was to him.

'It will probably be for good Mailen.' Her eyes filled up and the first of many tears started to fall down her face. Max put his arms around her and hugged her tightly. He whispered in her ear.

'You know I care for you very much Mailen. I am going to take an envelope out of my bag and give it to you. There is fifty thousand dollars in the envelope. I want you to build a house in the country and be happy.' Mailen started to tremble, her body quivering under the tears. Max felt the emotion, she did her best to control the tears, but she loved him and his shoulder became a blanket to soak up the tears.

'Please don't go.' She cried holding his body tight. Max gently stepped back.

'Please Mailen take the envelope and be happy, it would mean everything to me.' Mailen took a napkin from her pocket and blotted the tears rolling down her face. Max took that opportunity to bend down towards his bag. He unzipped it and took out the fattest of the brown envelopes. He put it into Mailen's hands and squeezed them together.

'Thank you so much Max, I will never forget you.' Mailen had turned into a wreck, her make up cracking under the relentless tears. Max put his hand up and wiped away two smudges of makeup; an excuse to feel her skin.

'I will have you in my heart forever Mailen.'

'Why do you have to go Max?'

'A long time ago a very close friend of mine saved my life. He now needs my help; I need to repay the debt I owe him.' Mailen put her head down and moved into Max's chest. She lifted her head and tilted it up to his ear.

'Please come back to me Max, I love you.'

'I will think of you every day for the rest of my life.' Max put his hands up to her head and tilted it back gently. He stroked her hair then kissed her softly on the forehead, three kisses, one kiss for each year he had known her.

'I need to go now. Goodbye Mailen, take care and please for me, be happy.' Mailen's tears started to roll down her face again.

'You are a good man with a good heart Max. Wherever you go and whatever you do I will be sending my love over the ocean to keep you safe.'

'Goodbye Mailen.'

'Goodbye Max.' Max lifted his holdall, slung it over his shoulder and walked back to the reception to see Jose, who was just finishing a phone call when Max approached him.

'Is everything in order Jose?'

'Yes Senor Max.' Jose pointed to the nearest taxi. 'This taxi will take you, it's around a thirty minute drive to my cousin's home and he is expecting you. He will take you to the boat and have someone drop you in Florida.'

'Good Jose, I thank you for your help.'

'Hope to see you again Senor Max.' Max gave him a warm handshake then stepped into the taxi and slammed the door. He looked out of the open window.

'You never know Jose, you never know.'

Chapter 30

The phone was ringing; Jack and Holly were really upbeat about their breakthrough. They were certain it was enough for the President to change his mind and get the search back on track.

'Hello.' Johnson's voice sounded flat, even from just one word. Jack took the lead, a real excitement in his tone.

'Johnson, we have the breakthrough we have been looking for. Tell the President to get the search back on track.'

'What breakthrough, what have you found? Johnson's voice lifted for a brief moment.

'We have cracked part of the coded message sent to Mike Fox by the Butler. He was sending him to a location called Penshaw Monument. It overlooks the village of Washington.' Johnson's voice sank back again.

'Is that it Jack?'

'Are you kidding me, C'mon Johnson, we can go there and look into this. We are flying over the north of France as we speak. We are just around the corner from where we need to be. I can't believe your reaction; we thought you'd be thrilled.'

'I'm not so sure.' Johnson declared, I cannot see the President budging over this turn of events. Holly was incensed.

'What if someone is waiting there for him and they do not know he is dead? What if the Butler had a backup plan or something?' Jack nodded, Holly was right. Johnson had the feeling there was something else.

'Is there something you are not telling me?' Jack gritted his teeth and shook his head at Holly. *Don't blow it now Holly.*

'What are you talking about Johnson?' Holly asked.

'You just said to me, what if the Butler had a backup plan? So I am asking you. Is there anything you are not telling me?' Holly looked at Jack; he was still shaking his head. *No Holly.*

'No, there is nothing, we just strongly believe we should go there and investigate this further. It warrants that, don't you think?' There was a pause in the verbal tennis match, too long a pause for Holly.

'Jesus Johnson, we really thought you would be delighted with this news.' Johnson did not reply. Jack decided to put in his two cents.

'Johnson. What's wrong, something is wrong, I know it is, C'mon level with us, you owe us that at least for all this mess you have forced upon us?' Johnson had bought himself some thinking time. He had made his decision, a decision that would not go down well with Jack and Holly.

'The President will not change his mind based on what you have just told me. The operation has been closed and that was a direct order.' Jack looked away in disgust; Holly put her head in her hands. Johnson though, had one last piece of news for them.

'I am prepared to do one thing for you, but it is strictly off the record, is that clear?'

'What is it?' Jack asked dismissively.

'The pilot has orders from me to take you anywhere in the world when he is provided with the appropriate code. I will not cancel that code. That means you can land at your destination. I have to make you aware of one thing though. You are on your own; no rescue party will be there for you should you get into trouble.'

'It appears that we have been on our own from the start.' Jack said angrily.

'Now is not the time to vent anger Jack, you have a decision to make. Do you want to be hidden away in a safe house, or do you want to land in England and do your own thing?' Jack looked at Holly and then spoke to Johnson.

'One moment Johnson.' Jack pressed 'Mute' on the call.

'Well Holly, what do you think? Are you in or out on Johnson's terms?' Holly looked out of the window; they had now passed France and were headed across the English Channel.

'Well Jack, I have come this far and let's face it, my holiday is ruined, so why not see a bit of England?' Holly looked back and smiled at Jack. He held his arm up high, his palm facing her. She did the same and then gave him a big high five. Jack pressed 'Mute'.

'Johnson.'

'Yes.'

'We go on, we land, we find the *Document of Truth* and we all live happy ever after, ok?'

'Maybe you two were the right people for the job after all, I had my doubts, but you make quite the double act.' Jack looked at Holly and smiled.

'Yes we do.'

'One last thing Johnson, is there any news on the professor yet?'

'Heenan has captured him, so there is a real chance that he could find the *Document of Truth* before you. Heenan's methods are brutal, he will confess to anything I guess.'

'Poor Gordon.' Holly Said.

Chapter 31

The professor was ordered to go outside by Yuri. Heenan was having his afternoon snack out there. A plain ham and cheese sandwich, cut into quarters, with the crusts removed and a side plate of green olives. He was reading a copy of the New York Times, seated under his bright red parasol, by the poolside. He read this newspaper for two reasons, firstly, to laugh at the arrogance of how America reported its woes and secondly to look out for opportunities and in particular, money making opportunities. His parasol was angled just enough to shade him from the sun and just enough to read his newspaper.

The sound of footsteps began to dominate the atmosphere, drowning out the sounds of bird noises and the play fighting hamsters Bonnie and Clyde. Heenan slowly lowered his newspaper just past the bridge of his nose. He peered over the newspaper to see the professor. He was stooped, tired and dirty and trundling behind Yuri. He folded the newspaper in half then placed it on the round smoked glass table.

'Ah professor, how are you getting on?' Heenan looked happy with himself; a rare smile accompanied his rare calm tone. His legs were crossed, his right leg sitting over the left, showing off the huge heel of his leopard skin cowboy boot. Yuri manhandled the professor into position, pushing him to make him stand opposite his boss.

'It is a slow process; it will take me a bit of time, I am trying my best to match up some threads.' The professor looked shattered, sounded shattered, he was desperate for sleep. If he wanted to buy more time with Heenan, this was not the way to go about it.

He stood hunched over; swaying slightly, his stubble starting to show. The bags under his eyes were sagging further by the hour, changing to a deeper shade of grey.

'Tell me professor, how long can you hold your breath underwater?' Heenan smiled, as he glanced round to his swimming pool, the sunlight appearing to dance over it on cue.

'I don't know, why do you ask?' The professor was so tired that he did not even pick up on the obvious.

The professor came from good stock; he was educated at Oxford and received many accolades over the years. He had taken many tests in his studies, through his life, but he had never faced a test like this. A test that had him petrified for his safety, but even more so, his family's safety. Heenan craved some good news and craved it now. His new best friend's clock was ticking and ticking fast.

'Well professor, I will let you into a little secret. The record for holding your breath in this pool and surviving, I may add, is three minutes forty eight seconds.' The professor looked at Yuri; the lap dog was unmoved, just staring at his boss, awaiting his orders.

Heenan picked up his newspaper, unfolded it and proceeded to read it for a few seconds. Enough time for him to make a decision.

'If you do not have a breakthrough for me, by the time tomorrows copy of the New York Times arrives, then professor, you will attempt to break that record in the swimming pool. Do I make myself clear?' The professor clenched his fists together, a moment of defiance, his anger poking through the fear. *Who the hell do you think you are? You know nothing about what it takes to work on something like this. It takes time; it could take weeks, months, even years to crack this.* The professor rocked on his feet, he was close to passing out, he needed food, he needed water and most of all he needed sleep.

Heenan signalled to Yuri, he was finished with his new best friend. Yuri took him by the arm and marched him off. Heenan turned the page of his newspaper and offered the professor one last reminder, as he shouted over his newspaper.

'Remember professor I have your family hostage. I decide who lives and who dies. I want answers professor, answers, do not disappoint me.' The professor looked up at the bright blue sky, squinting, as the brightness was too much for his tired eyes to cope with. The defiance he felt sweep through his body a moment ago was still festering, fighting to rise up and burst out again. He could wait no longer.

'Wait!' The professor shouted, as he yanked his arm away from the grip of Yuri. His outburst caused Yuri to draw his gun and point it at him. The professor swung around to face Heenan. He yelled out, desperation, fear and exhaustion all playing some part in his state of mind.

'Do it, go on do it.' He said as he slumped to his knees. Yuri looked at Heenan for an answer, his gun still pointed towards the professor's head.

'Go on then kill me, go on do it. You won't though, will you, you need me. You're not going to kill me, how else are you going to decipher this, you're nothing but a common thug, a bully and a bad one at that.' The professor's emotions collapsed on top of him. He cried into the floor tiles, his eyes closed, his haunting thoughts terrifying him.

Heenan calmly wiped his lips with the outside of his hand, brushing the edge of his moustache.

'Come and sit down next to me professor, you're right, let us talk about it.' Heenan folded down his newspaper once more. Yuri holstered his gun and helped the professor to his feet. He walked him back to the table, Heenan pointing to the seat next to him. Yuri pushed him down on to it, the professor was sucking in what air he could, trying to catch his breath.

'Please professor, accept my apologies, of course you are right. I cannot do this without you.' Heenan stood up and offered the professor his right hand, the professor lifted up his arm. It felt so heavy, his strength wilting by the hour. The professor was about to clasp Heenan's hand to shake it, when Heenan suddenly pulled it back. He lashed out and kicked the professor smack in the centre of the chest. The professor cried out as his chair tipped backwards, causing him to fall into the swimming pool. Heenan stood by the poolside, as the professor scrambled back to the surface. He leaned down over him as the he clung to the edge. He poked the professor in the head.

'Now, do not disappoint me anymore. If you do I will kill your youngest child, this is your last warning, is that clear professor?' The professor coughed up a mixture of water and chlorine, as he gasped for breath.

'Yessss.'

Chapter 32

Around the same time that Holly and Jack were landing at Newcastle International Airport, Max was hiring a car to take him to see his dear friend Senator Natalie. It was a two hour drive from his drop-off point and Max took in every metre of the journey. It brought back so many memories to him, he had wondered many times over the last three years if he would ever set foot in these parts again.

As he arrived at Senator Natalie's summer house, he noticed how lush and well-kept the area was. The gated entrance to the Senator's residence was covered in pink coloured Bougainvillaea. He stopped and pressed the window down, the hot air he felt was an instant reminder of how refreshing the air con was in his car. He leaned out of the window, inhaling, taking in the smells from the shrubs and plants. *You always had the best gardens.* He rolled the car on a few more yards until he reached the intercom.

'Hello, can I help you?' Max released his finger off the button.

'Tell the Senator it is Max.'

'Right away Max.' The excited servant replied.

Max watched as the grand half-moon tops of the wrought iron gates opened slowly. He drove in, the weight of the car crunching the loose stone chippings underneath it. He parked to the side of the house, nothing much had changed since his last visit that he could see. His military background, forcing him to monitor every little detail of the surroundings he was in. He got out of the car and walked around to the trunk. He popped it open and lifted up his backpack. He double checked the contents, another habit he could never break and then left it there, slamming the trunk shut.

The great canopy that covered the front door had two brilliant white sculptured pillars which supported it. Max looked down at the brown veined floor tiles, which were reflecting his healthy look. The sound of the door clicking open was enough to make Max look up. There he was, the man he owed his life to. The Senator leaned back on his heels; his face broke into a big smile. He opened his arms out for a seriously big man hug. Max smiled and happily embraced him.

They loosened their embrace, but held onto each other, the years of great respect for each other held dear.

'Good to see you Senator.' Max said, as he leaned forward and hugged the Senator once more, it felt long overdue. As they unwrapped themselves from the hug, the Senator pointed at Max and smiled.

'Max, drop the Senator. You know it is Nat to you.' The Senator's voice was deep, his tone raspy, coming right from the pit of his stomach. A stomach that had been well looked after over the years. Max let out a cheeky grin.

'I know Nat, I was only joking.' The Senator waved Max in.

'Let us go into the lounge for a chat. I'm having a Scotch Max, so I trust you will join me.'

'Of course Nat, it would be rude not too.' Max followed the Senator into the lounge, a majestic square room; which also had not changed since Max's last visit. The sixteen feet draped purple curtains that covered the sash windows did not look like they had been used once. The Senator opened his huge, brown, mahogany, globe drinks cabinet. He took out one glass for Max and filled it, two fingers deep, a lavish measure; the lead cut crystal glasses were big enough to stuff an orange into. He started to top up his own glass, when he realised he had forgot to ask Max a very important question.

'Do you want your Scotch neat or on the rocks?'

'I like to keep things as neat as possible Nat, my Scotch is no different.' Max was serious in his reply.

'Neat it is Max.' The Senator handed Max his glass and chinked it, both raising their glasses together.

'Cheers Nat let us drink to old times.'

'To, old times Max.' They both raised their glasses again and gulped the whisky down in one go. Max winced then put his glass down on the perimeter of the globe cabinet. It was like Saturn's ring, a swirl of cylindrical glass around the wood cabinet. The Senator followed suit.

'Please Max, sit down and we will talk.' The Senator pointed to the sofa that Max was to sit on. The Senator sat down facing Max, his two cream leather sofas sitting opposite each other. As the Senator crossed his legs, Max's attention was drawn to his bright green socks. They were no match for his brown trousers and canary coloured shirt.

'Your dress sense is no different to your surroundings Nat, nothing has changed I see.' The Senator smiled.

'Let's get down to business Max.'

'Let's.'

'Max, I said in my email this is about Holly and it is. The thing is Max.' The Senator adjusted his seating position, he was uncomfortable, not from the sofa, his discomfort came from what he needed to say to Max.

'I recently discovered some disturbing news about your past.' Max jumped straight into the conversation.

'Disturbing news about my past? You know I am straight up Senator.' The Senator adjusted his position once again; it was not getting any easier.

'Max, please let me speak and I will not tell you again, it is Nat to you.' Max put his hands up as an apology.

'Sorry Nat, please go on.'

'Thank you. The operation you led down in Panama.' Max again jumped in.

'What about it?'

'Two of your team survived Max.' Max stood up and put his hands together and looked up to the sky.

'Thank God.' Max looked back at the Senator who was showing no positive emotion. He knew the Senator well enough to know there was some bad news coming his way. Max sat back down.

'What is it Nat, spit it out.' The Senator looked down at the floor then looked back up at Max.

'They set you up Max. You were supposed to have been killed in that operation, all four of you. The three men you led inside are dead and luckily they think that you are too.' Max stood up again.

'I know you would not lie to me Nat, but is your source positive about this? Could there be any mistake?' The Senator stood up and rubbed his brow.

'It is a good source Max, there is no mistake. They earned a cool half a million dollars each to double cross you.' Max held his breath and he relived the moment of the explosion, his mood instantly changing from anger to revenge.

'Who ordered the hit Nat?'

'It is complicated Max.' Max looked Nat straight in the eyes.

'Try me.' The Senator pointed to the sofa.

'Please sit down Max.' Max sat back down, almost hovering on the edge of the sofa, ready to spring off it at any second.

'You thought you were working on a private contract for the United States Government on that mission. This was not the case. You were in fact working for a consortium of sorts.' Max looked understandably confused. Two of his hand-picked team and so called friends had tried to kill him for a bounty; knowing he would be totally expendable, the perfect crime, no blowback.

'What type of consortium? Who was involved? And who was in charge Nat?' The Senator walked behind the sofa placing his hands on the top of it.

'I believe there were three main parties to this. Conrad King, remember him?' Max shook his head in disbelief.

'That snake.'

'Yes indeed, that very snake. He did some contract work for a man called Folis Heenan who is based in Northern Cyprus.' Max looked surprised, a name he did not know. He thought at least he would know the people behind his assassination attempt.

'Who is the Heenan guy?'

'I have recently been building a picture up on him. He has built up quite an empire for himself. Mainly from dealings in Russia, the Ukraine, Baltic States and most recently Western Europe, but he expanded into South America three years ago. Your operation in Panama was his first and last venture in South America. Why? I am not sure yet?' Max wanted answers, his blood beginning to simmer.

'What was his connection to Conrad King?'

'King did some private work for him. He became close to his inner circle, but it was short lived.'

'Short lived, what happened?

'You know Conrad King, Max. He could not keep his big mouth shut. A few months after your operation in Panama, Heenan apparently overheard King on the telephone to an advisor of the President.' Max cut in quickly.

'The President? The President of the United States?'

'Yes, I have heard the call, we intercepted it. I did not know at that time that any of this was linked to your operation Max.'

'Of course not, please go on. Wait! You just said we intercepted it. Who are we?' Max walked around to the back of the sofa and mirrored the Senator. It was a subconscious use of body language; years of training had programmed his muscle memory to do this.

'I will come back to that question when I have finished telling you about this. You may want to sit back down for the next bit Max.' Max shook his head intently.

'I am fine Nat, please go on.'

'Well, the third person involved in this plot was in fact the President himself.' Max stood looking at the Senator. *Not possible, it must be a mistake.* Max respected the Senator far too much to rule out that was indeed the truth. *Why would the President collude in my assassination?* Max looked down at the sofa, then back at the Senator.

'I would not have believed this story from anyone else but you Nat.' The Senator walked around to the drinks cabinet and opened up the globe.

'I think I will give us a refill Max.' The Senator poured two more large whisky's and handed one to Max. The Senator continued to explain in detail how complicated the situation was.

'Conrad King had something on the President from years ago, back in their college days, something the President thought was dead and buried. He used this information to bribe him.' Max took a swig of whisky. It was a two second welcome distraction from the headache he was quickly developing.

'What did he have on him?'

'It was a photo of him doing the Nazi salute dressed in the full Nazi uniform. He even had the stereotypical short moustache. It was probably a fancy dress stunt, but that's not the point when you're the President of the free world.'

'He was impersonating Adolf Hitler? Jesus Christ, how long ago was this?' The Senator peered into the bottom of his glass. He watched as he rolled around the dregs of the liquid gold in his glass.

'Not long enough for his liking. We both know how strong the Jewish sentiment is at the top of American politics. He will be slaughtered if that photo ever became public knowledge.'

'Where is the photograph now?'

'I will give you one guess.'

'Folis Heenan?'

'You guessed it. The call we intercepted was King speaking directly to the President, he must have gone through one of the President's aides first, but no doubt he would have had something on him too. He gave the President just enough information to reel him in. The President was panicked, really panicked, he needed the situation resolved and quickly.'

'I think I can work out the next bit for myself.' Max said.

'Please, after you.'

'Conrad King bribed the president with this photo. The bribe involved Folis Heenan and the operation down in Panama; Folis Heenan then kills King for the photograph. How am I doing?' The Senator nodded his approval.

'You always were the quickest to work things out Max, but there is a few little details missing from your summary.'

'I'm listening.'

'We intercepted another call, this time from Folis Heenan to a cell phone. We have identified that call was made to the President himself. The President had made a deal with the devil; he had colluded with Heenan on the Panama operation. It was all made to look like the Panama underworld was behind it, but we have since learned it was the President, Heenan and King.'

'But why Panama?' Max asked.

'The President knew you couldn't be bought and knew we were close, so he handpicked Tweedle Dee and Tweddle Dum, your two weakest and greediest buddies to do the dirty work. Half a million dollars each is a hard pay day to refuse, when you're a mercenary. They have since gone on to organise their own elite team, working directly for the President.

'I know there is no love lost between you and the President Nat, so I just need to ask you one more time. Are your sources nailed on with this information?'

'I am one hundred percent sure Max.' The Senator finished his whisky and smiled at Max.

'Now for part two Max which involves Holly. This is where I need your help.' Max was apprehensive. *What has Holly got mixed up with?* His apprehension was quickly confirmed by the Senator.

'The President used the Secret Service to track down Holly along with a man called Jack Hammonds. He abducted them and persuaded them to pursue his sickening agenda.'

'Wait Nat, I don't understand, why Holly and this Jack guy? The Senator started to pace the floor.

'Folis Heenan has infiltrated a secret group that were protecting a special piece of our history.' The Senator paused. Max asked the obvious.

'What secret group, what are you on about Nat?'

'They were called the Presidents Shield, but they are all dead now, killed by Heenan's men. They all carried markings on their soles, a cryptic puzzle of sorts. Each message is useless on its own, but together all four carry a message.' Max was dumfounded, three years relaxing in Cuba had weakened his focus a little. His brain was working overtime, computing the amount of life changing information he was being informed of.

'What message, I'm sorry Nat, but I am struggling with this. First I'm double crossed and the President is involved. Then Holly goes missing, a secret group has been murdered, by a man who was also involved in my attempted assassination.' Max watched as the Senator walked over to his window. The Senator turned and looked out of the window, his eye line obstructed by the sash bar.

'What message Nat?' The Senator conceded.

'The *Document of Truth*. The message describes the location of the *Document of Truth*. Of course it needs to be deciphered first and only a handful of people in the world could stand a chance of doing that'

'The President wants Holly and Jack to find the *Document of Truth* I take it?'

'He did, but I've just been informed he has since closed down the operation and left her high and dry.'

'The son of a bitch.' The Senator swung around to face Max.

'Heenan had his men dismember all four feet to retrieve the tattoos. He has also kidnapped a leading academic, a professor from London. He is renowned for his knowledge in ancient scripts etc. He was second choice to Holly and Jack. It pains me to say it, but luckily the President got in there first. If the professor fails, Heenan will go after Holly and it scares me what he is capable of.' The Senator's cell phone started ringing; a tune Max was very familiar with, his dear friends favourite. The first line of the lyrics, something the Senator drummed into Max on the battlefield. *Wise men say, only fools rush in.* The Senator looked at his phone; it was a call that couldn't wait.

'Excuse me one moment Max, I'll take this call and then I will tell you who we are…'

Chapter 33

'Where yees gannin? The taxi driver asked in a broad local accent. Neither Jack nor Holly had come across a Geordie before. He was looking at them in his rear view mirror, wondering why they had no suitcases and why they were not answering the most obvious of questions. Jack and Holly looked at each other wondering what language the taxi driver was speaking.

'I'm sorry, what did you say?' Holly replied. The taxi driver picked up on the American accent coming from the back of his cab and adjusted his tone.

'Where are yee gannin to?' Was the slow verbally exaggerated question from him.

'Penshaw Monument please.' Jack replied, looking at Holly. He started to reflect on a missed opportunity. *I wonder what my blind date was like, guess I will never know.* He looked at Holly as she blinked; he could see how long her eyelashes were. Not something that Jack had ever looked at in women before, but he found himself admiring them. *I would never have met you if I had gone on that blind date. It's true what my friend Gary says; it's a mad, mad world.*

'This is a first for me like bonny lass.' The driver declared.

'What is?' Holly asked.

'I have never picked up a fare here at the airport and then taken them to Penshaw Monument before.'

The smell inside the taxi was lavender, a present from his wife, something to relax his passengers she thought. The inside was spotless, cleaned almost hourly. The inside was almost entirely black apart from a green, white and black mini football scarf on his dashboard. It had a Spartan helmet in the middle of it, with only one word underneath it, Blyth. The outside of the white Ford Mondeo had a few dirty splash marks from his last fare. The rain had stopped, but the ground still held one or two puddles from the last shower.

'Are yous from over the pond then?' The driver asked as he drove off, switching between his rear view mirror and the road ahead.

'Yes we are.' Holly replied, but Jack wanted to change the subject.

'How long will it take to get there?'

'Well that all depends like. You see we have two choices. We can gan through the toon or we can gan rooound past the Metro Centre. Either way, the traffic will be a bit of a bummer. Just the time of day, ya nah what am sayin like?' The Geordie had returned, Jack wondered if he had been beamed up to Mars and flagged down a taxi there!

'Just tell me how long please. It has been a long trip.' Jack replied.

'Fine mate, we will gan through the toon, much nicer that way and I can show ya the sights on the way, be about half an oooahh, maybe a bit more.'

'I think that is thirty minutes in our world Jack.'

'Yes Holly, I had worked that one out thank you.' The taxi driver inserted his ticket into the exit machine. The red light turned to green and the barrier began to nod as it rose up to its temporary vertical position. As it closed Jack now had one question running through his mind. *What will the next part of our little adventure bring us?*

Chapter 34

'I have some more news Max. I have just been updated on the whereabouts of Holly and Jack Hammonds. They have just arrived in England, via Newcastle International Airport. The Senator had returned to the lounge, his phone call had given him positive news, they were alive.

'What are they doing there?'

'My guess is they are doing what they do best Max, they are following a trail. You know how stubborn she is, she will be searching for answers, even against the President's wishes.' Max nodded.

'I know how stubborn both of you are.'

'The thing is Max, Holly still hates my guts, but she is still my little girl. I want her back safe, before she gets caught up with this Folis Heenan.' The Senator was not one to let his emotional barrier down, but his concern for Holly's safety brought him very close to it.

'She loves you, you know that. She is just very focused on her career. You know what she's like Nat, single minded, intelligent, driven, sound familiar?' The Senator smiled at Max's comment, he could feel the sentiment behind it.

'One of the things I know I got right with Holly was to put a miniature tracking device in the locket that her Grandpa gave to her. I knew she would never take that off. That is how I am able to keep track of her.' Max was impressed at the Senator's ingenuity.

'What do you want me to do Nat?'

'Before I tell you that Max, I owe you an explanation. What you asked earlier, remember when you asked who –we- were?' Max nodded.

'Yeah I remember.'

'I never thought this day would come, when I felt the need to confide in someone, but Heenan has done some amount of damage to our organisation, in a very short space of time.'

'Organisation? Now, you are starting to scare me Nat, what are you wrapped up in.?'

'I want your word, that what I am about to tell you, will never be discussed with anyone, you will take it to your grave!' Max nodded, walking forward to shake the Senator's hand. He looked him in the eyes.

'You have my word Nat.'

'I am the leader of a secret organisation. It comprises of a group of very wealthy individuals and some business leaders that share a common goal. Our sole purpose is to protect, to protect our future, our history, our economy and most importantly our faith.' Max sat down, he had already received disturbing news from the Senator, that sounded impossible to contemplate. Now the latest revelations would be on a whole new level.

'Does this organisation have a name, will I have heard of it?'

'No Max, you will not have heard of it. The name of it is 1183.'

'1183? What does that mean?'

'We are a formidable and well-funded organisation that has protected the line of the Washington family throughout time.'

'The Washington family? Why?' Max asked, not knowing what to think about this new information, that had just been bestowed upon him.

'There is a power above Max, a power that leads us in our quest. A power not even the most famous Washington knew about.

'You're talking about George Washington right?'

'Indeed.' The Senator walked back to his window, he leaned on the frame, peering out at his cycad plants. It irritated him that some people referred to them as palms.

'It has been my job and the job of the leaders before me to be sure the President of the United States does not stray from the wishes of the 1183. Several have tried, but we have managed to stay one step ahead of the game.'

'I don't understand, what is this all about?'

'George Washington became the first President of the United States, because 1183 had planned it for centuries.'

'Oh, c'mon Nat, this sounds like codswallop.' The Senator turned around to face Max.

'The only reason that we are here Max is because of fate. That fate started in 1183. William de Hertburn was the chosen one. He was chosen to adopt Washington Manor in England. The records will show an exchange of land was involved, but the truth is, he was put in place to change the course of history. He was worthy of becoming the first Washington and his blood was spilt to honour 1183. Once the original consortium of 1183 members agreed the terms of existence, they put in place a plan to invest around the world. That day a Shield was created. That Shield carries the Washington Coat of Arms. 1183 is sworn to protect the coat of arms and everyone who represents it.' Max was lost for words; he classed the Senator as his closet friend, he had known him for so many years, yet he knew so little.

'Some people follow God in their beliefs, some a book, some a prophet, some Jesus, the list goes on Max. For us, 1183 is all that matters and like any other belief, we will do anything we can to protect it.' Max had gone from his care free days in Cuba, to a stunned silence in a matter of hours. *How did I not see this*?

'You need to understand the meaning behind 1183 Max. Just think about this for a minute. If 1183 did not exist there would have been no line of Washingtons throughout our history, which means no George Washington. There would have been no first President called Washington, there would have been no Washington DC' The Senator paused for breath. Max had never seen him so animated before.

'How much do you love our flag Max?' Max was puzzled, the question was loaded. *Why are you asking that*?

'You know the answer Nat, I love my country and I love my flag.'

'Of course you do, like every single decent American, you love your country and you love your flag. The Washington Coat of Arms from 1183 is the foundation of the *Stars and Stripes.* George Washington was not our President by accident Max. 1183 had been working towards this for hundreds of years.'

'I think I need another drink Nat.'

'No Max, you need a clear head, I know this must have come as a shock, but 1183 is in trouble, big trouble.

'Wow Nat, you really believe the history of the United States all started back in 1183 in a Village in England?' The Senator looked at Max and replied abruptly

'I know it did.' Max shook his head, his conscience struggling to allow his brain to believe such a claim. Something at the back of his mind was overlapping his disbelief, surfacing to the front, knocking on the door of reality.

'Wait a minute Nat. When I was a kid my buddies and I messed around in the school playground, playing this game. We all talked about this mystery superpower that protected the world. It was a story my father told me, when I was only five or six, God rest his soul. It was just comic book stuff though, something about The Washington Triangle' The Senator smiled at Max. He walked up to him, put his hand on his shoulder and said something that sent shivers through his body.

'You remembered.' Max took a step back, his body language changed. His tone became assertive, bordering aggressive.

'What are you saying Nat, what's going on?'

'Calm down Max.' Max was in no mood to calm down, his mind was having flashbacks. *You're not saying what I think you're saying are you?*

'You remember that story Max, because I told it to you.' Max turned away, his flashbacks increased rapidly; reality had collapsed as he knew it. He failed to make sense of the words he was listening to. The Senator called out to him.

'Max.' He ignored it, his flash backs too consuming for the Senator's attention. The Senator shouted louder.

'Max.' Max swung around, he was angry.

'What?'

'I am your father.' The flashbacks slowed, as the enormity of the Senators words sank in. He began to fightback tears. A dad and a sister he never knew he had. The Senator walked up to Max's face, he spoke from the heart.

'I have always looked out for you. You too are a chosen one and your time is nearly upon us. You will take the leadership of 1183 soon. I knew you were safe in Cuba all this time.' Max pulled out his lucky rabbit's foot from his pocket.

'There is a tracking device in here isn't there?' The Senator nodded. *Damn, all this time.* Max thought.

'I take it Holly knows nothing of this.'

'No and I want it kept that way.' Max knew deep down, that would be for the best under the present circumstances.

'I want to tell you everything Max.'

'Oh please dad, tell me more.'

'C'mon Max, you are better than that, sarcasm was never your thing.' Max dropped his shoulders, the tension slowly released.

'You're right, Holly is in danger; I should be focused on that. Tell me about this *Document of Truth*.' The Senator was relieved, he had not planned to have that particular conversation today, but he got caught up in the moment and dropped his guard. A guard he could not afford to drop again.

'The Washington Triangle was part of 1183. A part we lost control of for a while, when George Washington created the *Document of Truth*. He created a Presidents Shield to safeguard its location. Inside that little wooden box are secrets that will change history, if found.'

'Why did he do it?'

'He did it for the good of the people. It was a masterstroke to be honest. If he hadn't have given himself that leverage, he could have been assassinated.'

'Do you know where it was hidden?'

'No, only the President's Shield had that answer, they are all dead and Heenan has their markings, their tattoos.'

'I don't understand why you need me Nat? You say you are well connected and well-funded. Surely you must have other people who could find Holly and get her back quicker than I can.'

'Yes I do, but there is a problem. I have my suspicion that Folis Heenan has found a way to manipulate someone in 1183. If I send in one of my team, then there is a chance Heenan could find her first.'

'I understand.'

'I also believe the President is paying your two double crossing friends to put together a mission to destroy Heenan. Hopefully he succeeds, that will save us all a big headache.' The Senator handed Max a cell phone.

'It is safe, off the radar. Do you have passports, visas etcetera Max?'

'Yes.'

'Well in that case Max, I would like to wish you the best of luck. I will have the helicopter take you to the airport, where I have a jet standing by. God bless you son and bring my little girl back safe.'

'You can count on it Senator.'

Chapter 35

As the taxi approached the Tyne Bridge, in Newcastle City Centre, the driver decided to offer some of his local wisdom.

'When we get on the bridge you will have a sight to behold. There are seven bridges all within walking distance of each other, which link us with Gateshead. Tell me another city in the world where you can see all that then?'

The taxi driver was proud as punch of his city; he loved nothing better than to show it off, to anyone from outside the area. With one arm rested on the driver's window he rattled off a string of facts about Newcastle. His twenty year old faded tattoo of St George slaying a dragon, poked out of his crisp white, short sleeve shirt. Jack looked at Holly and raised a sarcastic eyebrow. The taxi came through the short tunnel and onto the Tyne Bridge and the view appeared in front of them.

'Wow that is fantastic.' Holly said as she pressed the button to pull down her rear window. She pointed to the Sage and Baltic buildings to her left, the Hilton Hotel to her right, all perched on the water's edge.

'Ya heard of Geordie Shore like? All gans off doon there?' He looked in his rear-view mirror willingly. No takers for his question. The trendy Quayside district sat underneath the bridge, home to one of Europe's hottest party scenes.

The taxi had slowed to less than twenty miles per hour, due to congested traffic on the bridge. A bright pink limousine, pulled up alongside the taxi. Two women dressed in nurse's outfits had their heads bobbing out of the sunroof, screaming an unrecognisable song lyric. Jack and Holly smiled at each other. Jack looked back out across the bridges. The taxi driver kept looking in his mirror, checking for signs of appreciation from Jack and Holly. He was not disappointed; both of them seemed lost in the moment, captivated by what they could see.

'Told yah's like.' He said smiling in to the rear view mirror.

'This reminds me of the Sydney Harbour Bridge.' Jack said warmly, finding it hard not to be drawn into the unique view out of the taxi window.

'Well actually mate; it is the Sydney Harbour Bridge that reminds you of this one. You see the Tyne Bridge was built long before the Aussie one. In fact the Aussie one was designed on this bridge.'

'It is a beautiful piece of architecture.' Holly said catching the last views as the taxi made its way off the bridge and into Gateshead.

'Where aboots over the pond yees from then?'

'I beg your pardon sir, what did you say there?' Holly asked struggling to make sense of the question. The taxi driver was getting excited, it was mission accomplished over the Tyne Bridge.'

'I'm sorry pet, our Helen is always gannin on at me to slow down when I speak to other folk like. I was asking where in the States are yous from like pet? My name is Frank by the way, my friends call me Pizza Frank, but that is another story.' The taxi driver burst out laughing at himself. The pizza story was a local legend with his friends, but he knew it was not the time for that one. Holly glanced at the taxi driver's name tag, Frank Murphy, licenced to carry four passengers.

'I am from Florida and Holly is from New York.' Both Jack and Holly were quickly warming to the taxi drivers charm.

'I love Florida man; it's the bee's knees. Me and our Helen have been twice. She has been to New York before, with her mates like, but me and the lads just gan to Benidorm for a good session if you nah what I mean?'

'Where is Benidorm?' Jack asked.

'Ah man, it's class there, It's on the Costa Blanca in Spain. Mind the price of a pint has gone through the roof in the last few years; it is all doon to the Euro.

'Benidorm sounds like it's a man's thing Holly, a way of letting off steam.' Jack said.

'Nor, it's not just a man thing, far from it. The women gan there in their droves. Me and the lads go every year, first May Bank Holiday weekend.'

'Even better Frank.' Jack said, laughing a little. Frank was on a role with his captive audience, but changed the subject back to his second passion of being an unauthorised local tour guide.

'You need to visit the Northumberland coastline up the road when you are here, seriously, it's breath-taking. There are some fantastic little villages supporting the coastline. Bamburgh is my favourite; it has a massive castle that sits on a hill looking out over the North Sea. Then you have Alnwick along the road from there, which has the most amazing gardens. It also has a famous castle. It was the home of Hogwarts in the Harry Potter films.'

'Really? Holly said with genuine excitement.'

'Why aye and if you go up a bit further to the border with Scotland you have Lindisfarne, known locally as Holy Island. But I suppose our best loved bit of history is Hadrian's Wall. It was built in AD 122 by the Roman Emperor Hadrian, stretches eighty four miles from Cumbria on the west coast of England, right through Newcastle alang to South Shields on our coast here. He built it to keep them Jocks oot like, ye nah what them lot are like.' Frank laughed at himself again. Both Jack and Holly found Frank a source of light relief and entertainment, lapping up his enthusiasm.

'Mind ya I should not complain too much as our lass is from Bonnie Scotland. She is always gannin on about the fact most of this area was part of Scotland a thousand years ago, blah, blah, blah, who cares about a thousand years ago anyway?' Frank laughed once again; he could sense his passengers were being suitably entertained by his humour and knowledge.

The rain had come in quickly and the sky had turned a deadly black colour. Frank removed his arm from the door and put up his window.

'So what is at Penshaw Monument that is so important? I mean ye have nee luggage with ya?' That question changed the mood instantly. It brought reality right back into the taxi.

'We are just meeting someone there Frank.' Holly said looking out of her rain soaked window. There would be no answers out of that window, but she suddenly hoped there would be one at the monument.

'Well you are about to get your first glimpse of it in a second or two.' The rain instantly eased, Frank reduced the wiper speed to intermittent. They turned off the A184 and on to the A195.Two sights became instantly visible as they left Follingsby roundabout. Penshaw Monument, standing there all majestic, perched on its hilltop with its chest puffed out. The second, a roadside sign, *'Welcome to the Original Washington'*. Underneath the words was a symbol, a symbol that had the Oracle's words ringing in Holly's ears. *The Washington Coat of Arms*.

They arrived at the footsteps to Penshaw Monument. Holly climbed out of the Taxi scanning the scenery. Jack paid the fare, along with a generous tip and gave him a warm handshake.

'Thank you Frank, that was a great journey, you were very entertaining.' Jack said patting the taxi roof. The rain had stopped, but no doubt it would be back.

'I wonder Jack.' Jack looked at Holly who was still fixed at the monument. *I know what she means*. Frank honked the car horn and waved as he drove off. Jack and Holly were oblivious; their attention was now on the Greek, God-like, stone structure in front of them.

Chapter 36

The President was sitting on his plump brown leather chair at his desk, in the Oval Office. Four of his staff sat opposite him, half-moon shaped around his desk. The briefing was about the escalation of cocaine, being smuggled via Mexico into America.

'You can see in paragraph four that we seized seven tonne of cocaine at Miami docks in just three months, at the beginning of the year.' The president ignored the comment. He felt the vibration of his cell phone, tucked away in his inside jacket pocket.

'Excuse me one second.' The President swung around and turned his back, took out his cell phone and looked at the text message. *Everything in place, target identified, two hours till impact, last chance to call this off!* He put the phone back in his pocket and swung back to resume the briefing.

This was highly unusual; in fact none of his staff had ever seen him with a personal cell phone before.

'Our sources tell us that the cartels are digging a series of new routes, investing millions in equipment to do so.' The President looked vacant, his mind was elsewhere.

'Is everything ok Mr President?' The President did not even hear the question.

'Mr President is everything ok?'

'Yes, sorry, please go on.' The briefing resumed, the President offered her his full attention, his full attention that lasted a mere thirty seconds. The message needed a response and it needed it soon.

'Sorry, can I have the room please. There is an urgent matter I need to attend to.

'Mr President are you sure everything is ok?'

'Yes, now please leave.' The door closed and the President wasted no time in returning a text message on his cell phone.

Destroy the target, that's an order.

Chapter 37

It only took just over ten minutes, to climb up to Penshaw Monument. There were fifty or more people mingling around. A group of ten or so were huddled together making small talk. Others were taking in the views, pointing out places of interest and taking photographs.

The views were fantastic. To the north, looking over the River Wear and the forest of trees, you could see the whole of the Sunderland Nissan car plant. Six thousand locals toil away day in day out, preparing and making various models of cars alongside their robotic friends. To the south was Herrington Country Park, which holds many national and local sporting and leisure activities. To the west was Washington. The whole of Washington was within their view, but for now their only interest was in the east.

Jack took Holly's hand and walked over to the east side and stood between the centre columns. He looked at the sheer scale of it, touching it, blackened in parts, tall, wide and hearty. Holly looked down at the swirl of grass banks that dropped away over fields, houses and roads. Jack squeezed Holly's hand, she looked at him.

'This is it Holly, this is the exact place where we believe the Butler's message was sending Mike Fox.'

The breeze that was unnoticeable at ground level had become an unwelcome distraction to Holly. She rubbed her arm for warmth.

'You cold?' Jack asked.

'A little, just feeling the breeze when it zips up.' Jack looked out into the distance.

'It's not until we are here now, that I wonder if we have got this all wrong Jack. I just cannot see anyone hiding around here, waiting for the Shield to turn up.'

'I can see where you are coming from, but now we are here, why not give it a go?'

'So we are just going to yell *OUT* and see what happens.' Jack nodded in agreement.

'Why not, after three?'

'One, two, three.'

'Out, out, out, out, out, out.' Their cries aroused some attention, although stranger things had taken place at the monument over the years.

Their cries echoed around the valley below them and out into the Penshaw air. They stood quietly and waited for what seemed like an eternity, nothing had changed, no one appeared.

Five minutes had passed, they gave it one last go, but the result was the same, nothing but a few funny looks.

'What's next then Jack?'

'Well, I need something to eat and drink. There was a sign for a tea shop, at the garden centre that we just passed on the way in. Shall we go there and have a talk about plan b?' Holly was disappointed with the outcome, but she knew in her heart it was a long shot.

'Come on then Jack, I could murder a good cup of English Tea.'

Inside the garden centre was a modern and impressive looking tea shop. As they walked up to the front door they could see the service counter through the glass. A mouth-watering selection of homemade pastries and sandwiches, teased them.

'Oh my God I am gaining weight just looking at them.' It was Jack who suggested the tea shop, but it was Holly who was showing her intention to indulge in the delights on offer. Jack opened the door for Holly; the assistant was finishing off her last customer.

'Good afternoon what can I get you my dear?' Her voice was warm and pleasant.

'These look fantastic.' Holly said to the lady, pointing at the cakes.

'Thank you my dear, is there a favourite I can tempt you with?' Holly scanned the selection for a second.

'I want that one please.' Pointing to her selection.

'Good choice, I made that myself. That is a walnut and ginger.'

'May I have a cup of tea with that please?

'Of course you can my dear and what is your husband having today?' Holly almost laughed at the innocent question. She looked back at Jack and winked.

'What are you having Jack?' Holly teased in a suggestive tone.

'I will have a latte and the ploughman's sandwich please.

'Coming right up my dears.'

Their disappointment from yelling at no one was temporarily put on hold. Hot drinks and homemade food became a welcome distraction. Jack peered out of the big glass windows at the assortment of colourful plants on show. While he was looking at the plants, he was also talking to Holly

'Should we give it another go once we have had this? We have come all this way, we need to keep trying.'

'I suppose it won't hurt to give it one more go Jack, although you must admit this looks like a waste of valuable time.' Holly joined Jack in gazing at the plants. One in particular caught her eye, a plant that thrust her back to her childhood. She rubbed her locket, the heart shaped silver locket that held more than a lifetime of memories to her.

'Japanese Acer.' She smiled. Jack looked at her, she appeared so ladylike at that moment to him, poised beautifully, as if waiting on a portrait being completed.

'Holly... Holly.' His voice rose slightly.

'What?'

'I have noticed when you are thinking, you rub your necklace over and over. Is it from an ex-boyfriend or someone? Holly smiled and then let go.

'No Jack, it was someone far more important than that.' Jack smiled, that was a good enough answer for him. As they stood up from the table, they noticed how busy the place had become. Every table was now taken and the tea chatter levels had increased two fold. As Jack and Holly left the tea room, the lady serving called to them.

'Bye dears, thank you.' Jack gave a thumb up, Holly smiled and then waved. Jack nipped in front of Holly to get the door. He was beaten to it by a man coming into the shop.

'After you marra.' He said warmly, holding the door wide open for them. He had one hand on the handle, the other grasping a copy of a newspaper. He was wearing a striking red and white football shirt that curved over his impressive mid-section and sat below his waist, resting on his jeans. Jack let Holly walk through first.

'Thank you.' She said, as she stepped out. Jack nodded.

'Thanks dude.' Holly suddenly stopped in the doorway. Something swam around her subconscious; her mind was racing. Not from Jack's comment, but from what she was trying to process, from what she had just seen. It was the name at the top of the newspaper that suddenly got her attention; she spun around, bumping into Jack.

'Excuse me sir, is that a local newspaper you have?' She asked hastily. He turned around; double checking the question was aimed at him.

'Why aye man flower.' He replied, holding a big grin.

'Is it a daily paper?'

'Indeed, it is pet.' Jack wondered if he was back on Mars. Holly was in her zone, she was on to something and Jack knew it, he had quickly learned when Holly was serious.

'Do you know the nearest place I can get one?' The man looked at her for a second.

'Here man, just take this one.'

'Gee thanks, that is very kind of you.'

'It's nowt man, divent worry about it.' *What on earth is he saying and what is Holly onto here?* Jack thought.

'One last question if you don't mind?'

'Shoot pet.' Holly pointed up at the monument.

'You see up at Penshaw Monument. If you were to stand up there and face east, what would you see beyond those hills?' Holly's arm was at full stretch in that direction, to emphasise her point. The man's smile grew even bigger, if that was possible. He looked down at the badge on his football top and kissed it.

'That my darling is God's country. Sunderland! It is home to the most humble and friendly people on our great earth.'

'Thank you so much for your help.' The man had not finished.

'My pleasure sweetheart, you see this badge, it has four segments.' The man pointed to one of the segments.

'See this one? That is the sun setting over Penshaw Monument right there.' Holly beamed, the writing under the badge read Sunderland A.F.C.

'Mr, you have just made my day, what is your name?'

'Colin, but my friends call me Captain.'

'Well Colin, a thousand thanks to you. If the people of Sunderland are half as sweet as you, I look forward to meeting many more of them.' Colin offered Holly a cheeky wink as they walked out of the tea shop.

'You mind telling me what all that was about Holly?'

'Jack, look at the name of the newspaper.' Holly held it up like a trophy. He said the name out loud as if compelled to.

'The Sunderland Echo.'

'Yes Jack, the Sunderland Echo. Remember the line in message. *Stand between the centre columns facing east, shout out and listen to the echo.* We have been looking at this the wrong way round. The newspaper has the answer. There must be something in here. Sunderland is east of the monument and this is the Sunderland Echo.' Holly and Jack raced over to a wooden bench in the garden centre and took a seat on either side of it. They divided a few pages each and started to sift through the paper.

'Got it.' Jack said in an excited voice. He pointed to a section in the centre of the paper called 'SHOUT OUT.' It is where locals can have their say on local matters.

'This must be it. *'Shout out and listen to the echo'* was the message.'

'Yes Jack that must be it. At last we have a real breakthrough. Is there anything in the shout out column that may help us?'

'There is a message here asking to hear from any brothers coming from abroad to meet up and cleanse their soles.' Jack looked at Holly.

'This must be a reference to the markings on the soles of their feet.'

'There is a phone number Jack, call the paper and put in a reply.'

'What shall I say?'

'I don't know something like, *'Just arrived from Majorca and hope to meet up at the first opportunity, to share my story with you.'* Jack took the phone out of his pocket and dialled the number.

It was pretty straight forward to place the advert, but their excitement was tempered after hearing there was no Sunday edition to the Echo. It was a daily newspaper, but Monday to Saturday editions only.

Holly asked the manager of the garden centre for a number of a local taxi firm. There was one in Penshaw village a few hundred yards away, he called one for them and it arrived within minutes. They walked across the road to the oncoming taxi; Jack turned to Holly and poked her gently in the back.

'Why did you not phone Pizza Frank, our personal taxi driver?'

'It would have taken him too long to get back here.' Holly replied half serious. Jack just smiled as he opened the back door for Holly.

'Did you notice the owner's surname Holly?'

'No and what is it with you and people's name badges?' Jack ignored her reply.

'Green.'

'What?'

'His surname was Green and he runs a garden centre. Have you never noticed how many people have a surname linked to their line of work.' Holly shook her head in bewilderment.

'Where would you like me to take you?' The taxi driver enquired. The smell of lavender was evident as Jack closed his door.

'Sunderland please, a nice hotel would be great.' He said stroking his hair back. *Jesus I can actually understand this guy*, Jack muttered under his breath.

'Is there any particular hotel you would like me to take you?' The taxi driver was a little bemused by the generalisation of the request.

'Just a nice one that we could book straight in to when we arrive please.' Jack replied, still messing with his hair. Holly looked at him with a hint of contempt.

'Sorry about my husband driver, is there a hotel you could recommend?' Holly said poking her tongue out at Jack.

'Yes, the Marriot at Seaburn; the Hilton is very nice but the location of the Marriot is right on the seafront.'

'How far is it?' Holly asked

'It is only five or six miles from here, it will take about fifteen minutes or so to get there.'

'Great thanks that will do nicely' Jack said as he leaned forward, finished with adjusting his hair. He looked at Holly and smiled. He held this particular smile a little longer than normal, long enough for Holly to notice.

'What was that smile for?' Holly asked. Jack leaned over and gave her a gentle kiss on the cheek.

'I have just realised Holly.' Jack continued his smile and then extended it even further.

'Just realised what Jack?' Holly smiled in anticipation. Jack leaned over and kissed her once more on the cheek. He looked her in the eyes and then whispered in her ear.

'Happy birthday Holly.' Holly glowed, although the planned celebrations in Mexico seemed light years away.

'Gee Jack you remembered.' She said in a girly tone.

'So what does the woman that has everything want for her birthday then? Jack asked, running his hand through his hair once more.

'Apart from finding the *Document of Truth* you mean? Well some new clothes would be nice as I have had these on for two days now.' Holly pointed to her clothes, which were carrying one or two reminders of their adventures. *White cotton pants with a pink off the shoulder blouse were more suited to Mexico than Sunderland.* She thought to herself. The only thing that had kept its appearance was the small black shoulder bag. It held all her ladies essentials and the fax from the Butler, the same fax that could maybe lead her to her birthday wish. Jack leaned forward to the driver.

'Is there somewhere on the way you could drop us off to get some clothing? We will be quick, maybe you could just wait for us?' Holly mimed *Thank you* to Jack. He mimed *your welcome* in reply.

'Yes sure, the Bridges Shopping Centre is on the way. There is a Debenhams there, nice classy shop'

'Great thank you, can you take us there first please.'

'No problem.'

'Well Jack, I don't know about you, but I could get to like this place, everyone we have met has been very sweet and kind.' Jack laughed.

'We have only been here two hours or so Holly.' Holly looked at Jack and screwed up her face at him.

'Don't mess with the birthday girl Jack!' Jack smiled and then looked out of the taxi window, as the view of the monument was slowly disappearing.

Chapter 38

The faintest droning noise had emerged way beyond the hills; it soon grew louder and meatier. Within seconds the unmistakable sound of the helicopter was evident, the propellers waltzed and fizzed at a speed, just enough to thrust it through the air. An old farmer on the ground stood and watched it rage overhead, he had not seen the likes of this for a long time.

Leading the operation to kill Heenan and his men were former Special Forces Sergeants Iain Brennan and Yogi Nadler, the two soldiers that had double crossed Max.

'We are two minutes to landing, is everyone ready?' Several shouts of 'ready' went around the helicopter one by one, each shout accompanied by a thumb up. Yogi put his hand on Brennan's shoulder. He shouted above the dense noise that bounced around the inside of their flying metal beast.

'Make this quick, in and out, minimum noise and fuss ok?' It was greeted by a firm nod.

'We will collect our bounty and have a very long holiday.'

'I will 'yee har' to that my friend.' Was the brief and dour response to Yogi. Iain Brennan had always been super serious; Max once joked that his face would crack if he ever smiled. He was very good at his job, clinical, they all were and that is why they commanded very good paydays.

Everyone on this trip had a price. This included a no questions asked, full on assault of a civilian target. They all wore full military uniform, blacked out faces and carried automatic weapons, pistols, knifes and grenades. They had a backpack full of explosives; this was destruction on a grand scale.

The pilot advised of the descent for landing. They were being put down on the blind side of Heenan's mansion. There was a plot of land that had been identified as suitable for the drop.

Ten men exited the helicopter as it bumped down. Brennan hand gestured the way forward, while Yogi whirled his hand around, signalling for the pilot to go. They all jogged off, hunched down as the helicopter made a steep right turn, quickly disappearing over the hill. Suddenly the noise that was left was peaceful, wildlife, mainly birds tweeting innocently, as they went about the daily grind for food and survival.

Yogi signalled two men abreast, as they marched up the hill towards the mansion. The fields were a mix of rough grass and weeds, scorched in parts due to the intense summer they had suffered. Apart from the odd goat, everything was very calm, just as they liked it. They stormed up the hill like Noah's assassins.

Twenty four hours ago two men were sent ahead to do a reconnaissance on the property. They had identified where to land and where to gain entry. The pre-operation had gone smoothly. All information was received on time and was now being played out perfectly. The two men, who had carried out the reconnaissance, were now sat parked up in a truck just over a mile north. They awaited final instructions to extract the rest of the death party, once the mission was complete.

Both parties had their GPS co-ordinates locked on each other. Yogi had decided it would have been too risky to use a helicopter for their escape. The route back down the hill would have exposed them and they would have been easy pickings for any resistance.

At the point of entry, was a solid steel barrier about four feet high. The barrier was inserted into the imposing stone wall, which wormed around the whole estate. It was originally designed to allow animals to be let in and out. This was well before Heenan took residence. It has since been welded and bolted shut; only Bonnie and Clyde ever roamed the inside of this mansion now.

Brennan ordered the explosive device to be placed into position. A stock of sandbags to be used as a soundproofing barrier, were dropped off in advance. They built up a wall in front of the blast area. They calculated that the reduction in noise by using the sandbags, would cancel out any echo back to the main residence.

The order was given and the barrier was blasted; enough space was created for a point of entry. The sandbags had worked, although their contents were deposited all around them.

They had rehearsed the operation until they could do it in their sleep. Five teams of two in their primary position, ready for the assault inside. Their mission was simple. 1. Take out Heenan and his men. 2. Destroy all computers and devices that they could find. The professor was to be unharmed and released if possible, but it would be overlooked if he became a casualty of war.

Yogi checked his watch and then checked the GPS of the getaway truck .Everything was in place. *It was all very quiet, maybe a bit too quiet.* He thought to himself. Brennan broke the silence.

'I know what you are thinking Yogi, but this is too big a payday to stop now, let's do this.' Yogi nodded and then signalled for the other teams to go in.

All five teams slowly made their way through the tunnel that led to the main residence. The tunnel finished on the blind side of the swimming pool outhouse, around twenty metres behind Bonnie and Clyde. Two teams were ordered either side of the swimming pool, two either side of the entrance stairs. Brennan and Yogi moved around to the side and entered close to the central stairs.

Suddenly, a shot was fired from inside the house. They scrambled for safety, looking for signs of the shooter. Yogi checked with each team, nothing. Yogi whispered to Brennan, as they found cover against the wall at the bottom of the main outside stairs

'They must have heard the helicopter.'

'It sounded like the bullet stayed inside the property, maybe a warning shot?' Brennan whispered back.

Two minutes had passed since the single shot was fired. Yogi and Brennan agreed it was time for entry, he signalled to go in on five. His right arm up, five fingers displayed, the countdown made, four, three, two, one. His clenched fist signalled go, go, go. They rushed to the main door, both turned and stood with their backs to the wall, one either side. Yogi slapped an explosive on it, no need for sandbags now. He signalled two teams to do the same, on the windows either side of the main door. The final two teams were ordered behind the wall in front of them to offer extra eyes and cover fire.

Five more fingers signalled countdown again. A rush of dust swept inwards and upwards, as the entrance doors were blown. Two seconds later the grand windows to the sides met the same fate. The three teams held cover, as their comrades shot open rapid fire through the clouds of dust. Yogi signalled stop!

'I say three teams in, split left, right and centre.' Brennan agreed. The signal was given; they stormed into the building, the other two teams taking cover at the entrance.

Automatic fire rained down on them, through the clouds of dust, the noise far too great to communicate with words. They opened fire in return, as they ran for cover. Brennan pointed out a blind spot from the balcony above. The bottom of the staircase would allow cover from the sniper. As Yogi prepared to signal, Brennan noticed a second sniper from the angle of gunfire. He grabbed Yogi just in time; he held two fingers to his eyes and then pointed to a location in the balcony above them. Yogi nodded then noticed a shadow behind a stone pillar, in the floor above the two snipers, now there were three.

Silence descended as the dust settled, Yogi signalled to all teams, three snipers identified, locations noted. The six of them ran into open space and opened fire at the three targets. The second floor sniper took a hit, twice in rapid succession, once to the arm, once to the head; he stumbled forward and rolled over the balustrade, the sound of bones cracking and crunching were clear, as he landed on the stone floor in front of them. A signal by Brennan ordered a stop to the gun fire. They ran back for cover.

'Time to smoke them out Yogi.' Brennan advised. Yogi nodded and then signalled for two teams to land grenades on the first floor. Four grenades were unclipped, Yogi threw a canister of gas upstairs, it bounced once then landed. It started spinning around, gushing out a thick green mist. Another signal was given and then simultaneously four grenades were thrown, landing within several feet of each other on the first floor. The sound of metal clunking onto stone was quickly followed by mayhem. One of the main stone pillars that supported the staircase was taken out; the floor above dropped a few inches. A mass of stone fragments and dust bellowed out a mushroom cloud across the entrance. The two teams at the entrance rushed in and then upstairs, followed by the rest of them.

A single shot was fired down on them, it hit a comrade in the arm, a tirade of return fire ensued. The wounded soldier signalled to the rest to go on, he would live. They stormed to the top, three men swooped left and two to the right.

To the right lay a body covered in blood, dust and stone. To the left sat a man, a door that hung off its hinges was the only thing keeping him up, he was paralysed by a combination of gunfire and shrapnel.

'Boss.' Yogi and Brennan jogged up the stairs and stood over the dying man. Yogi ordered they check the floor above. The man looked up and made half an attempt to smile. His teeth more red than white, his black shirt and black combat trousers ripped down to his boots and covered in thick dust with red blood visible to his chest, he was bleeding heavily. His shirt absorbing the after effects of the bullet wound.

The floor was given as safe; no further signs of life were located around them. Brennan lent over the dying man, his rifle pointed down at him.

'Where is he?' The man spat at him, a mix of blood and dust only reaching as far up as his legs. He looked over his blood soaked body and then pressed his boot hard into his chest, twisting it on his wound. He cried out as he squirmed with the last drop of energy his body would allow. Brennan removed his foot and asked again.

'Where is he?' The man closed his eyes and pointed above to the staircase that led to the top floor. Brennan offloaded two quick shots into his chest and then signalled to clear floor two and move to floor three.

They all stood at the bottom of the stairs to the third and final floor. Yogi took the lead and one by one they made their way up the eighteen stone steps. In the silence they all took positions outside the door.

Two men stood behind the door at right angles, two on the top stair and two more three steps down. Brennan made his way up the final few steps and signalled his entry instructions. They burst in one by one, guns sighted ready for action. Quickly they lowered their weapons; there would be no further gunfight today. Brennan walked past Yogi to see what they all were looking at. Slumped to the side of his desk with a gunshot wound to the side of the head was Heenan, his gun lying on the floor next to him. Brennan bent over and picked it up. He put it to his nose and drew a breath; it had indeed been fired recently. Blood had swamped the table and covered the area where his face lay.

'Guess we know where that single gunshot came from now.' Yogi said sarcastically.

'Is it him?' Brennan asked looking at the blood covered body, his white shirt covered in red matter, his jeans wet with blood as it dripped off the desk and found its way to the floor.

Yogi grabbed his hair and lifted the part of head that was still intact; his moustache carried a crimson tinge to it now. He squinted down at the little puffy features that were left.

'Yeah it's him. The coward was not even ready to put up a fight, hard to believe he would take his own life, what a loser.'

'So much for the big bad ass we have heard so much about.' Brennan quipped.

'It is payday now boys, round up all the electrical equipment you can find and put it on the ground floor.' Yogi took two photographs on his phone of the blood stained body and sent them along with a message to the President.

Target eliminated with photos to confirm. All equipment will be destroyed once funds are received. No sign of the professor. You have five minutes to deposit funds into the Cayman account. Time for a long holiday sir, we are done now.

The sweep of the property took less than four minutes. All the equipment recovered was piled up as instructed and awaited its fate. Yogi then made the call to Seth, the man in charge of their getaway who sat waiting in the truck.

'Seth, get the truck down here now it is time to go home.'

'Roger that sir.'

Yogi's phone beeped with a message from his bank in the Cayman's

4.000.000 dollars deposited into Cayman account RD36729980

'Money's paid guys, burn all this stuff, we are done here.'

'Not a bad return for such a big payday, one gunshot wound to the arm.' Brennan said.

Chapter 39

All the men were assembled and waiting for the truck to arrive. Spirits were high, very high. This was a very big payday and the operation a resounding success.

'Hey Connor, what was that boat you said you were going to buy? Jimmy J asked. He was his best buddy in the troop. Connor smiled broadly at Jimmy J.

'Well Jimmy, if you're planning a trip with me, I guess it will be a rowing boat.' Everyone laughed; Sims patted Jimmy J on the back. It was all good lads banter, the pressure was off.

A faint noise from a diesel truck could be heard. Here is our ticket out of here.' Jimmy J piped up. The truck noise grew louder, the dust cloud that followed, grew bigger. The windscreen was covered in thick dust; only allowing the outline of two people in the front to be made out.

'Look at the state of the truck; the least they could have done was clean the windscreen so they could see out of it.' Connor said laughing at himself and the state of the truck. The truck trundled down the road and rolled through the front gates, which had been opened a few minutes earlier. Most of the men were sitting on the steps to the entrance, watching their chariot arrive as Jimmy J piped up again.

'Seth seems to be getting fatter by the day.' Yogi and Brennan laughed, but suddenly that comment produced a very unwelcome question. They squinted into the front of the truck analysing Seth. Brennan removed his glasses.

'Something is not right Yogi. That is not Seth, that dust is hiding something.'

'Take cover men, it is a trap.' Brennan shouted to his troop. Eight soldiers jumped from the back of the truck. They opened fire, catching the troop off guard. Sims was the first to be hit, his cries echoing out as Brennan, Jimmy J, Connor and three others fell. Yogi found cover inside, two comrades took cover near their stash of weapons, but it was exposed, too exposed, they were picked off easily. Brennan and his five comrades were finished off, as the onslaught continued, Sims lay screaming with pain.

Yogi had quickly become alone and isolated. He ran upstairs, searching for a weapon. He spotted a handgun, sticking out of one of the dead bodies on the first floor. He rolled him over, grabbed the gun and took cover. He sat to the side of a window, one of the six glass panes still hanging on by a thread. He looked on as another vehicle approached the main gates and pulled up behind the truck. Seth got out of the driver's side, rifle in hand. *You have got to be kidding me, you double crossing good for nothing scum bag.* The double crosser had been double crossed.

Yuri got out of the back of the car and opened the passenger door; Yogi slumped to the floor, the realisation of how well he had just been played. Heenan stood there, hands in pocket. He marched over to Sims and pointed a gun to his head.

'The man inside, what is his name?'

'Yogi.' Sims whispered to him through the pain. Heenan shouted inside to him.

'Yogi, you can see I'm a man of resources. Your friend here is about to have his brains blown out, unless you come out in five seconds. You cannot escape, so I would like to propose a deal.' The words were unexpected. *It's another trap,* he thought. Heenan counted down, taunting Yogi.

'Five, four, three, two.' Yogi yelled out.

'Wait, wait a second. How about you and me settle this man to man?' His Tennessee droll echoing around the grounds outside. Bang! Heenan finished off Sims. Yogi started to hit himself with his gun, his squad completely wiped out, well the ones he could trust. Heenan called out to Yogi.

'I need you to do something for me and if you do it, I will let you live.'

'What is it?' Yogi asked with a hint of disgust.

'I need you to call the President.'

'No way.' Yogi slammed.

Two of Heenan's men now had a clean shot of Yogi, he was cornered.

'We are good to go, repeat, we are good to go.' Was the message in Yuri's earpiece.

'Boss, we are in position.' Yuri said to Heenan.

'Good.' Heenan looked up at the window.

'Have a look at the red dots on you; I can kill you at any time. This is your last chance to take my deal. All your men are dead, all except Seth here, who now works for me.' Yogi looked at the two red dots, both aimed on his chest. He knew this was it.

'You have nowhere to go, take the deal.' Yogi looked up to the skies, his heart told him to shoot himself, his head said take the deal.

'You think I did not anticipate this would happen. You think I did not have men looking out for this. Your two men stuck out like a sore thumb yesterday. They gave you up very easily.' Heenan scoffed.

'Seth you rat.' Yogi yelled. Seth yelled back.

'Look man I'm sorry, I really am, but it was this or a bullet to the brain. If you haven't noticed, it looks like I made the right choice.'

'Hey Yogi, your friend Seth here told me it was you who was the double crosser down in Panama. That job was mine, so thank you.' Yogi banged the back of his head in frustration and desperation at his plight. He looked down again at the red dots, two had become five.

'Yogi, if you call the president for me I will let you live, this is your last chance.'

'I don't believe you.'

'That may be true, but what have you got to lose. I will also let you keep all the money from this operation if you do one job for me; you will be a rich man.'

'You give me your word?' Heenan let out a big grin and opened his arms so Yogi could see them.

'Of course.' Yogi took a deep breath and looked around at the collection of dead bodies outside. They were his friends, his troop and his life, but so was the money.

'Ok I will make the call.'

Chapter 40

The President was flanked by two aides as he strode down one of the many corridors of the White House. He was upbeat, almost giddy. He passed Johnson's office and then stopped. He took a couple of steps back and then peered in.

'Ruby.' He shouted. Johnson's personal assistant was lost in her typing and startled at the Presidents tone.

'Tell him fifteen minutes in my office and tell him it's good news Ruby, very good news, wonderful news.' Ruby looked shocked; this was way out of character for the President. She shouted back at him as he shot off down the corridor.

'But Mr President he is in a meeting with the Russian ambassador.' The President stopped once again and backed up to the door. He leaned back in and grinned, his giddiness rising by the second.

'Make it ten minutes and that's an order.' Ruby smiled and nodded. *You're the boss.* The President looked back at his aides.

'Where were we again?'

'We have found two tunnels coming in from Mexico, the drug cartels are ramping up their operation.' The President felt his cell phone vibrate, he ignored it.

'Who have we got down there, who can get us inside their operation?' The questioned stunned the aide. His cell phone continued to vibrate.

'You will need to take that up with the FBI Director sir.'

'Get me a meeting with him tonight, that will be all, I have an urgent matter to deal with.'

'Yes sir.' The President shot back into Johnson's office.

'Ruby, I need to use the bathroom.' Ruby was shocked. In the sixteen years she had been an assistant in the White House, she had never witnessed any President dash into an office bathroom before.

'Of course Mr President, straight through.'

'Thank you Ruby.' The President slammed the door, causing Ruby to jump. *My God what has he ate? Someone in the kitchen is in big trouble by the sounds of it.*

The President dug into his pocket for his cell phone. The vibrating had stopped; the screen offered no clues to the caller. *Beep Beep. A voicemail, who would leave me a voicemail on this phone?* He pressed the button and put the phone to his ear.

Mr President this is Yogi. I am standing with Folis Heenan. He is alive and well and has a gun to my head. He has ordered me to read the following message to you.

The President could hear Yogi clear his throat, he was panicked. He stood up and banged the door with the side of his fist causing Ruby to jump again. *Maybe I should call a doctor, this is not good?* She thought. Yogi began the message, his tone had dropped.

Mr President I'm going to expose you one way or another. I'm going to find the Document of Truth, but if I don't, I will release the photograph of you, you know the one. Once you have been stripped of your Presidency, I am going to kill you. It took me three years to get my body double exactly like me and because of you he is now dead. Watch your back I'm coming for you.

Utter disbelief rained down on the President. He banged the door again. *That's it I am calling the doctor.* Ruby announced to herself. Rage and fear filled the face of the President. He circled the bathroom and then looked in the mirror. His tie had been twisted to the side, his top button undone, without him realising he had done it. He spoke to the mirror. *Jesus Christ, think man, think. Who can fix this mess?* There was a knock on the bathroom door, it was Johnson. Ruby had excused him out of the meeting and showered him with concern for the President's wellbeing.

'Mr President it's Johnson, is everything alright?' The President took a breath.

'Come in Johnson.' He replied, staring at himself in the mirror. He stood tall, his persona returned, calmness restored. Johnson walked in as the President straightened his tie and fastened his top button.

'Are you sir? Ruby said you were ill.' The President turned away from the mirror and looked at Johnson. He put his hands in his pocket.

'You know it's funny. Five minutes ago I was ready to tell you Heenan was dead. Now, I need to tell you something completely different, something you are not going to like. My only hope is that you will work with me to restore justice.' Johnson felt a rush of adrenalin pass over him. He thought the President had finished with the name Heenan, but had no idea why!

Chapter 41

She had an Irish look to her. Jack thought to himself as he looked at the pretty lady. Pure white complexion with long strawberry hair, a hint of fresh looking freckles, added to the beauty of the lady, standing behind the check in desk of the Sunderland Marriot Hotel.

He noticed her name, her badge pinned to her navy blue jacket, *Shoreen. That name sounds Irish to me.* Holly was more interested in the obligatory process of checking-in. She had just realised they had not discussed the room situation. It caused her the faintest of blushes, as she thought about wanting two separate rooms.

'Welcome to the Sunderland Marriot Hotel, how can I help you today?' Shoreen said, smiling as she waited for an answer. She was warm and friendly, her accent not Irish in the least.

'We would like.' Jack paused and looked at Holly, who immediately raised an eyebrow, guessing his intention. He turned back to look at Shoreen and offered her a cheeky smile.

'Two separate rooms please.' Shoreen remained professional; she had seen most things in this job before.

'Would you like two singles or two doubles?' Shoreen asked, knowing from her very brief encounter with Jack and Holly the response could be amusing.

'Single.' 'Double.' They answered together. Shoreen waited for one of them to claim victory in the war of the rooms.

'Double please Shoreen.' Jack said, rolling his eyes in a playful motion.

'Yes sir, I can do that for you. Is it just for the one night?' Shoreen enquired.

'Can we keep our rooms open for now? We are undecided on how long we are staying.' Holly asked, hoping that would wrap up the room formalities.

'Of course you can. Would you like to reserve a table for dinner tonight?'

'Erm, you know what, we will just hang fire for now thank you.' Holly said.

'That is no problem; can I have your passports please?' Holly delved into her black shoulder bag and fished out the two passports that Johnson had given them.

'Ok, one double en suite for Simon Yeoman and one for Katie Yeoman.' Holly felt the need to clarify the situation.

'We are brother and sister.' Shoreen smiled, as she completed the formalities.

'We will pay by cash if that is ok?' Jack requested, still admiring the view.

'Of course.' Shoreen tapped a few buttons and then presented them with their room cards.

'You are in rooms 214 and 216 on the second floor. You can access your rooms by the lift just behind you or via the stairs to your right. The rooms are double en suite with sea views. You can use the leisure facilities until 9pm tonight and they open again at 7am. Breakfast is served from 7am to 10am and included in the price. If I can be of any further assistance please dial zero from the phone in your room. Thank you for choosing the Sunderland Marriot for your stay.' Shoreen had rolled off those words a thousand times before, but they were warmly appreciated by Jack and Holly.

'Thank you so much.' Holly replied smiling.

'Damn, I should have bought some swimming shorts when we stopped at the shops, could have had a dip later. Jack said, teasing Holly, she was unimpressed. Jack winked at Shoreen and then took off to the stairs.

Jack stood right behind Holly, as she inserted her key card into the door of room 214. She paused and turned to him.

'Jack, you're 216 next door.'

'Spoilsport.' He turned away and walked the ten yards to 216. Holly walked into her room, but stuck her head back out and shouted to Jack.

'What is the plan now?'

'You mean your place or mine?' He teased.

'I mean we need to step up a gear and work on the code.' Holly came back out to the corridor, propping her foot in the door to keep it open.

'Look, I'm starving, why don't we get freshened up, have a bite to eat then get to work on the code?'

'You are always starving Jack. There were a few restaurants that we passed on the seafront, I noticed as the taxi pulled up. Why don't we try one of those?'

'Fine with me Holly, I could really murder a curry.'

'No chance, you're not working alongside me stinking of curry. We can go to one of the Italian restaurants.'

'Fair enough, I will stink of garlic working next to you then.' Jack scoffed. Holly shook her head. *Always the joker.*

'Thirty minutes Jack, be ready in thirty.' She yelled as the door closed on her. *Women, can't live with them, can't live without them.*

Chapter 42

Bridie was presented to Heenan by Yuri, a welcome sight for them both. The mansion had been cleaned of all the death and destruction. His original chair and desk put back in his office. The risk of his body double spilling blood on his prize possession was not an option.

Heenan wanted a second opinion on the professor, whose time had just about run out. Bridie was the only living person he rated smart enough to give him an answer to the question he kept asking himself.

'Bridie, I have a problem and it needs your special skills shall we say.' Heenan outlined to Bridie the timeline of events of everything that had happened over the last few days. Bridie thought she had seen it all with her employer over the last few years, but even she was surprised at the prize on offer.

'I will give you ten minutes with the professor. At the end of that, I want to know if I should stick or twist.' Bridie sat crossed legged, slightly twisted to her right. She puffed on a cigarette, her expression emotionless. She licked her lips and then uncrossed her legs and stubbed out the cigarette.

'I will only need five minutes with him, let's not waste any more time.'

'Yuri, take Bridie down to see the professor.' Yuri nodded.

Bridie knocked on the door twice before she walked in, her heels slowly scratching the stone floor. The professor was hard at work; he looked up and was surprised to see such beauty before him. He stopped his work and sat back. Bridie pulled up a chair next to him. His body odour was evident as she got up close and personal.

'Get this poor man a shower and some food as soon as I leave here Yuri.' Yuri was happy to follow Bridie's lead. She had taken the pressure off him for now. She took hold of the professor's hand.

'How are you?' She asked tentatively. The professor was about to give her an answer, but Bridie stopped him by putting her fingers to his mouth.

'Ssshhh, don't answer that, let me speak honestly to you. I only have a couple of minutes before that monster returns. I can help you but you need to help me first, do you understand professor.' The professor nodded slowly. *What is going on, who is she?* He was suddenly lost in the moment, a mix of kindness and hope had descended up on him.

'What do you want?' He enquired gracefully, his shattered exterior giving way to a burst of adrenalin.

'Are you able to crack this riddle for the man upstairs?' Bridie stroked the professor's face gently; she gazed at him, her eyes rolling over his face. His senses were heightened; his words slow to come out.

'I believe it is possible ye yes, ber but it will take time.' The professor stumbled over his words; his fear had turned into exhilaration. Bridie's spell was well under way. She looked deep down into the iris of his eyes.

'How long do you need professor, be honest and let me help you.'

'I am frightened to say the truth.' He whispered to her, under the radar of Yuri's ears.

'Whisper it in my ear.' Bridie leaned forward to absorb the professor's words.

'Two weeks, probably three, maybe even months, I really don't know.' Bridie kept stroking his face as she gazed closely into his eyes. She whispered to him, putting her hand firmly on his thigh and squeezing it softly.

'Don't you worry professor, I am going to put an end to all this nonsense and anguish for you my poor thing. It will all be over soon, trust me.' The professor filled up with tears. The thought of a positive outcome, a reunion with his family, was not something he had held out much hope for.

Bridie removed her arm and stood up; she smiled down at the professor, who sat staring at her with renewed hope.

'Yuri, throw me your gun.' Yuri unclipped his gun from his belt and tossed it to Bridie. She caught it one handed, spun it around her hand and then cocked it. She pointed it at the professor. He pushed back off his seat and fell backwards, pulling the table over with him. Bridie took two steps to get a clear view of the professor. He screamed out.

'No, no, what are you doing.'

'I told you it will be all over soon didn't I?'

Bridie walked into Heenan's office, flanked by Yuri, not overly concerned how he may take the news. She wore a light brown, almost see through blouse. Heenan could see the outline of her bra underneath it as she took a seat. Part of her locks swooped around her front and dangled down her left shoulder. Her matching light brown trousers and shiny cream boots completed her outfit. Heenan stubbed out his cigar and then sat back in his seat.

'Before you start yelling and shouting, I did you a favour by killing the grey bean pole. He has no value to you, it is better to focus on a new approach. Yuri has informed me about these two other specialists that the President recruited; we need to track them down.' Heenan looked serious; he contemplated the offer, but wanted to know more and just what it would cost him.

'What is your plan Bridie, I know you will have one, you would have had it before you killed the professor. Remember I know you.' Heenan folded his arms, his mind not made up. Bridie looked around at Yuri who was deadpan and then looked back at Heenan.

'Two million euros, Yuri, three of his best men, plus the two yanks you have just recruited. I trust they are expendable should it be required?' Heenan pushed back on his chair, he rubbed his stubble. Several seconds of silence passed before he replied.

'How long do you anticipate it will take you to apprehend them?'

'Twenty four hours, I will personally oversee the operation.' Bridie replied without even a twitch. The seductive siren was chilling in her appraisal. Heenan felt vulnerable without Yuri by his side although in truth he treated his hamsters better. Yuri was the safety blanket he could always rely on. The prize though was too tempting, his mind was made up.

'Do it. You have twenty four hours, not a minute later.'

Chapter 43

The Sunderland Marriot Hotel sits proudly on the seafront in the suburb of Seaburn. Between there and it's next door neighbour Roker, they have over two miles of golden sandy beach. The North Sea is all that separates them from Scandinavia, Germany, Holland and Belgium. Seaburn and Roker beaches are home to Europe's biggest free airshow, which attracts over half a million visitors, flocking there to see the Red Arrows and a host of other classic displays.

Today though, it is like every other Saturday evening along the promenade. The restaurants and bars are buzzing with the happy sounds of chatter and good humour, mainly from its local population, although a sprinkling of visitors are made very welcome by the locals and businesses alike.

Jack and Holly made their way to the cluster of eateries on the promenade. Holly had changed into her new purchases, a black cotton vest, black tight jeans, a red cotton cardigan and of course her Converse trainers. Functional was her mandate for this occasion.

There were four Italian restaurants in close proximity to each other, Little Italy, Martinos, Gabrieles and Santini's. They all looked as good as each other, so they plumped for the nearest, Gabrieles.

Jack too had dipped into the funds Johnson had given them. He was now sporting a multi-coloured floral shirt, which was currently hidden inside a new black leather jacket.

They were greeted by the owner, Nevio. He offered them the last available table with a seaview. Once seated, they were handed two menus, one for food and one for drinks.

They settled on a bottle of crisp chilled Pinot Grigio. It was placed on the table inside a steel cooler. Their wine was poured into the glasses by the waitress, a third full. The wine glass instantly misted up below the level of the chilled wine. They agreed it was a good choice, quaint, authentic and very chatty. Although it seemed dimly lit at first, it was in fact the dark interior that created the warm ambience inside.

They decided to share a starter, cheese and tomato garlic bread. For main, Holly went traditional with a lasagne. Jack was more adventurous and plumped for the hottest dish on the menu, pollo etna.

Holly dipped into her shoulder bag, took out the fax and then rolled it out on the table. Jack moved his chair; he could now look at the fax and the sea.

The starter was served on a round plate, cut into eight pieces. The smell wafting up was too much for Jack. He took the first slice, salivating as he took his first bite. The melted cheese turned to string as he ate it slowly to see how hot it was.

'We need to look at this differently Holly.' He stated pushing a piece of cheese back into his mouth.

'How do you mean Jack?' Holly had placed her first piece of garlic bread on a side plate and used her cutlery to dissect it.

'Neither of us has ever seen anything like this before, agreed?'

'Agreed, but what has that got to do with anything?'

'We have nothing to go on, so we need to think outside the box.' Jack took a sip of his wine and then wiped away the rich tomato sauce, which had dripped onto his chin.

'I once solved a case in Africa by working backwards. I am not saying that we do that here, what I am saying is that by thinking outside the box I got a result.'

'Actually Jack I think you may be right.'

'Let's start with the Zodiac signs.' Holly said.

'First, we have Aries, the Ram, the start of the Zodiac calendar. Then we have Leo the Lion, Sagittarius the Archer and finally Virgo the Maiden.' Jack took a sip of wine and then began to focus.

'Do we look at the names, where in the calendar they are, the animal or what?' As Holly looked down, deciding where to focus her energy first, Jack had a revelation.

'Wait a minute Holly; I can't believe neither of us has spotted the obvious here.' Holly looked intrigued. *What has he spotted?* Jack tapped his finger on the fax.

'These are not markings, they are mirrored numbers. You put a mirror to these and it will reveal a set of numbers.'

'My God Jack, you are right, well spotted. A school girl error on my part, Grandpa will be turning in his grave at me for not spotting that sooner.' Holly took a gulp of wine and then dipped into her bag for her vanity mirror.

'Well Holly, do him proud and solve the significance of these numbers.' Holly angled the mirror over the fax; it did indeed reveal a list of numbers.

The first tattoo was 139-1319-1320-1411.
The second tattoo was 194-1913-219-2124-2211-237.
The third tattoo was 264-265-2612-2613-278-2716.
The forth tattoo was 295-296-3314-3417-359-3510.

'They appear to be in some sort of order, but I have no idea what order yet.' Said Holly. The empty pizza plate was removed and the wine topped up without either one of them blinking an eye.

'What about the cities? Only three of the tattoos have the names of cities on them. We have Reykjavik on the first tattoo, nothing on the second, Madrid on the third and Oslo on the fourth. All of them are in central Europe, but why is there only three?' Jack looked at Holly; he felt the first effects of his wine, a warm glow and a sense of freedom flashed across his mind. Holly was still consumed by the fax.

'I don't know, but they are there for a reason, that's for sure.' She replied.

'The last thing we have are numbers, the zeros stand out for me, lots of them, just don't know why yet.' Jack nodded and then read each one out loud; he hoped in vain that it would help solve the puzzle.

Tattoo one 00600010011001800050
Tattoo two 00200090004000400220
Tattoo three 00400010017001300050040
Tattoo four 01700140002000500170019 0

Nevio arrived at their table, two plates of steaming hot food, one in each hand. He looked down at the fax and asked if it could be moved to make room for the food. His wife Christine stood behind him, armed with a ten inch wooden cylinder full of black peppercorns. It was tucked under her arm, ready to be ground over their food on mutual agreement. She then offered both of them a silver bowl of parmesan cheese, generously sprinkled over their food.

'Bon appetite.' She said, as she backed away gracefully.

'Thank you.' Holly smiled

After the obligatory food tasting and hand wafting gestures across the mouth, to establish that the food was as hot as the steam suggested, the conversation rallied again.

'This was put together back in 1789, so we need to think what was available to George Washington at that time. It's pointless thinking post that date.' Jack tapped his finger on the paper four times to cement his point.

The next ten minutes were taken up with questions, questions and more questions, answers were scarce. The only thing that had become definite so far was that the wine was getting low and the food was disappearing off the plates.

Having clearly established that they were now dealing with two sets of sequential numbers and not a symbol, along with a set of zodiac signs and three cities, they divided their focus. Holly zoned in on links to anagrams, reverse sequences, word association, clusters and number groups. Jack looked at possible link patterns, running number patterns, location dating, pattern plays and historical word plays. No matter how much Jack looked at the fax, only one thing was nagging at him.

'Holly, these zeros, so, so many in these number sequences. The only time I have ever seen anything like that is in a binary sequence and it's obviously not binary code.' Holly looked at Jack, she grinned widely, her brilliant white teeth, freshly cleaned by the wine sparkled at him.

'That's it Jack, the zeros, that's the key to this, they are nothing more than a wraparound.' Holly leaned forward and pointed to the first sequence. *Tattoo one 00600010011001800050.* She carefully placed a finger over the first zero and then a finger over the third zero.

'What is left in between them?'

'Zero and six.'

'Exactly, that relates to the number six, double digit number 06. The zeros are just inserted before and after the two numbers. What we have here is an alphabet wraparound zero sequence.' Holly said, as genuine excitement rolled across the table. She was two steps ahead in her mind, it had already been decoded.

'I see.' Jack said, hoping to catch on to Holly's way of thinking.

'Look, by following my theory, tattoo one leaves us with is 06-01-11-18-05.'

'Yes, I can see that now, you said an alphabet though, where does that come in?'

'Simple, number one is A, two is B and so on. All we do is align each number with the alphabet letter it relates to and bingo!' Holly passed Jack the pen and paper. He scribbled away, quickly coming up with the first word.

'The word makes no sense to me Holly, I have never heard of it.' Jack was puzzled by the puzzle.

'Show me Jack.' Jack lifted his paper up to show Holly, who burst out laughing.

'C'mon Jack you should be using the _Alphabeth de la Bourbonnoise._ This is 1789 remember, there was no J, U or W attached to the _Alphabeth de la Bourbonnoise_ at that point. Washington would have used this alphabet, I'm sure of it. Jack smiled; he liked the way Holly was pronouncing the name of the alphabet with the effects of two large glasses of vino.

'You know I was just messing with you Holly right?' Jack chuckled.

'Tattoo one spells _F A L S E._' Holly said, still chuckling.

'Do the other three then smarty pants.' Jack said.

'Already done Jack.' Holly wrote them out for them to look at.

Tattoo two is B I D D Y
Tattoo three is D A R N E D
Tattoo four is R O B E R T

A moment of silence descended on them, the noise of chatter, laughter and cutlery clinking had disappeared as they contemplated a breakthrough.

'Ok Holly, what is this saying to us?' Holly was blunt, positive and certain in her appraisal.

'My money is on Robert, why else would a name be in there unless it had true meaning?'

'It would be a good way to throw us a bone.' Jack said stabbing the last piece of chicken on his plate.

'You have a real way with words Jack.' Jack opened his hands out and then dabbed his serviette to his mouth.

'We need to see if there was any Robert close to George Washington, maybe even a relative.' Holly said.

'You think the other three words are just fillers then?'

'I do and it would make sense, it was 1789 when this was done. Robert was a significant name then, all we need to do is work out who Robert is. When we do, we will have our first true lead.'

'Oh Holly I forgot to say the battery in Johnson's phone died, I left the charger on the plane, we will need to try and pick one up tomorrow.'

'I bet you did that on purpose.' Holly joked. Jack sipped back the last of his glass of wine; he lifted the bottle, empty. He signalled to Nevio, who walked to their table.

'Can we have the check please?'

'Of course.' Nevio looked down at the fax. It had aroused his attention earlier and he had a question to ask them about it.

'I take it from your accent that you are American yes?' They both smiled and nodded.

'Are you over here for the Washington Heritage festival tomorrow?' Nevio grabbed their full attention in one brief sentence.

'Why do you ask?' Holly enquired politely, ready to hang on to every word he said.

'I am very interested in the heritage of my adopted country and one of my regular customers here, Danni Grundy is the main speaker. He told me last night, he had a special guest coming from America, accepting an award on behalf of one of your Senators, who has made several large donations to charities here in Washington.' Holly looked at Jack, while she replied to Nevio.

'No, it's not us, but can I ask, do you know which Senator it is who has made these donations?' *Surely it couldn't be him, I would have known.*

'Yes, it is Senator Natalie.'

Chapter 44

Jesus, who the hell is Sam? Was the question swilling around his fuzzy mind. Jack lifted his head from his pillow and squinted through one eye. A few feet away, he could slowly make out a white curtain dancing back and forward from the breeze. His subconscious had ordered him to investigate the cries. He prized open his other eye with a gentle rub and then sat up.

He had slept well, a mix of drink, stress and fatigue had seen to that. He swivelled around and placed his feet on the carpet. He looked up at the flat screen television on the wall. He sat mesmerised for a few seconds at the news channel, struggling to read the headlines scrolling across the bottom of the screen. He noticed the mute sign in the corner of the television. *Where is the remote?*

Sam, Sammm. Were the cries coming from somewhere outside. *There it is again.* Jack jumped up and rushed to the window. He pulled back the curtain, pushed the window open and looked out. The sun was coming up over Roker Pier to his right, the brightness made him shield his eyes for a second. He looked down to the promenade in front of him. A couple of joggers and a lady pushing a pram were all that was on view. Sam, Sammm, come on boy. *Where are you?* Jack scanned around to where the voice had come from. He looked out at the beach, the tide was right out. *Got you, I see you Sam, so you're a dog; a golden retriever by the looks of you. Your mother sure has a voice on her old boy.* He looked down at his watch, 06.35am, *who walks their dog at this time on a Sunday morning anyway?*

Jack walked back to his bed and pulled back his quilt, the remote control now visible. He picked it up, looked for the mute, pointed it at the television and changed the channels. He flicked through a few channels but nothing caught his fancy, he was still in a daze. He sat on the bed and rubbed his face. *I suppose I should shower now I'm up.* He changed to a music channel, Smooth Radio, Sunday love songs. Barry White's deep voice ushered him to the bathroom.

As he opened the bathroom door, he realised he was still holding the television remote. He threw it towards the bed for a soft landing, but it bounced up and hit the bedside cabinet. Button number nine, on the remote was the point of impact as it bounced off the cabinet. It was enough to change the channel, this time to Sky Sports News. *Couldn't have done that if I had tried!*

Fresh from a power shower Jack donned his flowery shirt and finished getting ready. His mind began to refocus on the job in hand. He reflected on last night's events and the progress that they had made. He looked in the mirror to straighten his hair and spoke to his reflection. *The Washington Triangle, I wonder what the Oracle would make of this heritage festival today, be right up his street I reckon. And who is this Senator Natalie, the great philanthropist? Need to Google him.*

It is over to the Sky Sports Centre for the news headlines. The television broke his concentration; he looked at his watch, 7 AM.

Essex look set to clinch the County Championship, after a ninth wicket haul yesterday by the twenty-one-year-old debutant that everyone is talking about. His first three overs resulting in two wickets and a maiden over.

British summer sports, I mean cricket for God's sake, what sort of sport is that? Jack said to himself. He looked back at the mirror, vainly admiring himself. *Wait a minute, what did he just say? Maiden over, maiden over, maiden, maiden. That's it! Maiden.* His senses were heightened, his adrenaline kicking in. *Of course, bloody maiden.*

Jack spun round and grabbed his key card and wallet, stuffed them in his pocket and then rammed his trainers on. He took one last look in the mirror, running his hand through his hair. He pointed at the mirror, *looking good Jacky boy, looking good.*

He knocked loudly on Holly's door, then again, then again. He knocked again this time calling out her name. He knocked once more, still no answer. *Where is she?* He shot off down the corridor and took the stairs, jumping them in blocks of two. He caught sight of Shoreen as he reached the bottom of the stairs.

'Your partner has just gone in for breakfast sir.'

'No, no she is not my partner.' Jack stated quickly.

'Of course, sir.' Shoreen smiled and then looked down at her computer.

Jack paced through into the breakfast room. He glanced around; it was quiet, still very early for a Sunday morning breakfast sitting. Holly was seated with her back to him; her hair was enough for him to rush over. He tapped her on the shoulder.

'Holly I have got something.'

'Jesus Jack, you scared the hell out of me there and good morning to you too.'

'Sorry Holly, but this can't wait.'

'What is it?' Jack took a seat opposite Holly.

'Well I was going in the shower and remembered the remote was in my hand, so I threw it towards the bed. It ended up hitting the bedside cabinet and that changed the channel.' Jack was rambling in his excitement. Holly was bewildered.

'Slow down Jack, you are not making any sense.' Holly looked down at her toast and then dobbed a knob of butter in the middle of it. She began to spread it into the corners.

'Holly, pay attention.' He demanded.

'Ok Mr Grumpy, go on.'

'One-word Holly, maiden!' Jack tapped the table then leaned back and waited for the fanfare.

'I have five words for you Jack, what are you talking about?'

'My little trick with the remote is what I'm talking about. I had a music channel on and after it hit the cabinet, it switched to a sports channel. They were reading the sports headlines, which were about cricket; you know that stupid game for gentlemen.' Jack smiled, waiting for Holly to laugh. She looked blank.

'Anyway they were discussing the latest events and there it was.'

'What?' Holly shrugged.

'A maiden over, meaning no runs were scored! You get it Holly?' She sat looking at Jack shaking her head in bemusement.

'C'mon Holly wakey wakey. A maiden, meaning nothing happened, a first, a virgin, the chosen one. Do you not see the link here?' Holly smiled and put her hands together.

'Well done Jack, I get it now; you're talking about the Zodiac signs.'

'Yes, at last.' Jack slammed his hand down on the table causing the cutlery and crockery to jump. The waitress arrived at their table to check if everything was ok. Jack nodded and then moved the conversation along.

'We have four Zodiac signs, but I think one of them is irrelevant to the equation, just a red herring so to speak, or to give it it's real name, a maiden, a nothing.' Jack picked up a sausage from Holly's plate and stuffed it in his mouth.

'Sounds feasible, that means we can focus on the three Zodiac signs for clues, but we need to work out which ones first.'

'There is something else I have been thinking about.' Jack said.

'The Oracle kept banging on about that the Washington Triangle. What if this Senator has something to do with it, what was his name again? Holly cut in and answered for Jack.

'Senator Natalie, born 1st July 1958, height one metre ninety, weight around two hundred and thirty five pounds.' Holly looked Jack straight in the eye. He put the remainder of the sausage back on Holly's plate.

'What's going on Holly, how do you know so much about this dude?' He asked.

'Because Jack.' Holly took a breath and then let it out, the words she detested making public.

'He is my father.' Holly put her cutlery down and looked out at sea.

'Senator Natalie is your dad? Why didn't you say something last night?' Jack shook his head, more news that made no sense to him.

'I don't understand Holly, what's the big secret?' Holly kept looking out at sea for an answer.

'I suppose I was in denial. Somehow I would wake up today and it all had been a bad dream. I have not spoken to him in a long time, it's personal, I swear to you Jack, I know nothing about his dealing. Last night's revelation came as a shock to me, although it shouldn't have. He was always having secret rendezvous. I need you to believe me Jack.' Jack picked up the half eaten sausage and munched down on it.

'Yeah I believe you Holly.' He said chomping away.

'Not even you would make that up.' Holly looked at him, his mouth bouncing up and down as he devoured the sausage.

'Thank you.'

'Right let's get ready to rumble.' Jack said.

'Have some breakfast first Jack, it's still early.' Jack signalled a waitress over and then pointed at Holly's plate.

'Can I have the same please?'

'Of course you can sir.' The waitress replied.

Johnson walked into the Oval Office, a glum look for a glum day.

'Any news?' The President asked.

'Mr President I have been trying for hours to contact them, but the phone I gave them is just constantly on answerphone.'

'Keep trying Johnson, I owe it to them to bring them back safe and I owe it to them, to tell them the truth.'

Heenan was standing staring at a small tree on the far side of his swimming pool. There was a bird staring back at him, a red-footed falcon. His attention was distracted by Yuri's stand in.

'Boss.'

'Yes, what is it?'

'I have Bridie on the phone for you.' Heenan nodded and signalled him to bring the phone.

'Yes.'

'Jack Hammonds and Holly Macdonald went to England via Spain on a private jet arranged by your friends in the White House.'

'Good work, find their exact location and let me know immediately. Remember they are not to be harmed, I need them alive, both of them.'

'Understood.'

Chapter 45

'Doors open at 11am, with games, stalls and concessions all day.' Jack said, researching the day's itinerary at the Washington Heritage Festival. It was the 1pm slot that aroused their attention, something that was unmissable. *A history of the Washington Triangle by Norman Stocks, followed by a presentation from Danni Grundy to a VIP from the United States who is representing Senator Natalie, for his continued, generous contributions to various charities in the local area.*

'We should call Walt; this is his domain. He also mentioned something about knowing someone here. They could be involved in the festival, you never know.' Holly said. Jack dialled the number and Holly whispered to him while the phone was ringing.

'We need to get a charger for Johnson's phone as a matter of urgency.' The Oracle answered, he was suspicious, a Spanish number showing up on his phone, who could it be?

'Hello.'

'Hey, Mr Oracle, it's Jack here, we need your help with something.'

'Jack who? Do I know you?' The Oracle replied.

'Sure you do, we met at the library on Friday.' The Oracle was silent. Jack pressed on.

'You helped us with a government matter, remember?' Holly grabbed the phone from Jack.

'Hi Walt, it's Holly here.' She did not have to wait long for his recognition.

'Hey, yes I remember you, sorry I'm half asleep.'

'We would like to ask you some questions about the Washington Triangle.'

'Ah, the baby is coming home to roost is it?' The Oracle sounded a touch smug. 'What would you like to know?'

Several thousand people were already in attendance at the festival, on Albany Park, as Jack and Holly arrived. The weather was undecided, clouds massed, but the rain that was promised had not materialised.

There were three marquees at the festival. Two of them focused on Washington's history. They were both named after locals who had become famous after leaving the town. Marquee one was named Heather Mills, the walking medical miracle, human and animal rights campaigner.

Marquee two was named after George Clark, the well-known and popular television presenter.

Rows of white clothed trestle tables displayed a timeline of the local history, along with its success and challenges. It was however Marquee three that they were interested in. This was where the speeches and awards would take place. As they approached it, Jack pointed out to Holly, the name above the door, Marquee Bryan Ferry.

'Go to where the Ferry departed. Do you think we got that wrong? It could be here.'

'I don't think so Jack, everything has fallen into place so far.' Holly popped her head inside, only a handful of people were on view.

'We have about fifteen minutes to wait before the speaker comes on, fancy an ice cream Jack?' Jack looked up at the cloudy skies. *Not exactly ice cream weather, but why not?* He nodded to the ice cream van.

'After you.' Holly pointed to a juggler on the way to the van. He was sat bobbing back and forth, balanced on a unicycle. His eyes fixed on the three red and white skittles, which he revolved with his hands at great speed. A round of applause followed his latest stunt and he allowed himself to take a quick bow, from his constantly moving position. He called out to his assistant, who strutted over, carrying three metal rods in her hand, with one end of them wrapped in cloth. She took the skittles from him and handed him the rods. He shouted out loud for his audience to hear.

'Suzannah, light them up.' One click of her little wand was all it took to set them alight. A ripple of applause was offered by the crowd in anticipation of his next stunt.

'Thank you Suzannah, now stand back. He looked around the crowd and pointed to the flames.

'Please do not try this at home.' He half joked.

The ice cream van was baby blue and white with a huge poster on the side displaying the various items on offer and their prices. The hefty fella inside the van was sporting a four day old unshaven look. He handed over change to his last customer, a little girl bouncing on the spot waiting for her treat.

'Yes please, what can I get you?' The ice cream seller asked. Holly looked at the poster for options. Jack was more decisive.

'A 99 please.' Jack looked around at the daredevil juggler; he winced, as he threw the mobile mini rockets into the air. *He could do some serious damage to himself if he dropped one of those on his clown's suit. Third degree burns all day long.*

'You want monkey's blood with that?' Jack swung back around to Mr Creamy, he was gobsmacked.

'Do I want what?' Mr Creamy pointed to a large plastic bottle container in front of him.

'Monkey's blood man, strawberry sauce topping.'

'Sure, why not.' Jack replied. Mr Creamy squirted a healthy amount of the red liquid sauce, enough for it to drip onto Jack's hands as he received it.

Mr Creamy was a stand-in today, much to his annoyance, as Mrs Creamy had branched out into a cupcake stall.

'Help yourself to hundreds and thousands over there.' Mr Creamy nodded in the direction of an enormous stash of the multi coloured sprinkles in a glass bowl. Holly was oblivious to the fact monkey's blood was an option, but her mind was now made up.

'Magnum please.' She declared.

'Dark chocolate, milk chocolate, almond or plain? Holly had not noticed the list of sub choices under the photograph.

'Err almond please.'

'Coming up.' Jack handed over the money and told Mr Creamy to keep the change and then guided Holly back towards the flame thrower.

'This guy has some balls, imagine if his Andy Pandy outfit caught fire? That would be the last juggling act he would ever do.' Jack chuckled to himself as he tackled the monkey's blood with his tongue. As he bit into the end of his chocolate flake embedded in the ice cream they were greeted with an announcement.

Attention please ladies and gentlemen. Came the voice through the tinny speakers, sited around the grounds of the Festival.

You have five minutes to get to the Bryan Ferry Marquee for the next exhibition. Norman Stocks will be giving a talk on the trail of the Washington Coat of Arms and enlightening you on The Washington Triangle. We also have a special guest today who I'm sure you will give a warm welcome to. They havs come all the way from the United States to collect the award on behalf of Senator Natalie, who most of you know has done so much for our great town. Five minutes ladies and gentlemen, five minutes.

'Wow your dad is quite the celebrity in these parts and you never knew, so much for Holly the super sleuth.' Jack ribbed.

'You know you can be a real pain in the butt sometimes.' Jack grinned and tucked back into his 99.

'Let's head over to the Bryan Ferry Marquee and make sure we get a front row position. I want to see everything that is going on.' Jack said.

'I wonder who this special guest is then Jack?' Holly asked as she pulled back the door to the marquee. There was a modest gathering, increasing by the second. Most huddled around the stage area, standing on flattened grass.

'It is nice and warm in here anyway.' Holly said as she looked about. There was piped music coming from the speakers, today's sponsors were also the local radio station, Sun FM

Next, a song you will be familiar with, from 1993, it's D:Ream and Things Can Only Get Better.

'That sounds like it could be our soundtrack Holly.' Jack joked.

You can walk my path. You can wear my shoes. Learn to talk like me and be an angel too, But maybe, you ain't never gonna feel this way. You ain't never gonna know me, but I know you. I'm singing it now. Things can only get better, can only get better...

Tall, bigger than average, balding with round rimmed glasses, dressed in denim jeans, a burgundy shirt, with matching burgundy V neck pullover was Danni Grundy. He was a local historian, fundraiser, Rotary Club chairman and part time self-confessed political activist.

'This is the guy Nevio told us about last night in the restaurant. It's one of his regulars, in fact that looks like Nevio standing to the side of the stage.' Holly said, pointing over. Jack was distracted as a ram raid on his calf was taking place by a passer-by with a wayward child's buggy.

'Eeeeee sorry pet.' The lady said.

Danni Grundy held the centre of the stage. His commanding thespian tone shuddered around the marquee.

'Ladies and gentlemen, thank you for coming. Shortly we will have the presentation and I am delighted to announce that I have just received a call from Senator Natalie confirming that our special guest is right here in the marquee.' Several whoops circled around the marquee. Jack looked at Holly.

'Who has your dad roped in to do this, do you recognise anyone?' Holly looked about and shook her head.

'No, no one.'

'Although I have never met this special guest before, I am truly excited that they have made the journey from America to see us today. Firstly though, I would like to welcome a great bloke and a great friend to the stage. One of our own sons is here today to give a small insight into ''A Trail of the Washington Coat of Arms''. Ladies and Gentlemen I present to you Norman Stocks.' Warm applause greeted Mr Stocks, Jack and Holly amongst them; keen listeners to what he had to say.

'Hey Holly, if Stormin Norman here is a font of knowledge we need to grab him for a chat.'

'Yes, we need all the help we can get at the moment.'

Norman dazzled in an outrageously clean white sweatshirt, emblazoned with a blatant advertisement across the front of it. www.thewashingtontriangle.com.

'Before I start ladies and gentlemen, I would just like to say that my talk today is only the tip of the iceberg. If you like what you hear and you are interested in finding out more, please visit our website.

I'm sure you can read it on the front of my jumper here. It has everything you need to know about Washington and more!'

'We need to check out that website Jack,' Holly said

'I'll have a look on the phone.' He replied.

'I want to start this talk, not at the beginning but at a point of historical significance. This jewel of our history is so overlooked that it is a crime. From there I will take you back to the start and guide you through time.'

'I'm looking forward to seeing what Mr Stocks has up his sleeve here Jack.' Holly said, but Jack's focus was searching for the website on the phone. *Yeah can't wait.* He said under his breath.

'I'm also intrigued to see who my dad has got to stooge for him. He was always getting other people to do his dirty work.' Holly said looking at Jack. He looked up and nudged her.

'I thought you wanted me to look at this website Holly.'

'I do, but can't you multi task?' Jack ignored Holly's sarcasm and looked back down at the phone.

'I have in my possession a Purple Heart that was kindly donated by Senator Natalie.' Norman Stocks proudly announced. Holly stood with her mouth open, looking at Norman. *What did he just say?*' Jack missed it; he was still waiting for the website to load.

'He was awarded this for service to his country. Now, what is so special about this medal of honour I hear you ask? Well this particular medal is only awarded to soldiers who are injured or killed in action against the United States of America. It dates back to 1782 and it bears our coat of arms, the Washington Coat of Arms.' Holly was frozen to the spot, dumbstruck at the words coming from Norman Stocks mouth.

'Tell me you just heard that Jack?' Holly looked on in disbelief at the medal hanging from Norman Stocks hand. Jack was oblivious and getting very irritated that the internet was not connecting. He knew Holly was talking, but no idea what she was saying.

'I am struggling to get a connection to the internet Holly; I will need to try again later.' There was no response. He looked at Holly who was totally mesmerised at the piece of jewellery hanging there.

'Holly, what were you saying?' He asked as he stuffed the phone away.

'My god, I didn't even know my dad had been awarded that medal. I had no idea he was ever injured in battle either, my god.' Holly said transfixed. Jack suddenly joined the party.

'What, what are you talking about?' He grabbed Holly by the arm.

'Are you serious, that medal is your dad's?' Holly looked at Jack.

'Not only is that Purple Heart medal my dad's, it also carries the Washington Coat of Arms.' Jack shook Hollys arm, a bit too rough for her liking.

'Stop it Jack.'

'Who the hell is your dad really Holly?' Holly pulled her arm away from his grip, her face filling with anger.

'Well it looks like I really know doesn't it?' Jack backed off; he knew he was out of line.

'C'mon Holly, I didn't mean it like that.'

'Sshhh Jack, we are missing his talk.'

'The original Purple Heart was designated as a Badge of Military Merit and was established by the man himself George Washington. At that time he was Commander in Chief. This medal was only awarded to three war soldiers by General George Washington himself, but he went on to authorise his subordinate officers to issue them as appropriate. The legend of the Purple Heart grew over the years. Although it was never abolished as such, it was not proposed again officially until after The Great War. After I finish my talk I will put the medal in this display cabinet to my right where everyone can take a look. You will also notice the outline of George Washington himself on that medal.'

Holly looked down at the grass on the floor, a sense of guilt surrounding her.

'Maybe I have been a bit too hard on my dad.' Jack offered a sympathetic look and took Holly's hand. Holly was still focused on the talk.

'Now ladies and gentlemen I would like to move on to the Trail of the Washington Coat of Arms. Danni Grundy and I started **thewashingtontriangle.com** website originally to offer people the chance to follow us on the trail. I know it's a bit of blatant self-advertising, but we do have great fun doing them.' Norman pointed to the website address on his jumper once more.

'You can view the tour details on our website along with a host of memorabilia that you can buy.'

'He certainly sells his product well I will give him that.' Jack said looking around the marquee. He noticed the juggling fire master had entered the great tent. *Don't tell me the fire juggler is going on this stage now.* As his eyes followed him something twigged deep into the depths of his mind. *Wait a minute! We have been looking at this all wrong. The zodiac signs, they are fire signs, they must be. I need to speak with the Oracle again.*

'Holly, I will be back in a minute.' Jack shot off outside, away from the hustle and bustle to make the call. Norman Stocks was now in full swing on stage.

'1183 is the date you should concern yourself with ladies and gentlemen. That is when our history can be truly identified. A mere twelve hundred metres from where we stand is our true birthplace, Washington Old Hall. Our National Trust has done a magnificent job in holding its authenticity and heritage. The Trail of the Washington Coat of Arms starts right on that doorstep. We gladly display the Star Spangled banner there and why do we do that? Because it's ours, yes that's right, ours.' He paused for breath and then continued.

'Our coat of arms, The Washington Coat of Arms was carried through time. The mullet and bars as it were, or to give it the more up to date name, the stars and stripes! This bore the basis for the American flag.' Danni waved over to Norman and pointed to his watch. Norman acknowledged his friend. He had a habit of getting a bit too excited and overrunning his slots.

'I am being told to wrap up ladies and gentlemen so please go to our website www.thewashingtontriangle.com to find out more or come and join us on a tour. Thank you for listening, my name is Norman Stocks.' A roaring round of applause was a fitting send off to Mr Stock's passionate talk.

Holly looked around for Jack but the thick cream drapes around the marquee had him hidden well out of sight. Danni Grundy had made his way back to the stage.

'One more round of applause for Norman please, great guy, be sure to check out the website. Now, as I mentioned before we have a very special guest about to join us on stage.' Holly kept looking around for Jack. *Where is he?*

Jack pressed call on the phone.

'Oracle, listen I need you to do me a favour. Pull up a map of Europe on your computer.'

'Why?' He replied.

'Look, I don't have much time, are you going to help or not?' Jack snapped.

'Of course, keep your hair on. Ok go ahead, map of Europe displayed.'

'Great, I want you to plot three cities, Oslo, Madrid and Reykjavik. Once you have done that put a line to each so you have a triangle, then tell me what sit's in the middle of it.' The Oracle murmured away in the background before confirming his answer.

'Ok, so I have put a point at Oslo, another.' Jack cut in abruptly.

'Just tell me what you see in the middle of the damn triangle.'

'Jesus, you are such a bad tempered boy Jack. Scotland, that's what sit's bang in the middle of the triangle.'

'I knew it.' Jack said.

'But this has nothing to do with The Washington Triangle Jack.' The Oracle said, dismissive towards Jacks insight.

'Thanks for your help, but I need to go, I may call again.'

'Can't wait, my dear boy.' *So rude that man.*

'Ladies and gentlemen please welcome on stage to collect the Honorary Doctorate award on behalf of Senator Natalie, his daughter Holly.' A warm round of applause swept around the marquee. Holly was shocked, she looked around for Jack.

'C'mon up Holly the stage is yours.' Danni was looking around waiting for someone to climb the three steps up to the stage.

'Put him on the phone.' Bridie announced to Yuri's stand in.

'Yes, what is it.' Heenan bellowed.

'I have my team in place, we will have them shortly.' Bridie announced.

'Where are they?'

'They are staying at the Marriot hotel in Sunderland, North East England. We are waiting for them to come back; we have checked their rooms, only one change of clothes in the wardrobes confirms it is them.'

'Good work Bridie, I knew I could rely on you.'

'Of course, I will be in touch soon.'

Standing in utter shock as he stared up at the stage was Jack. He could not believe what he was looking at. There was his sidekick Holly collecting the Honorary Doctorate on behalf of her dad. *How did he know we are in this marque? We must have been followed, that is the only answer.*

Handshakes by several people took place before Holly climbed back down the three steps. The obligatory official photographs were snapped by the appointed Washington Festival photographer along with media representatives from the Sunderland Echo and Newcastle Chronicle newspapers, along with hundreds of onlookers. *What are you doing Holly; these photos are going to be on the internet shortly.* Jack was rattled, he knew Holly had been romanced into accepting the award, a mixture of that and the guilt she now felt had summoned her up there, even though she knew it would put them in instant danger.

Jack ran over and collected Holly as she came back down the steps. He squeezed her hand and yanked her along towards the exit. Holly looked around at the masses of smiles focused on her, Honorary Doctorate in one hand, outstretched arm with Jack's clamped hand in the other.

'We have to get out of here Holly.' Jack's tone was definite and eager.

'Sorry Jack, I don't know what came over me there, one minute you were talking to me about something and the next I was on stage with everyone clapping and cheering.'

'Snap out of it Holly we are being followed, how else could your dad know where we were at that exact minute?' Jack pulled Holly harder.

'Jack your hurting me, stop!' He stopped, not because he was hurting Holly, but to convince her that he was protecting her.

'Jesus Holly, don't you get it? Me hurting your precious arm should be the least of your worries. We could be killed at any minute.' Holly was angry, she retaliated.

'My dad would never hurt me Jack, how dare you.' Jack raised his voice even louder and shouted in her face; scores of people now watching.

'For the love of god Holly it's not your dad that I am worried about, it is that lunatic Folis Heenan. If your dad knows we are here then I'm damn sure Heenan will, or at least he will soon when your face is splattered all over the papers.' Silence fell on the marquee. Holly looked deep into Jack's eyes, she leaned her head into his shoulder.

'I am really sorry Jack.' Jack lifted her head back up to look at her eyes.

'It's ok Holly; this has been intense for both of us.'

'Where did you go anyway?' Holly asked quietly. Jack smiled.

'I have worked out what the zodiac signs represent and what relation the cities have to the puzzle.

'My, you have been a busy boy Jack.' She said as she rubbed his face.

'We really need to get out of here right now Holly. Washington Old Hall is just down the road. Let's run down there and I will tell you all about it.'

Chapter 46

Majestic, quite majestic, was the first thought from Holly as they approached the entrance to Washington Old Hall. Jack reduced the pace from a jog, to a slow walk. He double-checked behind them, that they were not being followed. They finally stopped at the entrance, to take in the significance of where they were and what they were looking at. British and American national flags fluttered side by side above them. They were breathing heavy from the swift run down Spout Lane to the village. Holly took a breath, a smile appeared from within.

'Could this really be the start of our history Jack?' Her focus remained on the stone structure begging them to go inside. The two entrance pillars framed the view to the west side of the building. Jack turned and looked at her; he could sense the bond that Holly had instantly struck up, with the old fella she stared at. *Mythical and mysterious* she thought.

'This is the ancestral home of arguably the most significant person in American history. George Washington's family can be traced back to this very building Jack, how cool is that? Jack looked up at the climbing hydrangea that covered the great chimney breast. Holly was still lost in its spell.

'They took their name from this manor house; they created a coat of arms from here, carried it through time and put it on my dad's Purple Heart. It is the basis of our national flag; our capital city is named after it.' Jack burst out laughing.

'You sound like the Oracle.' Holly looked at him and smiled.

'Seriously though Jack, we are well educated people, how are we not told about this at school?' Jack looked up at the stone beauty.

'C'mon, let's go in, I want to know all about what you have found out about the fax.' As they walked up the entrance path a small party of students were starting a tour of the grounds. The guide was dressed up in clothes from back in the day, a sea of dirty red, white and blue adding to the theatre of the experience. As the guide addressed his little party he pointed to the Stars and Stripes above him.

'In the words of President Jimmy Carter when he arrived here in 1977 'HA'WAY THE LADS.' Those were the first words he spoke to the people here in the North East, as he stood and addressed them at Newcastle civic centre.'

'Jack, do you remember the Oracle said something like Carter had a message for here, or brought a message here, or had something to do with this? Why don't you call him and ask?'

'Once we get sorted I will, I have already spoken to him.'

'You have, when?'

Jack ushered Holly to a table in the grounds of the garden, he looked around again checking that the coast was clear.

'Take a seat Holly; I want to explain what I have found out.' Jack pulled back his seat, took one last scan around and joined her, sitting at the table.

'The common theme in all this has been a triangle, triangle this, triangle that.' Holly nodded, an obvious statement, what could come of that she thought.

'I called the Oracle and asked him to plot a triangle from each point of the cities on the fax and tell me what was in the middle of it, guess what it was?'

'Washington, here?' Holly replied with great excitement. *That is why he has dragged me here.*

'Scotland.' Jack said staring at Holly. She turned her head away in confusion.

'I don't understand the connection with Scotland. That has never even come into any equation so far.' Jack raised a finger; looked around once more and then whispered to Holly.

'Remember that nutcase juggling the fire sticks?'

'Yes, but why are you whispering?' Jack rolled his head, a drum roll echoed in his brain.

'Because my dear Holly, I have cracked most of the code.' Jack sat back and milked his moment. Holly jumped up from her seat, a burst of adrenalin screamed through her veins.

'I've got it Jack, Burns!' She punched the air and set Jack up for a high five, he was having none of it.

'Sit down Holly, someone might recognise you.' *Fire signs, you get burnt from fire, Scotland in the centre of the triangle of cities. Robert was the name we deciphered from the number sequence, bloody Burns, Scotland, Robert bloody Burns from Scotland.'* Holly repeated the words to herself. Jack looked about in a mild panic.

'Let's get inside; we need to work out the last part, but with what we know now we can surely do this Holly.' Holly leaned forward and kissed Jack smack on the lips. The master had been mastered, his love of control swept out over the garden that surrounded him.

Chapter 47

Bridie sat staring out of the great windows of Fat Buddha, legs crossed, eyes fixed, flat white coffee in hand. The North Sea in front of her was rough today, menacing. White horses rallied at a relentless pace to lavishly crash into the sea wall. Seagulls swarmed the skies, looking for any scraps of fish and chips, dropped by the throngs of people that had previously queued up at Minchellas and Queens Cafe to indulge in their seaside treat.

Fifteen minutes had passed since Bridie was made aware that Holly had been spotted on local social media sites at the Washington Heritage Festival. She had demanded answers.

If Bridie's looks and height were not enough for her to stand out from the crowd, then her bright red lipstick was. That splash of colour became even more striking, against the backdrop of her brilliant white cat suit, silk scarf and knee length boots.

He approached Bridie from behind, his black leather jacket fully zipped up. His peaky white bald head was overshadowed by the tattoo on his neck, two doves kissing, not the average tattoo for a great hulk of a man with shovels for hands.

'I have an update for you.' Yannis whispered.

'I'm listening.'

'They have been spotted entering Washington Old Hall. Yuri, Seth and Yogi are on their way.'

'Find them, but do not apprehend them. Get Yuri to place a listening device on them. I want to know what they are saying and get me his frequency, so I can listen in.' Yannis nodded and then retreated outside to make the call.

Bridie picked up her coffee cup, eyes fixed on the crashing waves. She took the smallest of sips, as large spots of rain began to appear on the window. She put her cup down and looked skywards. *Get me out of this country.*

Chapter 48

139-1319-1320-1411.
194-1913-219-2124-2211-237.
264-265-2612-2613-278-2716.
295-296-3314-3417-359-3510.

That is all that stood between Jack and Holly cracking the codes and locating the *Document of Truth*.

They had found a little corner inside, calmness had settled upon them, a renewed desire to finish, what they had been ordered to start. A crack of thunder whiplashed high above, was it George Washington's ancestors talking to them? Jack wondered. As Jack glanced through the window; a beam of white light appeared from nowhere, split off into the sky and then disappeared as quickly as it arrived. The dangling ornate glass lamp shade twisted around, reflecting pearl shaped shadows.

Jack looked at Holly expecting to see a hint of fear; there was none, she had slowly reduced her heart rate, a technique taught by grandpa. He watched as she took a large intake of breath and then closed her eyes. She sat silent; eyes closed and then bowed her head. She rested her palms against her knees, she wanted to visit grandpa, he would know. *Grandpa, I need your help, give me a sign, show me the way, let me hear your voice.* Jack looked at Holly. *What is she doing, has she fallen asleep?* He nudged her gently; not wanting any more unwanted attention being drawn to them. He could hear Holly murmuring to herself.

'Holly, wake up, you're dreaming.' There was no response. Jack nudged harder.

'Holly you're dreaming, wake up.' Holly jumped back on her seat, her eyes sparked open.

'What, what did you just say there Jack?'

'Keep your voice down, I said you were dreaming.'

'That's it, it must be.'

'What is, what are you talking about?' Holly pointed to the cell phone.

'Look up any reference to Robert Burns that you can find to do with dreaming.' Jack shrugged his shoulders, but one look into Holly's eyes and he knew she was serious.

'Holly, you're not making any sense.'

'Just do it Jack. I asked grandpa for a sign and he has sent me one. You said I was dreaming, right?' Jack shook his head in disbelief.

'Really Holly, is this what it has come to?'

'Give me the phone and I will do it myself.' Holly was furious, she lunged for the phone, but Jack pulled it back and she missed her chance.

'Ok, ok Jesus calm down, I will do it.' Another flash of lightning, this time it appeared to have come from a different direction. Rain began to stream down the glass panes, the sky had turned from grey to black in minutes.

'Looks like it's in for the day this weather.' The stranger said, as he leaned on Holly's shoulder, looking out of the window. Holly twisted in fright. *Jesus, where did he come from*?

'I'm sorry madam; I did not mean to frighten you, please accept my apologies.' Holly took a second to think. *A fellow American, he must be harmless, it's that Russian fella that is after us.* The stranger smiled and then wished them a good day. The bug was planted, a neat manoeuvre, one done many times before, just under the neckline, attached to the inside of her top.

'Excuse me.' Jack had a question for the stranger. He stopped and looked around; he smiled at Jack, confident and manly.

'Yeah, what is it?' The stranger put one hand in his pocket and the other behind his back, sliding his hand around his gun that was tucked in his belt. He cocked it slowly and quietly.

'Which part of the States do you herald from and what brings you to these parts?' Jack had noticed his watch, a Rolex, limited edition. It seemed out of place with his green combat pants and green sweater. The stranger slid the gun out of his belt and let his hand dangle free behind his back. A voice appeared into his hidden earpiece. ***They are not to be harmed, repeat, they are not to be harmed, put away your gun and exit immediately and that is an order.*** Yuri had eyes on Seth through his single lens camera, his orders were clear, their orders were clear.

'I am actually from Canada.' Seth replied, as he wiped a drop of rain from his nose with his sleeve. A nose that was bull shaped, flattened from years of amateur boxing.

'My dad is from Utah, I have a mix of accents, he was in the forces, and we travelled a lot. Anyway gotta go.' He slickly housed his gun and spun around to walk off.

'You never said what you were doing in these parts?' Jack's pressing question was ignored by Seth as he strode off.

'Jack, leave the guy alone and look up 'dreaming' as a reference to Robert Burns.'

'Inform Bridie we have ears, switch to frequency 410-430 MHz.'
'Roger that.'

'I don't believe it, I take it all back Holly.' Jack was flabbergasted. *It's surely a coincidence.*

'What is it Jack, tell me?'

'It appears your grandpa has indeed spoken to you. Robert Burns wrote a poem called *'A Dream'.' Thank you, grandpa.* Jack read out what his Google search had uncovered.

'It says here that on reading in the public papers, the Laureate's Ode, with the other parade of June 4th, 1786, the Author was no sooner dropt asleep, than he imagined himself transported to the Birth-day Levee: and, in his dreaming fancy, made the following Address in 1786:

'Are you getting this Bridie?'
'Yes, be quiet.'

Holly closed her eyes once more. *Hi grandpa, I need one last thing from you, let me see how to attach these sets of numbers to reveal the last piece in the jigsaw.* Jack was silent this time, grandpa was silent, Holly was silent, nothing. She opened her eyes in disappointment.

'I need the bathroom Jack, back in a second.'

'You want me to come with you?'

'Noooo, don't be silly.' It was a genuine question, not understood. Jack's previous sarcasm and smugness had overshadowed the intent on this occasion. Holly stood and rattled through her bag; she pulled out the trusty pen and an unused piece of paper and put it in front of him.

'Do me a favour Jack; write out the first verse of the poem, I need to see it in 3D so to speak.' Jack nodded, still in semi-serious mode.

'Ok Holly, sure thing.'

Holly sat on the toilet, rocking gently back and forward talking to herself. A strike of lightning flashed through the window, but it was not even enough to break Holly's concentration. *Ok Mr President, Mr General George Washington, Mr Commander in Chief. What is it you have hidden in that poem? Talk to me I'm here to help.*

Jack watched as Holly walked back to the table. He smiled and pointed to the paper.

'The first verse of the poem is there Holly, good luck.'

Guid-Mornin' to our Majesty!
May Heaven augment your blisses
On ev'ry new birth-day ye see,
A humble poet wishes,
My bardship here, at your Levee
On sic a day as this is,
Is sure an uncouth sight to see,
Amang thae birth-day dresses
Sae fine this day.

'Make sense of that what you can Holly, it is double Dutch to me.' Holly rolled her finger over the paper; she wanted to touch the words, to absorb their meaning. Jack pointed to the fax.

'The numbers don't run in order, they don't represent a sequence, but yet they have a meaning. They have a three and four number flow run to them.' Holly squeezed her eyes and tapped her fingers on her forehead. *Think Holly, think.* She stopped and looked at Jack.

'What did you just say there Jack? Repeat what you just said.'

'Erm, the numbers don't run in order and don't represent a sequence.'

'No, the second bit you just said.' Jack took a second to think.

'That they have a meaning and have a three and four number flow run to them.'

'Yes, they do have a meaning Jack, you're right and they do have a flow. It is not what is said in the poem as such, it is the flow of the poem and number that represent the flow.'

'I know it was me that said it Holly, but you have lost me.'

'Ok, break down the flow, make it as small as you can, strip it back and what do you get?'

'If you strip it that far back there will be no poem left, no meaning, just letters.' Holly beamed, her green eyes lighting up the ever darkening room.

'Exactly Jack, letters, the letters are the meaning, they must be. These blocks of three and four numbers represent the letters and the run of number blocks represent a word, I am certain of it.' Holly placed her hand gently on Jack's arm.

'The last game I played with my grandpa before he died was a basic word search. It was just a bit of fun to pass the time away. We would photocopy one from a book and see who could do it the quickest. Well I won by a couple of seconds and I was in the middle of ribbing him, when he came out with a pearl of wisdom.'

'What did he say?' Holly rubbed Jack's arm gently.

'He said, it's good to win my dear, but can you name those twenty one words that you have just found and do it in alphabetical order like I can? I was dumbfounded, I thought to myself, how on earth he could have possibly remembered all those words, let alone in alphabetical order.' Jack was drawn in, the answer was close.

'How did he do it?' Holly let go of his arm and sat back for the reveal.

'He didn't.'

'He didn't?' Jack was confused.

'No he didn't, he did it to teach me a lesson, but, he let me think he could do it, he played a trick on me.' The penny was not dropping with Jack, he shook his head.

'Nope, still don't get it.'

'He gave me a fresh word search puzzle and said I had an extra one minute to do it again. This time though, I was to turn the page over and recite the words in alphabetical order. Obviously I tried and failed miserably. Grandpa burst out laughing at me; gave me a great big hug, squeezed me so tight and told me he was only joking, he whispered in my ear. "My darling Holly, when you make fun of the opposition, you will never see what is hidden in front of you, be it a letter, a number, a word or a collection of them."

'That is all very interesting Holly, but I hope there is a moral to this story?'

'Look at the first set of numbers here Jack. Holly underlined the numbers with her finger. *139-1319-1320-1411.*

'The moral of the story is that it is a collection of the above. I will bet my bottom dollar that the first number in the block relates to the verse within the poem. The second will relate to the line of that verse and the third and fourth numbers will relate to the letter on that line.' Jack interrupted.

'So if we take the first block, number 139. You are saying that 1 is verse 1 of the poem and then the number 3 is line 3 of the first verse?'

'That is exactly what I'm saying Jack.'

'We are then left with the number 9 and that must represent letter 9 on the 3rd line of the 1st verse. You then do the same with 1319-1320-1411 and that gives you a word. You then do the same with the other blocks of numbers and you end up with four words.' Holly clapped to herself, a small display of satisfaction.

'And those four words will give us the location of the *Document of Truth.*' Jack said, the penny well and truly dropping now.

'Write down the first three verses of the poem together please Jack.'

'Done, here we go Holly.'

Guid-Mornin' to our Majesty!
May Heaven augment your blisses
On ev'ry new birth-day ye see,
A humble poet wishes.
My bardship here, at your Levee
On sic a day as this is,

Is sure an uncouth sight to see,
Amang thae birth-day dresses
Sae fine this day.

I see ye're complimented thrang,
By mony a lord an' lady;
"God save the King" 's a cuckoo sang
That's unco easy said aye:
The poets, too, a venal gang,
Wi' rhymes weel-turn'd an' ready,
Wad gar you trow ye ne'er do wrang,
But aye unerring steady,
On sic a day.

For me! before a monarch's face
Ev'n there I winna flatter;
For neither pension, post, nor place,
Am I your humble debtor:
So, nae reflection on your Grace,
Your Kingship to bespatter;
There's mony waur been o' the race,
And aiblins ane been better
Than you this day.

Jack and Holly jumped up in unison, embracing each other, dancing up and down like a pair of hyper children, overdosed on E numbers and lost in the moment. They had cracked the code and found the location of the *Document of Truth*!

$139 = W \ 1319 = E \ 1320 = S \ 1411 = T$ WEST

$194 = F1913 = A219 = C2124 = A2211 = D237 = E$ FACADE

$264 = H265 = Y2612 = L2613 = T278 = O2716 = N$ HYLTON

$295 = C296 = A3314 = S3417 = T359 = L3510 = E$ CASTLE

'Did anyone make out the location?' Bridie asked, still listening to the shrieks over the radio.

'No location was given, they just spelled out letters.' Yuri replied. Bridie raged back, her tone screeching.

'Did anyone bother to write the letters down?' Radio silence followed as Seth, Yogi and Yuri looked at each other.

'You fools, do I have to hold your hands for you?' Bridie ranted. Yogi had heard enough from the walking wardrobe, his pet name for Bridie.

'Hey lady, I don't know who the hell you think you're talking to, but you heard the same as us.' Bridie's response was ice cold.

'I am the lady that decides if you live or die sweet pea. Speak to me again like that and you will have made my mind up for me, capeesh?' Yogi bit his lip, screwed his face up and spoke through gritted teeth.

'Yeah sorry, no offence lady.'

'Follow them and keep the radio open. Is that clear enough for you to understand?'

'Yeah, sure.'

Chapter 49

It was less than four miles to Hylton Castle, the final resting place of the *Document of Truth*. The taxi journey was quick and Penshaw Monument was on view to them for the most of the journey. Was it keeping an eye on them Holly wondered?

They were on the verge of finding the most important document ever written affecting American history. That would be their ultimate prize, but could that prize prove that the Constitution was faked? Could it be the downfall of America as a superpower?

Bridie had ordered a *watch only* operation until she gave the word to go in. She wanted hard evidence that the *Document of Truth* was buried there.

It was just like Jack and Holly had imagined it to be. Originally built of wood around 1066, the modern day stone beauty still carried over 600 hundred years of memories.

'Isn't it just beautiful Jack?'

'It is Holly and I bet this baby could tell a few tales.'

'Is everyone in place?' Bridie asked

'Yes, we are good to go on your say so, digging equipment at the ready.'

'Remember nobody touches either of them until I say.'

'Roger that.'

As the taxi pulled away from the entrance to Hylton Castle, Jack and Holly walked up to the information board. They studied the map of the castle and all its markings, along with a huge timeline of the history, displayed in full colour on six foot boards.

'There it is Holly.' Jack said, pointing to the map.

'The Washington Coat of Arms, above the entrance on the west facade. We are stepping on the toes of history by walking through these gates.' Jack sounded nervous for the first time. Holly turned and faced him; she stroked his face, wiping away a few raindrops. The thunder and lightning had moved on, but the rain on its tail was only beginning to slow down.

'Don't worry Jack, I will look after you.'

'I never know which Holly is going to turn up to these mini adventures; you have a habit of surprising me.' Holly smiled at Jack's comment.

'Funny, my grandpa said that to me once.' Jack nodded for Holly to walk in through the gates. There was no fanfare, no drawbridge to lift, just a handful of people walking the grounds in the rain.

'It is very quiet here Jack.'

'Who goes out in this weather Holly? You need to be crazy.' Suddenly there was a great roar in the distance, they both stopped in their tracks.

'What was that Jack?'

'I don't know, it sounded like a rush of voices.'

A couple leaving the castle overheard their question and the man was happy to give them the answer.

'Sunderland has just scored, that's what the noise was pet, the stadium is just along the road. That's why it's quiet around here, everyone is at the match.'

'A soccer match?' Jack questioned.

'No man, a footie match, football, not soccer.' The man said playfully. He pointed at Jack.

'You should have a proper coat on man; you'll catch your death in this weather.' Jack smiled, nodded his acceptance of the local man's comments and walked on. *Another Martian.* As Jack and Holly gracefully moved on, the man shouted skywards. *HA'WAY THE LADS.*

'Did you hear what he just shouted there Jack?'

'It sounded like 'away lats' or something like that. Might be the team they are playing, who knows?'

'Everyone be ready to move on my order.' Bridie instructed.

'Roger that.'

'Jesus, she likes the sound of her own voice.' Seth whispered to Yogi off radio.

There it was in all its glory, the Washington Coat of Arms carved into the stonework hundreds of years ago. They both looked up at it; one of many that adorned the west facade. *Was this an old meeting place?* Jack thought. He turned around and looked at the two areas of grass in front of the west facade.

'Well Holly, any ideas which one it is buried in?'

'As it happens I do, it will be in that one.'

'Can you see where she is pointing to?' Bridie asked.

'No, she had her back to us, sorry.'

'Damn it, one of you get in there and find out.'

'Roger that.' Seth climbed out of the van and ran around the far side of the castle. He jumped over the perimeter fence and made his way to the side of the castle to get his eyes on the prize.

'I have a visual, repeat I have a visual.'

'What's happening, which grass area are they looking at?' Bridie demanded. Another great roar in the distance could be clearly heard.

'Sunderland has scored again by the sounds of it.' Jack said, as they both looked in the direction of the noise. Holly looked back at the castle and caught sight of something that disturbed her, she screamed and grabbed Jack.

'Jack, it's the man from the Washington Old Hall, over there, watching us.'

'C'mon Holly run.' Jack grabbed Holly's hand and ran across the car park to the exit. A van outside swung around and raced to block their exit. Yogi and Yuri jumped out of the van and ran to the gates. Jack looked for another route.

'Up the hill Holly, run, I will stay here.'

'No Jack, they will kill you.' Jack pushed Holly away as he faced the oncoming pair.

'Just go Holly.' He shouted, as he took up his boxing stance. Holly ran, getting a head start. Jack squared up to Yogi and Yuri as they ran through the gates. Yogi swung his rifle around and hit Jack on the side of the forehead with the butt of it. Jack fell to the floor, Yogi stood over him, he was not getting up, he was out cold on the tarmac.

Holly slipped on the wet grass, as she ran up the hill. She looked around to see Jack lying on the ground. *Jack, no.* She jumped back to her feet, only to see Seth standing in front of her, his gun pointed at her head. A young family ran away into the field behind the castle when they saw Seth with his gun. An elderly man shouted at Seth from a distance.

'I will call the police.' Seth fired a warning shot in the air and the man scuttled off in terror. Seth grabbed Holly by the arm.

'You're coming with me.' Holly resisted, her arms flying about. She caught Seth with a soft punch to the side of the head. Seth swung Holly round and head butted her, knocking her unconscious to the floor. He picked her up, put her over his shoulder in a fireman's lift and ran towards the van.

'Get Jack in the back of the van.' Yuri ordered Yogi. 'We are compromised here; we can come back when it's dark.'

'*Can't you idiots do anything without attracting attention to yourselves?*' Bridie raged. *No wonder Heenan treats him like a dog. She thought to herself.*

'*We will be back in three hours when it's dark and dig for the box, I'll handle it.*' Yuri replied, as he jumped back into the van.

'*You had better hope that the box is there when you do, or I will have 2 million reasons to put you in that hole.*' Bridie threatened.

Chapter 50

Handcuffed and feeling sick as he regained consciousness, Jack's concern was for Holly, not himself. They had been given a sedative by Yuri that rendered them lifeless since their capture. Jack rolled onto his side, but could not make out the person lying next to him. The body was warm, they were alive. *Is that you Holly?*

A small orange glow from a street light in the distance was enough for Jack to know that there was life outside. They were gagged, hands and legs tied together. Jack's right eye was badly cut; blood that had spilled out of it had dried down the side of his face.

Yuri had hidden the van in Cranberry Road, amongst a residential housing estate close by the castle.

'It's time, let's go.' Yuri commanded Seth. The van pulled away and turned left into Craigavon road, twenty seconds later they were turning right into Hylton Castle. Seth jumped out of the van, bolt cutter in hand. The lumpy chain that wrapped around the iron gates was cut off easily. Seth pushed the gates open, one at a time.

Jack was talking to Holly, not that she could make out anything that he was saying through his gag. *Don't worry, I will work something out.*

The van pulled into the car park, drove around the back and out of sight. Seth closed the gates and ran towards the castle.

'Get them out.' Yuri ordered Yogi. *I'm alive.* Was Holly's first thought, as the doors to the back of the van were opened. The moon was in view, along with the street lights on Washington Road. It was very quiet; the odd vehicle in the distance was the only distraction. The air had cooled several degrees, the grass still wet. Jack looked at Holly. *Don't be scared, I will protect you.* Holly was dazed, petrified and cold.

'Untie their legs.' Yuri ordered.

Jack and Holly were marched in front of the castle. They were put in exactly the same spot where they had been discussing the location of the *Document of Truth*. Seth lifted his gun and pointed it at Holly's head.

'Tell me where this box is Jack, or I will blow her brains out.'
Holly screamed into her gag, closed her eyes, her breathing
accelerated rapidly. *Don't tell him Jack.* Her muffled terror was hidden
behind her gag. *Look at me Holly, look at me.* Jack shook his head in
defiance. Seth was chillingly calm; he cocked his gun and began to
count down. Holly was shaking her head. *Jack, don't do it.*

'Five, four, three, two…' Jack looked up to the sky then pointed his
arms to a patch of grass.

'Just in the nick of time, yee har.' Seth yelled, his celebratory tone
echoing around the grounds.

'Dig up this grass and find me that box.' Yuri demanded. Holly
looked at Jack, her eyes filled with tears. Jack's head was bowed, he
was defeated. Yuri took out a cell phone from his pocket and called
Bridie. She had now settled for the night on-board a superyacht, a few
hundred metres into the North Sea off South Shields, seven miles
along the coast from Sunderland.

'We have the location and the dig has started, I will call you when
we have found it.' Bridie was peaceful, glass of champagne in hand,
looking back at the twinkling lights along the coastline.

'Good boy, I will be waiting for your call.'

The recent days of rain had softened the ground. The hole had
reached nearly a metre deep, but still nothing. Seth was starting to lose
his cool, his ten minute digging stint over for now. He climbed out of
the hole and pulled the gag from Jack's mouth. Jack immediately
gasped for air and spat the dirt back out from Seth's hands. Seth
grabbed him by the throat and then pointed his gun at Holly. He thrust
his head into Jack's face, his anger building, he wanted his money.

'If you're lying to me I am going to kill her first and then I am
going to torture you, just for the fun of it. Now, this is your last
chance, where is the box?' Jack's head dropped, his eyes rolled, he
needed air.

'Seth.' Yogi shouted up from the hole.

'What is it?'

'I have found something, get yourself in here.'

'Yuri, shine that torch over here.' Yogi shouted. Jack and Holly
stood looking into the hole, the darkness offered them nothing. Seth
started to shuffle dirt to the side; he could feel something cold and flat.
He ran his fingers over the surface; it was bumpy in the middle.

'There is something here, shine that torch on my hands.' He shouted. Yuri moved the light of the torch to exactly where Seth had his hands. Seth dusted off the last bits of soil. As the torch light illuminated the object, jubilation set in for the treasure hunters, their prize awaits. Holly dropped to her knees, they had come so close. She knew her life was over, Jack's life was over. She wondered in that moment about her dad. His Purple Heart, his war wound, so many regrets flooded her mind. She sat looking at the dirty box. The dirty box that had the Washington Coat of Arms clearly visible on the top of it. She looked up at Jack and nodded, a nod of rejection, of failure, of history being hijacked. Seth turned away and called Bridie, his excitement uncontained.

'We have bloody found it; we have only bloody found it.'

'Great job, really great job.' Kill them both and bring it to me straight away.'

Holly wept, the tears flowed. *I am sorry grandpa, I have let you down, but it looks like I will be with you in heaven soon, I love you grandpa.* Suddenly, the torch light disappeared as Yuri fell, face down into the hole. Seth was next, knocking the box back into the hole. Jack dived down and knocked Holly to the floor and positioned himself on top of her. They could here bullets whizzing past, but could not make out where they were coming from. Yogi jumped back into the hole and recovered the box, only to instantly take a shot to the head. He fell backwards, the box still cradled in his arms.

Holly could feel the fear in Jack. They could hear footsteps crunching against the tarmac approaching their position. *It was pitch black, maybe they couldn't be seen now?* Jack hoped. Jack rolled Holly into the hole and then followed for cover.

They huddled up close, the footsteps getting closer. A figure stood over the hole, too dark for Jack or Holly to see. Jack could just make out the shadow of his night vision goggles from the moonlight.

'Hello Holly, I see you've been busy.' *That voice is familiar, Max?*

'Your dad is worried about you; let's get you out of there.' *Max, it's really you, thank God, we're safe.* Holly mumbled into her gag. Max lifted Holly out of the hole, took her gag off and cut off her hand ties. She yelled out, as she squeezed the life out of Max with joy.

'Max, thank you, thank you, thank you.'

'It's your dad you have to thank.' Max replied, smiling through the darkness at Holly. *Hello, what about me?* Jack muttered to himself.

'Oh God, Jack I'm sorry, Max help me with Jack.' Holly said. They lifted Jack out; Holly took off his gag as Max untied him. Holly and Jack embraced, they were dirty, smelly and wet, but they were together and they were alive. Max slapped Jack on the arm.

'Well done big fella; thank you for keeping her alive long enough for me to rescue you.'

'Hey, thanks man, they would have killed us, you saved our lives, seriously man, I'm in your debt.'

'C'mon Jack, man up, you have your girl here to protect.' Holly threw her arms around Max once more and leaned into him.

'Thanks Max.' She spoke quietly into his chest.

'Right, let's get the hell out of here guys, I have a car outside. Max lifted his rifle over his shoulder and showed them the way.

'Hey Holly, aren't we forgetting something?' Jack jumped back into the hole and grabbed the box from the arms of the dead Yogi. Max looked around, shining his torch on Jack. *Now that's Karma, that's for my men you killed in Panama Yogi, you scumbag!*

'I thought we were going to die Holly.'

'Me too Jack.'

'Kinda makes you think about stuff.'

'What kinda stuff.'

'You know, like what's inside the box.' Jack joked. Holly slapped him on the arm.

'That bang to the head sure did nothing to help your sense of humour I see.'

'There is something rattling inside the box when you shake it.' Jack said as they ran.

'Be careful Jack that is the *Document of Truth* in there.'

Max waited for the automatic barrier to lift at the Marriot Hotel.

'How did you know we were staying here Max?' Holly asked.

'Your dad told me.' *How does he know?* She asked herself.

'I have some equipment in the trunk that will open the box for you.' Max said.

'We will do it in my room.' Jack offered.

'We need to call Johnson, we never did get a charger for the cell phone.' Holly said.

'After we open the box, I'll go to the bar, see if anyone can help us out with a charger for it.' Jack put his hand in one of his pockets, looking for the cell phone, he double, then triple checked all his pockets.

'Jesus Holly, Johnson's cell phone is missing; I must have dropped it when I was in the hole at the castle.' Jack declared.

'Look Jack, don't beat yourself up about that now, we are alive, that is all I care about to be honest.'

The three of them walked into the warm and welcome lit foyer of the Sunderland Marriot Hotel. Shoreen was on duty. *Doesn't she have a home to go to?* Holly thought. Jack waved as they took the stairs. Shoreen waved back. *What have they been doing, they are filthy?*

They stood staring over the lead box that was sat on Jack's double bed. Max removed a pad saw from his tool kit and began to cut it open. Once he had sliced it all the way around he stood back.

'It is all yours guys, knock yourselves out.' He said.

'That would be the second time today!' Jack said.

'Jesus Jack, a time like this and you're still cracking jokes.' Holly laughed. Jack turned and looked at Max, who shrugged his shoulders, his job was done.

'After you Holly, lift the lid.' Holly looked at Jack, his once red blood stained face, now blurred by the dirt.

'Ok, here goes.' She ran her fingers over the coat of arms softly and then put her hands either side of the box. Her fingers gripped the edges; she lifted it up very carefully. She winced as she felt the top come way from the rest of the box. She tilted the lid, so only she could see what was inside. Her pupils burst to life at what she saw.

'Oh my god.'

'Is it the wooden box with the *Document of Truth*?' Jack asked, his words rushed, he needed to know. Holly gently put the lid back down and then turned to Jack.

'What is it Holly, what's inside?' He asked.

'We need to call Walt.'

Chapter 51

Although Walt's number on the piece of paper in Jack's pocket was wet, it was still readable. As the Oracle had not been available to answer, he missed the most important phone call of his life. He had taken himself off to play poker at a friend's house, down in his bunker, with no phone signal. The poker game had no time limit, they played until they dropped and then they slept.

Max handed the cell phone to Holly.

'It's your dad.' Holly took the phone from Max and walked to the bathroom for some privacy.

'Dad?'

'Holly, I'm so sorry my little princess, I'm so glad you are safe.'

'Dad, it's me that should apologise. I have been an idiot and I am so, so sorry.' Her eyes filled with tears.

'I thought I was going to die tonight.'

'Don't be silly Holly your old man wouldn't let that happen to you.' Holly looked in the mirror; she was covered in dirt, but suddenly had never felt so alive.

'Holly, there is something I need to tell you, something I should have told you years ago, but I didn't, only because I wanted to protect you.' Holly could hear her dad's tone drop, she sensed bad news.

'What is it dad, you're scaring me.'

'Max is going to take you to meet someone tomorrow, someone very special.'

'Who dad, what are you talking about?'

'Your Uncle Albert and Aunty Linda.' Holly looked back in the mirror; she put her hand over her mouth, the shock made her tearful again.

'They are alive? They are really alive?'

'Yes Holly, they are alive and well and living close to where you are, in a village called West Rainton, near Durham. The tears began to roll down through the dirt on Holly's face.

'I can't believe they're alive, why have you not told me before?'

'They will explain everything tomorrow, when you see them. Look Holly I have to go, I have an important meeting to attend, I will speak to you soon.'

'Ok.' Holly sniffed back the tears.

'I love you dad, I'm sorry for the past few years.' Holly sobbed.

'It is me that should be sorry, about a lot of things, bye darling.'

'Bye dad.'

Chapter 52

As the electric gates began to open, Holly was transported back in time. Her thoughts raced back to the last time she had seen Albert and Linda. Her 13th birthday party was still etched in the depths of her mind. She was excited, very excited, but she had no idea what her relatives had been up to since that day.

Max pulled on the handbrake and Holly got out of the car. She looked around, something she was programmed to do by Grandpa. She was surprised as two speakers, either side of the house, burst into life. *Happy birthday to you, happy birthday to you, happy birthday dear Holly, happy birthday to you.* Canned applause followed the rendition. *They remembered.* Max pointed Holly to the side of the house; she walked round the garden and down to the rear of the property.

'I'll wait in the car Holly.' Max said. Holly nodded, as he walked back down the garden.

Holly had changed from the wet, dirty attire of the night before. Now blue jeans, her trademark Converse cream trainers, a tan coloured polo neck jumper and a black leather jacket had become her party outfit. Her trusty black leather bag freshly cleaned sat over her shoulder.

Holly had shed a few tears over the last couple of days, tears of fear and tears of joy, now it was tears of wonder. She stood and looked at the table in the middle of the garden, all dressed in red, white and blue bunting, with a stunning three tier chocolate birthday cake in the middle of it. The writing around the side displayed the message. *Happy belated birthday to the most precious child on the planet.* Holly stared at the cake in sheer delight; it brought back so many happy memories.

'I think I have waited long enough for one of your cuddles young lady?'

'Linda!' Holly screamed and then ran to her, nearly knocking her off her feet in the process. As Holly and Linda rocked side to side hugging tighter and tighter, Albert appeared from the conservatory.

'I was going to reply to your message in the *Shout Out* column of the Sunderland Echo, but seeing as you're here, I'll not bother now.' He said, tongue and cheek.

'Uncle Albert.' Holly switched relatives and dived into Albert's chest. Albert held her so tight and kissed the top of her head.

'I think we have some explaining to do Holly.' Albert said. Holly wiped away a tear.

'I think you do.' Holly replied.

'Take a seat my sweetheart; I think you will need one.' Linda said.

As Holly took a seat she got her first real view from the garden. It had an elevated position, overlooking farmland, but positioned there for one special reason. They could see the Angel of the North directly ahead and Penshaw Monument, off to the right. *Was it a lookout?* She thought.

'I gather you have had quite an adventure my princess.' Albert said.

'That is putting it mildly to say the least.'

'Has Jack looked after you well?' *Strange question Linda, what's going on here*?

'Yeah, I have grown to really like him, he has his moments, you know, but yeah, he's cool.' Holly ran out of words, she could sense something was coming her way.

'Holly dear.' Linda said. Holly interrupted immediately.

'Yes.'

'We are not really your Aunty and Uncle.' Linda said.

'What?' Holly never saw that coming, she had thought that maybe, they had been in some kind of trouble and gone into hiding.

'Then who are you?' Holly asked, puzzled at another twist to her past. Albert took Holly by the hand. He leaned into her. He lowered his voice.

'This will come as a bit of a shock to you Holly, but, we are your parents.' Holly shook her head, it was half-hearted.

'No, this is not possible; I spoke to my father last night.' Holly pulled her hands away from Albert and looked away, the hurt, the confusion and the lies. Linda pulled her chair around next to Holly and put her arm around her.

'We had no choice Holly. Not long after you were born, the operation we run here was compromised. Cracks started to appear after Carter's visit in 1977 and over the next few years it just got worse. Our lives were in danger; we could not take the chance that you would get caught up in it.'

'Where does dad, err Senator Natalie, I don't even know what to call him now. Where does he come into it?'

'He is still your dad princess.' Albert said. Linda continued.

Senator Natalie is a wonderful man, a great leader and his commitment to you is absolute.'

'But who is he?' Holly said, now shedding tears of bewilderment. Linda looked at Albert. *Your turn dear.*

'He is our boss, our leader and more recently our saviour.'

'Look Holly, knowing every little detail today is not going to change anything overnight, but I do want to tell you about your family.' Linda said, delivering her words gently.

'Family? I have siblings?' Albert butted in.

'No princess, but you have some cousins, based in South Africa and I know they will be beside themselves with excitement to meet you.' Holly looked down at the lush grass, she wiped a tear away. *I have had a family I did not know about all this time.*

'Jennie and George are based in Johannesburg and Elize and Mike are based in Cape Town. Jennie and George's son Kevin has just moved to London, he's in training with us.'

'Training, for what?' Holly asked.

'The same training you had when you were younger.' Those words brought her world crashing down. She had just realised, if the Senator was not her real dad then grandpa was not who she thought he was. That thought was one too many.

'No, please no, don't you dare tell me grandpa is not real.' Albert stood up and cuddled into Holly. He spoke softly into her ear.

'Your grandpa was the one real thing in all of this; he was your real grandpa and my real dad. He agreed to go with you to America as a baby. That was our deal with the Senator. Senator Natalie is not a blood relative; but your grandpa is.'

'You're not just saying that?'

'Princess, I will never ever lie to you again, I'm telling you the truth.'

Chapter 53

As Holly and Max walked through the foyer of the Marriot Hotel, Shoreen shouted over.

'Mr Yeoman is waiting for you in the bar.'

'Thanks, said Holly'.

'Yeoman, who came up with that name?' Max laughed, teasing Holly.

'I'll have you know that research of the name tells me that Jack and I are the Duke and Duchess of Rutland.'

'Blimey, someone in the Secret Service had a sense of humour.'

'And what name are you trading under this week, Max?' Max tapped the side of his nose.

Jack looked quite relaxed as he sat reading a copy of the Sunderland Echo.

'You will not find a reply in today's *Shout Out* column Jack.' Holly said as she approached his seat.' Jack lowered his paper.

'And you know because???'

'It is a long story, believe me.'

'Look, I'm going to leave you two love birds and call the Senator, put my head down for a bit, I have been travelling for some time.' Max said.

'Give him my love.' Replied Holly.

'I will.'

'Max.' Holly shouted as he started to walk off, Max turned and looked back.

'Thank you.' Max blew a kiss back towards Holly and disappeared from view.

'So Miss Macdonald, what has been going on with you?' Jack asked.

'Let's just say, you couldn't have made this story up if you tried Jack.' Holly took a seat.

'Did Walt call back?' Holly asked.

'Yep, he certainly did.' Jack replied.

'And?' Holly asked.

'He gave me a number for some guy called Shaun Duffy. The Oracle claims Shaun knows where the *Document of Truth* is. He met him on the Washington Triangle forum. It was Shaun that told the Oracle about the 1183 conspiracy thing.'

'What did Shaun have to say Jack, c'mon spit it out?'

'He said that he was in the crowd when Carter came to visit this Washington in 1977. He said the motorcade stopped suddenly down in the village, not where it was planned to stop at Washington Old Hall. Carter gets out totally against protocol. He walks into the crowd shaking hands and he was about to shake little Shaun's hand when some random guy pushes in and hands the President a note. According to Shaun, the President was visibly shocked at what was on the note.'

'We need to speak to Shaun.'

'C'mon Holly, this is a goose chase, I don't even think this is real anymore.'

'Trust me Jack, it's real, I am living proof of it.' Jack put the paper to one side.

'What do you mean by that Holly?'

'I mean, trust me, it's real, I'll explain later. What else did Walt say?'

'I told you so.' Holly laughed; she could hear Walt saying that.

'Call Shaun Jack-arrange a meet, today if possible.'

'Who made you the boss all of a sudden?' Jack joked. *My father, my real one, Holly thought.* As Jack dialled Shaun's number he pointed to the back page of the Sunderland Echo.

'Sunderland won two goals to one yesterday, in case you were interested. Came from a goal behind, two goals in two minutes in the second half, there is a full page report in the paper.'

'Are you an English soccer fan now Jack?' Holly asked sarcastically.

'I am now Holly, always pick a winner.' Holly rolled her eyes. *Soccer, what's that all about?*

'Hello, is that Shaun?'

'Yes, who's this?' Shaun Duffy had been expecting this call, but he didn't know when it would come and certainly didn't know who it would come from. What he did know could change everything!

3pm, before the school run, was the time Shaun had agreed to pick up Jack and Holly from the Marriott Hotel. Shaun got out of the car to greet Jack and Holly. *Look out for the lady with the converse trainers on and the black leather bag over her shoulder, it will be us.* Shaun remembered his instruction.

'You must be Jack and Holly I take it?' Shaun said, as he put out a hand of friendship to shake both their hands. 'Pleased to meet you both, c'mon lets go, we can talk in the car.' Jack and Holly both took their place in the back seats of the car.

Shaun drove round to the exit barrier. While he waited for the barrier to lift he noticed a BMW SUV parked on the opposite side of the road. The engine was still running and the windows were blacked out.

'Do either of you recognise that car?' Shaun asked. They both looked, but it looked harmless enough to them.

'No, why, what's up?' Jack asked.

'Ah nothing, you can't be too careful these days, the Silver Fox has eyes everywhere, thought it could be one of his spotters. Holly leaned forward to speak with Shaun.

'Who is the Silver Fox?'

'He is the person that runs this city; I only know his first name, Albert.' Holly looked shocked, yet another revelation. *Dad?*

'Can you tell me about him?' Holly asked as Shaun looked in his rear view mirror.

'I can do better than tell you about him Holly, I can show you.' Shaun turned right onto Whitburn Road then right at the roundabout onto Seaburn Terrace. Jack and Holly watched out of the windows as he passed the Lemonfield Hotel and followed the road up to the next roundabout. He took another right onto Chichester Road. Three hundred metres further up the road it merged into Sea Road. As he drove up the hill he pointed to a street sign.

'If you look at the name of that sign it says Sea Road.' Jack and Holly had no idea where this was going.

'Yeah ok…' Jack replied.

'It's really **See** Road, because the Silver Fox has spotters at the top and bottom of it. This is one of the main roads in and out of the city and he has spotters at every other main road. He always uses women, less conspicuous that way.' Everything seemed ordinary and harmless to Jack and Holly.

Three rows of red brick terraced houses lined the road along Sea Road before the Royal Marine public house came into view, although it was Subway and Dominoes that Jack switched his attention to. Holly smiled and pointed out a cafe to Jack, it was the name, the Mad Hatter. Shaun slowed the car and pulled up outside STIRKS family butchers shop, just avoiding the bus lane.

'This all sounds a bit far-fetched Shaun.' Jack was dismissive to the theory. Shaun picked up a pair of binoculars from the passenger seat and handed them to Jack.

'You see Zest Ladies Only Fitness Club on the first floor across the road?' Jack looked through the binoculars.

'Yeah I see, so what?'

'The Silver Fox has two spotters there, McBride-Donaldson and Moyse, with an apprentice lurking in the background, someone who has been a big noise in London. I only have her initials at the moment, KBC. I guarantee you; they will both be standing looking out of the window for anything or anyone suspicious.' Jack zoomed in and then adjusted the lens to get a clear view. There they were, one standing at the far left window, one at the far right. They had matching black T shirts on. Jack adjusted his view once more, he wanted a closer look. Suddenly, he sat back in his seat and looked at Holly. He handed her the binoculars.

'You need to take a look and pay close attention to the little logo and writing at the top right of the T shirts.' Holly knew it must be significant by Jack's reaction, but what? Shaun smiled; he knew Jack recognised the message.

'You have got to be kidding me?' Holly said.

'Something familiar?' Shaun asked.

'Very.' Holly said.

'The exact same message that was in the box we retrieved from Hylton Castle. How can that be?' Holly asked.

'Watch, I will drive to the bottom of the street now. Look to the left this time, ground floor, the bay window, the barbers, Fellaz. It is next door to the Doggie Diner we are approaching. Hepton will be in the window, same T shirt, same message.' Holly took a deep breath, looked towards the window and there Hepton stood, scanning the area. Holly nodded to Jack. *What is going on? Just when I think I have all my ducks in a row, someone throws a stone in the water and causes a big splash.* Holly thought.

'I found out last week that Hepton has a connection with MI5, I don't have any further details yet but that's 100% confirmed.' Shaun revealed.

Holly sat back and then put the binoculars down, lost in a collection of thoughts. In just a few days, her life had become alien to her. It seemed so strange to her that the one person on the planet that now knew more about her life than anyone else, was the man sitting next to her, Jack Hammonds.

'Tell me about this Washington Triangle, 1183 conspiracy you have going.' Jack asked.

'I will, but I need to take you somewhere first, there is something you really need to see, it's only five minutes away.'

Jack looked at Holly, she was miles away. Holly looked up as the car passed the Blue Bell public house. Her mind was asking questions and only one person could answer them, grandpa. *Please show me the way; I am hanging on by a thread here. Help me make sense of all this.* Shaun quickly grabbed Holly's attention.

'I'm not sure what the Oracle has told you, but I have spent forty years working on a theory.'

'I'm listening.' Holly said, as she looked back at Shaun.

'On the 6th May 1977, I witnessed something I was not supposed to. Something totally against protocol, something that was even reported in the Washington Post in DC, you can check.'

'We will, please Shaun, go on.' Holly said.

'Carter jumps out of the car and heads for the crowd shaking people's hands. He was just about to shake mine, when a man pushed in front of me and handed him a note. The President was shocked at what he read, I could tell. His security detail rushed over and ushered him back in the car and then sped off down the street. I looked around but the man was gone.'

'Nobody else saw this?' Jack asked.

'No, it all happened so fast. I only saw what happened because he pushed me to the side to get the note to the President.' Shaun paused; he was transported back to that moment in time, hand out ready to shake the President's hand. He could still see the note in his mind's eye.

'As I said, the Washington Post did report that Carter broke protocol, but there was no mention of the note.' Holly leaned forward.

'Did you see what was on the note?' Shaun looked in his mirror.

'I saw the front of the note and it was exactly the same as what you have just seen on those T shirts. A triangle of the Union Jack and a triangle of the Stars and Stripes locking together, with the Washington Coat of arms in the middle with 1183 above it.' Holly looked up to the heavens and smiled.

'Of course. It's still here Jack, they are still protecting it. They must have moved it from Hylton Castle.'

'Are you talking about the *Document of Truth* by any chance?' Shaun asked.

'Yes, do you really think you know where it is?'

Shaun pulled into a car park and pulled up the handbrake. Jack and Holly looked out of the window; neither of them had expected to be parked up at a location like this.

'What are we doing here Shaun?' Jack asked.

'There is something inside this building I need you to see, the sign that has been guiding you.' He replied. Holly looked for an entrance, it was very quiet, the car park empty.

'How are you going to get us in here? It looks like it is all locked up.' Holly asked.

'That's easy, my best mate from school is the maintenance manager here, he will let us in.' Jack shook his head, a wry smile appeared. *Of course he is. Everyone seems to know everyone in this place.* Shaun placed a call; the caller display read 'Stanga'.

'Hi mate, can you meet us at reception, I've just parked up.'

As Jack and Holly climbed the few steps up to the main entrance from the car park, Holly was first to get a clear view.

'This is quite an impressive building Shaun.' Shaun smiled. He looked at Holly.

'It's a stadium Holly. If you come from these parts, then it's more than a stadium. It is your Church, your Chapel, your Mosque, your Synagogue, your Temple; this is our Religion, this is where we come to pray.'

Jack's sport was baseball, although in a very short space in time, he had got to know the local team. The giant sign above the main entrance said it all: Sunderland A.F.C.

Stanga stood waiting for his guests, holding the full length glass door open. He smiled as Jack and Holly walked in, both thanking him as they made their way into the entrance.

'Cheers Stanga mate, I owe you one.' Shaun patted Stanga on the back.

'Not a problem mate.'

'Ok if we head on through?' Shaun asked.

'Fill your boots mate; you know the way by now.' Stanga replied. As Stanga closed the door, he could see a car entering the car park. He stood on his toes to get the best view over the bushes that were blocking his sight. *That looks like a BMW X5 if I'm not mistaken, not my choice of motor, but nice all the same.* As Stanga locked the entrance door, the driver of the BMW stepped out. *Dear me, I think you may be lost my darling, this is a football stadium, not a catwalk.* Stanga muttered to himself. He watched as she quickly looked around and then got back in the car. He could see she had put a phone to her ear.

'I have found them.' Bridie said.

'Where are they?' Heenan replied.

'At the local football stadium. They are with some other guy, I don't know who yet, his face does not appear on any of my databases.'

'What's your plan?' Heenan asked.

'I have a new team arriving any minute. There is no football game on today, I just checked, so I can only assume one thing, the treasure is buried here. I will deal with them my way.'

'Good, keep me informed.'

'I will.'

Shaun led Jack and Holly out of the player's tunnel and onto the pitch at the Stadium of Light.

'Holly looked to her right and then behind her at the executive boxes.

'It looks bigger when you're inside the stadium than it does from the outside.' Holly said.

'It is, the bottom half of the stadium is built underground.

'What's going on Shaun, why are we here?' Jack asked.

'I told you I wanted to show you something.'

'Yeah, but what?'

'Turn around and look at the north stand, there is a message there that I think you might recognise?' Shaun put his hands in his pockets and watched on as Jack and Holly looked to the north stand, moving a few steps closer, as if the message wasn't big enough to see already.

'Just when you think that nothing else can surprise you.' Holly said, as she stood looking at the three words written in the seats.

'You really think it's here?' Holly asked Shaun.

'I'm certain of it Holly. When the stadium was built, there was an official time capsule buried under the stadium. The *Document of Truth* was hidden with it, I'm positive.'

'What makes you so sure?' Jack asked, still mesmerised at the message in the seats.

'There was an official burial, photographs were taken and it was big news at the time. There is a man on the official photograph that had nothing to do with this football club. No one has ever been able to identify him, or where he came from. He had a badge on his jacket; you can guess what was on it.' Holly nodded.

'The same as the message that was on the box at Hylton Castle, what was written on those T shirts we have just seen and the same message that was on the note that was given to Carter I'm guessing?'

'Correct and there is one more thing.' Shaun said. Jack spun around.

'The man on the official photograph with the badge on was the same man that handed President Carter the note.'

'Unbelievable.' Holly said. *I need to phone my dad, I need answers*. She thought.

Jack and Holly took one last look at the message written in the seats, the message that had been repeated to them several times now. HA'WAY THE LADS.

As Shaun escorted Jack and Holly back down the tunnel, Holly noticed a picture on the wall, a giant photograph of a footballer cuddling a child on the football pitch.

'I recognise that boy, Bradley isn't it? Wasn't he the club mascot?' Shaun looked up at the photograph, his eyes glazed over.

'He was more than a mascot to the people of Sunderland Football Club, more than a mascot to clubs all over Britain and around the world Holly, he was our superhero.'

Stanga was waiting to unlock the door for his guests as they entered the main reception area. Shaun stopped and addressed Jack and Holly out of earshot of Stanga.

'I have an idea on how to confirm that the *Document of Truth* is hidden here.' He said.

'How?' Jack asked.

'There is a hidden shaft area underground that runs under the stadium from back in the mining days. I think we could access the time capsule from there. C'mon I'll tell you the rest in the car.'

Bridie had been busy while they had been inside the stadium. She called Heenan and told him her crude plan.

'I have planted a bomb under their car.' She said.

'You had better be confident you can find the treasure.' Heenan replied.

'It's here, I know it! When they reach the corner of the stadium I'll trigger it. That will cause massive damage to that side of the stadium and allow us access.'

As Shaun unlocked his car, his mobile phone rang. He excused himself to Jack and Holly to answer it. They climbed into the car. Shaun looked at the caller display before answering, it was a withheld number.

'Hello.' Shaun said cagily. The reply was definite and abrupt.

'Someone has planted a bomb under your car and if you don't do what I tell you, the three of you will be killed.' Shaun quickly looked around, he could see nothing alarming. He spoke quietly into the phone.

'Is this the Silver Fox?'

The End

Please visit – www.thewashingtontriangle.com to see what is proven, what is debatable and where you can find out more about us!